Tossed Overboard

Tossed Overboard

Garibaldi Sabio

Library of Congress Number:		2017901441
ISBN:	Hardcover	978-1-5245-7976-0
	Softcover	978-1-5245-7975-3
	eBook	978-1-5245-7974-6

Rev. date: 01/30/2017

To order additional copies of this book, contact:
Xlibris
1-888-795-4274
www.Xlibris.com
Orders@Xlibris.com
756438

Acknowledgments

Thanks to my colleagues in the Jackson Hole Writers Group for their useful pre-publication feedback. And I acknowledge immeasurable gratitude to Maruka for her thorough editing and proofreading.

Previous novels by Garibaldi Sabio

~ *Action* (2014)

~ *2358* (2015)

~ *Behind the Curtain* (2016)

DEDICATION

This book honors the Elegant Eight:

Maryjo A. K. W.

Caroline K. W. D.

Meeja S. W. M.

Sabrina K. W. O.

Elena M. W.

Annie E. W. M.

Nancy W.W.

Dubravaka B. J.

CONTENTS

Chapter 1: The Irish Sea

SHORTLY AFTER 0930 HOURS CAPTAIN Eliopoulos ordered the engine room on the container ship, *La Galissionière,* to slow down to three knots. Standing in the Pilot House, he lifted his cap, which was the pre-arranged signal to the First Mate on the deck. They were in the Irish Sea; the water was choppy, and the clouds portended rain.

The First Mate balled his hand into a fist and pumped his right arm. "Bring 'em out," he said in Spanish, the official language on board, and the Third Mate and the boatswain dragged two hapless sailors to the port side of the ship. "Lower the Minnie!" the First Mate barked. The Minnie was the nickname that the crew gave to the smallest of the lifeboats, really just a skiff with room for four or five men. Today the Minnie would have only two passengers, Moises Delgadinho, from the Azores, and Leonicio Muñoz, from the Canary Islands.

[TRANSLATION FROM SPANISH]: "All right, you two, climb down into the Minnie," said the First Mate.

"Why are you doing this?" asked Delgadinho..

"It's no use begging, Delgadinho. It ain't manly. You two been nothin' but trouble since you boarded. Now get off the frigging ship!"

The two sailors dug their heels in and resisted climbing over. "Listen, you dipsticks! You got two choices," snarled the First Mate. "You can freely and voluntarily climb down them ropes; or the third Mate and the boatswain'll throw you overboard. You might land in the water, but there'd be no way to dry off; **or** you might land on the skiff and break three or four ribs. Which is it gonna be, sailor boys?"

Reluctantly, Delgadinho and Muñoz climbed down the webbing into the Minnie. As they were gaining their footing in the webbing, the Third Mate hung a sack over Muñoz's neck. "Just to show how generous we are, in the sack you got a Number 10 can for bailing water from the waves and rain plus a knife to cut up any fish that you catch. If the fish tastes funny, it's the plutonium: There's more nuclear waste in the Irish Sea than anywheres else on the planet."

The boatswain added, "The sack also has your lunch and supper. It's unlikely you'll make it past tonight, so that's all you get; and there's a canteen of water in there too. By the way, when you stick your backsides over the gunwales to take a dump, be careful: The sharks in this sea don't like being mooned, and they're very likely to wanna take a bite. Also, it would be wise to avoid the oil drilling platforms you might see on your journey. If you show up in a skiff, they'll think you're a couple of fart-lollies from Greenpeace, and they'll use your boat for target practice."

The Third Mate laughed. "Exactly so. Now, you can either row west toward Ireland or east toward Wales, but the wind shifts will probably take you into the opposite direction, no matter how hard you pull on them oars. Just hope that you don't meet up with a nor'easter. If you get swept to the southwest, past St. George's Channel, you'll be in the Celtic Sea. If none of them whales over there swallow you, the next stop'll be Canada."

From the skiff, Muñoz yelled up to the crew members. "HELP US! YOU COULD BE NEXT!"

Nobody moved. The Third Mate and the First Mate exchanged glances. This was an important object lesson for the rest of the crew. The two officers suspected that either Delgadinho or Muñoz, or maybe both of them, had witnessed "the midnight swim," where the officers had tossed overboard a deckhand who was too sick to work and who might be spreading disease to the other crew members. Besides, the best way to maintain discipline on a long voyage was to punish a couple of "problem" crew members; and they couldn't think of a better example than putting these two jokers into a rowboat just before a storm hit. Although the ship really couldn't afford to lose two deckhands, the officers knew that they'd only be light-handed for one day because they planned to pick up a couple of newjays when they got to Scotland.

The First Mate ordered release of the ropes holding the skiff to the ship and then raised his cap to the Pilot House. The Captain nodded and yelled into the speaker: "Proceed to the north, at 14 knots."

"What are we going to do, Leonicio?" asked Delgadinho, as they watched the ship pull away. He spoke in a pidgin hybrid of Spanish and Portuguese, which the two of them had created as their means of communication after they met as crew mates on *La Galissionière*.

"Beats me, man. I gotta admit I'm scared shitless. The wind seems to be coming from the east. So, let's head west and hope we get to Ireland. You look even more frightened than me, so I'll take the first shift at the oars."

They figured that they would make landfall by the end of the day, so by twilight they had eaten all the food and had drunk all the water in the canteen. However, just as the Third Mate had predicted, as soon as the skiff had made several hundred yards in one direction, the wind shifted, and they were forced to row in the opposite direction in order to avoid being sucked into St. George's Channel. Neither of them could navigate by star clusters, so they stopped rowing when it got dark.

Taking turns staying awake at night in order to deal with unexpected winds or storms or waves, they started Day Two very tired and unaware of how far they were from either Ireland or Wales. They were also hungry, thirsty, and afraid. Luckily, one of the Irish Sea's famous flying fish jumped up in the air and landed in the Minnie along with one of the big waves. So they were able to have something to eat on Day Two, even though the salty fish flesh made them even thirstier. They also had to bail a good deal of water from the sloshing waves.

On the third day they saw the outline of land to the east, which they figured, correctly, was Wales; but it was difficult rowing because the wind kept pushing the water against them. Without fresh water and not having had any food other than the one fish on Day Two, they were both low on energy. They took turns at the oars every half hour. When Delgadinho saw that Muñoz's hands were blistered, however, he ignored his exhaustion and took extra shifts on the oars. A too-curious sea bird, a Manx Shearwater, landed on the skiff and provided their only nourishment on Day Three. By late afternoon, they could tell that they would make it to shore, which they did, finally, at Cardigan, an ancient market town on the River Teifi estuary.

Some good-hearted Welshmen pulled them from the skiff, gave them water, and brought them to the local Anglican parish church, St. John the Baptist. However, no one there could speak either Spanish

(Muñoz's language) or Portuguese (Delgadinho's language), nor did anyone know of any Spanish- or Portuguese-speakers in the area.

The parish priest, Father Roberts, telephoned his counterpart in Cardiff, where, he had read, some sort of international gathering of Anglican clergy was going on. He asked if anyone attending could speak Spanish or Portuguese. It just so happened that one of the attendees was Elizabeth Sánchez-Ríos, an Episcopal priest from the U.S.A., who, to the great relief of Father Roberts, spoke English, Spanish, and Portuguese.

She came onto the phone, spoke briefly with the two sailors and assured them that they were now safe. She asked Father Roberts to make sure that the two men would have a hot meal, warm shower, a place to sleep that night, and asked him to find someone to drive them to Cardiff the next day.

When they arrived in Cardiff, Muñoz and Delgadinho immediately and gratefully attached themselves to "Madre Elisabeta," to whom they told their story; and she determined right then to find a way to get them to the United States.

Chapter 2: The Litigation Steering Committee

"I THINK WE SHOULD TAKE the case," Alvin Shanks declared. Despite his current status as "of counsel," which meant that he was semi-retired and no longer among the real power-wielders in the law firm of Dornan, Frager, & Paloma, Shanks still attended meetings of the Litigation Steering Committee, of which he was once Chair, and where, from time to time, he tested his residual influence.

Seven partners were seated around the cedarwood conference table in the Dakota Conference room on the 43rd floor of the IDS Tower in downtown Minneapolis, reviewing prospective new cases. One of the rain-makers in the firm, Phillip Traxel, had just completed his presentation to the Committee about a possible, new matter. It was, Traxel conceded, "a difficult case as well as one of high risk." The potential clients did not have much money, and the litigation would surely take a substantial amount of resources, both in lawyer time and in funds. "Nevertheless," Traxel claimed, rubbing his bald head, "it is a high risk/high gain opportunity, one that this firm should have the courage and foresight to undertake."

The current chair of the Committee, Frank Bear, whose size and shape conformed to his name, usually withheld his comments until other members had their say; but in this instance he jumped all over Traxel. "Damn it, Phil, this is precisely the kind of case that would be a steady drain of time, money, and energy. If we jumped in with both feet, we would be slipping into quicksand – tens of thousands of dollars, maybe hundreds of thousands, plus an enormous amount of partner time, associate time, and paralegal time. It would require the hiring of all kinds of experts. The risk is outlandish, and the so-called gain is quite problematic."

"Yeah, I agree with Frank," said Norton Tremaine, a thin, nerdy looking fellow with thick glasses, who, everyone was aware, had ambitions to be the next Litigation Steering Committee Chair. "I did some preliminary checking on the potential clients," he said. "They maybe could at most scrape together fifty dollars by selling everything they own. After that, we'd be sailing on a rickety, contingency matter with lots of nasty waves."

In addition to subtly parodying Traxel's proposed case (for it involved matters on the High Seas), Tremaine was demonstrating his conservative credentials by declining to wax enthusiastic about this speculative case that Traxel was sponsoring. Tremaine had been a risk-taker when he was a brand new partner and had gotten burned. Over the intervening years, he felt compelled to prove to his fellow shareholders that he was actually a trustworthy and cautious protector of the firm's lucre.

A reluctant silence fell over the conference room after both Bear and Tremaine had spoken against the Traxel proposal. It was the white-haired Shanks who had punctured the quiet with his surprising announcement that he favored accepting Traxel's proposed clients. It was surprising because of Shanks's carefully-constructed reputation for fiscal caution.

"Our bank accounts are at the highest level that they have ever been," he said. "The associates we have selected over the last three years have all proven to be excellent choices; our partners' billable hours this year are already outstripping our predictions, and we have several corporate clients who provide us with steady business. A lot of our partners and associates have no experience whatsoever representing plaintiffs, and it limits our self-description as a full-service law firm when we only represent defendants. If we win this case, Dornan-Frager will not only reap a huge monetary award in attorney fees, but it will elevate our recognition among corporations that want to sue other companies but may be reluctant to hire us because of our reputation for only being a defense firm."

"That's a big 'IF,' Alvin." Joseph Benton, who wore suspenders but called them "braces," leaned forward and made eye contact with Shanks. "It's quite possible that we might *not* win. To be sure, the facts that Phil presented about the potential clients are egregious, but we may not be able to prove them. It involves admiralty law, about which no one in the firm has any expertise. There could be several defendants, each represented by other large firms and all of whom would chortle at the thought of nickel-and-dime-ing us as if we were a boutique, two-lawyer, plaintiffs' firm until we and our clients give up."

Before anyone else could jump into the discussion, Clifford Rehmel asked if he might have the floor. Rehmel spoke infrequently and then only when he was sure of his platform, his audience, and his facts. As a result, people paid attention to him when he did offer commentary. It helped that he had a basso-profundo voice and penetrating, blue-green eyes.

"There is a way to minimize the risk which Frank and Norton legitimately raise and which even Phil has acknowledged. Instead of jumping in with both feet, let's just dip one big toe." Rehmel looked around to make eye contact with everyone else and to make sure that they were all listening. "Why not tell the potential clients that we will *conditionally* accept the case, but that we will hire a private investigator with the clients' retainer payment to try to corroborate the asserted facts, and we will assign three associates to research the various areas of law involved in this matter. However, the Fee Agreement will allow us to withdraw if the investigator is unable to provide us with the necessary evidence."

"That sounds like a very reasonable suggestion," said Evelyn Granger, the only female member of the Committee and the only one who had not yet spoken. "Doesn't Cliff's 'Big Toe' idea in fact mitigate all of the objections that have bubbled up?"

A natural politician, Frank Bear knew how to count. Even if Benton voted against taking the case, Traxel, Shanks, Rehmel, and Granger would all vote "yes," enough for a majority. So, without consulting Tremaine, he smiled and responded, "Indeed it does, Evelyn. Let the Minutes show that the Litigation Steering Committee formally approved taking the case entitled *Delgadinho vs. Greenport Shipping,...* but with the 'Rehmel Proviso,' namely, that it is an acceptance conditioned upon a private investigator's bringing back a boatload of evidence sufficient to enable us to carry this matter to a successful conclusion."

Bear paused for effect and then added the coda: "Phil, you'll be the lead on this matter, and I assume that you'll collect the retainer from the clients and will hire the private investigator. Email the rest of us the names of the three associates whom you intend to assign the research roles." After the briefest pause, with not really enough time for anyone to interpose, Bear declared the meeting adjourned.

The members packed up their materials and returned to their offices, but Bear asked Rehmel to stay behind. When they were alone, Bear asked, "Damn it, Cliff! Why did you take Traxel off the hook?" I can't believe that you really think this case has a snowball's chance in hell of doing anything but drowning us."

Rehmel put his hand on Bear's shoulder and answered: "What if we had turned Phil down, Frank? Since we're using aquatic metaphors here, Traxel might very well have 'jumped ship' and taken the case to a friendlier law firm, probably with three or four junior partners and associates along with him. Not only would we look stupid if that other law firm were to win the case, but in the process we would have lost one of our biggest revenue-generators and would have given the green light to other client-magnets in the firm to try their luck in their own vessels."

The oscillation in Bear's temple movements indicated that he was biting down, hard, on his teeth. Then he stuck his finger in Rehmel's chest. "You better make sure that he doesn't screw up, Cliff. I'm going to let the Management Committee know that *you* made it possible for the firm to get stuck with this tar-baby." He then turned and walked out.

Chapter 3: Traxel's Office

PHIL TRAXEL SENT AN EMAIL on the firm's Attorney ListServ to all the other lawyers in the firm: "I'm in need, very quickly, of an experienced private investigator who has a wide variety of skills, who would be willing to venture outside of the Twin Cities, and who is comfortable with danger. Please respond as quickly as possible."

After four hours, only two lawyers had replied. Evelyn Granger wrote: "I have used the Gavercole Agency on several occasions. Jim Gavercole is quite competent and low-key, but he turns down cases that require any even potential confrontations. My guess is that you'll need someone different."

A transactional lawyer, Myron Ross, who officed one floor down from Traxler, wrote that he had used a female investigator named Lucy Vigdersen, who was great at doing document reviews, but she had three kids and would surely not want to travel outside the Twin Cities.

Then a knock at Traxler's door presaged rescue. "Come in," Traxel said..

A second-year associate named Ted Bruner, a sandy-haired six-footer who had been working on a few cases for Traxler, entered. "Hello, Phil. Have you had any luck in finding a private investigator?"

"As a matter of fact, Ted, I have *not*. I have a new case that requires a multi-talented investigator, but no one in the firm seems to have used or even to know of one that would fit the bill."

"That's why I came in. I know a guy who has *exactly* the kind of qualifications that you mentioned in the email. His name is Rocky Stonebrook."

"Never heard of him. Does he have an office here in Minneapolis?"

"Nope. He offices in Cleveland."

"Cleveland! How do *you* know of him, Ted?"

"*I'm* from Cleveland. And in the summer after I graduated law school, he hired me to work with him on a case – in Wyoming, so I know that he's willing to travel. The case had a lot of danger: Stonebrook got shot – wounded – in Wyoming and almost got pushed off a cliff in Brazil; and I myself was kidnapped, hogtied, and threatened with death. The case involved hitmen, drug dealers, federal marshals, people in the Witness Protection Program, cops and robbers, and a set of very strange characters. Stonebrook seems to eat danger for his breakfast cereal."

"Sounds like you were in the middle of it too, Ted. Please sit down, and describe this man Stonebrook, if you would," he added, motioning Bruner to a couch. "Would you like some coffee?"

Bruner sat but passed on the coffee. "It was a wild excursion. And while I did not appreciate being kidnapped, I have to say, it was a very exciting summer. They broke the mold after Stonebrook. He's very smart and obviously could have had all sorts of careers, but he enjoys the freedom of being a P.I. He's a writer on the side: He has had some poetry published, and he is finishing a non-fiction work on weird Wills, a topic he got interested in while reading in the prison library in New Jersey, where he was an inmate for a year on a marijuana charge. You'd never guess any of that from looking at him or talking to him. He's allergic to ties, and he talks in whatever argot that he judges is comfortable for his conversational companion.

"He speaks at least three languages without an accent; he has a sharp sense of humor, sizes up people immediately, seems absolutely unafraid of anything, but does not suffer fools gladly. Additionally, he seems to possess an extraordinarily accurate bullshit-detector. He is fiercely loyal to his colleagues, friends, and employees. One of the assassins we encountered, the one who kidnapped me, threatened to slit my throat but offered to set me free if Stonebrook would surrender himself to be murdered. Stonebrook made the trade. He survived only because somebody else killed the assassin, but the point is that he was prepared to die in order to save me."

Traxel smiled. "He sounds like a very interesting fellow. And I already regret that what we offer you as an associate here in our law firm is a lot less swashbuckling than what Mr. Stonebrook provided for you in Wyoming."

Bruner wasn't sure how he was supposed to respond, but he said, "That was a great *summer* job. But here I'm doing what I need, and want, to do in order to have a long career as a skillful lawyer."

"And, if I haven't said this directly to you before, Ted, the litigation partners, and I specifically, have been very pleased with your work. Since you're only a second year associate, I can't guarantee you partnership, yet; but you're doing everything you need to do to be in line four years hence. You have convinced me to try this Mr. Stonebrook, and I'd like you to be here when I call him."

Traxel rose from the couch and went to his desk. "Do you have his phone number?"

"Yes. I keep it in my cell phone. Hold on." Bruner fished out his cell, made a few punches, and read the number to Traxel.

"Here," Traxel said, handing the land line receiver to Ted, "why don't you make the call and see if you can get Mr. Stonebrook on the phone. Oh, and before you dial, what are the languages in which he is fluent?"

"English, Spanish, and Portuguese." Bruner dialed, and pressed the speaker-phone button that would allow Traxel to hear both sides of the conversation.

Stonebrook's secretary answered, "Stonebrook Investigations, can I help you?"

He felt a little uncomfortable calling her "Aunt Carol" in front of Traxel, so he just said, "Hi, this is Ted."

"Hello, Ted. Are you in town?"

"No, I'm at work, in Minneapolis, but the firm may have a job for Rocky. Is he available?"

"He's out of the office at the moment, but I expect him to roll in shortly.... oh, wait a minute; I recognize his footsteps now."

They could hear the sound of a door opening and heard Carol say to Stonebrook, "Afternoon, Rocky, Ted's on the phone, calling from Minneapolis, about a possible assignment."

"Great. I'll take it in my office," Stonebrook replied. He strolled into his office, got out a yellow pad and a pen, leaned back in his chair, and picked up the phone. "Hello, Ted, how are those suits treating you?"

"Very well, Rocky. As a matter of fact, one of them is right here and wants to talk to you about a possible assignment.. His name is Phil Traxel." Ted stepped away from the desk and sat down in a chair nearby.

"Good afternoon, Mr. Stonebrook. Ted has been very complimentary about your skills, telling me thrilling tales about his summer job with your outfit."

"Ted Bruner is a very resourceful young man, as I'm sure you and your colleagues have figured out for yourselves. What's the assignment you had in mind?"

Leaning forward in his chair, Traxel replied: "My firm has agreed to conditionally represent some clients who claim that they were mistreated and underpaid by some shipowners on a boat in the Irish Sea. They also claim that the officers tossed troublemakers overboard. The condition is that we get to withdraw if the private investigator we hire can't bring in enough evidence to prove the case. Ted has recommended that we hire you to be that investigator."

"Umm. Can you amplify what exactly it is that you'd want me to do?"

"That's a fair question, Mr. Stonebrook. However, I feel uncomfortable discussing it over an unsecure, telephone line. If I send you an airplane ticket and book a hotel room for you here in Minneapolis, would you be willing to fly here this week, look over some materials, and discuss it? We'd pay your daily rate and compensate you for lodging, meals, and incidentals."

Stonebrook looked at his calendar. "There are some things I can't cancel for tomorrow or Wednesday. But everything else at the end of this week is postponable. The case sounds like it will be sufficiently complicated that I'd want my associate involved as well. How about if you have *two* tickets waiting for us at the Delta ticket counter in the Cleveland airport at a civilized hour on Thursday morning, and then email me the departure time?"

Traxel paused only a couple of seconds before answering. Stonebrook obviously could not see Traxel's raised eyebrows. "Ummm. That's acceptable. Does Ted know your associate?"

"Quite well. The three of us worked as a team on the case in Wyoming that Ted evidently described to you. Her name, by the way, is Lauren Marlo, M-A-R-L-O." Stonebrook purposely did not mention that Ted and Lauren had developed more than a professional relationship.

"When you land," said Traxel, "ask directions for the Metroliner, which runs two floors below the ticket counter level at the airport, and take the Metroliner to downtown Minneapolis. Get off at the stop on 5th Street and 2nd Avenue, then walk to the IDS tower. The law firm's name is Dornan, Frager, and Paloma. We're on the 43rd Floor."

"How do we get to this I-D-S Tower from the metroliner stop?"

"Just look up. It's a blue-glass office building, the tallest building in Minnesota. You can't miss it."

"Okay. Thanks for the opportunity, and please tell Ted that I intend to treat him to dinner Thursday evening."

After they hung up, Traxel turned to Bruner. "The Litigation Steering Committee has authorized me to utilize three associates to work on this case. Would you like to be one of them?"

An ear-splitting grin telegraphed Bruner's affirmative answer.

Chapter 4: Cleveland

"CAROL," STONEBROOK SAID THROUGH THE doorway from his office, "please come in here, and bring Lauren with you."

When all three were gathered around his conference table, he explained. "I have tentatively committed us to a big 'wing-ding,' but I can't really pull it off without your plural agreement." Carol raised one eyebrow, but neither woman said anything. They both were attuned to Rocky's efforts to sprinkle a democratic patina over his unilateral decisions.

"I just got off the phone with one of Ted's bosses at the law firm where he works in Minneapolis." He knew that that information would strike a resonant chord with both of them. Ted was Carol's nephew and, during their work together on the Turnbull case two years earlier, Ted and Lauren had ratcheted up their relationship from colleagues to intimates.

"The case involves investigating allegations that a shipping company murders crewmen whom it deems to be trouble-makers by tossing them overboard. Lauren, without a chance to consult you, I told the lawyer that you and I would fly to Minneapolis on Thursday for a long weekend to find out more details and to interview the clients."

"Well," she said, "I had a bunch of things on my schedule for the rest of this work week, but I can move things around; and I don't have any plans for the weekend. So, color me 'flexible,' even though I get seasick rather easily. And thanks for including me on the trip to the Twin Cities."

Looking at Carol, Stonebrook said: "Carol, by now you have certainly come to accept that your title of 'Secretary' scarcely describes the extent of your duties here. However, if we take this assignment, I'm guessing that it's going to be an almost full-time gig for both Lauren and me for several weeks; and both of us are likely to be out-of-town much of that time. We can't really do it without your taking on the effective responsibility for everything else, including holding the hands of present and future clients, following up as much as you can on pending matters from your desk here at the office, making phone calls and writing letters over my signature to show the current clients that we're massaging their files, and following up leads. I don't expect you to hit the streets, but I would expect that you would receive a substantial bonus from the revenue this case will generate."

"And how is that different from normal?" she asked.

He smiled with relief.

Lauren patted Carol's hand and then said, "I have a question, Rocky. What is it exactly that you think *I'll* be doing on this case? I am delighted to spend the weekend in Minneapolis, but you don't expect me to go to sea, do you?"

Stonebrook laughed. "At this point I have no precise idea. And they didn't reveal all that much on the phone. But I'm guessing that there will be plenty to keep both of us busy for quite a while because they didn't balk at my request that they have two plane tickets waiting for us Thursday morning. Additionally, I'm guessing that you may be able to get Ted to help fill in some of the blanks."

Lauren made a concerted effort not to display any facial reaction to the last comment. She assumed that while they were in Wyoming on the Turnbull case, Rocky had surmised the upgrade in her relationship with Ted, but she doubted that Ted was in the habit of revealing his extracurricular life to his Aunt Carol.

"Okay," Lauren said, "I'll try to wrap up my work on two – maybe three – of the cases on my desk between now and Wednesday afternoon, and I'll prepare status reports on the other matters for Carol."

"Great, Lauren. And I'll do the same for my cases, Carol. I expect that someone from the law firm in Minneapolis will leave a message about what time the plane departs on Thursday morning."

Tuesday evening, Stonebrook went to the ballet. The Cuyahoga Dance Company performed in other parts of the United States, and in other countries as well; but the home base was in Cleveland, and Stonebrook's Significant Other, Donna Putrell, was a ballerina who occasionally danced lead roles. That evening she was dancing the role of Myrtha, Queen of the Wilis in *Giselle*. She got two curtain calls and a standing ovation.

Because Donna never ate before performances, they had a late, cold supper of leftovers and went to bed. He reached for her, but she demurred. "I am totally exhausted tonight. However, I *do* want to give you a send-off before you abandon me for the weekend. So, if you can break free from the office over the noon hour tomorrow, we can have a matinee."

"That's perfectly acceptable... and if our performance is encore-worthy, we can have another *pas-de-deux* tomorrow night."

She kissed him on the cheek. "Although I may fall asleep during your explanation, why don't you tell me about this new case?"

He began to run through the little that he knew, based on the telephone conversation and his speculation about what might be involved. He tried to downplay the danger, but he needn't have worried. As Donna had forewarned, she had indeed fallen asleep.

Chapter 5: Dornan, Frager & Paloma

DELTA FLIGHT 5007 LEFT CLEVELAND at 9:10 a.m. on Thursday and, because of the time difference, arrived in Minneapolis at 10:07. Stonebrook and Marlo did not check their luggage and, so, managed to get to the metroliner quickly. They arrived at the 43rd floor of the IDS Tower just before 11:00 and approached the receptionist. "Good morning, we have an appointment with Phil Traxel. Our names are...."

"Oh, yes," she interrupted, very cheerfully, "you're Mr. Stonebrook and Ms. Marlo. Mr. Traxel is expecting you. I'll call him now and let him know that you have arrived. Will you have coffee or tea?"

Stonebrook looked over at Marlo, who nodded. "Yes, thank you. I'll have coffee with cream, no sugar; Ms. Marlo likes tea, with lemon."

"I'll have your beverages brought to the Ramsey conference room, which is behind me and to the right. Please feel free to make yourselves comfortable there."

The conference room window had a great view of downtown Minneapolis, and Stonebrook was studying the landscape when three lawyers walked in. One was Ted Bruner whom Stonebrook warmly greeted and then stuck out his hand toward the man who looked like he was in charge. "I'm guessing you're Phil Traxel. How do you do?"

"Yes, that's right. And this is my partner, Cliff Rehmel. He'll be working on the case as well." Stonebrook shook his hand too..

"And this is *my* associate, Lauren Marlo," Stonebrook said, bringing Lauren into the small circle by the door. Although Stonebrook was dressed in his trademark, casual threads – khaki pants; a button-down, slightly wrinkled, oxford blue shirt; a western vest; and tennis shoes; Lauren could have passed for a junior associate at the law firm. She had on a black pants suit, a printed yellow blouse, and a black scarf that matched the barrette at the back of her flaming, red hair.

They all sat down at the conference table and checked each other out while a staffer brought in and served the coffee and tea.

Rehmel looked to be 60ish, about 5'11", had large, brown eyes, gray hair, an aquiline nose, high cheek bones, and a well-trimmed moustache. His fingernails were obviously accustomed to being manicured, and he wore a watch with a glittering gold band. Traxel was late 40s, about the same height as Stonebrook (6'3"), had an athletic build, blue eyes, and was bald. Both partners wore expensive, pin-striped, blue suits, starched white shirts, and appropriately conservative, striped ties. Bruner looked just he had looked two years ago but, instead of wearing jeans and loafers, he was suited up, albeit in a much less expensive cut than those of the two partners.

After waiting for the guests to take a sip of their beverages, Traxel opened the conversation with an encomium of gratitude. "Thank you both, Mr. Stonebrook and Ms. Marlo, for dropping whatever you had on your plates in Cleveland to come here with very little information to go on. We very much appreciate your flexibility. I'm going to hand each of you a folder with the information that we have so far. I'm certain that as private investigators you understand confidentiality protocol; so, if you ultimately decide not to take the assignment, may we count on your not revealing any of the information about this case?" Stonebrook answered "surely," managing to convey in just that one word both assurance and slight offense at having to be asked.

"Our clients are Moises Delgadinho and Leonicio Muñoz. They are pick-up sailors, one from the Azores and one from the Canary Islands, who were taken on as crewmen on a French ship flying a Bolivian flag called *La Galissionnière* owned by *Hestia Etoupeía*, a Greek corporation with an American subsidiary called Greenport Shipping Corp. The clients claim that the officers mistreated and abused all of the crewmen, used whips and withholding of food to impose discipline, refused to let crew members disembark in port, and threw those perceived as problems or troublemakers overboard to their deaths. Those who survived were not paid. They want us to sue the company for back pay and for compensatory and punitive damages for their horrendous treatment."

Traxel paused to allow Stonebrook and Marlo to digest the information.

"How did these clients find a Minneapolis law firm?" asked Marlo, letting everyone know that she had no compunction about speaking up.

"An appropriate question, Ms. Marlo. It turns out that...."

Stonebrook interrupted. "We're used to being called Lauren and Rocky. I don't know how important it is for lawyers at Dorken and Forken to be formal, but if we're going to be working together, may we call you 'Phil' and 'Cliff'?"

Traxel did not bother to correct Stonebrook's purposeful misnaming of the firm. "Of course," he answered, in precisely the same tone that Rocky had employed in answering the question about confidentiality. Ted suppressed a smile, both at Rocky's intentional tweaking of the firm's name and at Phil's prudent decision not to rise to the bait.

"Delgadinho and Muñoz were rescued in international waters off the coast of Wales and brought to a Church of England parish in Cardiff. A visiting Episcopal priest, who was about to return to her own parish in Wayzata, Minnesota, a western suburb of Minneapolis, agreed to bring them to the United States. Because this priest knew Senator Amy Klobuchar, she got an appointment with an Assistant Attorney General at the Justice Department and convinced him to get his boss, the A.G., to exercise his discretionary authority under the Refugee Act of 1980 to grant temporary refugee status to Delgadinho and Muñoz."

"Hmm." was Stonebrook's response. "Why not just stay in the UK?"

"That's a perceptive question, Mr... er, Rocky. And your former colleague, Ted Bruner, just did some research on that the last two days. Please explain, Ted."

Making eye contact with Stonebrook but frequently veering his vision toward Lauren, Ted began: "Both the U.S. and the UK are signatories to the UN Refugee Convention of 1951. The Convention authorizes, but does not require, signatory nations to grant asylum if the person seeking refugee status genuinely fears persecution based on one of five protected categories: race, religion, nationality, political opinion, or social group. Our clients genuinely fear persecution because the officers on the ship told them that if they showed up back in the Azores or the Canaries, they would be killed, and their family members would be tortured in front of them before they were put to death. The winning argument to the Justice Department is that Delgadinho and Muñoz fit into the fifth category, a 'social group' of shanghaied sailors.

"One of the key provisions of that Convention is the concept of *non-refoulement*. That's French for...."

"No forced return," Lauren interrupted.

"Exactly so," Ted agreed, with a nod of appreciation. "I remember, now, that you speak French, Lauren. At any rate, the target nation will not deport the asylum-seeker if his or her home country is either involved in the persecution or is unable to control private actors. We have contacted some lawyers both in Portugal and Spain who evidently have proof of other shanghaied sailors who returned to the Azores and the Canaries, respectively, and were in fact tortured and killed. Neither Portugal nor Spain seems to be able to interdict that kind of private conduct on her island possessions."

Lauren caught Ted's attention with a chin movement. "I think it's great," she said, "that the U.S. Justice Department is flexible enough to allow these guys in." Then, after a well-timed pause, she added, "But that still doesn't explain why they didn't just stay in the UK."

Ted nodded, acknowledging the relevance of the question. "The answer is that British law on refugees at the time of their rescue, when the UK was still a member of the European Union, allowed for *non-refoulement* to certain parts of the world but explicitly requires forced return to countries that are members of the European Union, including Portugal, of which the Azores are a part, and Spain, which owns the Canary Islands."

Traxel resumed control of the meeting. "It turns out that the State of Minnesota is a grantee of the Department of Homeland Security for refugee settlement, and St. Edward's-by-the-Lake, an Episcopal Church in Wayzata, is a sub-grantee of the State of Minnesota under that grant to provide instruction in English and other social services, such as housing assistance, to refugees. One of the firm's partners is a member of the congregation, and that's how the plaintiffs came to us."

"Aha," said Rocky. "I understand, now, the complicated way that these two guys found their way to Minneapolis and to this law firm. But, even though I'm not an attorney, I'm sufficiently familiar with the principle of 'jurisdiction' to have a question: How does a court in Minnesota acquire jurisdiction over something that happened on the High Seas between Ireland and the UK, on a French ship flying a Bolivian flag, owned by a Greek company?"

"May I?" It was Rehmel, who had looked at his partner as he asked the question and, having received an affirmative response, went on. "That's an astute question, Rocky. The asylum part of the case is a federal matter, and we must make our case to an Immigration Judge in

St. Paul in order for the Attorney General's temporary grant of asylum to be made permanent. But the demand for money damages would be in state court against the American subsidiary, Greenport Shipping Company."

Stonebrook leaned forward and spoke directly to Rehmel. "And why in the world would the *Hestia* Corporation need an American subsidiary, and if so, why would it be incorporated in a state in the middle of the country? And even if it *were* a Minnesota corporation, how could it be held liable for something on the High Seas?"

Traxel turned his head just a few degrees toward Bruner and pushed his lower lip out, his way of saying non-verbally that, so far, he was quite impressed with Ted's recommendation of this obviously perceptive, private investigator.

Rehmel thanked Stonebrook for the questions. "Those are all very pertinent queries, Rocky. It turns out that the Greenport Shipping Co., though nominally the subsidiary, actually pulls the strings in this complex corporate conglomerate. Greenport is incorporated in the State of Delaware, like many American corporations. Its headquarters and executive officers, however, are all in New York. Greenport is *not* going to want to litigate this case in New York because recently there have been some adverse decisions against companies that play hide-the-pea under ships with nominal ownership in one country, that are flagged in a second country, and which try to evade liability by incorporating so-called subsidiaries in the United States."

Lauren was taking notes and creating a diagram that tried to account for all of the pieces of the puzzle. "And Minnesota fits into this maze, how?" she asked.

"If we agree to take the case, we'll serve the Summons and Complaint without filing it, something we call 'vest-pocket service' here in Minnesota. We'll give the defendant two different first pages – that's the page that sets out the jurisdiction and venue – with a cover letter giving them a choice: Delaware or Minnesota. If they choose Delaware, we'll be prepared to litigate there and hire local counsel to help out; if, after considering the alternatives, the defendant decides to litigate in Minnesota, we'll ask them to sign a waiver of jurisdiction."

Lauren followed up. "Why would they ever agree to litigate in Minnesota?"

Rehmel replied. "The plaintiffs live here now, but they're not citizens, so the defendant won't have to worry about being 'home-towned.' It's more convenient for us, of course, to try the case here; but just as we would hire local counsel in Delaware, the defendant would have no trouble hiring local counsel in the Twin Cities. The best reason, though, is that precisely because Minnesota is in Fly-over Land, judges here in Hennepin County will have had little or no experience with admiralty-type cases and, therefore, no matter who gets assigned, he or she is unlikely to have any prejudices. In Delaware, there's a big risk that the judge randomly assigned to the case might have opinions about such cases."

"One more procedural question, if you don't mind." Lauren addressed her question to Ted. "I kind of remember from a poly sci course on the Constitution that admiralty cases get tried in federal courts."

Smiling, Ted said, "Wow! You had a very sophisticated political science prof, Lauren, Normally, admiralty cases are *indeed* tried in federal courts, particularly if the dispute is over property on board the vessel; but if the matters in controversy are about personal injuries to sailors aboard ship, then, under the Jones Act, they can be tried in either state court or federal court. We want it to be in state court because we get a jury trial in state court, and we think a jury that hears the evidence will award big punitive damages."

Stonebrook got up to refill his coffee cup, asking a question on his way to the table with the beverages. "Does the eventual jurisdiction make any difference in the assignment you're hoping we'll take?"

"Not at all," answered Traxel. "However, the assignment we are hoping you accept will make all the difference in our deciding whether we would proceed with the case."

"What precisely do you want us to do?"

"We need verification of the assertions made by Mr. Delgadinho and Mr. Muñoz: Documents, films, personal testimony."

"So, you expect us to testify at trial?"

"Precisely."

Lauren spoke up. "Do you have specific notions about how you think we ought to go about gathering such evidence?"

Rehmel answered. "We figured that that's within the bailiwick of a private investigator agency."

Stonebrook scrunched up his eyebrows, rubbed his chin, and stared intently at both Rehmel and Traxel. "When can we meet Delgadinho and Muñoz?" he asked.

Traxel tried not to show his exhalation of relief. Stonebrook hadn't rejected the idea; he was asking a question that made sense only if he were actually considering taking the assignment. "I have invited them both, along with the Episcopal priest who serves as their interpreter, to come here at 2:30 this afternoon. That will give you time to have lunch and review the documents in the folders. Then you can ask them whatever you'd like."

"Say some more about the priest, if you would," Stonebrook said. "How is it that an Episcopal priest in Minnesota is tri-lingual?"

Rehmel flipped opened a file. "Here's what we know: Her name is Elizabeth Sánchez-Ríos. She grew up in Artigas, Uruguay, right on the Brazilian border. Her father was a jeweler, and her mother, who grew up right across the bridge in Quarai, Brazil, was an interpreter for the courts on both sides of the border, which is how her parents met and why Elizabeth speaks both Spanish and Portuguese. During Uruguay's military dictatorship in the 1980s, the family decided to flee the country. Her father's jeweler connections in the United States enabled them to emigrate to Chicago. Elizabeth was about 10 when they arrived, so her English sounds like that of a native speaker.

"Although she was raised Catholic, she wanted to be a priest, which is still not possible for a woman in the Catholic Church. So, at age 19, while in college at the University of Wisconsin, she started attending Episcopal services and converted. Following in her mother's footsteps, she became a court interpreter, in Milwaukee; but in her 30s, she decided to fulfill her ambition to become a priest. She matriculated to the General Theological Seminary in Manhattan, and was ordained an Episcopal priest in the year 2012. Her first assignment, as an assistant pastor, was in Wayzata, Minnesota, a very liberal congregation that appreciated her vivaciousness, her feminism, her competence, and her people skills. Because of her, the congregation has not only grown but has taken on additional social justice missions, including sheltering and supporting these two potential clients. She's the one who got the member of the congregation who is a partner in this firm to convince Phil Traxel to take on the case."

Traxel looked at his watch. "It's almost noon. We can order in lunch, if you'd like, or there are at least a dozen restaurants within a three block radius. What's your pleasure?"

Lauren turned to Rocky and asked with her eyes if she could answer. He gave a nod that only Lauren and Ted could recognize. Then she said: "How about if we check into the hotel and come back for sandwiches in a half hour?"

"That would work out well, Lauren," Traxel interposed. "I've booked your rooms at the Radisson, which is a 10-minute walk through the skyway. As soon as you let Sylvia know what you'd like to order, Ted can walk you over to the hotel."

"Sounds like a plan," said Stonebrook.

Once they had checked in, Stonebrook said, "I'm going to let you two catch up privately. I'm going for a walk outside. I'll find my way back to Dorken and Forken. I'll see you at 12:30."

Lauren invited Ted to her room, where they embraced and kissed. "Will you stay here with me tonight?"

"I thought you'd never ask." he replied.

"What?! We've been alone for a whole two minutes, including the elevator ride."

"The answer's 'yes,' emphatically 'yes!'"

"Okay, we don't have time for any hanky-panky right now. I want to tell you that it was really nice of you to recommend Rocky and me. So, thank you. But I'm not sure, yet, what we're supposed to do. And even if there's something for Rocky, I don't really see any role for me in this case."

Ted drew back about a foot, so that he could look at Lauren's whole face. "I'm guessing that Rocky has figured out that the only way for him to obtain evidence to corroborate our clients' allegations is to go undercover as a seaman on a Greenport Shipping vessel. I think that there are a lot of things that *you* can do – – research on the corporate shells to demonstrate that Greenport is only nominally the subsidiary; check out the International Maritime Organization to find us the perfect expert witness, and hang around Miami lawyers to get the skinny on admiralty law firms, so that we get the right attorney in the right law firm to advise us since nobody in Dornan Frager has any experience in this field; and, also, find us an economist who can both do mathematical magic *and* not turn off the jury."

"Hmm," she replied. "Those sound like genuine tasks. This may actually be a fun set of assignments."

"Yes, but, not unlike our case in Wyoming two years ago, Rocky's part could be very dangerous. If the officers, or even the fellow crew members, suspect that he's some sort of spy, they would have no hesitation about tossing him overboard. I had no idea what the assignment would entail when Phil Traxel sent around an email asking for an experienced P.I. who wasn't afraid of travel or danger. Now that I know, I'm a little embarrassed at being the one who may be responsible for Rocky's potentially having to walk the plank."

She kissed him on the lips. "As you know, Rocky can take of himself; and I'm assuming that your law firm will have some resources available in case of an emergency."

"I, of course, will do everything I can to make that possible, Lauren. But, remember, this is a law firm with a very clear hierarchy. And I am a private first class."

"More like a second lieutenant, I should think," she answered.

"Well, yeah. I do have the authority to request that the receptionist bring coffee into a conference room."

She smiled. "We should get back for lunch before people notice our being tardy, together."

Chapter 6: Meeting The Clients

TED HAVING GONE OFF TO some associates' luncheon, and the partners having disappeared, Rocky and Lauren had lunch alone in the conference room and perused the folders that the lawyers had provided. "Rocky, do you have any idea, yet, what they want you to do?" Lauren asked.

"The signs all point to their wanting me to play sailor on one of the Greenport ships."

"Yes!" she replied. "That's what Ted told me this morning. How did you know?" "I don't know for sure; but how else would I possibly corroborate the clients' assertions? Interviewing Greenport officials would not likely be a useful exercise."

"After Wyoming, aren't you a little gun-shy?" she asked. "I mean, getting tossed overboard in the middle of the Atlantic sounds a lot more dangerous than hanging around a park on dry land in Monroe, Wyoming, dodging a hitman with not-so-good aim."

Stonebrook patted her on the wrist. "If I had wanted a job in a risk-free environment, I would have become a bookkeeper and have spent my work weeks preparing long lists of revenues and expenditures. But I would have had to say 'no, sir' and 'yes, ma'am' all day long; and, besides, I'd be bored by 9:15 every morning. Being a P.I. is a lot more fun." He paused and then asked, "Are you becoming anxious about our line of work, Lauren?"

"Not at all, Rocky. And you are very protective of your staff. But *you're* the one who keeps getting shot at. Carol and I both worry about you."

"I'm flattered and appreciative. But danger is literally an occupational hazard for a P.I."

The two of them strolled around the law firm after lunch to get a feeling for what Stonebrook called "the lay of the turf." Apparently, neither the lawyers, the paralegals, nor the support staff were accustomed to having unaccompanied guests walking through the offices, but Rocky and Lauren just smiled at the people who stared at them with puzzled looks on their faces, sometimes waving, Elizabethanly, as if he and Lauren were visiting royalty.

"What'd you notice, Lauren?" Stonebrook said after they had completed their tour.

She stopped and curled her lip. "I was not surprised that all of the secretaries and paralegals were women, but it was serendipitous to see several women in the offices reserved for lawyers. And the firm seems to take diversity seriously because I saw a significant sprinkling of racial minorities here as well. Of course, the corner offices on all the floors we traversed were occupied by upper- middle-aged, white males."

"Did you also notice that all the people in the lobby areas of each floor were very well-dressed, obviously either wealthy clients or attorneys from other firms here to negotiate, merge, or acquire?"

"Yes, I did," she answered. "My guess is that the clients in the case for which they're hiring us probably don't fit the stereotype of the typical folk here at ...." She looked around to make sure no one was listening.... "Dorken and Forken."

"I think you're right, Lauren. Which means that there was probably some resistance to the idea of the firm's accepting this case. My guess is that even Ted is not privy to the internal discussions of the heavies in the firm."

"No matter. What they're all counting on, however, is what you can provide after they send you on ...uh, their little cruise."

"Yeah, I got that. Did Ted indicate to you what kinds of tasks that you might undertake while I'm on the High Seas?"

"Yes, he did. A lot of non-legal research, some of it requiring travel to Florida. That should impact what we charge them, right?"

"Absogigginglutely, Lauren."

They were already in the conference room, sipping coffee with Ted and the two partners, when the receptionist escorted Moises

Delgadinho, Leonicio Muñoz, and the Episcopal priest into the room and offered them beverages.

"Hello," the priest began, "My name is Elizabeth Sánchez-Ríos, and these two gentlemen are Moises Delgadinho and Leonicio Muñoz," she said, pointing to them individually. She was dressed in a gray skirt-suit, a black blouse, and a clerical collar. Delgadinho and Muñoz were clothed even more casually than was Stonebrook -- Delgadinho in cargo pants and a dingy, gray shirt tucked in, exposing a belt made of rope, Muñoz in jeans and a brown, slightly torn, cotton, V-neck sweater over a T-shirt.

Rehmel had a big smile pasted on his face, even if it didn't look genuine. "Welcome. Thank you all for coming." Looking at the priest, he said, "My name is Clifford Rehmel; is it more appropriate to call you 'Rev. Sánchez' or 'Mother Ríos'?"

"Actually," she answered, "'Pastor Sánchez-Ríos' would be the appropriate moniker; but if we're all going to be working together, 'Elizabeth' will do. Shall I call you 'Clifford' or 'Cliff?'"

Stonebrook hid his grin. He liked this woman already.

"Umm, 'Cliff' is fine," said Rehmel. "And, uh, this is my partner, Phil Traxel, to whom you have spoken on the telephone; and over here is our associate, Ted Bruner." They both shook hands with the priest and with the two clients.

Elizabeth's face had an expression that was somewhere between a smile and a smirk. It conveyed that she understood the obvious hierarchy embedded in the introductions – Rehmel had the highest status, Traxel was up there ("my partner"), and Bruner was a young, worker-bee ("our associate"). She then turned dramatically to face Stonebrook and Marlo. She waited just a moment, but when no information about them was forthcoming, she sallied forth: "Hello, you two must be the private investigators. I'm Elizabeth."

Lauren stood up, took her hand, and said "Very nice to meet you, I'm Lauren Marlo."

Stonebrook also stood. He grasped Elizabeth's hand in both of his and said, *"Encantado. Me chamo Rocky Stonebrook; y penso que deveríamos traducir para os clientes."* [**Enchanted. My name is Rocky Stonebrook, and I think we should translate for the clients**]. He had spoken in a mixture of Spanish and Portuguese.

She had a look of both delight and surprise on her face. *"Obviamente, você sabia que eu falaba Portuñol, pero como es que Vd. aprendía a hablarla?"* **[Evidently, you knew that I spoke Portuñol, but where did you learn to speak it?]**

Without answering her directly, he turned to the two clients, extended his hand to each of them, and said *"muito prazer"* to Moises Delgadinho and *"mucho gusto"* to Leonicio Muñoz, the appropriate Portuguese and Spanish equivalents, respectively, of 'nice to meet you.'

Elizabeth translated for the lawyers, and then added: "You didn't tell me that the investigator you hired spoke fluent Portuguese and Spanish as well as a hybrid of the two languages that those of us who grew up on the Uruguay-Brazilian border call *Portuñol*. I am *very* impressed."

Turning to Stonebrook, she asked, "You not only speak both languages fluently, but your Spanish is *Porteño*, and your Portuguese is *Carioca*. How did you manage that?"

Stonebrook first answered in Spanish and Portuguese for the clients and then translated into English: "My mother is Argentine, so I came by the *Porteño* accent, spoken in Buenos Aires and Montevideo, naturally. I did a junior-year-abroad in Río de Janeiro when I was in college, hence the *Carioca* accent of those in that city; and I picked up *Portuñol, the hybrid,* in prison where it was a kind of creole spoken by the New Yoricans and some Portuguese-speaking guys from eastern Massachusetts."

The reactions around the table varied: Rehmel hadn't known of Stonebrook's prison record and couldn't hide his shock; Traxel grinned and blushed slightly: Ted had forewarned him, but he, Traxel, had forgotten to clue in Rehmel, whose mouth dropped open. Lauren kept a straight face, as if Rocky had merely said that today was Thursday, but winked at Ted, who returned the gesture. Delgadinho and Muñoz had broad smiles on their faces – Rocky's "confession" clearly made them feel a whole lot more comfortable than they had been when they entered the law firm's fancy portals. And Pastor Elizabeth looked downright pleased.

"I shall sit down now," she said, "and just play translator for Moises and Leonicio; but your language skills, Rocky," she said, turning to him, "are a great relief to me... and to the Congregation sponsoring them and providing their retainer.

"In order not to embarrass the clients, I shall not translate this or the next sentence. All of you should know that neither of these men has any money, so the $10,000 retainer that the firm has requested comes from a special collection provided by the parishioners of St. Edward's by-the-Lake. After my initial conversation with Phil, where he sought to explain the difficulties presented by this case, Rector Daniels and I – and the Vestry Committee of the parish – were all worried that the lawsuit might not have much chance of success. That the firm has hired a polyglot investigator will be a source of enormous reassurance to us all."

Rocky acknowledged her compliment with a teasing reply. "That the Assistant Rector ably forms noun clauses in her explication is an excellent start." He gave her a thumbs up, and she stuck her tongue out at him, so that only he and Lauren could see it, and then smiled.

"Well," interposed Traxel, "now that the introductions are complete, why don't we start. Pastor Elizabeth, will you make sure that our offer of coffee or soft drinks is legitimate. I'm aware that in some cultures, one feels obliged not to accept hospitality until the third offer."

She gave a quick look at Stonebrook, just partially rolling her eyes, but translated. Moises got up, and brought back three soft drinks, one for Leonicio, one for himself, and one for Pastor Elizabeth. He turned to Traxel and said, "*obrigado*," which Traxel figured out meant "thank you" without Elizabeth's having to translate.

"Let me begin with a very brief overview of the two island groups," Elizabeth began; "and, Rocky, would you be good enough to translate for Leonicio and Moises?" In English, she explained to the lawyers:

"Ever since 1494, the date of a treaty between Spain and Portugal, the Azores – a group of volcanic islands several hundred miles to the west of Portugal – have been Portuguese, and the Canary Islands, off the coast of Morocco, have been Spanish. They both have tourism and agricultural-based economies, but because they are islands, they have also been fishing sites and shipping ports. The Azores have about 250,000 people while the Canaries have almost 2.5 million. The Canaries are much further developed, and tourism is a much bigger deal there, partly because of their closer location to the mainland; and lots of Brits, Germans, and Spaniards show up every year. You should hear Leonicio's and Moises's stories directly from them."

Chapter 7: The Plaintiffs' Stories

MOISES BEGAN, AND ELIZABETH TRANSLATED simultaneously:

[**TRANSLATION**]: "My name is Moises Delgadinho. I am 27 years old and come from the island of São Miguel in the Azores. My father is a fisherman. I am the youngest of five sons. My oldest brother is a fisherman like my father. The second brother works as a clerk in the local government, and the others are dairy farmers, with just a few cows. There was no room for me in the fishing business, and I cannot afford to buy cows. So, I had several jobs on boats going from island to island in the Azores. I got to know a lot about working on boats. My brother the government clerk finds out when bigger boats and ships are coming to São Miguel, and I began hanging around the port and signed on bigger vessels. At first I work on ships that go from the Azores just to Portugal and Spain.

"The work was hard, but it's easy to save money because there is no place to spend the salary except when we land in ports-of-call. Then one day I hear in a bar rumors of a big merchant ship coming to São Miguel from Africa and traveling to northern Europe that needs extra sailors. It has a French name, *La Galissionnière*, but it is owned by a Greek company, *Hestia Etoupeía*.

"I went to an office in *Ponta Delgada*, the largest town on the island, and I gave a list of all of the boats and ships where I have worked. They seem impressed and promise me a better position than just deckhand. They say I could be in the engineering department, working in maintenance of machinery and appliances, which pays better than deckhands. So, I say 'yes' even though you have to sign up for two years at a pay rate of 60 euros per day or almost 44,000 euros for the two years. The crew was from many countries: The captain was Greek, the other officers were from Spain and Portugal, and at least one department head was from Burma. The sailors were from all over.

The language for giving orders was Spanish. That was hard for many of the sailors from Africa and northern Europe but okay for me because I had picked up some Spanish working on the boats that went from the Azores to Spain. Besides, Spanish and Portuguese share a lot of words.

"The first day the officers all seemed okay, and they served good food. But as soon as we were out on the ocean, beginning on the second day, things got ugly. The officers were mean. Some of them whose Spanish was not their first language were hard to understand when they gave orders, but they got very mad when sailors couldn't understand them. They had whips and lashed sailors on their bare backs whenever the sailors did something wrong or didn't carry out the orders fast enough. Besides whipping sailors, they denied food to crew members who the supervisors thought were not working hard enough. If they thought deckhands or maintenance crew were not working fast enough, they made us sleep on deck, which was impossible to do with the wind and waves.

"By moving quickly and working hard, I avoided getting beaten at first; but part of my job was to keep the life-saving equipment and fire-fighting equipment in good shape. I discovered that there were not enough life jackets for everyone, and many of the life jackets were torn, and the buckles had rusted off of some, and so they were useless. I also noticed that the ship was missing some of the lifeboats it was built to have. And the fire-fighting equipment was several years old. I brought this to the attention of the Chief Engineer, who told me to 'forget it.'

"I made the mistake of going over the supervisor's head to the Third Mate that if we had a fire or a serious storm, there would not be enough life jackets or boats and that the Chief Engineer was not interested in the problem. After that I was demoted to deckhand and given double shifts. They took away some meals, and I got whipped. I still have scars."

He unbuttoned his shirt and turned around. The rows of welts on his back generated involuntary gasps among the lawyers. He put his shirt back on and continued.

"We crew members grumbled more and more to ourselves. Some talked about getting off at the first port and not coming back. But the officers must have had spies because they never let us off the ship. We docked in Leixoes, Portugal; Vigo and Bilbao, Spain; Ghent and Antwerp, Belgium; Rotterdam, the Netherlands; Southampton, UK;

and we were on our way to Greenock, Scotland, when Leonicio and I were dumped off. They never paid me."

Elizabeth could see that Moises had finished. "Before Leonicio speaks, do you have any questions for Moises?"

Rehmel asked, "So that we have some precision about the compensatory damages, what is the conversion rate from euros to dollars?"

Elizabeth said, "I can answer that since I was recently in Europe and had to deal with exchange rates. One dollar is equivalent to .8 euro; so 44,000 euros would be $55,000 for the full two years."

"Thank you," replied Traxel, so that he could ask the next question. "How was the treatment on *La Galissionnière* different from that on other merchant ships on which Mr. Delgadinho worked?"

Elizabeth translated the question and Delgadinho's answer.

[TRANSLATION]: "Treatment varied, depending on the owner, the captain, the flag, the mates, the common language, and the ports of call. But nowhere was there flogging; on no other ships were sailors denied food as a punishment; and on no other ships were sick sailors or crewmen who the officers thought were trouble-makers tossed overboard."

"You personally observed that?" It was Ted who had asked the question, the incredulity showing in his tone of voice.

[TRANSLATION]: "Yes. One of the deck-hands got some sort of stomach poisoning after we had left Antwerp. Nothing the ship's paramedic gave him helped. He began to stink, really badly, and the crewmen who shared his cabin all demanded to be moved. I happened to be coming off a shift at midnight when I saw the Third Mate supervising two sailors carrying the sick man, whose name by the way, was Mohammed Belkoja, up to the deck They gagged him, so no one could hear him scream; then they bound his hands and feet and threw him overboard."

"Did you try to interfere?" It was Rehmel who asked it in a soft way, so that it wouldn't sound like cross-examination. The effort at softness failed.

[TRANSLATION]: "No. I had hidden in the shadows, so no one saw me. Because I had been recently demoted, I was sure that if I made any protest, I would have joined Belkoja overboard."

Traxel tried to shift the tone. "Were there any other atrocities of which you have personal knowledge?"

A short colloquy ensued between Pastor Elizabeth and Delgadinho. "He's asking me to request you to be clear about what 'personal knowledge' encompasses."

Ted opened his mouth as if to answer but, looking at his boss, thought better of it.

Traxel answered this way: "Why doesn't he tell us what other events he knows about, and we can then decide if they fall within the perimeter of 'personal knowledge'?"

[**TRANSLATION**]: "There was one sailor from Italy, the only Italian-speaker on board, a man named Marcantonio, whose Spanish was weak. When he didn't know Spanish, he just used Italian words. Unless they were almost the same as Spanish, no one understood him. I never found out his other name. Most crew members called him 'Marco' or 'Antonio' because when he had introduced himself as 'Marcantonio,' they thought he had said his name was 'Marco Antonio,' and he just accepted it because it was too hard for him to explain. So he was pretty frustrated most of the time. He let out his anger by complaining a lot: He complained about the food, about the work assignments, about the close quarters in the cabins, about the shortage of water, about the rats and mice, about supervisors not explaining their orders in a way that he could understand, about their not giving him time to study Spanish, and about the Burmese supervisor. He spoke up, angrily, when they wouldn't let us off the boat in port.

"After we left Vigo, on the way to Bilbao, he disappeared. Maybe on land, an employee can walk away and disappear. But on a boat, that can't happen. If someone is on board one day, and the next day while we're at sea, he's not there, it means somebody tossed him overboard."

"Is it possible," asked Rehmel, "that Mr. Marcantonio was so frustrated, or so angry, that he jumped overboard and tried to swim to shore?"

[**TRANSLATION**]: "Not possible. Marco told us he was not a very good swimmer, and he also had an unusually large fear of sharks."

Ted thought that he could interpose a question here. "Did any of the seamen ask an officer what ever happened to Marcantonio?"

[**TRANSLATION**]: "Of course. We asked various supervisors, the Mates, and even the Captain. All the officers and supervisors shrugged their shoulders and pretended that they had no idea. If the goal was to cut down on complaining, it sure worked!"

Delgadinho sat down, and Elizabeth nodded at Leonicio, who stood up and opened his mouth to speak; but before he could say anything, Traxel assured him that he could stay seated while he spoke. Elizabeth translated what Traxel had said, and Leonicio sat down with a palpable sense of relief.

[**TRANSLATION**]: "Thank you to this law firm. I am Leonicio Muñoz, age 29, from Spain, specifically the Canary Islands. I grew up on Tenerife, the largest island, but I moved when I was 21 to *Gran Canaria* because it has the biggest freight port. I always liked the water, and I started as a teenager working on the ferries that took passengers and cargo among the seven islands. I was a hard worker, and one of the ferry captains hired me to work for his brother on cargo boats from *Gran Canaria* to Morocco and to the Spanish mainland.

"As I gained more experience, I managed to get hired on bigger ships. Deckhand work is very hard, so I was hoping to get an easier job. The brother recommended me to another boat to be a steward, where I learned how to serve meals. So, when I read the announcement that *La Glassionière* was looking for stewards who spoke Spanish, at good pay, I signed up. At first, everything went fine. Then one day, about three weeks out, the boatswain got up from his chair in the dining room very quickly and bumped into me, and made me spill a bowl of chili on the First Mate. He didn't care how or why I spilled the chili. He yelled at me to get out and to never show up again in the dining room as a steward.

"So, I got demoted to deckhand. The closest friend I made was this fellow here, Moises. He and I figured out how to communicate in a mixture of Spanish and Portuguese, in what Madre Elisabeta calls *Portuñol*, although we didn't know there was a name for it. The officers did not like that we spoke the hybrid and told us not to do it. The Second Mate overheard me talking to Moises in the hybrid and hit me on the head and in the jaw with a blackjack. It broke two of my teeth. Because I was bleeding, Moises took me under the arm and started walking me to the first aid station, but the Second Mate yelled at him to let go of me. When Moises did not move fast enough, the Mate pushed him down and kicked him. I crawled to the first aid station, but the guy in charge really had no training to be a nurse, so he gave me two aspirin and a tumbler of water and told me to go back to work.

"After that, the officers looked at us suspiciously whenever they saw us together and would smack their blackjacks into their hands to threaten us. When we had left England, sailing toward Ireland, they put us into a small lifeboat with a jug of water and enough food for one day and told us to row. They warned us that if we survived and ever showed up anywhere in Spain or Portugal, including the Azores or the Canaries, we would be marked for slow and painful deaths. They also said that it would be a big mistake to contact our families because the Company was going to tell them we died at sea. We asked about our pay, and they laughed. The Third Mate said, 'You should be happy that you get a boat and one day's food; we could have sent you to join the fish with Belkoja and Marcantonio.'"

"It took three days to get to Wales. We made a net out of my shirt and caught a fish that flopped on the boat with a wave, and we also managed to capture and kill a sea bird. So, we had raw food to sustain us, but once we drank up the water, we had no liquid and were ... how you say? ...*dehydrated* ...when we made landfall. If it was not for Madre Elisabeta, we would have been shipped home and killed. We have been afraid to contact our families. We have nothing except what the members of the St. Edward's Church give us."

When Muñoz finished, no one said anything. The stories of the two men were compelling, credible, and frightening. There was no appropriate response. Elizabeth looked over at Stonebrook, who grimaced, signaling that both men – and her translation --were impressive.

Traxel caught the exchanged look and asked Stonebrook: "Well, Rocky, what questions do you have of either Pastor Sánchez-Ríos or of Mr. Delgadinho or of Mr. Muñoz?"

Stonebrook answered: "I'll need to speak at length to both men about how the ships operate, so that I don't look like a neophyte when I board *La Galissionière*; but we certainly don't have to do that here. Let me get directions from Elizabeth, and I'll make an appointment to chat with Moises and Leonicio at St. Edward's-by-the-Lake."

"Does that mean you'll take the assignment?"

"The short answer," he replied, "is 'yes.' Of course, we have to negotiate the specifics of our contract, the limits on out-of-pocket expenses, Lauren's role, and several other items, including the firm's back-up resources here in Minneapolis. But those are details. Lauren and I are both on-board, as it were, and look forward to doing what we can for señores Delgadinho and Muñoz."

Chapter 8: St. Edward's-by-the-Lake

THE LAKE NEAR WHICH ST. Edward's sits and which gets included in its name, is Lake Minnetonka. The ninth largest of Minnesota's famed 10,000 lakes, Minnetonka is surrounded by 13 municipalities, all western suburbs of Minneapolis and all populated by well-heeled denizens.

St. Edwards-by-the-Lake has a reputation of attracting congregants whom the envious members of other churches in the area characterize as "Limousine Liberals." They have an intensive social justice program, led the struggle within the Anglican-Episcopal community to support an official approval of same-sex marriages, and happily hired Elizabeth Sánchez-Ríos as their assistant pastor..

Ted received permission to accompany Rocky and Lauren for an all-day visit on Friday to St. Edwards in the suburb called Wayzata (*correctly pronounced "Why-zett-ah;" locals easily spot outsiders by the way they mispronounce the name*). They met the two families that had provided housing for Moises and Leonicio, chatted with Rector Daniels and with the President of the Congregation to gauge the level of support for the two refugees, and had lunch with the Dornan-Frager partner who had convinced Phil Traxel to take the case. Most of the day, however, they spent with Moises, Leonicio, and Pastor Elizabeth.

Lauren and Ted both took careful notes – each of them with slightly different perspectives about which facts were pertinent – while Rocky purposely made eye-contact with the two clients during the conversations. Because of Stonebrook's Brazilian accent in Portuguese, Moises and Leonicio both urged Rocky to pretend that he was from the Canary Islands. There had been a long history of *Canarios* going back and forth to Latin America such that the accents of Canary Islanders and those of Latin Americans were almost indistinguishable, and if he were to say that he was from one of the two smaller Canary islands, *La Gomera* or *El Hierro*, no one would likely challenge him.

At about 3:00 o'clock, two interpreters showed up, one bilingual in Spanish and English and the other bilingual in Portuguese and English. "My brain is frazzled from translating since 9:00 this morning," Elizabeth announced as she welcomed the translators. "Lauren and Ted, each of you pick a plaintiff, and feel free to continue asking him questions, using the translators. There are soft drinks in the refectory. Please help yourselves."

She then turned to Stonebrook. "I'm going on coffee break; would you like to join me?"

"Indeed!" he answered, rising from his chair and stretching. "Make mine a double."

"Do you want to drive?" she asked. "There's a lovely bakery and coffee shop a short distance from here." He nodded, and as they climbed into his rental car, Elizabeth removed her collar.

"Is this bakery anti-clerical?" he asked with a smirk.

"Nope," she replied, "but when I'm on break, I prefer to wear civies."

She made small talk about Lake Minnetonka and St. Edward's until they arrived at the Wuollet Bakery on Lake Street. They each ordered a coffee and a muffin; they sat in a secluded corner.

"Shall we exchange autobiographies?" she asked.

"Well, I already know something about you," he replied, seemingly unsurprised by her query. "You're the daughter of a Brazilian-Uruguayan couple, emigrated to the U.S. as a child, were raised Catholic, converted to Episcopalian at the University of Wisconsin, matriculated to an Episcopal seminary in New York, and landed the St. Edward's job right after ordination."

"Quite right. And this job turns out to have been a perfect placement for me. Now, all that I know about you is that you are a private detective from Cleveland, Ohio. How'd that happen?"

"Right after graduating from Ohio State," he began, "I got caught in a marijuana sting and got sent to prison in New Jersey for a year. Because of my degree, I was put in charge of the prison library and spent a lot of time there reading. I wrote some poetry, which got published after I got out; but almost all of my employment interviews ended abruptly when I told the interviewer where I had spent the previous 12 months. A nice chap took pity on me and hired me to work the cash register at his hardware store, but I was not really cut out for retail work. I had developed a lot of street smarts in the slammer, and I decided to hang out a shingle as a private detective. Turns out to be what you would call 'the perfect placement.'"

"What do you like about it?"

He looked at her and smiled. "You tell me yours, and I'll tell you mine."

Elizabeth laughed. "Okay. You can take the girl out of the Catholic Church, but you can't pull the Church totally out of her. Episcopalianism is...umm,. close enough for religious work. It's Catholicism without the Pope, and although I admire Francis, he still won't let me be a priest merely because I have two X chromosomes. So, in this church, I *can* be a priest, and this particular congregation is very supportive about my various social justice causes. The collar allows me to accomplish a whole lot of things I would not be able to do as a civilian. Besides, I've gotten to be very close to many of the members of the Congregation. They are family. And I feel like I'm making a significant contribution."

She paused and then asked, "And where are you, spiritually, Rocky?"

Stonebrook leaned back in his chair and spread his hands, as if stunned. "Whoa! I thought you wanted to know what I like about being a private detective."

"Well, I am interested in your answer to that question, but the spirituality question seems more pertinent. First things first."

He fidgeted, scratched his neck, looked her in the eye, and curled his lip. Finally, he said, "You know, for most people I wouldn't answer that question and would change the subject. I find it intrusive."

Elizabeth put her hands on her hips. "Well, of course it's intrusive. Isn't that what's in the very nature of intimate conversation?"

"Oh? And what constitutes an *intimate* conversation?"

She caught herself formulating an answer to his question. "No, that's a clever diversion, Mr. Private Detective. I acknowledge that my question was indeed intrusive. Your response should be either to divulge or to say that the question is out of bounds. However, if you had really thought it was out-of-bounds, you would have said so. And your reply that you wouldn't answer it for *most* people implied that you would make an exception for me."

"My hunch is that you are a lot more indirect with your parishioners, but I find your forthrightness to be quite charming." He took a deep breath. "All right: I not only regard the question to be intrusive, I'm uncomfortable with the term 'spirituality' – I find it to be vague, vapid, and void of genuine meaning. It seems to be a carefully calculated, euphemistic way of asking someone about his religious beliefs, practices, and affiliations, which are personal."

"Exactly so. But euphemisms are useful, linguistic lubricants. If a teenage parishioner, for example, comes to Confession and is obviously hesitant about discussing sex, I am more likely to elicit a helpful answer from her if I ask if she's 'sexually active' than if I were to ask if she's been laid recently."

Stonebrook guffawed. "Yeah, I can appreciate that," he said.

"If this were a first date," she went on, "the question might be inappropriate. However, in a conversation between a member of the clergy and someone whose duties impact her work, I think it should be deemed permissible."

"You took off your collar, remember?"

"I saw you eyeing the other customers in this bakery as we sat down. You don't stop being a detective even when you're on coffee break, do you?"

"*Touché*. Nevertheless, the real reason that I am hesitant to answer your question is that no matter how I try to explain it, my answer is likely to come off as insulting to you, precisely because I recognize that taking off your collar is merely symbolic."

"Tell me if I have accurately reframed what you just said: You don't trust that I can accept you as a colleague or friend or ally or even as a working partner if your religious views fall outside the corners of what you evidently deem to be a rigid rectangle or triangle."

"Ouch! I suppose that your 'translation' is quite reasonable. However, I *do* trust you, so I *shall* respond as you have asked. My father was Jewish, my mother Catholic. They sent me to a Unitarian Sunday School. I have attended various Protestant churches with friends, mainly to get a handle on what and how they do things rather than to seek ...mmm... spiritual sustenance. I have concluded that almost all of the religious outfits invariably fall back on the same arrogant premises."

"Sorry to interrupt," she said, "but how are religious premises 'arrogant'?"

"The shared premises among all of them are two-fold: First, there is, or are, one or more omniscient and omnipotent, supernatural entities who, or which, have a divine Master Plan so complex, universal, and comprehensive that puny humans can't possibly comprehend it; and Second, notwithstanding the first premise, if a puny mortal repeats the right words (written long ago in some other circumstance) or sings the right hymns (composed in response to some previous crisis), then he or she can cause the supernatural(s) to modify his, her, its, or their Master Plan. That's what's arrogant."

"Oh, boy!" she replied. "I look forward to many, long, stimulating conversations about the universe, about life, about supernatural Beings, and about arrogance. But," she said, looking at her watch, "it's time to get back to St. Edward's." She got up, grabbed the check, and paid the cashier.

As he started the car, she asked, "Have you ever been married?"

He turned to look at her as he answered. "No,.. however,..."

"However, you are in a committed relationship. I can read it in your eyes. And from the vibes between Lauren and Ted, I'm fairly certain that your woman is not Lauren Marlo."

"'Yes' to both surmises. But I acknowledge a special connection between the two of us, a certain resonance in our brain circuits. That's so rare and too valuable to ignore."

"Aha! It sounds as if you're propositioning a kind of emotional adultery."

He pulled over and stopped the car. "Listen, I don't want there to be any tension between us. Our chemistry is palpable. If we were the same gender, we would be hang-out pals; if I weren't in a committed relationship, and if we didn't live 1,000 miles apart, I'm confident that we'd become lovers. As it is, we are on the same team and have a mutual goal of getting justice for those two guys who washed up in Wales on your watch. I take delight in your mind, I find you very attractive, and I appreciate both your unpredictable personality and your expansive world view. I'm very pleased to be working with you on this case, and I look forward to finding legitimate reasons to spend time with you. How's that for candor and transparency?"

"Let me respond in kind," she answered. She leaned over and kissed him softly. He kissed back, and they locked lips for a long time.

She pulled back and felt her face. "This doesn't happen very often, but I can tell that I'm blushing."

"It flatters you, ... and it flatters me. I wonder if the vibes that *we* give off are as noticeable to everyone else as those that emanate from Lauren and Ted."

They both laughed in order to shift to a less uncomfortable mood, and Rocky started the car.

Chapter 9: Preparation

ROCKY, LAUREN, AND TED WERE in a small conference room at Dornan Frager, and Lauren was reading from a checklist she had prepared. "You have both passports?"

"I will. My real American passport, under the name of Pedro Fishkin, is in my dresser drawer back in Cleveland; I'll retrieve it when I get home to pack. A forger I met in prison, who owes me some favors, is, as we speak, creating a Spanish passport, under the name of Julián Arroyo and showing an address in *San Sebastián* on the island of *La Gomera* in the Canaries. I'll pick it up from him in Boston on the way overseas."

"Where will you keep your American passport, Rocky?"

"In a hidden compartment in this wide belt I bought at an Army-Navy store this morning and that I have pounded, scratched, smashed, and dirtied up to make it look old and well-used."

"What about a tracker?" asked Ted.

"It's not going to do any good while I'm on the ship, but I'm going to take one like we found in my shoe in Wyoming. But instead of putting it in my shoe, where, as you will both remember, it felt like a stone, I'm going to have my dentist embed it in one of my wisdom teeth. It will be rigged to send off sound waves when I bite down on it as hard as I can."

"How far will the signal reach, Rocky?"

"According to the ex-FBI dude in Philadelphia who's arranging for me to get it, the signal can be heard 100-150 miles away, but it needs a receiver."

"What kind of receiver?"

"Any kind of military installation that uses radar will see it on their screen."

Lauren spoke up. "How will that find you? This is not a governmental operation."

"By a back door. Elizabeth has asked Senator Klobuchar, who sits on the Senate Commerce, Science, and Transportation Committee, which, among other things, oversees the Coast Guard, to have a sealed order sent to all military installations. It will say that if and when they receive a weird ping on their radar screens, they are to establish its location and report to a Commodore Costaign, the military attaché in London."

"And what will this Commodore Costaign do with the information?"

"Not sure. But it's the best we could arrange on the fly."

Lauren put a question mark next to the tracker on her list. "What about money?"

"I don't know what good money will do on a cargo ship, but Spain uses euros, so I'll change dollars into euros at Logan on my way out."

"Item No. 4:" she said, "the itinerary. What do we know about *La Galissionière*?"

"I have that one," said Ted. "A law school colleague of mine working for the Navy Department was able to get the information for me. It's not classified, so he was able to email it to me within an hour after I inquired. *La Galissionière* is scheduled to stop at the port of *Santa Cruz* on the Canary Island of Tenerife a week from Tuesday to pick up cargo and crew. It is bound for various ports in the Mediterranean – *Casa Blanca* (Morocco), Tangier (Morocco), Algiers (Algeria), Tunis (Tunisia), Alexandria (Egypt), Bodrum (Turkey), Samos (Greece), Siracusa (Italy), and Ajaccio (Corsica)."

"Next on the list is contact information other than the tracker," read Lauren. "How will we know where you are or if you are in trouble?"

"I've given some thought to that question," answered Stonebrook. "At first I figured that I should have a regular check-in time; however, if everything were jim dandy, but I didn't have a way to communicate it, you guys would jump to the wrong conclusions and try to send in the cavalry. On the other hand, if things were awful, and the bad guys surrounded me as I tried to contact you, you would also make the wrong inference and do nothing to rescue me.

"So, I've come up with a code that only you two and Donna will know.

~ If I mention food, assume that I'm going to have trouble sending another message in the near future.

~ I'll throw in a number, which will represent the number of days before any communication will be possible. Saying that my buddy and

I drank four grogs of rum between us means that you shouldn't expect any more messages for four days.

~ If I mention rain, that means that I think they are on to me and are likely to try something unpleasant very soon.

~ If I mention a name (of an uncle or a sister or my dentist or of a geographical site, it will really refer to the place where I'm sending the message. You'll need to decode it because it can't be as obvious as 'I miss the White House' to refer to *Casa Blanca*, Morocco."

Ted interrupted. "Give us an example of the kind of code you would use, Rocky."

Stonebrook paused and then said: "If I ask you to send a birthday card to my niece Patracleo, what would you guess that meant?"

After an excruciating silence of about 25 seconds, Lauren answered: "I know – it means you're in Egypt—because Patracleo is Cleopatra reversed."

"Right on, Lauren! Very good," Rocky said with a big smile. "Let's try another one, a little more difficult: If I were to write that I'm looking forward to one of Grandma Barbara's mackerel dinners, what would I be saying?"

He sat patiently while Lauren and Ted struggled to solve the riddle. Finally, Ted said, "This may seem far out, but then, *you're* far out, Rocky: 'Grandma Barbara' refers to the Barbary Coast, an 18th century term for North Africa; and as an amateur angler, I'm aware that the largest fish in the mackerel category is the tuna. So, together, they spell 'Tunis.'"

"Bingo!" said Stonebrook. Lauren jumped up and impulsively kissed Ted on the cheek. "That was brilliant!"

"It appears as if the two of you together will have no problem decoding my messages. That's very good."

"However," interposed Lauren, "just how do you expect to send us messages from a ship in the Mediterranean Sea?"

"I don't," replied Stonebrook. "But I'm hoping to be able to disembark at each port and to find my way to a post office."

Ted shook his head. "Based on what Moises and Leonicio have told us, they may not let you off the boat, Rocky, and even if they do, you are likely to have minders."

"That's true, Ted. And there are two other dimensions that spring from that. First, if I do manage to get to post offices, I'll have to send the messages in Spanish, since it is unlikely that a deckhand from a small island in the Canaries would know English, which means that you'll need to have someone translate the messages. And second, I would, for sure, send off alarms if I sent letters or postcards to the United States."

"Dornan Frager," said Ted, "has law firms with which we have collaborative relationships in Paris, Lisbon, and Madrid. I'll get you an address – at the Madrid firm – and a name you can use as the addressee for any letters or postcards."

"That would be super, Ted. Thanks."

"Next," read Lauren, "I've booked you on a flight and some ferry boats, so that you can make a quick tour of both *La Gomera* and *El Hierro* islands before you show up at the recruiting office in Tenerife... just in case somebody on board asks you questions."

"A prudent plan, Lauren. Thank you. And what are you going to be doing?"

"I'm going to Miami, to Dover, Delaware, and to London to check out admiralty lawyers, corporate schemes, and the International Maritime Organization."

"How about you, Ted?"

"I'll be in the law library, doing research for you."

"Okay, I guess we're all in this up to our necks." He extended his arm, and the three of them stacked wrists, gesturing as if they were The Three Musketeers.

Chapter 10: On The Way To London

STONEBROOK INVITED LAUREN TO JOIN him and Donna for supper the night before he took of/f for the Canary Islands, so that Lauren could, in a private setting, explain to Donna what the communication system would be. Lauren had met Donna, remembering that she was a Eurasian beauty; and episodically they had crossed paths enough to say "hello" and "how are you," but they had never really had a chance to chat. In the informal setting at Rocky and Donna's apartment, the two women took an immediate liking to each other.

"So, how will this guy in the Madrid law firm contact us if he gets a coded message?"

"His name is Andrés Janer, at the law firm of Fernández y Asociados. He speaks English and will be able to translate Rocky's messages and to email the translations to the three of us. I'm going to send him our email addresses – Ted's, mine, and – with your permission – *yours*. Janer will not know the codes, however, so we three will have to do that and share our guesses electronically."

"What if the three of us have different interpretations of the message, or if Pedro is so recondite in his message that none of us can figure it out?" Donna called him Rocky in front of other people, but used his real name, Pedro, at home. It was a sign of trust that she referred to him as "Pedro" in front of Lauren.

"Yeah, that's always possible. We can chat electronically, or over our cell phones, until we reach a consensus"

"Fine. But even if we are in agreement about the meaning of Pedro's message, what do we do with it?"

"If he mentions 'rain,' we need to call in the cavalry."

"And where might the corral be?"

Lauren gritted her teeth and nodded. "Donna, you have identified a weakness in our plan. The closest thing we have to back-up is this guy

Commodore Costaign, who *may* – and I emphasize *may* – be able to call in some markers for a platoon of marines or sailors."

Donna smiled. "'Markers,' eh? Ol' Slyboots here has obviously been teaching you prison slang."

"Occasionally, he drops a *bon mot* or two, and I scramble to expand my street vocabulary."

"Well, let's get back to the decoding operation. When are we going to have a chance to practice?"

"I suggest that we do it on the plane," Lauren answered. And before Donna could frame a question, Lauren explained: "Although I had intended to go to Miami and Dover before hitting London, when I discovered that your ballet company was flying to London, I figured that I could reboot my itinerary. So, I booked passage on the same flight that you are on, and I wangled the seat next to you. We'll have the long flight over the Atlantic to practice a variety of scenarios."

"That sounds wonderful, but how did you manage to exchange seats with my dancing colleague?"

"Using Stonebrookian techniques."

"Aha. Well, Pedro has been encomiastic about your work. I should have inferred that he meant that you have learned how to do things his way." Donna hoisted her wine glass in recognition of her two skillful dinner companions.

On the plane, after sharing background info and telling stories about Stonebrook, they turned to the task at hand. "How about," suggested Donna, "if each of us pretends to be Pedro, writing a coded message in hopes that Donna, Lauren, and Ted will be able to decipher it without tipping his hand to the bad guys?"

Working separately for about 15 minutes, they exchanged messages. Donna's said,

"Dear Andrés – I can't wait to see you again. We can help Grandpa pick oranges unless it rains like it did at Eduardo's farm at the lake."

Having read it three times, Lauren said, "Let me think out loud: At first I thought 'Grandpa' was significant, but I'm leaning toward its being a red herring. After all, if Andrés is supposed to be his cousin, then they would indeed have a grandfather in common. I'll hazard a guess that 'the oranges' are a substitute for tangerines, which is a substitute for Tangier, a port in Morocco. Rain, as we know, means that he thinks they're on to him. And I believe that 'Eduardo's farm at the lake' means St. Edward's-by-the-Lake, which, in turn, means Leonicio and Moises. So, he's telling us that he thinks they have figured out that he's not who he is pretending to be, that he'll be getting off in Tangier, unless they throw him overboard somewhere between *Casa Blanca* and Tangier."

Donna's eyes widened with admiration. "You are really good at this. I shall trust your judgment when we get an actual message from Pedro. Now give me yours."

Just then one of the dancers came back to Donna's row and asked, "Fred, do you have any aspirin? I have a terrible headache."

"Sure," Donna answered. "Hold on." She reached for her purse and handed two aspirin to the woman, who thanked her and returned to her seat.

Lauren gave Donna a puzzled look. "That woman called you 'Fred!'"

"Yes, she did. My professional name here in the ballet company is Frederika Roxon. A few of my fellow dancers feel that they are close enough to call me 'Fred.'"

"Why do you need a professional name that's diffferent from your real name?"

"Why does Pedro Fishkin need a professional name like 'Rocky Stonebrook'? It helps to compartmentalize our lives."

"All right," said Lauren, recognizing that she may have already stepped over a boundary line. "If you're ready for a possible coded message, here's my offering. I should warn you that it is intentionally difficult," and she handed her the coded message. It said: "If we go to the islands in the summer, not the ones where the dogs play, but where they have the sandy TV news programs, I may feel it necessary to stay longer than you would like."

Donna put her hands up to her temples, as if her fingers were able to channel some brain waves. "I'll think aloud, as you did, Lauren. 'Islands which are not the ones where dogs play' must refer to the Canaries, so named, according to Pedro, not because of birds but because of dogs found there by early explorers. *Canaria* derives from *canis,* the Latin word for dogs. So, it refers to some *other* islands. Next, he mentions 'sandy TV news programs,' which I'm guessing refers to Al-Jazeera, the TV news station that broadcasts from Qatar. I was curious when I first heard of Al-Jazeera, about the derivation of the name, and an Egyptian friend of mine told me it meant 'island' or 'peninsula.'

"Initially, I thought that the message must refer to Corsica, which is the only island that *La Galissionière* will be visiting. But, then, there would be no reason to throw in the sentence about the sandy TV news. So, I have an idea, but I need to do what I would do when Pedro sends us actual messages, and that's look on Google. I'm going to look up something on my cell phone; please don't let the flight attendant interrupt me." She whipped out her cell phone, clicked on Google, and, after a moment, said "aha!"

"Al-Jazeera sounds suspiciously like 'Algiers,' and Google confirms that 'Algiers' in Arabic means 'the islands,' referring to some small islands in the Algiers harbor. In sum, I think that the message means that he's involuntarily getting off the ship in Algiers but may not be able to re-board."

"Wow," Lauren said. "That was waaaaay impressive. I am in awe of your decoding skill. Once I recover from my naive incredulity, let's try some more." And they practiced on each other for another hour and a half, when the flight attendants served dinner and then turned off the lights, so that everyone could try to sleep.

Chapter 11: Santa Cruz de Tenerife

Shaped like a duck facing northeast, the island of Tenerife seems to have as its bill, the capital city, *Santa Cruz*, which, along with its adjacent city of *San Cristobal de Laguna*, has a combined population of almost 400,000. It sits off the coast of Morocco even though it belongs to Spain, 800 miles to the north. It is a modern, port city, with sculpture parks, restaurants, museums, theatres, parliamentary buildings, and perpetual spring weather.

Stonebrook took the tram from the airport to the *Plaza de España* near the harbor. He found the *Pensión Cejas* on Calle San Francisco. He spoke in English, so that the concierge would think he was a tourist. "I'd like to be able to store a suitcase for a few weeks, please."

The concierge looked him over and saw a well-dressed man, whom he assumed to be an Englishman or maybe an American. "Are you a guest here?"

"No," but I'm going on a boat trip for a few weeks, and my travel agent recommended this *pensión* as a friendly and flexible place that would let me store my one suitcase."

"Two euros per day with a down-payment of 30 euros."

Stonebrook responded in perfect Spanish: *"Le ofresco un euro cada día, con un pago inicial de quince euros."* [**I'll counter with one euro per day and a downpayment of 15 euros.**]

The concierge could not conceal his surprise. "Habla español... sin un acento! Es usted un Canario?" [**You speak Spanish...without an accent. Are you from the Canaries?**]

"Gracias por la alavanza. No, pero estaría agradecido si me permita a dejar mi maleta aquí mientras que estaré al mar." [**Thanks for the compliment. No, I'm not; but I'd sure appreciate it if you let me store my suitcase here while I'm at sea].**

"*Por seguro, señor. Y no tendrá que pagar más de 1.50 cada día y con un pago inicial de solamente diez euros.*" [**Of course. And you won't have to pay more than 1 ½ euros per day with a down payment of only 10 euros.**]

"We have a deal," replied Stonebrook, and he offered his hand to shake on it. "I would like a receipt, though, and a favor. I need to change out of my traveling clothes."

"*Por supuesto a los ambos. Hay un cuarto de baño a la izquierda.*" [**Of course to both. There's a bathroom to the left.**]

Stonebrook changed into a seaman's outfit --loose, bell-bottom trousers with a draw string over which he wore his wide, black belt, a loose over-shirt, canvas shoes, and a beat-up, straw hat. He emerged from the bathroom with his suitcase and 10 euros, which the concierge took and gave him a receipt.

"Is that how you plan to dress for your voyage?" the concierge asked in English. "You look like a deckhand instead of a traveler."

"It's a very informal cruise," Stonebrook answered, pleased both that the concierge thought he might be a local and that his outfit appeared to be that of a deckhand.

He walked to the Restaurante Anatolia, where he engaged the cashier.

[**TRANSLATION**]:

Stonebrook: "Can you please tell me where the recruiting office for the merchant ships is?"

Cashier: "Walk over two blocks to the *Farmacia*. Between it and the *Casa León* is a doorway. Go through it and up a flight of stairs. Good luck."

Walking to the *Farmacia*, Stonebrook took a long look at the boats in the harbor. There was a cruise ship as well as two ferries and a couple of merchant ships. One bore the label, *La Galissioniere*. He located the doorway that the cashier at the restaurant had mentioned and walked up the stairs into a dingy office waiting room. He sat down on a bench where three others were sitting.

A woman appeared from a side door and said in a loud voice, "Gómez." The man next to Stonebrook got up and followed the woman into another room. Then she returned to a desk in the waiting room. Stonebrook approached the desk and asked her if he was supposed to "register."

[**TRANSLATION**]:

"There's no registration, but you have to be referred by someone. Who sent you here?"

"Carlos Santander," answered Stonebrook.

The woman looked suspicious. "Oh, yeah? Who the hell is Carlos Santander?"

"My boss on the main ferry from *El Hierro* to *La Palma* and from *El Hierro* to *Gran Canaria*."

"What'd you do on the ferry?"

"Everything. I started off as a deck hand, worked in engineering, spent time as a steward, and ended up as a greeter for the passengers."

"So, why come here?"

"My girlfriend's husband threatened to kill me, so I needed to split. Santander figured I'd do well here."

The woman laughed. "Your girlfriend's husband, eh? There won't be many chances for that on board *our* ships – they have all-male crews and are at sea for months."

"That's okay. I need to get out of the Canaries. That husband is a very jealous man."

"How soon can you go?" she asked

"I'm ready now."

"Well, there are two cargo ships leaving tomorrow. *La Galissionière* goes east to the Mediterranean and *O Setubal* is going north in the Atlantic."

Stonebrook scratched his chin. "Well, that's *where* they're going, but what nationality are they?"

The woman looked at her clipboard. *"La Galissionière* is either French or Greek, I'm not sure which. And the *Setubal* is Portuguese."

"Oh, boy," Stonebrook replied. "The girlfriend's husband is Portugee; I better not go on that one!"

The woman giggled. "Okay, I'll sign you up for the *Galissionière*. They're short of deckhands. Maybe after a couple of weeks, you can work your way up. Show up tomorrow morning at 7:30."

"Thanks much. Where, exactly, do I show up."

"Pier No. 5. And take this Note of Introduction." She signed a form letter and handed it to him.

Stonebrook thanked the woman again and headed off to the post office where he sent a note to the intermediary in the Madrid law firm. *"The French lady has invited me accompany her on her voyage to the Rising Sun."*

Chapter 12: Aboard La Galissionière

ARRIVING AT THE DOCK A half-hour early, Stonebrook waited and watched other crew members amble up the gangway. At about 7:20, he walked up himself. At the top was a grizzled-looking sailor, with a three-day beard, a dirty shirt which stank of cigarette smoke, and a clipboard.

[TRANSLATION]:

"Who are you?"

"My name is Julián Arroyo. I'm a deckhand."

"Oh, yeah? Well, you ain't on the roster," he said, pointing to some papers on his clipboard.

Stonebrook took out the note he had received from the woman at the recruiting office and showed it to the man, who read it very carefully.

"All right. I'm adding you to the roster, but you have to go do some paperwork with the Third Mate. Turn right, and go up the first flight of stairs. Next!"

Stonebrook followed the man's directions, and entered a small cabin, where a large man sat behind a small desk, "What do you want, sailor?" He said in Spanish with an unmistakable, Portuguese accent.

[TRANSLATION]:

"I'm a new deckhand. Name's Arroyo. The man at the top of the gangway told me to see you. Here's the note from the recruiting office."

The Third Mate inspected Stonebrook from head to toe, looked at the note, and looked back at Stonebrook again. "Where're you from?"

"From *La Gomera*, here in the Canaries."

"Do you speak any languages besides Spanish?"

"No. Is that expected?"

The Third Mate ignored Stonebrook's question. "And what's your background working on ships?"

"I have worked on ferries between islands in the Canaries – as a deck hand, in engineering, as a steward, and as a greeter of guests."

"And what did the Recruitment Office tell you you'd be doing here?"

"She said I'd be a deckhand at first, but if I showed you how good I was, there might be a chance for better jobs after we're underway."

"She was wrong. The only openings we got are deckhands. Take it or leave it."

"I'll take it."

"Okay. Sign these papers." And he handed Stonebrook a thick contract, about 10 pages long.

Stonebrook started reading it, and the Third Mate said, "Sign at the bottom of page 10."

"Do I get to read it first?"

"You been on board five minutes, and already you're a trouble-maker. It's standard language. Everybody signs. If you want the job, sign. Otherwise, get off the ship."

"If I can't read it now, do I at least get a copy I can take to my cabin and read later?"

"Sure. Sign there on page 10, and I'll give you a copy."

Stonebrook signed (as Julián Arroyo), and the Third Mate pulled a copy out of a drawer that sounded like it had rarely been opened. "Here's a copy. Deckhands are in the bunkhouse aft of amidships. You'll be in Cabin 6, lower bunk, right side as you walk in. Stow your gear, and show up for orientation at 0800."

Stonebrook took the contract and found his way to Cabin 6. He started to unpack his satchel, when a tall man, with a bushy beard, approached and said,

[TRANSLATION]: "That's my bunk, buckaroo. Go somewhere else."

Stonebrook answered. "I don't want to cause any trouble, but the Third Mate said the lower bunk, right side, Cabin 6. was mine. If there's another bunk you would suggest, I don't really have any strong feelings about this particular bed."

"That's good. 'Cause you're not sleepin' in my bunk. I don't give a rat's ass where you *do* sleep, but it's not going to be here."

Stonebrook tried to sound fair-minded. "Hey, if it's that important to you, we can certainly swap. Just tell me where your *other* bunk is, and we can switch."

"I ain't tellin' you jack shit, boyo, except that that's my bunk. So move away." He stepped toward Stonebrook, menacingly.

Four other sailors had gathered round. Stonebrook read their facial expressions as *Is this guy gonna wimp out before we even leave the dock?* Stonebrook didn't back off. "You know something? Your breath stinks. I'd appreciate if you'd step to the side."

The bearded man pulled a knife out of his belt and said, "How does this smell, boyo?"

With lightning speed, Stonebrook grabbed and bent the index finger of the man's hand that wasn't holding the knife, and applied pressure to the top 1/3. It looked like a fairly benign grip, but it was very painful. "Drop the knife."

The man obeyed and started to scream. Stonebrook released some of the pressure, but held on to the man's index finger. "Okay. Let's start over. My name is Arroyo. What's yours?"

The man didn't answer, and Stonebrook applied a little more pressure. "Donohue," the man said in a loud voice, louder than he intended.

"Where did you learn Spanish, Donohue?"

"In Spain."

"And where did you learn to be an asshole?"

The other men laughed. Donohue turned red, but then he laughed too. "I was just giving you the guff we give to all first-timers. You passed the test, boyo. You didn't take any shit."

Stonebrook let go of the man's hand. "Am I the only new man on board?"

"No, we've been going from cabin to cabin, initiating all the newjays. You did good.

Some of the other new guys are still lookin' for bunks to sleep in."

"I like jokes, myself. But I don't think it's a good idea to joke with knives. I know some dudes who wound up dead or one-armed because they didn't know where the boundary was between jokes and seriousness."

A short, fat guy with long black hair, who had been watching the fracas, jumped in. "This guy Arroyo is right, Donohue. The knife bit did cross the line." He bent over, picked up the knife, and handed it to Donohue. Once Donohue re-inserted the knife in its scabbard, the short guy turned to Stonebrook. "My name's Jesús López. Welcome aboard!"

At 0800 the crew gathered on the main deck. The Captain said a few words in heavily accented Spanish, which almost no one understood, and turned things over to the First Mate.

[TRANSLATION]: "Welcome aboard *La Galissionière*. The ship language is Spanish. If you don't understand it, you're in deep shit. It's less important for you to be able to *speak* it. We mainly care that you can obey orders... quick. There are a bunch of newjays on-board – four deckhands, two stewards, and one engineering assistant. You'll have a day or two to figure out how we do things here. After that, don't expect no slack. We carry just enough crew to get the job done, so nobody gets a free ride.

"If you do your job, work hard, don't make trouble, you'll get along fine, and you'll be able to get off the ship in every port. Screw up, and you'll be waving to your crew mates from this here deck as they walk down the gangway for a day of fun-and-fuck.

"You got about an hour before we cast off. Familiarize yourself with the whole ship. So, when an officer or supervisor says, 'Hey, you, wipe the crud off the sponson,' you'll know where to go without asking any dumb questions. Just to make sure, we're gonna have a group quiz a half hour after we're underway. Crewbies who know the answers get more free time; those who have the wrong answers get extra duties.

"Now, let me introduce the supervisors, so you'll know who you report to. The Chief Engineer is Mr. Pimental. The supervisor of the deckhands is Mr. Thura. He reports to the Third Mate, Señor Cano...." He went on, but Stonebrook stopped listening after "Cano."

When the so-called orientation ended, Stonebrook started wandering. The Third Mate called Donohue over. [TRANSLATION:] "Donohue, I want you to bird-dog that new crewbie, Arroyo. Feed him dog turds about the ship, so he answers all the questions wrong."

"Aye, aye. Mate."

Donohue caught up with Stonebrook in the engine room. [TRANSLATION]: "Hey, Arroyo, I'm sorry we got off on the wrong foot earlier. It was just our initiation ritual. To make up for it, I thought I'd help you out with info about the ship. That way when the officers throw questions at you new grundoons during the quiz, you'll know all the right answers."

Stonebrook put on a grateful face. "That's very generous of you. I'd appreciate that."

Donohue looked all around, as if he were making sure no one was listening. "Rule Number One – unless ordered to go there, stay out of the deckhouse close to the bow – that's where both the Pilot house and the cabins for the officers and the Chief Engineer are – all singles."

Stonebrook's thought was – *A good con always starts off with the truth. So, Donohue's 'Rule Number One' is probably good advice. Maybe his second statement will also be in the vicinity of verisimilitude. But I'll expect nothing but bullshit after that.*

"Rule Number Two," Donohue continued, "is make sure you don't sit at the supervisors' table in the crew mess. That's a big no-no, and the supers take delight in embarrassing the newjays who unknowingly violate that rule."

"That should be easy enough – I'll just sit with the other grundoons."

Donohue laughed. "Good plan. Now, let's talk about the ship... because the officers take great pleasure in making grundoons look stupid during Quiz Hour. First of all, the ship is an SL-7 class, built in Rotterdam; its propulsion is diesel with a bow thruster, and it...."

"Whoa, Donohue. Let me make some notes here." Stonebrook took out a pocket-size notebook and began writing down some of the things Donohue said, even though he knew what the man was saying was completely bogus. On the plane, Stonebrook had read *Box Boats: How Container Ships Changed the World,* by a director of the Steamship Historical Association, a man named Brian Cudahy. Much of the book was so technical that it helped Stonebrook fall asleep, but he learned a lot about cargo ships and had figured out *La Galissionière's* lineage.

"Okay, I'm ready now, and I have a question. The First Mate mentioned 'sponsons;' what are they?"

"Ah, yes," replied Donohue. "They are the fasteners that hold the lifeboats onto the sides of the ship. We need to wipe them frequently to make sure they don't rust. Now those huge jobbies sticking up from mid-ships – they're called 'Darnby Winches.' Another thing they ask is the dimensions of the ship – the right answers are '390 ft. long and 58 ft. wide.'"

Stonebrook wrote down the information in his notebook. "That's really helpful, Donohue. Thanks." Stonebrook stuck out his hand.

"We're not done yet, boyo. Let me show you the hold. The Mates are likely to ask you how many containers are stacked." When they got there, Donohue said, "Notice that they're stacked four-high here in the hold and two-high on the deck."

"I see," said Stonebrook, feigning wonderment, "and how many total are there?"

"A full load on *La Galissionière* is 192 containers." Stonebrook knew Donohue was lying through his teeth. A brochure at the Recruiting Office indicated that it held 226 conatiners.

"Okay, I'm going to go back to the cabin and review my notes. You sure have been a big help."

Donohue smiled. "Glad to do it, boyo. We're all in this together."

Chapter 13: London

CAROL HAD MADE A HOTEL reservation for Lauren at the Park Plaza Riverbank because it was near to the Vauxhall Underground Station and on the same block (Albert Embankment) as the office of the International Maritime Organization. After checking in, Lauren wisely slept without setting an alarm and took a day to re-set her body clock and overcome jet-leg.

On her first full day she walked around the neighborhood to get her bearings and located the IMO office. Serendipitously, she would not have to take a taxi or bus or tube.

On Day Two, refreshed, she entered the IMO building, hoping to find someone on the staff with whom to chat. Without any real basis, she had envisioned a small, wooden-structure office, squeezed between two other nondescript buildings and just large enough for a half dozen staff members and, therefore, informal enough to make someone available to chat with a visiting American. To her chagrin, the IMO had its own, very large brick building, facing the Thames.

A security guard asked with whom she had an appointment.

"I don't have an appointment and didn't know that I needed one," she answered. "I just flew in from the United States, and I thought that I could get some information about the IMO by coming to its office."

"I see," answered the security guard, making clear that he totally disapproved of what to him seemed to be a naive, if not pushy, American expectation. "Let me make a call for you. Please have a seat over there."

She sat and waited, reviewing her research notes about the IMO. It was not, as she had surmised before she began her research, an independent non-profit organization but, rather, a specialized agency of the United Nations. Except for landlocked countries like Afghanistan and Belarus, all the UN member nations (171 of them) belonged, and the organization was governed by a 40-member Council – which always included the Big 10 Merchant shippers (the U.S., the UK, Russia, China, Japan, Korea, Panama, Norway, Greece, and Italy). It worked through a Secretariat of permanent staff here in London.

Just then the security guard approached. "If you can wait, Miss Paula Ross will be available in half an hour."

"Oh, good," said Lauren, trying to sound enthusiastic and grateful. "Can you tell me who Ms. Ross is?"

"Ms. Ross is an assistant cataloguer in the MKC."

"Umm,... and what is the MKC, please?"

Without attempting to hide his disdain for her ignorance, the security guard said, "The MKC is the Maritime Knowledge Center. You may wait for her in the Library on the second floor, and you're welcome to look at materials about the IMO while you're waiting."

She ignored his patronizing tone, thanked him, and got up. He pointed the way to the elevator, saying that she had to pass through a metal detector "before boarding the lift."

Turning toward him just before the metal detector, she asked, "Oh, and *if* you know, how many staff work here at the IMO?"

"There are 265 permanent employees and another 34 temporary employees, including us security guards." He smiled oleaginously, and she smiled back, trying not to let him see her surprise.

Lauren had read rather aimlessly for about 20 minutes when a young woman of about her age, brunette, green eyes, conservatively dressed in a skirt and sweater tapped her on the shoulder and said, "Good morning. My name is Paula Ross. I understand that you wanted some information." There was a tone of forced cordiality, which Lauren read as *I pulled the short straw and was obliged to come chat with the silly American.* So, she decided to do something unexpected.

Standing and extending her hand, Lauren, said, "Hello, my name is Lauren Marlo. Let me begin with an apology. I didn't do enough homework to understand that I was supposed to make an appointment. I just showed up at the IMO office, which I foolishly thought would have just five or six employees and asked to chat with someone. Had I done sufficient research, I would have figured out that this is a 300-person Secretariat, with very busy staffers, and I would have written for an appointment while I was in the States. How about if I leave now and make an appointment for later this week?"

Her apology and self-deprecation did in fact disarm the assistant cataloguer. Ross sighed. "That's all right. You're here now, so what I can do for you?"

"What I need is the name of someone who can testify at a trial in a case I'm working on."

Ross looked around, surreptitiously. "Would you like to go for a snack? There's a tea house about a block over."

"Uh, sure," said Lauren, not quite sure why this woman had suddenly invited her to leave the building and have a chat. But she was determined to go with whatever flow that Paula Ross had in mind for their conversation.

When they got outside, Ross walked as if she were a bird just let out of a cage. "You look about the same age I am. Are you?"

"Well, I'm 24," answered Lauren. "I graduated college two years ago and have been working for a private detective agency ever since."

"Yes, we *are* the same age," said Ross, with a kind of happy lilt. "I graduated three years ago from university, but I had no idea what I wanted to do. Interviews didn't go so well, so I reluctantly asked my parents for help. It turns out that my mum's best friend is married to a bloke in the Admiralty, and he arranged for an interview with the IMO. At the time, I had no idea what the IMO was, much less that it had its headquarters here in London. They offered me this job, and I greedily accepted.

"If you made a hierarchy of all 116 job-titles in the Secretariat, Assistant Cataloguer would probably be No. 114, barely above janitor and cafeteria server. I can do it easily, but it is sort of boring. On the other hand, I am grateful to have found anything at all, on a professional level. The pay is decent, the hours are reasonable, and, if I can just be patient, there will likely be opportunities for advancement."

She looked around to make sure no one was in ear-shot. "The bad news is that none of my friends, and no one I ever meet at parties, has ever heard of the IMO; and I really get knackered trying to explain to the wankers where I work."

By this time they had reached the tea house and had sat down. Lauren looked at the menu. Paula asked, "Do you mind if I make a suggestion?"

"That'd be good, Paula," Lauren said, purposely calling her by her first name.

"Yorkshire and Twinings are the best teas; and the scones here are blinding."

"Uh,... 'blinding'?"

"Sorry, that's British for 'superb.'"

"Sounds good. Let's go for it."

Once served, Paula leaned over, after looking to both sides. "The reason that I invited you to come to the tea house was to get you out of the IMO building. You had no way of knowing, but it would have been a major cock-up for you to have asked anyone with more chevrons for the name of someone to testify."

This time Lauren looked from side to side. "What's a cock-up, and who are the people with chevrons, the security guards?"

Paula giggled. "A 'cock-up' is a big mistake. 'Chevrons' means people with higher rank than Assistant Cataloguer. The IMO has a 45million pound annual budget, 171 member nations, a Council, five committees, seven subcommittees (all staffed by the Secretariat, of course), conventions, treaties, conferences, endless meetings, reports, audits, and inspections. However, it has no enforcement power, and, except when it beats the drum about the role of climate change on the oceans, it does nothing controversial. So, the chevrons would have deemed your request as 'taking the piss.'"

Lauren grimaced. "Taking the piss?"

"Seeking something quite unreasonable. Giving you a name of someone who would testify in a trial in a court of law in the United States, probably a big-dollars case involving companies in countries that are also members of the IMO, the chevrons would surely characterize as having 'lost the plot.'"

"Sorry, Paula, but that's another British slang term I don't know."

"I see.'Lost the plot' means, uh, acting irrationally or ridiculously"

"Oh!" Lauren paused. "I now understand why you hustled me out of the building. But do you have any suggestions of how I can find somebody to testify about all this IMO stuff of which the jurors in the United States will be as equally ignorant as your 'wanker' friends?"

Leaning over conspiratorily, Paula answered. "As a matter of fact, I do: The Secretariat has a group of consultants whom they call 'Ambassadors.' Recommended by their host countries, they are invariably smart, knowledgeable, and articulate. The reason they exist is to spread the word, as it were, because the Secretariat's chevrons are aware that they operate in a rarified atmosphere totally separate from the rest of the world."

"When you say that nations are members, what that really means is that each member nation has to designate an agency within its government to represent that country at the IMO, right?"

"Exactly so. The governmental agency that the U.S. has designated, by the by, is the Coast Guard."

"Do you know the name of the lead person from the Coast Guard who heads whatever team the U.S. sends to all these conferences, Councils, and Committees?"

"No, but I'll get it for you when we go back to the building."

"But will I be able to convince anybody on the Coast Guard team to testify about the IMO in our clients' trial?"

"I doubt it, but you'll be a better judge than I about that. It's *your* Coast Guard, after all, But here's what I want to suggest: Get someone from the IMAREST."

"Oh, great," said Lauren, "another alphabet-soup outfit. Is this IMAREST a sub-gizmo of the IMO?"

Paula laughed. "Not really. IMAREST is the Institute of Maritime Engineering, Science, and Technology. It's a non-governmental, professional organization of scientists and engineers and other maritime professionals. It is well respected and has consultative status with the IMO. Its HQ also happens to be in London, on Birdcage Boulevard. When we return to the IMO Building, I shall call Dr. Mackenzie for you."

"Who's he?"

"*She...* is Dr. Bev MacKenzie, the Policy Director for IMAREST and a very neat lady. I happened to have met her at a wedding, where we got to talking, and were delighted that we each had found someone who had actually heard of the other one's employer. So, even though she's a chevron, and I'm a mere bottom feeder, we have the kind of relationship that allows me to call her."

"Terrific."

They returned to the IMO building, and, making sure that no one could overhear, Paula called Dr. Mackenzie, "Bev, hi, this is Paula. I'd like to send over an American to your office. Can you see her today?"

(Pause) "She needs the name of an IMAREST luminary, someone who can speak understandably to laypeople, and who is an Ambassador for the IMO." (Pause). "Thanks ever so much. I'll send her over this afternoon, about 1:30. Her name, by the way, is Lauren Marlo."

Paula hung up and grinned from ear to ear. She then stood up, in the good-bye stance. Lauren hugged her. "I shall always be indebted to you, Paula. And I feel like I made a new friend."

"You did. Cheery-bye, Lauren. Oh, and I looked up the American delegation. The lead person is a Commodore Richard Costaign."

That afternoon Lauren had a pleasant chat with Dr. MacKenzie, who put her in touch with a man named Alfred Grindon, a Canadian by birth and an Englishman by choice. Grindon turned out to be exactly the kind of person for whom Lauren had been searching. He was tall, substantial, and ruddy, wearing a well-tailored suit and sporting an attractive mane of dark hair with a handsome dab of gray in the temples. He had a firm handshake, a ready smile, and a mellow, baritone voice that made you want to listen even if he were reading off the ingredients on a soup-can label.

He quickly grasped the task and agreed to testify, saying that he was quite sympathetic owing to the fact that his older brother, a sailor on a merchant marine vessel, had been killed by privateers, which is how he, Alfred, had become interested in maritime matters and had made them his career choice. He now worked full-time for IMAREST and was familiar with IMO operations because of his status as an "Ambassador."

He listened carefully to Lauren's explanations, took notes, and asked intelligent questions. They exchanged telephone numbers and email addresses, and he promised to be available whenever the trial took place.

Chapter 14: Quiz Hour

FIVE BELLS RANG, INDICATING 10:30, and the "grundoons," as Donohue called them, gathered on deck for the Quiz.

The First Mate called out, [**TRANSLATION**]: "Rodríguez. You're the new assistant engineer, right?"

"Aye, sir."

"You get the first question, Rodríguez: What's the propulsion system on this rust bucket?"

"Steam turbines, sir."

"That is partially correct. We also have some diesels – where are they?"

"Uh, powering those... uh... large windlasses."

"That's sort of right, but we have a special name for them. You know what they are?"

"No, sir. I thought they was windlasses."

"Let's see who else might know. Arroyo, how about you? Do you know what we call those thingamajigs that Rodríguez calls windlasses?"

Stonebrook said, "A guy in port told me they was called Gantry Cranes."

"Very impressive, Arroyo." Turning to the Third Mate, he said, "Make sure Arroyo is the first to disembark when we reach *Casa Blanca*." Then, facing the crew, he said, "I have another question.....let's see, for Fonseca, a steward. How many men do we have on this boat?"

Fonseca squeezed his eyes shut and then opened them. "There are four officers, the Chief Engineer, four supervisors, and sixteen crew members.. That's a total of 25."

"That's good, Fonseca. It's important for stewards to know how many men will be eating, isn't it? Your boss, the Second Mate, is busy checking supplies at the moment, but I'll tell him that you get the first mess shift off-duty. Mr. Cano, do you have any questions?"

"Yes, I do," answered the Third Mate. "Quintana -- you're a new deckhand. Why do we not go faster than 14 knots on this boat?"

Quintana grimaced. "I'm pretty sure that the faster we go, the more fuel the ship eats."

"That's correct. Follow-up question, Quintana: What are the dimensions of this boat?"

"Not certain, Mr. Cano I think it's about 450 feet long and 50 feet beam."

The Third Mate turned to Stonebrook. "Arroyo, do you agree with Quintana?"

Ah, here's the trap, thought Stonebrook. *The right answer is 460 feet long and 63 feet beam. But If I correct Quintana, I'm participating in the embarrassment of a crewmate. If I merely agree, then the Third Mate'll say that we're both wrong.*

So, he answered: "At sea some things, like the length of the containers have to be precise, but for most other things, approximations are close enough. Quintana's estimates sound like they're within 10 to 15 feet or so of the exact measurements."

The Third Mate frowned. "You lucked out on that one, Arroyo. Quintana is indeed within 15 feet of both dimensions. But I don't agree with you that things can be what you call 'approximations.' We have lunch exactly at eight bells. You better be there on time, not approximately.

"Are you a gambler, Arroyo?"

"Not with money, sir!"

"How about with 'good time?" When Stonebrook didn't seem to understand, the Third Mate went on. "I'd like to give you a really tough question. If you get it right, you get extra privileges the whole trip; if you get it wrong, you get assigned extra chores the whole trip. Are you willing?"

Stonebrook thought about it. "I'll counter-offer: If I get it right, I get extra privileges the whole voyage, but if I get it wrong, I get extra chores for the first week."

Everybody laughed. Even the First Mate. The Third Mate didn't think it was so funny, but he hid his discomfort. "Privileges for eight weeks, extra chores for four weeks. How's that?"

Stonebrook answered, "Deal!"

Licking his lips, the Third Mate said, "All right, here goes: What can you tell us about when this ship was built, and what class describes it?"

Donohue averted his eyes and tried not to show his smirk. He was sure that Arroyo would use the information that he, Donohue, had fed him... and, thereby, answer wrong.

"When I was in the Recruiting Office in Tenerife," Stonebrook began, "I was looking at photos of ships – *La Galissionière* looks exactly like the Wacosta, a Class C-2 ship that Sea-Lane had built in San Juan in 1970, except that it must have later been jumboized by splitting it in half and splicing a new mid-body section onto the hull."

Third Mate Cano turned beet-red and shot a look-to-kill at Donohue. The other grundoons whispered "Holy Shit!" to each other. The First Mate said, "That's exactly right, Arroyo. You're the first newjay who ever got that one right. Okay, Cano, you made the bargain. Make sure that Arroyo gets extra privileges for the first eight weeks of our voyage."

"Of course, First Mate. However, maybe Mr. Arroyo would like to go double or nothing."

"Why would I want to do that, Mr. Cano? I already won extra privileges."

"Just for the first eight weeks. At double or nothing, if you get this last question right, you get extra privileges for the *entire voyage*....BUT if you get it wrong, then you lose all those privileges from the last question and you have to have extra chores for eight weeks."

Sticking his tongue in his cheek, Stonebrook answered. "Umm. That's not a very good deal. But I *am* willing to risk this much: If I get the question right, I get extra privileges the whole trip; but if I get it wrong, my privileges from the last question are reduced from eight weeks to six weeks, and I get extra chores for three weeks after the six weeks of privileges run out."

Third Mate Cano was formulating a counter-proposal when the First Mate said:

"That sounds fair to me. Ask him the question, Cano."

The Third mate clenched his teeth. "Okay. What are 'sponsons'?"

"That's actually easy because Donohue told me what they were right after orientation." He paused, looking over at Donohue, who had a *I just ate the canary* expression on his face.

"Sponsons are outboard add-ons to the hull which give the ship greater stability and which increase the beam by about four feet on each side."

Donohue's mouth dropped open, and the Third Mate stomped off. "Well," said the First Mate, "you got that one right too, Mr. Arroyo, and you might want to share some of those extra privileges with Mr. Donohue, who evidently supplied you with the right answer."

Chapter 15: In The Quad

NOT HAVING ANY ASSIGNED DUTIES after the Quiz, Stonebrook went back to the cabin that he shared with López, Donohue, and a third man he had not yet met but who was lying in the bunk above Stonebrook's.

[TRANSLATION]: "Good morning," Stonebrook said as cheerfully as he could. "We're apparently bunk mates. My name's Arroyo."

The man leaned up on his elbow. "Nice to meet you, Arroyo. I'm de la Cruz. I listened to you during the Quiz. Where'd you learn all that shit, man?"

"A dude I met waiting in the Recruiting Office clued me in about the quizzes that the officers on most of these ships dish out to the first-timers. So, I boned up as much as I could about *La Galissionière* as soon as I knew my assignment."

De la Cruz, who had beady eyes and a triangular beard but no moustache, twisted the hair at the bottom of his beard. "I'm trying to figure out your accent. Where you from?"

"From *La Gomera*, in the Canaries."

"No way, man! *I'm* from *La Gomera*. Where on the island do you live?"

"In San Sebastián. I work on the ferries there."

De la Cruz frowned. "You must know a pal of mine. He works on the ferries in *La Gomera* too. Name's Alfonso Pintero."

Stonebrook shook his head. "Never heard of him. Sorry." He turned to his locker in order to end this conversation.

But De la Cruz persisted. "It's not possible to miss Pintero – he's huge, sings all the time – mainly to hide all his farts – and wears a captain's hat to look important."

"Maybe I'll run into him after this voyage. I actually grew up *El Hierro* and just moved to *La Gomera* three months ago."

"*El Hierro*, eh? What's the nickname of that island?"

Stonebrook looked de la Cruz straight in the eye. "What is this? Son of Quiz Hour?"

He tried to sound disgusted instead of highly anxious. "*El Hierro's* nickname is *El Meridiano,* and that's it! I've had enough quizzes for the day, *hombre.*"

Just then Donohue entered the cabin. Pointing his finger at Stonebrook, he said,

"You fucked me over, Arroyo!"

Stonebrook snorted. "What you really mean, Donohue, is that Cano told you to set me up, and, coward that you are, you fed me misinformation for the quiz. Then, when I got the answers right, Cano chewed you a new asshole."

López, who had walked in right behind Donohue, laughed. "You got that right, *hombre.* Cano's chewing was so loud, I heard it from 10 feet away." Then, turning to his bunk mate, López asked, "Why you screw a cabin mate, Donohue? How little will it take for you to rat *me* out... or de la Cruz?"

Donohue didn't answer. He stomped out of the cabin, slamming the door behind him.

López put his hand on Stonebrook's shoulder. "You did good this morning at the quiz, Arroyo. But neither Donohue or Cano is gonna forget it. You better keep eyes in the back of your head."

Chapter 16: Miami

Wearing a suit, in which she could pass as a junior lawyer, Lauren wandered into the federal courthouse on North Miami Avenue in Miami. She found the Clerk's office and chatted up a deputy clerk about wanting to watch some admiralty case hearings. There were two scheduled for the following Friday, and the deputy also told her that the Eleventh Circuit of Appeals, whose main courthouse was in Atlanta, had a satellite courthouse in Miami, at 99 N.E. 4th Street and that she should try there also.

Since there was nothing going on at the district court, she took a cab over to the Court of Appeals. As she went through the metal detector, she asked the deputy marshal if he knew of any admiralty cases going on. The marshal said that there was in fact an argument scheduled to start in about an hour in front of a three-judge panel that he thought was an admiralty case. It will be in Courtroom No. 2, one floor up."

Lauren wandered up to that courtroom and saw two separate groups of lawyers speaking in hushed tones. There was a 20-something woman sitting in the second row of the gallery with a notebook. Lauren approached her and asked, "Is it okay if I sit next to you?"

"Hi," the woman said, "what's your connection to this case?"

"None," answered Lauren. "I'm starting law school in the fall, and I'm just hanging out in courthouses to see how the system works beyond what I learned in high school civics."

"Then, please sit down. The reason I asked about a connection is that I'm an associate in the law firm that's representing the defendant in this matter. I'm not assigned to work on this case, but later this year they may let me second-chair a trial, and I need to see how things work in real life. The only reason that I wasn't more welcoming when you asked to sit down that I was afraid that you might be a witness for the plaintiff; and if plaintiff's counsel thought that I was somehow trying to influence an adverse witness, it would make a stink."

"I understand...I think," said Lauren, who then introduced herself. The young associate introduced herself too. "My name's Emily Cadwalader, and my firm is Anagnos, Iken, & Goldthorpe."

"Very nice to meet you, Emily. Can you tell me what's going on, please?"

"Sure. This is an admiralty case. It involves alleged injuries under the Jones Act.

We represent the shipping company, Blue Water Marine, Ltd. The plaintiffs are three seamen who used to work for the company on a ship called the The Barracuda."

"Who are the lead attorneys in this case?"

"Our lead attorney is Dylan Wentworth, the man in the gray suit and red tie. He's a partner who sits on the firm's Management Committee. He only handles big cases. The plaintiffs' attorney is Anthony Brindle, the African-American fellow with the moustache, in the black suit and yellow tie. He's the main reason I'm here today. The litigation partners all say that he keeps winning admiralty cases when the plaintiffs don't seem to have very strong facts. If I'm ever going to try one of these cases, I need to know how he operates, so I can figure out how to beat him in front of a jury."

"Well, this is an appeal, right?"

"Yes. Very good. This is the Eleventh Circuit Court of Appeals. Brindle won a very large verdict from a jury in the district court. And we filed an appeal on behalf of our client. So, today, there will be no witnesses. Both law firms filed briefs with the Court." She showed Lauren a copy of her firm's brief, in a blue cover and Brindle's brief, in red. "It's just an oral argument before the three appellate judges. All three are likely to interrupt both attorneys with questions. Oh, and notice those lights on the podium: They're warning signals to the lawyers that their time is about to run out."

Lauren stayed for the oral arguments. As Emily had predicted, neither attorney got out more than three or four sentences before the judges began to ask questions. Although Wentworth was no slouch, he often tried to evade the tough questions by answering a question he wanted to answer but that the judges hadn't asked. The judges invariably pinned him down.

Brindle was more believable because where a questioning judge pointed out a shortcoming, Brindle readily, and disarmingly, conceded that it was a weakness in his case and then articulated a sentence beginning with the word "however" that handily rebutted Wentworth's argument on that point. It was a *tour de force,* and though the judges had tried to project impassive and impartial facial expressions, it was clear that Brindle had been persuasive.

Lauren asked Emily for her reaction. Emily sighed. "It doesn't look good for the home team. I see why the defense bar has such grudging respect for Anthony Brindle."

"Is Brindle a sole practitioner, or is he in a firm?"

"He's in a small firm called Farrell & Brindle. Farrell does family law, and Brindle does employment law, mainly admiralty-related, employment law."

Over the lunch hour, Lauren looked up the firm's address and phone number, and through her IPAD got Brindle's email address also.

Chapter 17: Stormy Seas

A LOT OF WHAT DECKHANDS do when at sea is chipping, painting, scrubbing, sounding the ship (checking the ballast tanks), and making sure that the gear on deck is properly lashed and that the other gear is accounted for in the dunnage room. That's what Stonebrook, Donohue, López, de la Cruz, and the other deckhands did. López told Stonebrook that on most ships, deckhands work eight hours every day, from 8:30 to 5:00 (with a half hour for lunch), and then are off – except when in port, when "we work until the work is done, that's sometimes 10-12 hours." But on *La Galissionière,* the supervisors and officers called them "slugs, lazyboots, and drones" if the deckhands tried to quit before 10 hours.

Four of the deckhands took a smoke break about 1600 hours (4:00 p.m.), and Stonebrook went with them even though he didn't smoke, just to hear their conversation. The supervisor of the deckhands, Mr. Thura, happened by and began cursing them out – in a combination of Burmese and Spanish. Because López was closest to him, Thura began striking him with a billy club. López tried to cover his face with his arms and took the blows on his elbows and forearms. Stonebrook noticed that no one else moved to interfere. Stonebrook pretended to slip and fell against Thura, knocking the billy club out of his hand.

Thura blew a whistle, and the Third Mate and the boatswain both came running.

[**TRANSLATION**]:

Boatswain: "What's going on here?"

Thura*:* "The *Canario* assaulted me!"

Cano: "In trouble again, Arroyo?"

Stonebrook: "Actually, I intended to ask Mr. Thura why he was beating López when the boat pitched, and I accidentally fell against Mr. Thura."

López: "That's exactly right, Mr. Cano."

Boatswain: "What did you see, Fernández and Molinero?"

Molinero: "I didn't see nothin.'"

Fernández: "I dropped some cigarette ash on my shirt, so I missed whatever else was happening with the other guys."

Third Mate: "We don't put up with any disrespect toward supervisors. López – you got night watch from midnight to 0400 tonight — for lying, you son of a bitch. And you, Arroyo, the First Mate gave you first off in *Casa Blanca*, but in the two days between now and then, you're working double shifts; plus during the hottest part of the day, you're going to be painting the bow from the outside. And if you ever raise your hand again to Mr. Thura or any other supervisor or officer, you're going to get 20 lashes, understand, shithead? All of you, get back to work, and don't take any more breaks until you hear the bells for supper."

When Cano and the boatswain left, Stonebrook approached Molinero: "How come you pretended not to see that Thura was whapping a crewmate with a goddam billy club?"

"Listen, Greenhorn, you haven't figured out yet how things work on this boat – if you wanna survive, you say somp'n close to 'yezzah, boss,' whenever a supervisor says somp'n to you, and you don't make any waves. Whenever the boatswain or any officer asks what you saw when somep'n bad's goin' down, the right answer is 'I didn't see nuthin.'"

Molinero walked away, and Fernández said to Stonebrook: "Nothin' personal, but I'd be grateful if you didn't hang around me no more. From now on your ass is grass, and anybody near you's just lookin' for trouble. You might as well have a bell around your neck. I got a family to feed, and I can't afford to have the big shots put me off in the middle of nowhere. Sorry, man."

López got up, inspected the bruises on his arms, and said. "Thanks, Arroyo. You stuck your neck out for me, but Molinero and Fernández is right. You can't afford to come to nobody's rescue no more."

Two hours after supper, the winds were not only nasty, but they changed up. That meant that the ship alternated between rolling (tipping side-to-side) and pitching (tipping fore to aft). "Get out of those frigging bunks!" It was Thura, opening the door to cabin 6.

"Rain gear on; tighten hatch clamps, check mooring cables, make sure gear is secure!"

De la Cruz, Donohue, López, and Stonebrook swiftly donned their rain gear and moved as quickly as they could to the main deck, holding onto wall banisters for support as they trudged.

The four deckhands from Cabin 5 were already on deck when they arrived. Water had sloshed all over, and it was very slippery. Thura shouted something, but no one could hear him over the noise of the wind, the crashing of the waves, and the creaking of the wood.

Stonebrook was checking hatch clamps when he saw López slide by. "AYUDAME!!"

[HELP ME!] López shouted as the tipping ship carried him portside. A huge wave followed him. Stonebrook turned from the hatch where he was working and leaped to grab onto López's leg, but Thura threw his shoulder into Stonebrook's chest, as if he were a pulling guard for a professional football team, and Stonebrook went sprawling. He grabbed onto a mooring cable to keep from going overboard. But as he latched onto the cable, he saw the huge wave carry López into the ocean.

"Man overboard!" Stonebrook yelled (in Spanish). No one moved. Thura, who was also holding onto a mooring cable, said: [TRANSLATION:] "There is no way to get him now. Anyone who tries will join López at bottom of sea. I saved you, Arroyo. In Myanmar, you would be obligated to me all rest of your life. On board this ship, I expect complete loyalty rest of voyage."

Stonebrook looked around. The other deckhands were attending to chores and pretending not to notice that one of their co-workers had just been swept off the ship to his death in the stormy sea. One man from Cabin 5 was vomiting. When everyone signaled that the work was complete, they moved carefully into the crew mess for coffee and muffins. No one said a word.

Chapter 18: Minneapolis

TED AND LAUREN WERE DRINKING wine in his apartment in downtown Minneapolis. "You did really well, babe. The two partners who are honcho-ing this case, Phil Traxel and Cliff Rehmel, verified all the material in your report, and they are extremely impressed. They hadn't known about IMAREST, but they checked it out and investigated, and the feedback was that Alfred Grindon would be the perfect expert witness. They asked me how you managed to find him. I just said that the reason I had recommended you and Rocky was that I had observed your resourcefulness up close."

She leaned over to his side of the couch and kissed him, twice. "How's that for being resourceful?"

"Very," he answered. "And as soon as I get through complimenting you, I hope you will become even more resourceful."

She smiled. "Take your time with the compliments."

"The word on the litigation partners' old law school classmates' grapevines was that Anthony Brindle was probably the very best plaintiff's attorney around for admiralty law, and they flew him up here and locked him in as co-counsel for the trial. If you had just pulled off the Grindon and the Brindle coups, that would have been enough for them to think that you were marvelous, no matter what Rocky brings back from his 'cruise;' but your having wiped the cobwebs off the complex, cryptic, and inscrutable, corporate connections among all the companies created to hide Greenport's ownership of *La Galissioniere* has made them want to offer you a full-time job as an investigator for the law firm."

"Is that the real reason why they sent me a plane ticket?"

"Well, the ostensible reason is to prepare you for a deposition; but my hunch is that before you leave, they might casually mention a job offer."

"Why are they preparing me for a deposition before they even start the lawsuit?"

"Assuming that Rocky brings back factual support for our clients' allegations, and further assuming that we sue out the case shortly thereafter, things will move very fast. So, my fellow associates and I are doing prep work: I have drafted a Complaint; one of my colleagues is preparing a list of witnesses and a paragraph or so summarizing the facts about which each witness will testify. The defendants' attorneys routinely ask for that kind of information in their interrogatories; then they'll schedule depositions. You'll be one of the deponents when we tell them the nature of your testimony. After deposing you and Rocky and the two clients, the defendants'll bring a motion for summary judgment. One of my associate colleagues is already working on a brief to oppose their motion for summary judgment."

"What's summary judgment?"

"It's a standard technique in defendants' procedural tool boxes. It asks the Court to dismiss the suit, without a trial, just because the law, as applied to undisputed facts, is supposedly so clear that a trial would be a waste of time."

"That doesn't sound fair. Do judges grant those motions very often?"

"Sometimes. It helps to clear the judges' dockets of meritless claims."

"How can a judge know the claims are meritless if he or she doesn't hear any testimony or read any documentary evidence?"

"Well, it's true that there are no witnesses. But both the defendants' brief and the plaintiffs' brief will attach lots of exhibits to bolster the arguments that either summary judgment is appropriate or is not."

"Speaking of appropriate, isn't it a little sneaky for a law firm to try to hire an investigator away from an investigator's firm in the middle of the investigation?"

Ted blushed. "Uh, yes. That's why the job offer won't be explicit. It will just be an inquiry about how you learned to be such a terrific investigator and where you'd like to be five years from now, hinting that Dorken and Forken would be interested in having a full-time investigator."

"And you think that's an ethical practice?" She moved to the end of the couch.

Ted squirmed. "I don't see it as *un*ethical for them to plant some seeds, so that after this case is over, you might think about upgrading."

"I don't think I could do that to Rocky. I would never have had the opportunity to go to London and Miami and Delaware, without his having insisted that the law firm include me in the investigation team."

"Hey, Lauren. Rocky saved my life back there in Wyoming. I will always be grateful to him. But it is not the case that he has granted you tenure; nor do I think that he expects you to stay as his associate for the next 45 years. Some day – and I emphasize *some* day – you may want to have a different job. And I sure would not be unhappy if that new job were in the Twin Cities."

She looked at him for several seconds without answering. Then, she got up. "Well, we have two or three days to test-drive that idea." She grabbed his hand and led him into the bedroom.

Chapter 19: The Moroccans

CABIN 4 WAS A QUAD, in which there were four Moroccan deckhands. There was little contact between the Moroccans and the rest of the crew because only one of them, Hamdi Al-Dimashqi, understood Spanish, and he didn't speak it very well. No one else aboard spoke Arabic. The one who understood Spanish transmitted orders from the officers and the supervisors as best he could.

They were generally given the worst jobs to perform – refacing the exhaust valves of the main engine; chipping and cleaning the rust from inside the fresh water tanks; chipping and cleaning paint around the boilers when the boilers were idle; and scrubbing steel.

Scrubbing steel was the worst assignment because it was done with oakite, which could take the skin off your hand if it got on your skin outside the glove. One of the Moroccans, a man named Kaddouri, had been assigned to the task of scrubbing steel. Some oakite leaked onto his wrist and burned his skin. He screamed and ran to the infirmary. The ship had no medical officer, nor any nurse; but the boatswain, who had had some minimal first aid training, put some salve on the wound, wrapped it in bandages, and pointed to the single cot in the infirmary. He signaled for Kaddouri to lie down and then went to the First Mate to report the injury.

[**TRANSLATION**]:

First Mate: "Is the A-rab gonna be able to go back to work soon?"

Boatswain: "I doubt it. The wound looks nasty and is likely to get infected. The man is obviously in a lot of pain. I gave him some aspirin."

First Mate: "In two days we'll put into *Casa Blanca*. Put him off there. In the meantime, try to get a message to the Recruitment Office in Casa Blanca for a replacement. Give preference to somebody who can speak Spanish better than Al-Dimashqi."

Boatswain: "Roger that. I guess we'll have to assign Kaddouri's duties to some of the other deckhands."

First Mate: "Indeed. Tell Thura to give the job to whoever's been the biggest pain in the ass."

That same day, Al-Dimashqi, the one who spoke a little Spanish, complained to the Second Mate that the Recruiting Office had promised them food that would adhere to Muslim dietary standards, but most of the meat was pork. The Second Mate pretended that he didn't understand and walked away but discussed it with the First Mate, who mused that: [**TRANSLATION**] "The Arabs are a lot of trouble. And, as long as we're dismissing Kaddouri, we might as well dump all four of the bastards from Cabin 4."

"Well," answered the Second Mate, "but the Captain'd be pissed if we disembark the kid, Nimri. That's the cap'n's boy toy."

"Oh, shit, You're right. Okay, let's dismiss Kaddouri, Al-Dimashqi and Ghulam. But lock Nimri in the infirmary. Have the boatswain drug him while we're in port."

"Aye, aye, Mate. One last thing: How much are we going to give them in repatriation funds to get home?"

The First Mate smiled. "That's their problem. Besides, they'll all *be* home – *Casa Blanca*, after all, is *in* fucking Morocco."

Nimri, the seventeen-year-old Moroccan, came into Cabin 6 after work hours. He asked if anyone spoke Arabic, but since he asked in Arabic, no one understood him. He tried Berber – no answer. Finally, he tried Portuguese. When no one answered right away, he turned to leave. But before he had fully exited, Stonebrook replied in Portuguese:

[**TRANSLATION**]: "What do you need?"

"Oh, finally, someone I can talk to!"

"How do you know Portuguese, kid?"

"My father had a job as a fisherman in the Algarve region of Portugal for five years, and he brought the family to stay by Sagres Point, so he could spend time with us when he was off-boat. I learned Portuguese in school there. I was pretty sure that no one outside of Cabin 4 spoke

Arabic or Berber, and I was just hoping someone on the ship might speak Portuguese."

"Umm. The Third Mate is from Portugal."

"I am afraid of the Third Mate. I would not ask him anything."

Nimri looked around and saw that De la Cruz and Donohue were staring at him. **[TRANSLATION]**: "Can we go somewhere else and talk, in private?"

Getting out of his bunk, Stonebrook nodded and walked out the door with the boy. Continuing in Portuguese as they walked away from the cabins, Stonebrook asked, "First of all, what's your name?"

"Mahmoud Nimri."

"Nice to meet you, Mahmoud. My name's Julián Arroyo. What seems to be the problem?"

"I don't know what to do. The Captain orders me to come to his cabin at night and does... sexual things, that I don't like. I tell him to stop, and he laughs and makes signs that let me know that if I don't do what he says, he will throw me overboard. I told the older guys in my cabin, but they say that they have no way to interfere because, at sea, the Captain is all-powerful."

"How did you get a job on this ship?"

"A recruiter came to my village, Temara, not far from Rabat, and offered jobs to teenagers. They give us food and buy us clothes and tell us that there is more if we take the jobs in Rabat. Five of my neighbors agreed, and their parents signed. When the recruiter came by to pick them up, he told me to come along for the ride to Rabat, and he asked me my father's name. When we got to Rabat, he forged my father's name on the contract document. I don't know what happened to the other four boys, but the recruiter told me that I had to pay him back for the food, and clothes, and the ride to Rabat. I said I had no money. He said that I'd have to earn the money and took me to *La Galissionière*. They put me in the cabin with the Moroccan grown-ups, who try to protect me from being beaten by the supervisor and the Third Mate; but they do not protect me from the Captain's abuse." He burst into tears.

Stonebrook shook his head. "Let's go see if there's some coffee in the Crew mess" No one was there, and Stonebrook poured them each a cup. "What do you think I can do?"

"I don't know. I'm not sure I can take it anymore. They didn't let me off the ship at any of the ports. We are coming shortly to *Casa Blanca*. Is there some way you can help me get off?"

Stonebrook rubbed his temple. "I don't have a plan at the moment, but I'll work on it. I'll try to get...."

Just then the Third Mate burst into the mess.

[IN SPANISH]:

"What are you doing here, Arroyo?"

"We're both off-duty, and we're having coffee."

"Oh, yeah? Well, I happen to be from Portugal, and I overheard you speaking Portuguese to the A-rab. When you first came aboard, I asked you if you spoke any other languages besides Spanish, and you said 'no.' There's something about you that rings flat, Arroyo. You lied about the languages you speak, de la Cruz says you're not really from *La Gomera*, you know a lot more about container ships than a guy who worked on ferries would know, you assaulted Mr. Thura, and now you're hustling the Arab kid."

"I'm not 'hustling' Nimri. We're just chatting."

"Oh, yeah? What are you chatting about?"

"It turns out that he went to school in the Algarve, so we discovered that we share a language."

"And how is it that you know Portuguese, Mr. Canary Islander?"

"As I told de la Cruz, I live in *La Gomera* now, but until three months ago I lived on *El Hierro*, the smallest of the Canaries. When my sister and I were little, both my parents worked, so the lady next door took care of us. Even when we went to school, she fed us and watched over us after school. This lady was from Brazil, and we learned Portuguese from her."

The Third Mate just shook his head, in a gesture that signaled incredulity. Then he moved his lips to display his teeth. Finally, he spoke in Portuguese, so Nimri would understand too: "I've met some heavy-duty bullshitters in my time, but you would win the gold medal.

Now get out of here, and I'm ordering you to stay away from the kid."

Chapter 20: At The Pier

As the Casa Blanca harbor became visible to those on board *La Galissionière,* the officers and supervisors began issuing orders to prepare for docking. The Second Mate told the cooks to finalize the food lists they would need to pick up; the First Mate, who is traditionally in charge of docking, ordered Thura to assign deckhands to the mooring cables and the bosun's chair; the Third Mate alerted the engineers to stand by the machine levers to lift the gantry cranes. The boatswain was supposed to give the order to bleed the forward winches, but he wasn't on deck. Cursing him, the Second Mate gave the order in his absence.

Noticing that the boatswain had left his post, Stonebrook followed him with his eyes.

He saw him dragging Nimri toward the infirmary. Stonebrook approached Thura and told him **IN SPANISH,** "I'm really sorry. I know that docking is heavy duty work, but that rancid bacon we had for breakfast is backing up in my intestines. I've got the runs. I HAVE to go to the head."

"Hurry back, Arroyo, you goldbrick!"

Stonebrook dashed to his cabin and searched López's locker and found the large duffel bag he had noticed when López was still alive. He stuffed it about 1/3 full with López's clothes, took it to the dunnage room, avoiding anyone's seeing him, and found a 10-foot rope. He slipped into the infirmary, sucker-punched the boatswain, tied him to a chair, and gagged him.

In Portuguese, he said to Nimri, "Let's go!"

They went two cabins over to Stonebrook's cabin. Stonebrook said: **[IN PORTUGUESE]**: "Take out the clothing, and climb into the bag. I'm going to stuff the clothing around you and carry you off the ship. You'll have to get into the fetal position."

Nimri stood there, paralyzed. **[IN PORTUGUESE]**: "What'll happen to you when they find out you slugged and tied up the boatswain?"

"I'll worry about that later. Right now, let's just see if you fit and if I can carry it as if it weighs a lot less." Nimri climbed in, and, after stuffing the clothing around him, Stonebrook swung the duffel over his shoulder. It was heavy, but he thought he could manage it.

"Okay. Out of the bag until I come back for you when we dock."

Nimri shook Stonebrook's hand vigorously. "*Shukran! Obrigado*!"

"I take it that *shukran* means **obrigado** [thank you] in Arabic?"

"Yes. I am in your debt."

"Not yet, Mahmoud. We have to get off the ship first."

As the Captain brought the ship parallel to the dock, the First Mate yelled **[IN SPANISH]** "Deckhands! Ready the bosun's chair! Arroyo and Quintana go first."

Stonebrook started running to Cabin 6. "Where the hell are you going, Arroyo?"

"I have to get my laundry bag."

"What!? Do your laundry on the ship, dipshit!"

"Nah, the water is all rusty and leaves residue. I'm using shore leave to wash 'em good."

Stonebrook ran to the cabin, heaved the bag with Nimri over his shoulder and rushed back to the main deck.

[TRANSLATION:] "All right, Arroyo, you won 'first-off' in the Quiz. So, climb up on the bosun's chair, straddle the rod on the board, and we'll drop you onto the dock. Once Quintana follows, you two run the mooring cables through starboard chocks, and pull those suckers until you can get 'em around the bollards. It's harder than it looks."

Stonebrook climbed up with the laundry bag. "No!" shouted the First Mate, "you gotta hang on with two hands. We'll drop the laundry bag later."

"Frankly, I'm afraid somebody's going to drop it from too high up. I also have some breakable things in there that I intend to sell in the *souk*."

"I promise we'll drop it softly. Mount up!"

Stonebrook hesitated, but he had no good answer. As the First Mate had warned, it required two hands to hang on to the rod on the board, and it would be easy to fall off.

The First Mate called out: "Swing him out, boys."

They swung the bosun's chair out over the dock and winched it down to about four feet above the pier, and said "Jump." He did, and landed with his knees bent, so he wouldn't injure himself.

"All right, Quintana, you're next," the First Mate shouted.

"NO! My laundry bag, first" Stonebrook yelled back from the pier.

"Jesus H. Christ!" the First Mate swore. "All right. Tie that duffel onto the bosun's chair and dump it on the pier."

The deckhand on the winch moved the chair out over the dock and opened it for dropping about five feet from the deck. Stonebrook caught it, but it still crashed onto the pier.

Nimri muffled a groan.

Quintana followed, and the two men complied with the First Mate's instructions about the mooring cables. But as Quintana pulled his cable, he tripped and went into the water between the pier and the ship. Just then, the wind shifted, and the ship moved toward the dock with a loud crunch. Quintana let out a horrible moan and slipped beneath the surface. Stonebrook started to run to the dock edge to see if he could help, but there were only about three or four inches between the ship and dock.

"Get back to the mooring cable, you nitwit!" It was the First Mate.

"What about Quintana?" asked Stonebrook with an obvious edge in his voice.

"The man's dead. No one could survive that. One of these assholes forgot to throw out the safety blocks." Then turning to the crew, "De la Cruz! You hop on the bosun's chair. Take Quintana's place on the pier with the mooring cable. Don't trip. We can't afford to lose two deckhands today."

Once Stonebrook and de la Cruz managed to get the mooring cables around the bollards, the First Mate said, "All right we're going to unload the containers now. The other crew members can get off when that's done. But Arroyo and de la Cruz, you two can 'go on up the street.'" It's now a little after 0900. We shove off at 1600. Be back on board no later than 1530."

Chapter 21: In Casa Blanca

STONEBROOK HEAVED THE DUFFEL OVER his shoulder and started walking off, away from the ship. De la Cruz caught up with him and started making small talk.

[TRANSLATION] "Hey, de la Cruz," Stonebrook interrupted, "you act as if nothing happened back there. One of our co-workers just got killed, and you and the First Mate and everybody else treat it as if it was nothing more than somebody dropped an apple into the water."

De la Cruz stopped and turned. "Listen, man. Workin' on ferries is child's play compared to workin' on container ships. Men get injured. Men get swept overboard. Other men die on piers. It's what we call 'occupational hazards.' If you're gonna be a pussy about it, go back to working on the fuckin' ferries, but get off my back. *I* didn't kill Quintana."

"Well, who was supposed to throw out the safety blocks, whatever they are?"

"Safety blocks are large hardwood blocks which we're supposed to throw over the sides when we dock, exactly so if a crew member falls overboard — or trips on the pier – he won't be crushed between the ship and the dock."

"So, it sounds like everyone knows about the danger if they manufacture those safety blocks, and we keep them on board, precisely to keep from happening what did."

"And your point is... what?"

"Somebody neglected to throw those blocks, and as a result, someone else died."

"Maybe that was *your* job, Arroyo. In which case, *you're* the one who's responsible.

86

My guess is that if you try to complain to somebody here in *Casa Blanca*, the First Mate, the Third Mate, and Mr. Thura will all say that it was *your* assignment, and *you* blew it."

A long silence passed between them. Finally, de la Cruz changed the subject. "Where you goin' with that... duffel bag?"

"I don't know. I've never been in Morocco before. I'm going to look for a laundromat."

"I don't know what you got in that duffel, Arroyo, but if that's laundry, I'm the Pope."

Stonebrook decided not to respond. "I'll see you back on board this afternoon." And he took off in a direction different from the one de la Cruz was taking.

Once de la Cruz was out of sight, Stonebrook gently dropped the duffel to the ground.

[**IN PORTUGUESE**]: "Okay, Mahmoud, come on out."

"Okay. But I hurt my elbow when they dropped the bag on the pier."

He climbed out of the bag, holding his left elbow with his right hand.

"Other than the elbow, are you okay?"

"Yeah."

"Do you have any way to get back to your village?"

"No, I have never been to *Casa Blanca*. I don't know anybody. And I don't have any money."

"I'm going to look for a Port Chaplain's office. But the signs are apparently all in Arabic, so you're going to have to translate."

"What's a 'chaplain'"

"Yeah, well, it's usually a Christian priest or minister. But I'm going to look for a Muslim equivalent, but I don't know how to say it. Maybe, um, *mullah* or *sheikh*?"

Nimri looked puzzled. He thought about it and, then, with an "aha!" expression, said: "Perhaps a *qasis* or an *imam khatib*."

"I don't know, Mahmoud. But let's keep walking until you see an Arabic sign that might be one of those."

Stonebrook dumped the duffel bag into a trash container, and the two of them walked around for about 25 minutes until Nimri spotted a mosque. "Let's ask in there."

In the mosque, Nimri engaged in a long conversation with someone in Arabic, of which Stonebrook understood nothing. The man, whether he was a *qasis* or an *imam khatib*, Stonebrook didn't know; but Nimri said that he felt safe with the man, who had promised to find someone to take him to his home village of Temara.

"Oh, one last thing. I need to get to a post office. Can you ask this man how I can locate it since I can't read the signs?"

After a brief inquiry, Nimri said: "The *qasis* says for you to go two streets to the left, then four streets to the right, then turn right again for a half block. The post office has a Moroccan flag in front."

They shook hands. Nimri once again said, "*shukran. muito obrigado.*" [**thanks very much**]. In Portuguese, Nimri told Stonebrook that he had saved his life and that he would never forget him. He took a medallion from around his neck and handed it to Stonebroook. "My parents gave this to me when I turned 12. It has a prayer on one side, and my name on the other. It is all that I have to give you, but I want you to have it."

Stonebrook knew that it would be disrespectful not to accept it and, so, he graciously took it and put it around his neck.

After they parted, Stonebrook followed the instructions and managed, with great relief, to find the post office. He composed a message in Spanish to the lawyer in Madrid and asked in Spanish if anyone could speak either Spanish or English. An ancient looking fellow behind the counter indicated with sign language that he would fetch someone who spoke Spanish from across the street and went to find him. He returned in five minutes with someone in tow, equally old, to whom Stonebrook managed to explain that he needed to send a telegram to a law firm in Madrid. Rocky paid for it in euros, which the postman accepted.

Back outside, he breathed a deep sigh, and then asked himself: *Now, what am I going to do? I can't go back to the ship because by now they will have found the boatswain, fit to be untied; and, not speaking Arabic, I can't red any signs or talk to very many people here. I think I'll look for a police station.*

He wandered around, choosing streets at random. After about 15 minutes he came upon a building with signs in Arabic, French, and Spanish. He went inside and discovered that it was an office of the International Seafarers Union. He found a Spanish-speaking official and explained that he had just escaped from *La Galissionière.*

[IN SPANISH] "Yes, we have heard about that ship. It has a terrible reputation. It abuses the seamen and makes them sign contacts promising not to complain to the Union. We have not been able to make any headway with the company that owns the ship. We haven't even figured out what company *does* own it."

"Well, I need to get to the United States. How can I do that?"

"Probably the U.S. Consulate. But it is far from here and hard to find. The best I can suggest is that you go to the nearest police station."

"Fine. How do I get there?"

"Go around the corner to the right. Walk two blocks. Then turn left. You will see it. The last building on the right."

"Thanks much."

Stonebrook found the police station, walked in, and asked if anyone spoke Spanish, English, or Portuguese – in all three languages.

A man with two stripes on his sleeve held up his hand, turned around, and went to an office in back. He returned with an officer wearing something on his epaulettes.

[IN ENGLISH]: "I am Lieutenant Lutfi. How can I be of service?"

"Thank you, Lieutenant. I'm an American citizen, I need to get to the American consulate, but I don't speak or read Arabic."

"How did you arrive in *Casa Blanca*, sir?"

"It's a long story, but I escaped from a cargo ship called *La Galissionière*." "May I know your name, sir?"

"Oh, yes, sorry. It's Pedro Fishkin."

"Are you also known as Julián Arroyo?"

Stonebrook froze. *How would this man know my pseudonym. I got a bad feeling.*

He looked at his watch and said, "Oh, you know what? I'm late for an appointment. Thanks for your trouble." He turned to leave.

The Lieutenant blew his whistle, and two police officers appeared and blocked Stonebrook's exit. "Better than the American consulate, señor Arroyo," Lutfi said, "we shall provide you an escorted ride to your transportation – *a ship*. Captain Eliopoulos called to say that you might get lost here in *Casa Blanca*. Fortunately, we shall not have to waste any time searching for you, and the Captain, no doubt, will be grateful that we shall have returned you to him. Interestingly, he thought that you were a Spaniard. He will be surprised to find out that you are an American, *posing* as a Spaniard."

The Lieutenant smiled the way prison wardens smile at newly arrived inmates. He then said something in Arabic, and the two police officers took Stonebrook by the arms to a police car outside. They delivered him to the pier where *La Galissionière* was docked.

[**TRANSLATION**]: "Ah," said the First Mate, "you are back early, señor Arroyo, or señor Fishkin, whichever you prefer. Oh, and you apparently left your laundry in *Casa Blanca*. *Que lástima!*" [**what a shame**].

Chapter 22: Last Ride On The Ship

[IN TRANSLATION]

"Welcome aboard, señor Arroyo." It was the Third Mate, who had a nasty grin on his face to which it took all of Stonebrook's self-restraint not to make some belligerent reply. "You're a sick man, so we're sending you to the infirmary. You apparently were there earlier today. I have asked Mr. Donohue to escort you there, and I have told him that if you do anything other than walk gently with him to the infirmary, he has permission to break your ribs."

Donohue stepped into view with a billy club in his hand. "Hello, boyo." He signaled with the billy club that Stonebrook was to precede him. They walked to the infirmary without incident, and Donohue opened the door. The boatswain was inside, gathering anything that had a sharp edge or point. "This will be your single room for the two days it takes to steam to Algiers. You can piss in the sink, and you can take a dump in that waste basket. Donohue here will bring your food once or twice a day, depending on how he's feeling about you. I think you know how *I* feel about you after you fed me that knuckle-sandwich." With that, the boatswain hauled off and punched Stonebrook in the face, causing Stonebrook to fall over. "I guess we're even now." And he walked out.

"Well, Arroyo," said Donohue, "I had been thinking of ways to get you back for how you set me up during quiz hour, but this has worked out even better than my worst plan. All the officers and supervisors on the ship hate your guts, and I'm sure they will come up with something very ... appropriate, boyo." With that he walked out, and when the door closed, Stonebrook heard the unmistakable sound of a lock.

The boatswain joined the four officers, the Chief Engineer, and Mr. Thura in the Officer's Mess. **[TRANSLATION]**: "You want coffee?" asked the Second Mate

"Nah, I'm good. Arroyo is locked up."

The First Mate turned to the business at hand. "The Captain called this meeting so we can decide what to do with Arroyo-Fishkin, the American pretending to be a Spaniard, who assaulted Thura, and who smuggled the Moroccan kid off the ship."

"I say we feed him to the sharks." It was the Third Mate.

The First Mate shook his head. "There's a problem with that: Once we get through the Strait, we're going to be within a few miles of the North African coast until we get to Algiers. Given the currents, his body is likely to wash up somewhere on the coast of Morocco or Algeria."

"How about..." The boatswain paused and looked around the table, "...if we make a record of his crimes and have a little trial, and then hang him? Justifiable execution."

The Captain shook his index finger back and forth. [His Spanish had a very thick, Greek accent and was decidedly ungrammatical] "Nobody care if some *kathiki* [**scumbag**] fall off the boat and drowning. Nobody give shit if other *kathiki* washing overboard in storm, but this Arroyo must have friends who send him here. If we hang him, there will being investigation by the Seamen's Union, by the Port Priests, by the States of America Government, by the UNO, by police from whatever town we land. Speaking of police, boatswain, be sure the purser send nice gift to Lieutenant Lutfi. Now, we need better idea for Arroyo."

Thura offered: "What if he have serious injury when we unload in Algiers – bad enough to crush part of his brain, and we send home as... how you say, 'invalid'?"

"That's very creative, Thura." It was the Second Mate. "But everybody on the crew would see it. Some deckhand or steward is bound to spill the beans somewhere, and then all the investigators the Captain mentioned will be sniffing around."

After an uncomfortable silence, the First Mate thought aloud. "Let's be logical about this. We can't kill him, and we can't gin up a disabling accident without calling down all the people we don't want to see. We also don't want to arouse the crew. Except for those of us around this table, who really knows if Arroyo got fired or quit when we docked in *Casa Blanca*? After all, the four Moroccans all left."

"Only Donohue and de la Cruz know," said the Third Mate. "Donohue can't stand Arroyo. If we transfer de la Cruz to some other ship in Algiers, he'll be out of our hair and couldn't stir up anyone."

"Maybe," said the Captain, "once we figure out what we do with Arroyo, we have other meeting to decide if de la Cruz should live."

They all nodded. Some sipped their coffee. The First Mate took control again. "How about this: At the south end of Algiers there is a *souk,* an open-air market where you can buy fruits, vegetables, meat, jewelry, furniture, almost anything – including humans. The Tuareg send agents to buy slaves there. Of course, they don't call them slaves; they say they are looking for 'strong employees' to help with the camel caravans across the desert. We could sell Arroyo there. He could never escape from the Sahara, and he could never contact anyone."

"I like it," said the Captain, and slapped the table. That was his way of saying that the decision had been made.

"All right," said the First Mate, "when we get to Algiers, we'll find an Arabic translator, lease a jeep, drug Arroyo, and sell him in the *souk.* In the meantime, Arroyo stays in the infirmary, and he does *not* get off in Tangier. We speed up after we unload in Tangier so we can get to Algiers in two days."

The Third Mate interposed a question: "What if somebody else in the crew gets sick or injured between here and Algiers?"

"I'll treat him somewhere else," said the boatswain. "Nobody should go into the infirmary except Donohue to bring food, or one of the *new* Moroccan deckhands to empty the wastebasket full of Arroyo's shit, or me... to kick Arroyo in the groin if my foot itches."

The meeting ended in a big round of laughter.

Chapter 23: Nagorno-Karabakh

HE LAY ON A COT in a small, strange room. The walls were cement blocks, and the ceiling was vaulted. Looking around, he noticed that there were no decorations on the walls, and no window either. In one corner sat an empty bottle with an unusually long neck. Next to it was a large, black pot with a cover. There was a door, but it had no glass in it, just a narrow slot about knee-high.

There was no sink, no dresser, no other furniture at all... except a chair by the door. In it sat a man with coal-black hair, a large, hairy moustache, and dressed like... like something out of a National Geographic pictorial story of gypsies or of Bulgarian peasants. The man had a sardonic smile on his face.

Stonebrook raised himself on his elbows. His right eye was throbbing, and he could feel that he had a nasty shiner. *"Dónde estoy?"* **[TRANSLATION: Where am I?]**

The man answered in slightly accented English, but Stonebrook couldn't quite make out the accent. "You are in the village of Berdzor in Kashatagh Province of Nagorno-Karabakh."

Stonebrook answered in Spanish. *"Nagorno-Karabakh — reconozco el nombre — es una parte disputada de Azerbaijan.."* **[TRANSLATION: Nagorno-Karabakh — I remember the name - it's a disputed province in Azerbaijan]**

"Very good, Mr. Stonebrook. I suspected that you would be knowledgeable about geography. But you don't have to speak Spanish. I know who you are and that you are an American."

Stonebrook did not try to protest and figured that silence would be the best response.

The man continued. "Your political sensitivity is less developed than your knowledge of geography, however. It would be dangerous in this place, outside of this room anyway, to make what you think is a neutral statement, namely that Nagorno-Karabakh is a part of Azerbaijan. The three-fourths of the population who are Armenian would construe your observation as being pro-Azeri, and they would probably shoot you. There has been a civil war going on within Nagorno-Karabakh for many years, but the rest of the world is preoccupied with Syria and Afghanistan and Iraq, with the Chinese claims on the South China Sea, and with Russia's invasion of Crimea. Here, however, the planet boils down to only one thing: 'Will Nagorno-Karabakh remain Azeri or become Armenian?' And there are no neutrals."

"Who are you, and what is your first language? Your English is quite fluent, but I don't recognize the accent."

The man smiled. "I have two names – in Azeri, my name is Babar, which means 'Lion;' in Armenian my name is Sahak, which means 'he will laugh.' My father was Armenian, and my mother Azeri. Their marriage was not accepted by either ethnic group, and they fled to Canada, illegally, with me and my twin sister when we were teenagers. We both became fluent in English, but we retained our Karabakhi accents."

"Which side are you on?"

"I don't have a side... except to survive. An Armenian separatist group found our family in a suburb of Winnipeg and murdered my father. My mother and sister and I crossed the border to the United States, requested refugee status, but the American Government turned us down and deported us to Azerbaijan. The Azeris in Shirvan, where the Azerbaijani government sent us to live, denounced my mother as a whore for marrying an Armenian and stoned her to death after raping her. My sister disappeared the next day – which was three years ago, and I have not seen her since. Because I speak both Armenian and Azeri without an accent, I can pass for either, and I do – but very carefully."

"So, what is *our* connection, and why am I here?"

"Our 'connection,' as you term it, is that I bought you from a cargo ship captain when it docked in Algiers."

Stonebrook swung his feet to the floor and sat up straight. "What do you mean that you 'bought' me?" He asked with rising anger in his voice. "Do you think that you own me? That I'm your slave?"

Babar/Sahak raised his arms, palms up. "Neither. Actually, I saved your life. Had I not bought you, the Captain would have sold you to the other bidder, who traffics in slaves for Tuareg camel-drivers in the

Sahara. You do seem somewhat less than grateful. Think of it as a contract like that of a professional football player who is asked by the team that acquires rights to him to perform services, some of them dangerous and life-threatening."

Stonebrook was trying to think his way out of this predicament. He looked around the room, which seemed a lot more like a cell than a hotel room.

Babar/Sahak demonstrated that reading Stonebrook's mind on that point was rather easy. "I apologize for the accommodations, but it is the closest thing to a guest house in this village, even though it was built as a jail."

"So, you're going to have someone shove a tray of gruel through that slot in the door for me to eat, and I'm going to have to use that bottle to urinate and that pot to defecate. Is that the deal?"

"Not at all. If you prefer, you can use the latrine down the dirt path to the east. The door to this room is unlocked, and you are free to come and go as you please. I expect that you will take your meals with me in my cottage, which is a few hundred feet away; but doing so is not required".

Stonebrook stood up, moved his arms back and forth, checked his legs and trunk for bruises and cuts but found nothing other than the black eye. "I'm confused. Either I'm your slave, or I'm your guest. Either I'm confined to this cell, or I'm free to go. Which is it?"

Babar/Sahak remained in his chair, seemingly insouciant to Stonebrook's discomfort.

"Perhaps your impatience is a result of hunger. You were drugged and have been in a sort-of, induced coma for quite a while. Would you like something to eat?"

"Yes, I'm hungry...and thirsty," Stonebrook answered, trying to remain calm, "but I am even more starved for information. If the door is unlocked, what's to keep me from running off?"

"Why, your desire to remain alive, Mr. Stonebrook. No one else in this village speaks English, or Spanish for that matter. If you decide to run away, you will at some point encounter a patrol either of Armenian separatists or Azeri soldiers. Since you don't speak either language, as soon as you open your mouth, the members of the patrol will assume that you are an enemy spy and will shoot you...unless they decide to torture you first, for information that you can't give them."

Stonebrook sat back down and sighed. "Okay. If I stay, what sort of services do you expect me to provide to work off the contract price?"

"Excellent, Mr. Stonebrook. I think you finally understand the situation here. Here's what you Americans call 'the skinny:' I intend to purchase a container ship and to go into the business of transporting goods. I need a good deal of information about various ships in order to make the right purchase. You were a crew member of one of the ships under consideration. After you've had a meal, I'd like to bring in my battery-operated recording machine and have you talk into it. I want to know everything about *La Galissionière*, every detail that you know or observed, its owners, its flag, its officers, its crew, its operating procedures, its ports of call, its merchandise."

"And after I disgorge everything I know, then what?"

"Then you will have fulfilled your contractual obligation, I will have gotten full value for the contract price that I paid, and I shall conduct you, safely, to Tbilisi, the capital of Georgia, the country to the north, whose government cares not a whit about the Armenian-Azeri conflict. There you can contact the American embassy, show them your American passport, and fly home."

Pretending to scratch his stomach, Stonebrook checked to see if his black belt, containing the American passport, was still there. It was not.

"Oh, I removed your belt, so that its buckle could not harm you while you were in transport in the mule cart. Your belt and the passport in the secret compartment are both safe."

Stonebrook clasped his hands behind his neck and exhaled. Rummaging through the flood of information Babar/Sahak had thrown at him, he asked. "May I have the belt and the passport now?"

"Why would you need it? The belt obviously is not necessary to hold up your trousers, and your passport will of no use to you until and unless we get to Tbilisi."

"It would make me feel less of a prisoner if I had the belt ...and the passport, that's why."

Babar/Sahak thought about Stonebrook's response for a full minute. "All right," he said, "as a sign in the firmament, I shall return your belt and your passport right after dinner. Are you ready? Come."

He opened the door and led Stonebrook out. It was dusk. It would have been an exaggeration to refer to the dirt path winding its way among scattered huts as a street. But they walked down it, seeing no one

else. They entered a modest hut, and Babar/Sahak led him to a table and
bade him sit down. A woman entered shortly from behind a curtain,
and, without saying anything, she set down tumblers of lemon water,
which Stonebrook gulped down greedily. The woman then brought in
a dish of saffron-colored rice with various herbs and greens. Stonebrook
recognized the taste of parsley, tarragon, marjoram, and watercress.

"This is called *plov*," Babar/Sahak told him.

Then came a second course: Sturgeon with a pomegranate sauce.
Babar/Sahak told him, "This dish we called '*shashlik*,'" and the sauce is
called '*narsharab*.'" Stonebrook ate as slowly as he could manage, to be
polite, but he was, indeed, very hungry.

The woman, still not saying a word, cleared the plates and served
black tea and fruit preserves as dessert.

"Well, that was delicious, Babar. I have been in jails, and this
certainly beats any prison fare that I have tasted."

"I am glad that you enjoyed it, Mr. Stonebrook. Feel free to wander
through the village, but don't wander too far – there are likely to be
mines buried on the outskirts. Some of them are marked by flags, but
they are difficult to make out in the dark.

"Your 'guest cottage' is the fourth building on the right when you
exit. Oh, and, as I promised, I shall return your belt and passport." He
rang a bell, and an elderly man appeared with the belt and the passport,
which he handed to Stonebrook. The man nodded to Babar/Sahak and
said, quietly, something like *laylah sa'idah*, and then he exited the front
door.

"Was he speaking Armenian or Azeri?" Stonebrook asked his host.

"That was Azeri." He rose, shook Stonebrook's hand, and said
"*Buenas noches*."

Stonebrook took the hint, said "Good night," and walked out the
front door. He turned left, the opposite way from his "guest cottage,"
and strolled through the village. There was little to see – a few lights
in a couple of the huts, but no one was out walking around. He turned
around and found his way back to the cottage where he would sleep.

As he lay down on his cot and tried to re-play the events since he
had awakened, the room suddenly began revolving. *The tea*, he said to
himself... and then he passed out.

Chapter 24: The Recording Machine

WHEN STONEBROOK AWOKE THE NEXT morning, there was a table in the middle of the room with two chairs. On the table was a pan of water. Babar/Sahak knocked on the door and entered as if he had been given permission to do so. "Good morning, Mr. Stonebrook. I hope you slept well. I shall leave in a moment to give you privacy. Once you have urinated and washed your hands, just throw the pan of water out the front door. That will be the signal to bring in the breakfast. Since we had an Azeri dinner, we're going to have an Armenian breakfast – it is called '*khash*' - a porridge of bulgur and lamb over *lavash* bread. I'm afraid that there is no coffee, but you can have more tea."

"I'm worried about the tea, Babar. It knocked me out last night."

"I doubt that it was the tea, Mr. Stonebrook. Your body is still adjusting to the altitude, to the long trip in the coma, and to the food of the Caucasus. Besides I want you to be alert while you speak into the recorder."

Stonebrook nodded, waved Babar/Sahak off, and performed his ablutions. As soon as he tossed the pan of water out the front door, the woman who had served the dinner the night before, entered, with a tray on which were two bowls, two spoons, and a pot of *khash*. She left while the two men ate and chatted, but she returned in about 20 minutes, cleared the breakfast bowls without ever having said a word, and left black tea as she departed.

Babar/Sahak pulled the recording machine from a satchel and set it on the table. "Okay. Please begin, and tell me everything you know about *La Galissionière*."

Stonebrook spoke for about an hour and a half. He mentioned everything that he knew about the ship's ownership, the nationalities of the crew members, the peculiar culture of that ship, the discipline, the problems that had developed between him and the Third Mate, and sundry other details that Stonebrook thought that Babar/Sahak might want to know – things like the number of containers, the sort of merchandise unloaded in *Casa Blanca*, and the kinds of equipment on board.

When he finished, he looked up with a look of accomplishment. "Is that it?" asked Babar/Sahak.

"Yeah, that's all I can think of at the moment. What else are you interested in?"

"Well, you never explained why a private detective from Cleveland, Ohio, decided to sign on as a deckhand on a ship in the Mediterranean, did you?" The friendly, smiling face at dinner and at breakfast had disappeared, and an undertaker-solemnity had replaced it.

"Well," Stonebrook began, trying to think rapidly, "it didn't occur to me to talk about that since your articulated interest was in matters that might influence your purchase."

"If you were representing another prospective buyer and had pretended to be a deckhand in order to obtain an unvarnished picture of how *La Galissionière* operated, that would be very much of interest to me. So, who is your client?"

"Surely, Babar, you are aware that I am ethically obliged not to reveal the identity of any of my clients, but I can assure you that with respect to my passage on *La Galissioniere* the client – whether he, she, it, or they -- has or have nothing whatsoever to do with a potential buyer of container ships."

"I think that it is quite possible that your notion of protecting the identity of your client or clients would extend to denying that he, she, it, or they have anything whatsoever to do with potential purchasers of container ships. I am frankly disappointed. I rescued you from the Tuaregs, paid for you, have brought you to this safe haven, provided lodging and food. Yet, you withhold crucial information from me. That is *not* fulfilling your contractual obligation. It is analogous to your donning your football uniform, standing in the position of a linebacker, but refusing to tackle the fullback as he runs by you."

"Look, Babar, I want to be fully cooperative. I *do* appreciate what you have done and, despite your suspicions, I am indeed grateful. It seems to me that I have provided all of the information you need to decide whether *La Galissionière* would be an appropriate purchase.

You now have a complete picture of all the things that you told me you wanted – her owners, her flag, her officers, her crew, her operating procedures, her ports of call, her merchandise. You even have a notion about what the officers and crew deem to be inappropriate behavior by crew members. What more could you want?"

"The 'what more that I want' is that which my competitors are looking at – and at what other ships they are considering buying, and what criteria they are employing to make the decision. Several million dollars ride on this decision, and you are withholding essential information. You say that you are grateful, but you refuse to divulge – or 'disgorge,' to use your term – the key to the lock."

"I'm trying to tell you that the identity of my client or clients is irrelevant to the measures of comparison, to the touchstones that you will use to decide whether to buy *La Galissionière* or some other ship."

"You have *not* been persuasive, Mr. Stonebrook. You disappoint me greatly. I am going to leave you now, so that you can think over your obligation to me. Please reconsider whether not disclosing the name or names of your client or clients is more important than making sure that I have 100% of the information that I need to make a multi-million dollar decision. Think of it this way: I am, essentially, your *current* client, who has paid a great deal of money to bring you here and who has intercepted the destination that the ship captain intended for you, namely to wind up as a camel-dung shoveler for the Tuaregs in the middle of the Sahara desert.

"Come to my cottage if, *and when*, you have changed your mind. The next meal will be a celebratory feast, in recognition of your difficult determination to be completely candid with me." With that he returned the machine to the satchel, turned, and walked out the door.

Chapter 25: Wayzata, Minnesota

BECAUSE IT WAS ELIZABETH'S TURN to give the sermon on Sunday, she was in her study, researching appropriate Gospel passages to undergird her social justice message. A knock on the door interrupted her. "Enter," she said.

It was Leonicio. "*Buenos días*," she said cheerfully.

[IN SPANISH] "I must talk to you about something very serious, Madre Elisabeta."

"Of course, Leonicio. What is it?" He was still standing, literally with his hat in his hand, and she bade him sit down.

"I am very sorry to ask your help. You have done so much for me already. But I do not know where else to turn."

Elizabeth came around from behind her desk and took a seat right next to Leonicio.

"You may tell me anything, and if there's any way I can help, I shall."

He exhaled as if he were about to confess to having murdered Jon-Benet Ramsey. The lawyers have told me that there will be a… deposition, where the lawyers for the company that owns *La Galissionière* will ask me questions about what I know and saw." He looked into her eyes.

"And why does that make you afraid, Leonicio. They already did a dress rehearsal, right? And you told me afterwards that everything was good."

Leonicio put his hand over his mouth and shook his head. Elizabeth was very curious, but she knew better than to rush him if he was not ready. So, she just sat there, patiently.

"They tell me that a woman with a machine will record every word that I say, and that I must speak the truth because I will be under oath."

She nodded. "Yes, that's apparently quite regular in lawsuits."

"I asked the lawyers why I am under oath in the...deposition." He paused. "The lawyer say that at trial, the lawyer for the ship company will try to make me say something different from the deposition so the jury will not believe me and that if I lie in the court, I could go to prison."

She could see that Leonicio was quite agitated, but she still didn't understand why. She put her hand on his shoulder. "Leonicio. At a trial, every witness is a little nervous. I had to testify once, so I know the feeling. You really do not have to worry."

He had been looking down at the floor, but he now looked up and looked directly into her eyes. "Yes, I *do* have to worry. If I tell a lie, I could go to prison, and if I tell the truth, they are going to kill Sofía and Valentina!"

Elizabeth blanched. "Who will kill them? Who said such a thing?"

"Last Saturday a man came to the door of the family where I stay. He somehow knew when the Andersens would be out and that I would be home alone. He was in a suit and seemed polite. He greeted me in Spanish and asked if he could come in because he had some news about Sofía. I hesitated, but I said 'yes.'

"When he came in, he said, 'Listen carefully, señor Muñoz. We know that you plan to testify in a lawsuit about your experience on *La Galissionière*. It would be a big mistake if you say negative things about the ship, its officers, its supervisors, or anything that happened to you or anyone else aboard. If you do'— and here he leaned into me very close – 'if you do, you should realize that we know where your wife Sofía and your little daughter Valentina live in the *Arucas* municipality of *Gran Canaria*. It would be a shame because your daughter is only five years old. No one should have to die that young.'

"I let out a cry. The man stepped back. He showed no emotion. He just added, 'We are watching you. You must not tell anyone that I have brought you this message. Sofía and Valentina would suffer if you did. You will not see me again. You now know what to do. Good-bye.' And he left."

Although Elizabeth was trained in how to comfort parishioners for all sorts of situations, this was a brand new crisis. She put one hand over her heart and the other hand on Leonicio's wrist. "So, what have you done since Saturday?" was the best that she could think to say.

"I have not slept. I have not eaten much at all. I told Mrs. Andersen that I was sick and didn't feel like eating or doing anything much. I am afraid to tell anyone, even Moises. I finally decided that I can tell you, but I don't know what to do."

"Leonicio, I understand now why you are so upset. I can't think of anything worse. But first, it will not help Sofía and Valentina if you are not healthy. You must eat, and you must sleep. I have some herbal tea that I drimk when I have trouble falling asleep. I will give you a bag that you can make into tea and drink tonight. In the morning, you should tell the Andersens that you feel better and that you have regained your appetite. The trial is a long way off, and maybe we can get your deposition postponed. We will have time to make a plan."

"Will you promise not to tell anyone?"

She looked at him without answering for about 10 seconds. "If you tell me that this is a religious confession, then I will be bound not to reveal what you say. But I ask you not to call it a confession. Besides comforting you, I have no way to help you protect your wife and daughter, but señor Stonebrook might be able to, and, with your permission, I want to get a message to him in hopes that he can do something."

"What if he cannot?"

"He seems to be a very resourceful man, and he is a detective. Let me try that first, okay?"

Leonicio nodded. "Okay," he said. They rose and hugged. She went to her desk drawer and pulled out a tea bag and handed it to him. "For tonight."

Chapter 26: Passing The Word

As soon as Leonicio left, Elizabeth picked up her cell phone and called Ted at the law firm. "I need to talk with you as soon as possible about a very serious development concerning the case, but I don't want to say any more over the phone. I will come downtown. When can you be free?"

"I'll make myself free immediately. Do you want me to bring in Cliff? Phil's out-of-town."

"It's your call, Ted. I'll be there in 40 minutes."

She arrived when she said she would and was immediately brought into a conference room where Cliff and Ted were waiting. She accepted a cup of tea and proceeded to disclose what Leonicio had told her.

"Do we know where Stonebrook is now?" asked Rehmel.

Ted answered. "We got a coded message from him from *Casa Blanca*, Morocco, through the Madrid law firm. Lauren figured out that it meant that (1) he has verified everything that the clients told us; (2) that the ship's officers are on to him and that he expects trouble; and (3) they're not going to let him off in Tangier."

"What about that tracker in his teeth. Any soundings?"

"I don't know," said Ted, "but we're sure not going to hear it in Minnesota. We need someone closer."

"Who can we get to be listening... and where?"

Elizabeth interjected. "How about that Commodore Costaign? Isn't he posted in the Mediterranean?"

"Yeah," said Rehmel, "but I'm sure he's got a lot to do besides bird-dog our investigator. We can alert him. But we still need someone else to do something."

"You know, Lauren was in Europe recently. Maybe she has an idea. If it's okay, I'll call her." Rehmel nodded his assent.

Elizabeth reminded them of the purpose of the meeting. "So far, we've decided to let Ted call Lauren to see if she can figure out a way to have someone be available if we hear a signal from the tracker in Rocky's teeth. Even if this someone hears the signal, or if Costaign hears it, then what?"

Neither Cliff nor Ted had any answer.

She persisted. "I also want to return to Leonicio. Someone has found him and has threatened him. Who could that be? How is it possible for someone to have located him? We can move him out of the Andersen home, but that won't do anything to protect his wife or daughter."

Making a steeple out of his fingers, Rehmel spoke but didn't have a lot to offer. "Elizabeth, please find out from Leonicio precisely where the wife and daughter live in Grand Canary. Your idea of moving him is also good. Arrange it as soon as possible, and make the move at night."

When the meeting broke up, Ted called Lauren at the Stonebrook office in Cleveland.

After he relayed what had gone down, he asked her if someone she had met on her travels might be available to help. "The only person I can think of is Rocky's Significant Other, Donna. If I remember correctly, the ballet company has been in Paris and Brussels and Geneva and Madrid and that they're getting ready for some performances in Lisbon and Oporto. I'll call her as soon as we finish here. By the way, I miss you."

Chapter 27: In The Guest Cottage

STONEBROOK PACED BACK AND FORTH. Speaking to himself in Portuguese, a language he figured that no one in the village, including Babar/Sahak, would understand, he engaged in this internal, but aloud, colloquy:

[TRANSLATION]: *Here's what I know for sure: (1) There's not going to be any lunch and probably not any dinner if I don't "sing for my supper," as it were; (2) Babar believes, or says he believes, that I am withholding information about a potential competitor; (3) if he really believes that, there is nothing I could say that would convince him otherwise; (4) if he doesn't really believe that, then his real goal is get me to reveal information about Leonicio and Moises;*

(5) if that's his real objective, what would he do with that information, and why is it so important? (6) And if that's the real goal, then all the stuff about wanting to know about the crew and the owners and the officers and procedures is phony, even a supposed interest in buying a container ship is bullshit, just a pretense to get me to fess up about the real clients;

(7) Well, if the whole thing about the purchase is a sham, how much can I believe about what he's told me about where I am and about his background? (8) He has tried to convince me that I'm in Nagorno-Karabakh, in the Caucasus Mountains, in the middle of a civil war where I don't speak the language of either side. How do I know whether that's true?

(9), I believe I'm in the mountains: The altitude is different, more like I felt when I was in Wyoming during the Carvalho case, although not quite as high. But that doesn't mean I'm in Azerbaijan. (10) He has gone to a lot of trouble to convince me I'm in Nagorno-Karabakh by serving Azeri food and Armenian food, but what if we're not in Azerbaijan?

(11) Where else could I be? The only other people I've seen, besides Babar, are the woman who served food, who did not say a word, and the old man who delivered my belt and passport. The only words the man uttered were **laylah sa'idah**. *(12) That's an* Arabic *phrase! I don't read or speak*

Arabic, but I do know a few phrases, such as good morning, good evening, good night, thank you, and good-bye. **Laylah sa'idah** *means "good night." Of course, when I asked Babar what language it was, he answered, "Azeri." I don't know any Azeri, but I doubt that it would be the same as Arabic.*

(13) To be sure, Babar did not show through any facial tick that the man had made a mistake in speaking Arabic, but then, I didn't show by any facial tick that I recognized the words as Arabic. (14) Whatever research Babar has done on me, he would only know that I speak English, Spanish, and Portuguese. It is highly unlikely that he could have discovered that I can say "hello, goodbye, thank you, and how are you," but not much else, in four or five languages, including Arabic. It comes in handy as a private eye.

(15) All right. So, IF the whole set-up is bogus, where might I be? What place is Arabic- speaking and in the mountains? Well, the Atlas Mountains stretch from Morocco, across Algeria, to Tunisia and separate the ocean from the desert. All three are Arabic-speaking countries. (16) I suppose it could be anywhere in the Atlas Mountains; on the other hand, the last place I remember before waking up in this cell was hearing Donohue saying something to the boatswain about the port of Algiers. Why transport me to Morocco or Tunisia when Algiers lies at the northern foot of the Atlas Mountains? On the other hand, if he were afraid I might escape, it would be safer to be hundreds of miles away. (17) The story about both Armenian separatists and Azeri soldiers wanting to kill me would... did, in fact... initially scare me into not venturing very far. However, if we are in Algeria, and not in Nagorno-Karabakh, why not be just a province or so away from Algiers?

(18) If I am in Nagorno-Karabakh, I have no way to get out; and I have no way to elicit any help from Babar unless I divulge everything about Moises and Leonicio, which might result in their capture, or death. (19) But if I'm in the mountains outside of Algiers, I might be able to escape and get back to the coast. (20) If I'm wrong, of course, I'm likely to be killed, and neither Donna nor Carol nor Lauren will ever know what happened to me. (21) But if I don't take a chance, I'm likely never to leave here, wherever "here" might actually be.

(19) The least bad option is to wander off, as if I'm going to take a crap in the woods, and keep on going until I can hitch a ride. If Azeris or Armenians pick me up, then I'm going to have to do everything I can to convince them I'm an American and not a spy; if an Algerian picks me up,

I hope to get a ride to Algiers and send a coded message. (20) Since I don't have any food or water, I better leave immediately.

He put on his belt, covered it with his shirt, and walked down to Babar/Sahak's cottage.

"Well, have you made a decision to disgorge?" Babar/Sahak asked.

"Actually, I came to borrow a roll of toilet paper. I prefer to shit in the woods rather than in a pot in my guest cottage, or in that smelly latrine."

Although he frowned, Babar/Sahak fetched the TP and handed it to Stonebrook without commenting.

Chapter 28: Holding Up (In) The Atlas

STONEBROOK WALKED SLOWLY INTO THE woods without looking back. After about 100 yards, he ducked behind a large bush, that would have served as a privacy barrier if he were actually looking for a semi-private place to defecate and looked through its branches back toward the village. He saw no one.

Looking up at the sun, he guessed that it was about 9:00 a.m. and that the coast was perpendicular to the sun's position, to the leftt, north, and downhill. He wasn't sure if Algiers would be due north, northeast, or northwest, and he had no idea how far away he might be; but he decided that he would try to maintain a path that was due north by keeping the sun on his right.

In front of him were woods and ridges, but in the distance he could tell that the woods thinned out and that he would be in scrub, on the downhill side of the mountain. That would be easier to travel through, but he would also be easier to spot.

He took off at a jog, zig-zagged when he could until he got to the end of the woodsy part. There were no animal trails he could use, so he made his way down the slope by creating his own switchbacks.

Back in the village, the old man entered Babar's cottage and spoke to him in Arabic:

[TRANSLATION]:

"The American has not returned from the woods. I think that he is gone."

"Get the jeep. I will send a text message to Blida."

Meanwhile, Stonebrook had reached a promontory. Catching his breath, he saw what looked to be a walled city in the distance, which he gauged to be about 10 or 12 miles away. That would take him another three or four hours if he could maintain the pace, which he wasn't sure he could manage. He felt dehydrated and hungry and low on energy. As the sun approached noon, the heat would become oppressive, and he might lose his sense of direction. Scanning the horizon, he did not see any roads.

The mountains were coming to their northern terminus, and continuing due north would mean hiking down a steep slope, which could result in injury, a condition he could not afford. Tired as he was, he turned northwest, a direction that offered a longer distance but a more gradual decline. After an hour, he saw an unpaved road and a sign – in both Arabic and French. He couldn't read the Arabic, but the French was close enough to Spanish for him to understand the sign: 11 km to Blida and 56 km to Algiers.

That's seven miles to Blida, apparently the name of the walled city, and about 34 miles to Algiers. I'll never make it to Algiers, but I might just have enough energy to drag my ass into Blida..

He heard the sound of a vehicle before he saw it and dove into a ravine.

The jeep drove by, and Stonebrook could make out the faces of the driver and the passenger. The old man was driving, and Babar was riding shotgun, peering through binoculars, with a rifle standing tall between them.

He chose a route alongside the dirt road, weaving and ducking and listening carefully for the sounds of other vehicles. An hour or so later, he flagged down an old truck driven by a middle-aged man with a woman beside him. He shouted, "*Saba'akher,*" one of the half dozen Arabic greetings he knew, meaning "good morning." The looks on their faces were not friendly. He then tried the only word he knew in Berber, which was *tiffawn,* which he thought was the right way to say "good morning" in that language.

The man smiled and beckoned Stonebrook to get into the open, back end. As Stonebrook climbed up, he looked at the man and asked, "Blida?" The man nodded and smiled again. Stonebrook collapsed in the back of the truck but didn't dare close his eyes. As the truck got closer to Blida, Stonebrook saw that it, indeed, was a walled city, apparently a former French garrison. As they entered the city, Stonebrook observed modern streets, irrigated gardens, cedar groves, markets, mosques, and, after about a dozen blocks, he spotted what looked like a post office because it had a flag outside. He banged on the cab, and the man stopped. Stonebrook climbed out, grabbed the driver's hand, shook it, and said "*shukran.*" It was the Arabic word for "thank you," but he didn't know how to thank the man in Berber.

Chapter 29: Blida, Algeria

ONCE THE TRUCK DROVE ON, Stonebrook walked into the building he assumed was a post office. He asked in English, "Does anyone here speak English?" The clerks and the customers all stared at him without answering. He then tried Spanish. *"Habla alguién español?"* [**Does anyone speak Spanish?**].

One man, behind the counter, answered in heavily accented Spanish. *"Yo comprendo el francés, y conozco un poco del español. Pero, Usted debe hablar muy despacio."* [**I understand French, and I know a little Spanish, but you'll have to speak very slowly**].

With great relief, Stonebrook said, *"Muchas... gracias. Deseo enviar un mensaje a un primo en España."* [**Thanks very much. I would like to send a message to a cousin in Spain**].

The man scrunched up his eyebrows as if he were trying to solve a puzzle. Eventually, he inquired, in French, *"une telegramme a l'Espagne?* [**A telegram to Spain?**]

"Oui! Si!" Stonebrook exclaimed. The man handed Stonebrook a pen and paper and signaled that he should write out what he wanted to send. Stonebrook thanked the man, in Spanish, **and went over to a table, where, after thinking, wrote the following:**

"LLUVIAS INTENSAS. NUEVE GOLES DE CAMPO HACIA KENTUCKY DE LARRY PARKES EN EL ROSTRO NEGRO. DIGA SALUDOS A COSTAIN."

Stonebrook addressed the telegram to Janer in Madrid and paid the post office employee with euros that he had tied in a bandanna around his ankle.

He walked out, proud of himself and dead tired. He strolled down the street, found a market where he bought a raw carrot and chomped down on it with his wisdom tooth as hard as he could in order to loosen the tracker. On the third bite, he felt something move and hoped that the tracker had been activated. He saw a café across the street, entered it, and ordered the first thing on the menu without having any idea what it was. The waiter brought him couscous with chicken and garnished with dates. He devoured it.

He was trying to figure out how to order coffee when two men and a woman joined him at his table. It was Babar, plus the old man, and a woman with a scar on her face, a hijab on her head, and an upper body like that of a shot-putter.

"Well, Mr. Stonebrook, that was a long way to walk just to avoid the smell of the latrine in the village."

Stonebrook looked around and started to back his chair up when Babar leaned over and said, "You have already met Zaki," nodding toward the old man. "And across from you is Yasmine. She is holding a pistol with a silencer under the table and aimed at your family jewels. It would be unwise for you to make any sudden moves."

Stonebrook looked around. No one else seemed to be paying any attention to their table.

"And if I don't move precipitously, then what? Do we return to the phony Karabakhian village of Berdzor?"

"We plan to take you to a safe house here in Blida. That would save you a long hike, uphill, to your guest cottage. There we shall chat some more. Perhaps you will be more forthcoming."

"And when you're through with your interrogation, then what?"

"As I told you before, if you fulfill your contractual obligation, you will go free."

"And if I don't meet your standards of fulfillment, then what?"

"You will have every incentive to meet my standards. Yasmine, for example, has been instructed not to fire the pistol unless you make a sudden move."

"Point well taken, Babar. I am ready."

Stonebrook walked to the cashier to pay the bill for his lunch. While the cashier handed Stonebrook a receipt, he turned it over, and scrawled "M'AIDEZ" on the back. Although he did not know French, he had years before learned that "MAYDAY" was an Anglicization of the French word, 'm'aidez,' meaning "help me." He tried to hand it to the cashier, but Babar swiftly grabbed it and said something to the cashier in Arabic or Berber. Then: "Please stop playing amateur hour, Mr. Stonebrook. Are you ready now?"

Stonebrook let his tongue slide under his wisdom teeth but felt nothing. "I didn't get dessert. I'd like to buy some hard candy to take with, if that's all right."

"I'll spring for a lollipop for you." He said something to the cashier, who exchanged a lime lollipop for a coin that Babar handed him. Stonebrook removed the paper cover and bit down hard on the side of his mouth with the embedded tracker. This time he heard a pop.

"Delicious, Babar. Let me answer in Armenian: *Shukran!*"

"Ah, yes, you apparently do know a few words of Arabic, including '*laylah sa'idah.*'"

"Gee, I thought you told me that Zaki spoke Azeri."

"That was a serious mistake." Babar forced a grudging smile.

"Whose? – Yours for inadequate research? Or Zaki's for having said 'good night' in Arabic?"

"Both. However, Zaki's has created more difficulty for me, and he will have to pay."

"Poor Zaki," Stonebrook commented. "My hunch is that he has no idea that he made an error, and you're going to punish him anyway."

"Things work different here in Algeria than they do in the United States, or Canada, Mr. Stonebrook."

"Ah, you finally admit that we are in Algeria and not Nagorno-Karabakh."

By that time Babar had taken Stonebrook by the arm and had coercively moved him toward the front door. Yasmine took his other arm, and they forced him into the jeep, which was parked out front. Zaki, sitting next to Stonebrook in back, put a blindfold around his eyes; and, just to make sure Stonebrook didn't try anything heroic, Yasmine, riding shotgun, pushed the barrel of her pistol into Stonebrook's crotch.

Chapter 30: The Safe House

BASED ON STOP SIGNS AND time, Stonebrook guessed that the supposed "safe house" was no more than a mile from the coffee shop. The four of them alighted and walked into the building, Stonebrook still blindfolded. Once inside, they walked toward the rear of the house, and he heard the sound of curtains being pulled shut. Zaki removed the blindfold, and Babar invited Stonebrook to sit on a hard chair. "The leather chair is a lot more comfortable, and you will be allowed to sit in it as you provide useful information."

The room was minimally furnished – a couch on which Babar sat, the uncomfortable wooden chair where he had been "invited" to sit, the very comfortable-looking leather chair, empty, and a floor-to-ceiling bookcase, barely filled. Yasmine sat at a small table with the gun pointed at Stonebrook, and Zaki stood in a corner, whittling with a hatchet.

"First things first, Mr. Stonebrook. Please decipher the four messages that you sent to a man named Janer in Madrid. Here is the first one, sent from Tenerife: 'THE FRENCH LADY HAS INVITED ME TO ACCOMPANY HER ON HER VOYAGE TO THE RISING SUN.'"

"Well," answered Stonebrook, "that's pretty simple. I was telling my cousin Andrés that I had been hired onto a French ship that was heading east."

"I believe the American aphorism is 'Close but no cigar.' The French Lady referred not to *any* old French ship but, specifically, to *La Galissionière,* and Janer is not your cousin but, rather, an attorney in a Madrid law firm. I'm sure that you can do better on the next one.

"The second one you sent from *Casa Blanca*: 'THE WORK IS HARD. EXPECTING RAIN. I MAY MISS THE EXCURSION TO THE MUSEUM.' Please explain."

Stonebrook shrugged. "There's not much to tell. The work on board was, indeed, difficult, and since cousin Andrés had told me in advance that he wanted to hear about the Kasbah Museum, I was forewarning him that I might miss it."

"You are such a lousy bullshitter, Mr. Stonebrook. We have had a serious drought in the *Maghreb*. So, no one was expecting rain either in Morocco or Algeria. My guess is that 'rain' is a substitute word for 'trouble' in the form of the officers learning your true identity, and you predicted, quite accurately, that you might not get off the ship in Tangier. How'm I doing so far, Mr. Stonebrook?"

"You keep insisting that these are coded messages when they are simple expositions."

"Wordplay is over, Mr. Stonebrook. I am growing weary of verbally fencing with you. In *Casa Blanca*, you *did* disembark and you sent the following message: 'THE GOVERNOR IS, AS THE EDWARDIANS CONTEND, A TRIP TO HAVI LAND. THOMAS AND FRIENDS EXPECT TO RIDE THE TUBE.'"

"Gee," answered Stonebrook, "I think you confused my message with someone else's. That does not look at all familiar."

"My guess is that you never expected a Canadian to be checking out your messages, so you were sure that no Arabs or Greeks or Burmese would figure out that 'the Governor' refers to the ship, *La Galissionière*, because of Monsieur Galissionière, the French Governor of Canada in the 18th century. But I haven't figured out either 'the Edwardians' or 'Havi-Land.' The Edwardians ought to be some Englishmen, but I can't quite make the connection; and Havi-Land sounds like *Havana-Gila*, so, perhaps, Israel. I haven't shared that, yet, with your friend Yasmine. She doesn't like most men. She strongly dislikes European and American men. She hates policemen and quasi-cops; And she despises Jewish men. So, once I disclose that you are a half-Jewish, American, private detective, her trigger finger is likely to become itchy... if you get my drift."

"You know, Babar, ever since we met, I have been impressed with your vivid imagination, your command of English, your ability to spin tall – almost believable --tales, and your resourcefulness. But you are barking up the wrong tree here. That's not my message, so I can't help you."

In a command-form tone, Babar said something in Arabic to both Yasmine and Zaki. Yasmine came behind Stonebrook and put one arm under his chin, making it difficult for him to breathe, and clamped her other hand on Stonebrook's hand, balling four of his fingers into a fist. Zaki came over and, with his whittling hatchet, severed the pinky on Stonebrook's left hand in one blow.

Stonebrook screamed loud enough to startle neighbors half a block away, but Yasmine tightened her grip on his throat, so that he couldn't make any more sounds. Not being able to breathe, Stonebrook began stomping his feet, shoved his body against Yasmine's, and pushed her back into a wall. Zaki ran up and placed the blade of the hatchet against Stonebrook's left eye. Stonebrook froze.

Still sitting on the couch, Babar said calmly: "Phase One has now ended, Mr. Stonebrook. If you move without my permission, your eye will join your pinky as a *former* body part. Now, if you will slowly return to your chair, Zaki will bandage your wound, so that you don't bleed to death before I finish the interrogation. But you must end your stupid jokes and pretended ignorance and start telling the truth. Is that clear?"

"Yes!" said Stonebrook, slowly taking his handkerchief out of his pocket to stanch the bleeding on his hand.

"Now that you know that we are serious, let me point out the obvious: You have nine more fingers, ten toes, and...*additional appendages*...to offer. But, although I have never been accused of being a compassionate man, I would still prefer useful and truthful information over having to continue with these amputations."

He paused to let Stonebrook absorb what he was saying. "Now, here's the order of questions that I shall put to you. ONE, decode the *Casa Blanca* message; TWO, decode the Blida telegram; and THREE, tell me where Delgadinho and Muñoz are." How you answer will determine whether you retain all your remaining body parts. Nod when you are ready."

Zaki approached, poured alcohol on the wound, which elicited a loud groan, but not as loud as the amputational scream, and then wrapped the wound in a tight bandage.

Stonebrook looked at Babar and nodded.

"Let's try the Algiers message again, shall we? 'THE GOVERNOR IS, AS THE EDWARDIANS CONTEND, A TRIP TO HAVILAND. THOMAS AND FRIENDS EXPECT TO RIDE THE TUBE.'"

Stonebrook had to think fast. It was necessary to provide a sufficiently accurate decoding in order to prevent additional amputations but not so much as to endanger the clients. "You are correct about 'the Governors' standing for *La Galissionière*. Havi-Land refers to a famous American actress named Olivia de Haviland, who starred in a film called *The Snake-Pit*. I was conveying the report that conditions on board *La Galissionière* were, indeed, a snake pit.

"We had been in touch with some officials of the International Maritime Organization, whose headquarters, I'm sure you know, is in London. Hence, the nickname 'Edwardians.'"

"Now, that wasn't hard, was it? Who are the contacts at the IMO?"

"I really don't know. If you have managed to obtain copies of my messages to Madrid, then you certainly should have found out that I flew from Cleveland to Boston to Madrid to Tenerife. I never stepped foot in the UK. One of my colleagues did, and he passed on the information to the IMO and from there to a spy on La Galissionière."

"How was the information passed to you?"

"By a spy, an Irish-British sailor on *La Galissioniere*, named Donohue."

Babar made a note on a 3x5 card and then looked up. "The message you sent today from the post office here in Blida stated: 'LLUVIAS INTENSAS. NUEVE GOLES DE CAMPO HACIA KENTUCKY DE LARRY PARKES EN EL ROSTRO NEGRO. DIGA SALUDOS A COSTAIN.' In English, that means: 'Heavy rains. Nine field goals toward Kentucky from Larry Parks in blackface. Regards to Costaign.' I get the 'heavy rains' – you're letting *Licenciado* Janer know that you're in deep shit. The rest is unclear."

"I'm surprised, Babar. You seem to know about American, and Canadian, football. A field goal is three points. So nine field goals are 27 points, or miles, toward Kentucky – from the perspective of Ohio – means 27 miles south of Larry Parks in blackface. There was a Hollywood film in the 50s in which Larry Parks starred as a singer who appeared in blackface. His name was Al Jolson. I figured that Janer would recognize that 'Al Jolson' is a stand-in for 'Algiers.' 'Regards to Costaign' is a plea to get my colleague, Richard Staynco ('Costaign,' backwards), the one who interviewed the IMO officials, to get the U.S. Ambassador in England to get his counterpart in Algiers to alert the Algerian Government that someone in Algeria wanted to do me harm."

"Quite clever, Mr. Stonebrook. Except that you have grossly under-estimated the amount of time it would take for this fellow, Staynco, to make contact with the American Ambassador in London and convince him to contact his counterpart in Algiers. He, in turn, would have to use up quite a lot of diplomatic currency to lean on the Algerian Government to do something to an unnamed, bad actor here in Blida, a city of over 100,000, if in fact the Algerian Government figured out that Blida is the place to which you are referring. Blida is actually to the southwest of Algiers, and the Algerian Government might conclude that there is nothing 27 miles due south of Algiers.

"If everything worked at warp-speed, some minor functionary from Algiers would show up at the office of the Mayor of Blida two weeks from now, and the Mayor would say he knows nothing about any American adventurer."

Stonebrook appeared to actually be pleased with Babar's answer. "Ah, but the people in the Post Office know that an American showed up, and the people in the coffee shop know that three Algerians hustled an American out to the street."

"An interesting point, Mr. Stonebrook." Babar then gave a command to Zaki, who nodded and left the safe house. "If Zaki does this job right, I shall let him live, despite his gigantic foul-up in the village."

Stonebrook looked pained. "If it's really going to take two weeks for anybody from Algiers to come looking for me, is it possible to take a break now, drink some water, maybe get a doctor to sew up my hand?"

"You'll get water and medical attention once you tell me what I want to know. To whom do you plan to make a report of your escapades on *La Galissionière?*"

"I'm really feeling faint, Babar, and I'm losing blood through Zaki's bandage."

For the first time, Babar sounded as if he were losing patience. "I've had it with your bullshit, Stonebrook. I want you to know that Yasmine is talented with a knife, and I have no doubt that she would happily cut off another finger. All I have to do is say the magic words. Now, to whom do you submit your report." The last sentence was louder than its predecessors.

Stonebrook's head started to swivel in circles, and his body went limp. He fell off the chair onto the floor. A command from Babar prompted Yasmine to hustle to the kitchen where she obtained a tumbler of water and threw it into Stonebrook's face. He didn't move.

Another command. Another trip to the kitchen. Then, the sounds of helicopter blades. Babar rushed to the window and drew back the curtain. An explosive device blew open the front door, and five men dressed in identical, black outfits, with weapons aimed at chest level, poured into the house.

As they found the room where Stonebrook lay on the floor, Yasmine stepped into view and fired into the chest of the point man. He involuntarily said "*oof-dah*," and put his hand on the spot where the bullet had tried to penetrate the Kevlar vest. The second man taserd the woman. "Get her gun!" one of them shouted. "But don't kill the bitch. Remember, our orders are not to take out any of the locals."

The man tasered Yasmine a second time, grabbed her pistol and stuck it into his belt. He checked her body for other weapons and removed a knife.

The man who seemed to be in command of the fivesome knelt down and pushed back Stonebrook's eyelid. "Are you Mr. Stonebrook, sir?"

"Yes. And you must be the cavalry. Thanks for showing up."

"How're you doing, sir?"

"Except for an amputated finger, I'm all right. I was faking a blackout. I sure hope you have a medic on board the chopper."

"We always carry a medic with us, sir; we never know when a mission will give rise to injuries."

"'Give rise to..' That's an elegant phrase. I'll have to remember that."

The commander beckoned to one of the other men, and the two of them raised Stonebrook to his feet. "Can you walk on your own sir; we have a tight time-line, and we need to leave now."

Stonebrook looked over at Yasmine, prone on the floor and jerking. "Where's Babar?"

The commander asked, "Who's Babar? We weren't told of any companion."

"No, he's not a companion. He's the guy in charge of the kidnapping. He was just here. You got to find him."

"I'm sorry sir," said the commander, "we have to leave now and get you and your finger to Tangier," and he less-than-gently pushed Stonebrook toward the door. Another of the five rescuers entered the room and shouted "CLEAR!"

"Everybody out!" said the commander, and they hurriedly exited the house, pulling Stonebrook with them. Within 90 seconds they were all in the helicopter and airborne. The medic on board examined Stonebrook to see if there were any other injuries. Seeing none, she removed Zaki's bandage, cleaned the wound as best she could with water and alcohl, and then applied pressure to the wound to stanch the bleeding. She then applied some ointment, gauze, and a clean bandage. "I'm going to tie your hand to the fret by your head, so that you can keep it above your heart and slow down the bleeding."

She looked around. "Does anybody have the severed finger?"

"I do," said a young man, and handed her a handkerchief. The medic removed the finger from the handkerchief and inserted it into a plastic, sandwich bag, and covered it with ice from a cooler. Turning to Stonebrook, she said, "Apply pressure to the site of the wound with your right hand. We'll get you to a hospital as soon as we can."

Stonebrook thanked the medic and then turned to the unit commander. "You guys saved my life. I am immensely grateful." No one said anything.

"Are you guys Navy Seals? Marine Special Ops? Air Force Para-rescuers? What?"

No one replied. Then the one who was obviously in command answered, "You will notice that none of us has any bars or stripes, there are no badges or patches to indicate a branch of service, and none of us is wearing a nameplate on our jackets. Except for your last name, we don't know who you are or why you rated this mission. And you don't know who we are, our names, or our unit. The Government will never acknowledge that this mission took place. It never happened.

"We accomplished the mission, and, as instructed, we shall deposit you at the emergency room entrance of the Tanger-Túouan Medical Center near the Municipal Plaza in downtown Tangier. The guy with the phone over there is arranging for a Spanish-speaking surgeon. You are to speak only in Spanish and *not* reveal that you are an American. Here is a disposable cell phone. When they're ready to discharge you, press the blue button, and say '*listo*.'"

"Then what?"

"Today is Sunday. You will stay overnight in the hospital, and you should be discharged after breakfast tomorrow. The ferry to Gibralter leaves at 1:00 p.m. on Mondays. A taxi will pick you up at the entrance and take you to the ferry. Here is your ticket. It's about a 1 ½ hour ride across the Strait. Someone named Patterson from the U.S. Consulate in Gibralter will meet you at the dock and arrange for your return to the United States."

"Wow! I'm overwhelmed. How did Commodore Costaign arrange all this?"

"I have told you everything that I am authorized to say. We are glad to have helped out." Then he turned away, indicating that the conversation had ended.

Back in the safe house, Babar pushed open the secret door behind the bookcase as the helicopter took off. He stepped back into the room where he had been interrogating Stonebrook. "Tangier, eh?" he said.

Chapter 31: Tangier

CARTHAGINIAN COLONISTS FOUNDED TANGIER ABOUT 2,500 years ago. The city takes its name from a Semitic word, *tingis*, that means "harbor." Sitting at the peak of Africa, just west of the Strait of Gibralter, Tangier has been ruled by Phoenicians, Greeks, Romans, Portuguese, the British, and, in the 20th century, by France and Spain before it became part of independent Morocco in the mid-1950s. Its status as a smuggling and spy center throughout the 19th and 20th centuries is legendary.

The medic on-board the helicopter, wearing civilian clothing, escorted Stonebrook into the Medical Center's Emergency Room, where he was admitted under the name Julián Arroyo and attended by a Spanish-speaking physician. They sutured his wound but were not able to sew the pinky back onto his hand. As the anonymous rescue crew commander had indicated, Stonebrook stayed overnight, had breakfast, showered, dressed, and pushed the blue button on the disposable cell phone. The doctor made a final check of his hand, handed him some pain medication and the bag with his severed finger, and signed the discharge papers.

He made it to the entrance at 10:45, and got into the taxi which was waiting for him at the front door of the hospital.

The taxi driver tried Arabic and French, but Stonebrook shook his head and tried Spanish. The driver shook his head. Stonebrook showed him the ferry ticket, and the driver nodded and took off for a silent, 45-minute drive.

Stonebrook paid the driver and noticed that he had almost an hour before the ferry boarded. He had strolled for about 15 minutes when a man in a white robe and a *keffiyeh* around his head approached him and began speaking in Arabic.

"*Lah t'quelem arabiyah*" was Stonebrook's lame way of saying "I don't speak Arabic."

The man answered in English. "Oh, but you *do* know how to say 'good morning' and 'good night,' don't you Mr. Stonebrook?"

It was Babar! He stuck a pistol barrel into Stonebrook's ribs. "You have caused me a great deal of trouble, Mr. Stonebrook. And despite your ability as an escape artist and your access to outside resources, for which I tip my *keffiyeh*, you are now utterly alone."

"How did you find me?"

"Aha. *You*, now, want information from *me*. If I am as forthcoming as you have been, then you will learn nothing."

"Fine, Babar. What's your plan now? I've got a ferry to catch."

"I don't think so, Mr. Stonebrook. I cannot risk your preparing the report about *La Galissionière*, even though you only have nine fingers with which to type it, nor your drawing conclusions between me and Greenport Shipping. So, adjust your plans, and prepare yourself for death. You have two choices – - quick and painless, or prolonged and extraordinarily painful.

"This pistol-shaped instrument in your ribs does not hold bullets; instead, it holds fluids, two different kinds. If I pull back the hammer before depressing the trigger, it will inject phosphorous that will, within one minute, cause your blood to curdle, your mouth to foam, and pain to attach to every neuron, synapse, and joint in your body. You will be unable to talk, but the gurgling sound that involuntarily emanates from you will elicit help from naive tourists and locals in the form of offering you water. Water, of course, will react with the phosphorous to cause internal explosions all throughout your bloodstream and organs. But it will take you at least an hour of unbearable pain to die.

"Option Two is for you to tell me where Delgadinho and Muñoz are hiding and who is paying you; and I'll guarantee you a swift, painless, but fatal injection of 100mg of conium."

"And, given your multiple deceptions so far, Babar/Sahak, why should I believe that you will inject the conium after I have told you what you want to know?"

Babar shrugged. "It's a fair question. You can't *really* be sure. But I have no reason to lie about it, nor would I particularly enjoy making you suffer. Like you, I have a job to do. If you can help me attain my goal, why shouldn't I reward you with your objective, that is to say, a painless death? If you *don't* tell me what I want to know, then the chances of your dying in excruciating pain are 100%. However, if you *do* reveal the information, and I decide that you are being truthful, then the chances that I won't administer the painful poison drop considerably. Don't you see?

"By the way, while you're considering your options, including the one you are currently contemplating, that of trying to use brute strength to overpower me, you should know that I have pulled the hammer back. Any abrupt move on your part will ensure the injection of phosphorous. Now, why don't we slowly walk together to that bench and sit down — very carefully. Then you can make your decision."

He pressed the pistol-like instrument a little more forcefully into Stonebrook's ribs.

They sat down on the bench, carefully, as Babar had indicated.

"All right, Babar. You win. Delgadinho is in *Minas Gerais*, Brazil, and Muñoz is in the Dominican Republic. My client is the Messerleine Corporation, a German company with an American subsidiary in Cincinnatti, Ohio, which has been slowly acquiring merchant ships in its portfolio."

"Tch, tch. Even on the precipice of death, you dare to trifle with me. You have been a worthy adversary, Mr. Stonebrook. But this is where...."

Before Babar could finish his sentence, his eyes dilated, and his face froze. The injector-pistol dropped from his hand, and he toppled over. Sticking out of the other side of Babar's neck was the shaft of a dart. It had arrived silently and mysteriously.

Stonebrook jumped up and looked around. Although there were bushes and trees all around, he saw no one within 100 yards in any direction. He put his hand on Babar's jugular vein. The man was dead. He dragged the body behind a bush about 10 feet away and curled the legs, so that any curious, passing strollers would see a man in the fetal position and assume that he was sleeping or intoxicated. Removing one of Babar's gloves and putting it on his right hand, he removed the dart from Babar's neck and wrapped it in the other glove. Not finding any trash cans, he dug a shallow hole with the heel of his shoe and buried the dart and the gloves there.

Stonebrook hurried to the ferry entrance and asked to be admitted early because of the bandage on his hand. He was allowed to board, found a seat in a corner by the bow, and mentally replayed the events of his "cruise" and of the post-cruise "expedition" in North Africa.

Chapter 32: Gibralter

SHAPED LIKE AN APPENDIX, GIBRALTER is a small peninsula (2.6 sq. miles) dangling from the south coast of Spain. It was a Visigothic kingdom after the Romans pulled out in the fifth century. And, then, 300 years later, a man named Tariq ibn-Zayid led the Arab invasion of Iberia from North Africa. The invaders called the famous Rock there *Jabal Tariq* (meaning "Tariq's mountain"), which eventually got Anglicized from *Jabal Tariq* into "Gibralter." Castile captured Gibralter in 1462, but her successor nation, Spain, ceded the peninsula to Great Britain in 1713 at the end of the War of the Spanish Succession.

Thirty thousand people (a hearty mixture of Europeans, North Africans, South Asians, and Jews) live there and are self-governing under the suzerainty of the United Kingdom, which is responsible for foreign relations and defense.

The Gibralter Philharmonic Society had invited the Cuyahoga Ballet Company to perform in Gibralter's peculiar concert hall, St. Michael's Cave, halfway up the Rock. It was a single performance on a Monday evening, and when Frederika Roxon showed up an hour late for rehearsal, the director called for a break and chewed her out privately.

"Frederika, I concede that you were superlative in London and outstanding in Paris. But I think that you take advantage of me, and of your colleagues in the troupe, to unilaterally decide that you can miss an hour of rehearsal here in Gibralter."

"You have every right," she answered, "to be furious with me, and I need to apologize to all the other dancers in the company. Please understand that I wasn't being selfish or even inconsiderate. I had made a side trip to Morocco over the weekend, and, based on the posted schedule, I was sure that I could make it back on time. However, the ferry from Tangier was delayed. I'll make sure it never happens again."

"You almost didn't make it back in time for the performance: You probably haven't seen the newspaper today, but the headline story is that they've suspended the ferry operation temporarily after they found a dead body, very close to the ferry entrance in Tangier. Detectives say that the murdered man was Walid Al-Sinan, the reputed head of an Algerian smuggling and extortion ring with ties to ISIS and the Somali pirates. He had been shot in the neck with a poison dart. Police apparently have no leads."

"Holy smoke! I guess I *am* lucky," she responded. "Thanks for understanding."

She was spot-on during the remainder of the rehearsal and danced so well that evening that she received a standing ovation and a dozen roses.

Chapter 33: Dornan, Frager & Paloma

EXHAUSTED, STONEBROOK WAS ABLE TO sleep on the overnight flight to the States. He stopped off in Cleveland, checked in with his physician at the Cleveland Clinic to see if it were possible to sew the finger back on, but the bad news was that it was too late. Donna was still with the ballet company somewhere in Europe, so he called Phil Traxel in Minneapolis and said that he was ready to make an in-person report. Then he ordered a pizza. He called Lauren and told her to pack. They were on a plane the next day to Minneapolis.

The lawyers feted the two investigators as if they were visiting royalty. The suits in the conference room comprised Traxel, Rehmel, Ted Bruner, the other two associates working on the case, as well as Frank Bear, the chair of the Litigation Steering Committee, and two other committee members, Norton Tremaine and Evelyn Granger. They plied Rocky and Lauren with sweet rolls and coffee and generally treated them like long-lost cousins.

Everyone was cheerful, polite, and welcoming. *Foreplay*, Stonebrook said to himself. Finally, Traxel broke the revelry with the question. "What did you find?"

"It was even worse than what Delgadinho and Muñoz said," Stonebrook began. "One man was crushed to death between the ship and a pier just because no one bothered to throw out safety blocks. They treated his death callously. Another man was swept overboard in a storm, and no one looked for his body, much less tried to help. There were four Moroccans aboard whom they mistreated, one of them sexually abused by the Captain; and they were put off the ship without being paid. The food was deplorable, some of it out of rusted tin cans with expired dates. The water was not really potable, there were not enough toilets or showers, the work days were minimally ten hours a day; it was hard labor. I saw one man being beaten with a billy club; I don't really know how often others were beaten." He gave them more details and answered their questions.

"How did *you* manage?" Traxel asked.

"I interfered with the supervisor's beating of one of my cabin mates, and I was given extra duties. I hustled the Moroccan boy whom the Captain had been abusing off the boat in *Casa Blanca,* and they got the local *gendarmes* to bring me back to the ship, where they locked me in a room, punched me in the face, and told me to defecate in the waste basket. In Algiers they tried to sell me as a slave to some Tuareg camel drivers, but the Tuaregs were outbid by an Algerian who had lived in Canada and who set up an extraordinarily elaborate con so that I would reveal the clients' whereabouts. I only escaped by the skin of my teeth with the help of some mystery men, who I believe were somehow connected to the Coast Guard. Before the rescue, the Algerian amputated one of my fingers." He showed them his hand.

No one said a word, and they all sat there in shock. Rehmel shook his head. "That was way beyond what we had envisioned when we hired you. Not only are we going to increase your compensation – combat pay, if you will – but I want to offer to include you as a co-plaintiff in the lawsuit. If the jury awards you damages, you get to keep all of them in addition to the investigation fees that we shall pay you."

"Yeah, count me in," Stonebrook replied. "One thing I haven't figured out is how the Algerian knew about me or how he knew about Delgadinho and Muñoz. After two days of games and cons, he mentioned their names and demanded to know where they were. When I declined to tell him, he had one of his henchmen cut off my pinkie. The cavalry arrived just in time to save the rest of my appendages."

"How could he have known?" mused Rehmel. No one had the answer.

Traxel looked around the table. "We have a majority of the Litigation Steering Committee present," he said. "Does anyone doubt that Mr. Stonebrook has brought back precisely the confirmatory information we hired him to gather?"

No one spoke. So Traxel turned to Bear. "Hearing none, Frank, I ask that you formally take a vote right here."

Bear was not happy about being put into a corner, but he gritted his teeth and asked: "Evelyn?" She voted "aye," as did Rehmel and Traxel. "All right," Bear said, "let the Minutes read that on this date the Committee formally authorized taking on *Delgadinho v. Greenport Shipping.*"

Changing the subject quickly, Traxel turned to Stonebrook. "While you were gone, your associate, Lauren, did some superlative work, exceeding our expectations. She got us an expert witness from the International Maritime Organization, and she found us an admiralty expert in Florida to be co-counsel in the case."

"And..." added Rehmel, "she unraveled the puzzle of the 1,000 veils hiding Greenport's ownership of *La Galissioniere.*"

"Why am I not surprised?" is how Stonebrook answered.

"All right, Rocky," said Traxel, "we're going to put you in a room here in the firm with a laptop and ask you to write up everything while it's fresh. You may come up for air and coffee periodically, and when you're finished, we're going to treat you and Lauren to a steak dinner at Manny's. Ted, because you recruited these two fantastic investigators, you're invited as well. Oh, and we'll put you both up at the Radisson again, if that's satisfactory."

"Fine, by me," said Stonebrook.

"Thank you very much," said Lauren. "I'm happy to accept the steak dinner, but I don't need the hotel room; I've made arrangements to stay with a friend."

Chapter 34: Phone Call From Miami

WITHIN 10 DAYS OF STONEBROOK's report, Traxel and Rehmel had completed their final edits and polish to Ted's draft Complaint; Delgadinho and Muñoz, accompanied by Pastor Elizabeth, had come downtown to sign a formal Fee Agreement; Stonebrook had mailed back his signed Fee Agreement; and a deputy sheriff had served the Summons and Complaint on Greenport Shipping.

Sipping a cup of coffee and reading some Advance Sheets from the Eighth Circuit on a Wednesday morning, Traxel saw that his intercom was flashing. "Yes, Sylvia," he said..

"There's an attorney on the telephone from a law firm in Miami. He says that he's calling about the Greenport Shipping case."

"Thanks, Sylvia. Please put him through." And she did.

"Good morning, Mr. Traxel." There was a noticeable drawl to his voice. "My name is Brian Stemler. I'm an attorney in the law firm of Anagnos, Iken & Goldthorpe, and we're representing Greenport Shipping. I thought it would be professionally courteous to call you rather than just send you a letter or mail an Answer as our first communication."

"Well, I appreciate that Mr. Stemler."

"First, I have to admit that I never received a Complaint that contained alternative first pages before. It's an interesting approach."

"As you can see, we are offering you a choice of jurisdiction, either Delaware or Minnesota. If you prefer New York, we'll even send you a third alternative first page."

"I understand Delaware and New York, but what is Minnesota's connection?"

"There isn't any...except that our law firm is here. You're from Florida, so you're going to have to be trying this case out-of-town no matter where we venue it; and it's simply a convenience for us if you agree to venue it here."

"Aha," Stemler answered, as if what Traxel said were a revelation. "And what advantage would accrue to my client if we agreed to venue it in Hennepin County, Minnesota?"

"None of the judges here in 'fly-over land' has any experience in admiralty law, so there won't be any biases, such as you might find in Manhattan or in Kent County, Delaware."

"I see. Umm. Is there someone in your firm who specializes in admiralty law? I looked up your firm's listing in Martindale Hubbell, and I couldn't find anyone who includes admiralty practice in his or her bio."

"That's right. But I should let you know that we do have a co-counsel from your neck of the woods – Anthony Brindle from Farrell and Brindle."

There was an awkward silence on the other end of the phone line, and Traxel thought, but wasn't sure, that Stemler had involuntarily made a noisy inhalation.

"Well, I'll get back to you on the venue question. May I have an extension on the deadline for an Answer?"

"Of course. You should know that Minnesota has what we call 'vest-pocket service.' A lawsuit begins when it's served, not when it's filed. There's no statute-of-limitations issue in this case, so we can hold off filing it as long as we want. That way, you and I get to determine the timetable for discovery, whereas if we file it, then we're on the court's schedule. If one of us thinks we need judicial intervention, then either plaintiffs or defendant can file the Complaint and the Answer. If you decide that you're willing to venue it here, then just send me an Admission of Service and a Stipulation to Jurisdiction, and I'll send you a letter granting an indefinite extension to serve the Answer."

"I can see how not having to comply with the Court's schedule would be an advantage. While we're on the timetable question, I should let you know that it's our position that you have the wrong defendant. Greenport Shipping is a mere subsidiary of a foreign corporation."

Traxel smiled. "We understand that you'll want to bring a summary judgment motion at the proper time, and when you're ready to do that, we can both make our legal arguments to the Court on that issue. But maybe each of us could take some early depositions, so both law firms can get a handle on the facts."

"That's an excellent suggestion, Mr. Traxel. We would certainly be interested in deposing all three of the named plaintiffs as soon as you're willing to make them available. Are they there in Hennepin County?"

"We shall make them available to you here, but you should know that neither Mr. Delgadinho nor Mr. Muñoz speaks English. So, you'll have to arrange for qualified interpreters – Portuguese for Mr. Delgadinho and Spanish for Mr. Muñoz."

"I see. Hmm. I suppose that if we agree to venue the case in Minnesota, we would hire local counsel, and that firm could find interpreters for us."

"No doubt, Mr. Stemler. My hunch is that it may be a lot easier to find a Spanish interpreter than a Portuguese interpreter."

"That's true here in Florida, as well. Whom would you like to depose?"

"For starters, we would like to depose the CEO of Greenport Shipping and the Captain of *La Galissionière.*"

"The CEO, whose name, by the way, is Felix Benteen, you could depose in New York. Captain Eliopoulos doesn't speak English, either. Since he would have to come to the United States, I'd offer our law firm facilities here in Miami, but you'd have to arrange for a Greek interpreter."

"That would be agreeable."

"Well, I've enjoyed our initial conversation. I hope that, even if matters get contentious between our clients in this case, that we can keep the opposing counsel relationship on a professional basis"

"I would welcome that. Thank you, Mr. Stemler."

"Give me four or five days to consult with my colleagues and check out Minneapolis defense firms, and I'll get back to you on the venue question."

"Fair enough. Good-bye."

A week later, Traxel received a telephone call from Charlene Nelson, a partner in the Minneapolis law firm of Stevens, Denton, Brixius, and Marvin. "Hello, Phil. We may have another case together."

"What kind of case is it, Charlene?"

"It's an admiralty case, even though neither of our firms generally handles that area of the law. But you have already chatted with Brian Stemler from the Anagnos firm in Miami, and he has explained your unusual proposal to venue the case here in Hennepin County. They have decided to accept your proposal, and Stevens has agreed to be local counsel." Everyone in the Twin Cities abbreviated the name of the law firm to "Stevens," so even the firm's partners began doing it as well.

"That's good. I look forward to working with you again, Charlene. We managed to settle the last case; I'll hold out the possibility of settling this one as well."

"Oddly, our firm represented the plaintiffs in that case, and your firm represented the defendants. In the Greenport case we're in the reverse positions."

"Exactly so. Are you and the Anagnos attorneys ready to move forward on the depos?"

"Yes. Stemler has put the Admission of Service and the Stipulation to Jurisdiction in the mail along with a cover letter, identifying Stevens as local counsel. They're trying to get the ship captain and the Greenport CEO to find holes in their schedules for depositions in Miami and New York, respectively; but they'd like to get started on the depositions of the three plaintiffs as soon as possible."

"Have you already located interpreters?"

"I have someone working on that now. As you predicted to Stemler, it is more difficult finding Portuguese interpreters. One of my partners, who has deposed non-English speakers in other cases, admonished me that we'll need more than one interpreter. It is intense work, and none of them likes to translate for more than two hours at a time without switching off."

"So, will you be deposing the plaintiffs, Charlene?"

"Maybe of the Stonebrook fellow. I think that Stemler would like to conduct the other two depos and to get the lay of the land here in Hennepin County, but I'll be present at all of them. And, if you don't mind, I'd like to bring along an associate who'll be working on the case."

"Not at all. I want to bring an associate as well. And, just to let you know, I'll want to have a Spanish-and-Portuguese-speaking advisor present at the Delgadinho and Muñoz depos to make sure that your interpreter is translating accurately."

"Huh. I can't see anything wrong with that. We're no doubt going to have to do the same thing about Greek translators for the Captain's deposition."

"Would you like to set the date for the depositions now, or will you need to consult Stemler first?"

"Stemler has already shared his calendar with me. How about three weeks from now, one on Monday, one on Wednesday, and one on Friday, at 9:00 a.m.?"

"Tentatively, yes. Let me check on the Spanish-and-Portuguese advisor's availability, and I'll get back to you. By then may I assume that you' ll have some dates for the availability of Mr. Benteen and Captain Eliopoulos?"

"Sounds reasonable, Phil. See ya."

Chapter 35: Depositions of the Plaintiffs

With the assent of opposing counsel, Stonebrook was up first, on the Monday of "deposition week." He needed to get back to Cleveland on some other cases.

Ted Bruner and his counterpart associate from the Stevens firm shook hands, and Stemler introduced himself to everyone. He was slightly rotund, well-tanned, clean-shaven, with thinning blonde hair on top. He was dressed impeccably and kept his suit coat on, even though the Dornan lawyers took theirs off.

Facing Stonebrook, Stemler sat next to Nelson, who conducted the deposition.

"For the record," she began, "this is the deposition of Pedro Fishkin in the case of *Delgadinho et al v. Greenport Shipping.* The court reporter has already sworn Mr. Fishkin in. Good morning, Mr. Fishkin, my name is Charlene Nelson. My co-counsel, Brian Stemler, who is sitting next to me, and I represent the defendant in this case, Greenport Shipping. If you've had your deposition taken before, can you tell me the names of the cases and the circumstances."

"I have had my deposition taken before, three…maybe four times. In each instance I was not a party but a witness."

"What kind of witness?"

"I'm a private detective in Cleveland, Ohio, and in each instance I testified about my findings and conclusions."

"What is the name of your business?"

"Stonebrook Investigations."

"Who or what is Stonebrook?"

"My professional name is Rocky Stonebrook."

"Why do you need a different professional name?"

"I don't think that 'need' is the correct verb. I just prefer to compartmentalize my life. Authors, actors, singers do it all the time.

Samuel Clemens used the *nom de plume* Mark Twain; Marion Morrison was known professionally as John Wayne; Margarita Cansino became Rita Hayworth; Vincent Fornier uses the pseudonym Alice Cooper; and Martha Westmacott used the pen name Agatha Christie. Why shouldn't private detectives have the same prerogative?"

Nelson smiled, knowing that non-verbal behavior doesn't show up in a deposition transcript. "Can you tell me the names of the cases and the attorneys who took your depositions?"

"Not off the top of my head, but when I get back to Cleveland, I'll send that information to Mr. Traxel, and he can forward it to you."

"That would be good. Will you do that Mr. Traxel?"

"Yes," answered Traxel, even though he was not being deposed.

Nelson continued. "Before you were a plaintiff, you were a private investigator in this case, is that correct?"

"Yes."

"And how did the Dornan law firm come to hire you, Mr. Fishkin?"

"Objection, counsel." Traxel interceded. "You may certainly inquire about the nature of his investigation and about how he came to be a co-plaintiff, but I'm going to instruct the witness not to disclose confidential information about how this law firm hires investigators."

"All right," she said. "Of what did your duties as a private investigator consist, Mr. Fishkin?"

"I was hired to see if I could confirm the allegations brought to the firm by Mr. Muñoz and Mr. Delgadinho."

"How did you go about your work?"

"I flew to the Canary Islands and hired on as a deckhand on *La Galissionière*."

"Did you sign on as Pedro Fishkin?"

"No."

"As Rocky Stonebrook?"

"No, as Julián Arroyo."

"Why did you use a fictitious name when you already had two other names?"

"Based on what Mr. Delgadinho and Mr. Muñoz had told me, I suspected that your client only hired crew members from Third World areas so that they could pay lower than standard wages, require longer hours of work, not comply with the IMO standards for toilets, food, and potable water, and might mistreat crew members. I was fairly certain that they would not hire an American."

"What language did they speak on *La Galissionière?*"

"Spanish."

"And how did you manage to pass yourself off as a native Spanish-speaker?"

"I am half-Argentine and grew up in a bilingual home."

"Do you speak other languages besides English and Spanish?"

"Yes. I speak Portuguese?"

"And how did you come by that?"

"Junior year abroad in Río de Janeiro."

Nelson sat back, taking stock of this interesting witness. She looked at her notes and then asked, "Can you tell me in as much detail as you recall what you did on the ship, what you observed, your conclusions about the things you mentioned earlier – wages, work hours, food and water, sanitary conditions, any alleged mistreatment?"

Stonebrook looked over to the court reporter. "Ma'am, this is going to be a long peroration. Please let me know when you need a break, and I'll stop until you're ready again."

The court reporter had a look of relief on her face. Attorneys and deponents rarely took into consideration the needs of court reporters, and she nodded gratefully. Traxel and Bruner both suppressed grins. Although Stemler had a sourpuss expression on his face, Charlene Nelson smiled appreciatively. She respected this witness, even though his testimony was very likely to be harmful to her client. *Better to find out now than at trial,* she thought.

"That's very considerate of you, Mr. Fishkin. Why don't you just begin, and Ms. Talmadge can signal when her fingers need a rest."

With a break in the middle requested by the court reporter, Stonebrook spent about an hour and a half, essentially iterating what he had written up for the Dornan lawyers.

When he finished, she said: "That's very interesting, Mr. Fishkin. As I understand your testimony, you assert that an Algerian man – whose name you don't know and who is now apparently dead – ordered a colleague, named, 'Zaki,' which you aren't sure is a first name or a last name, to cut off your finger; and you are making a claim for personal injury against Greenport Shipping as a result of what you term an 'amputation.' Do I have that right?"

"It certainly *was* an amputation, and non-consensual at that. And you *do* have it right."

"Help me out here, Mr. Fishkin: Even if a jury were to determine that Greenport Shipping should be liable for any alleged mistreatment you claim that you sustained aboard *La Galissionière* – long hours, unpaid wages, and having to use a wastebasket as a toilet, why would Greenport Shipping be responsible for the amputation of your finger, far away from the ship in Blida, Algeria?"

Traxel had anticipated that question and had prepared Stonebrook how to answer.

"First, the only reason that the Algerian was able to falsely imprison me was that *La Galissionière*. Captain and First Mate *sold* me to the Algerian. Second, the reason that he gave for ordering my finger cut off is that I wouldn't reveal where Moises Delgadinho and Leonicio Muñoz were. The only way that he could have even known their names, much less that they posed a litigational threat to the ship owners, was through Greenport Shipping."

"Throughout what you call your 'peroration' you continue to assert a belief that Greenport Shipping is liable for what happened on board *La Galissionière*. Do you have any facts to back up that belief?"

Traxel had also warned Stonebrook that Nelson would ask this question and that he should concede that he has no personal knowledge about it, nor should he volunteer that his employee, Lauren Marlo, *did* have the facts.

"No, I have no personal knowledge about that" is how he replied.

"Thank you, Mr. Fishkin; I have no further questions."

Moises Delgadinho's deposition was uneventful except that it took a long time: Stemler asked a question in English, the interpreter translated the question into Portuguese; Delgadinho replied in Portuguese; the interpreter translated what he said into English for the court reporter.

If Delgadinho didn't think a question was clear, then his query about the question and Stemler's reply had to go through the double translation process. Additionally, at Traxel's suggestion, Elizabeth politely interceded once early on in the deposition to point out that the interpreter's translation was close but imprecise. The purpose was to alert the interpreter that the other bilingual person in the room was carefully monitoring what he said..

Delgadinho said the same things under oath that he had told the Dornan lawyers that first time in their conference room. And he answered Stemler's probes, which were similar to the questions the Dornan lawyers had asked, the same way. Generally he came off as sincere and honest, if naive. Traxler made a note to prepare him for trial in a slightly different way. Stemler had purposely not tried to confront Delgadinho with difficult questions, hoping that he would be discombobulated at trial when confronted with his deposition testimony.

Muñoz's testimony was a big surprise to everyone, except Elizabeth. Muñoz was articulate, at the beginning, in answer to questions about his age and domicile and marital status. But as soon as Stemler asked him about events on *La Galissioniere*, Muñoz was hesitant, nervous, and seemed to have lost his clear memory. When Stemler asked him about allegations set forth in the Complaint, which he had signed, Muñoz admitted that he had signed, but he claimed that he didn't really understand what the Complaint said when he signed. He did *not* have a recollection of being hit with a blackjack, by any of the Mates. He said that he had voluntarily switched from steward to deckhand because he liked the fresh air, and he denied that anyone forbade him to speak Portuñol with Delgadinho.

Obviously perplexed by this turn of events, Traxel asked for a break. "I'm sorry, counsel," answered Stemler, "we haven't been going long enough to take a break yet; you obviously want to coach your client, and I don't think it's proper."

Traxler replied, "This is not prison, counsel. If I want to take a break, or I think that my client wants to take a break, *we* shall determine that, not you."

"Off the record!" said Stemler. Once the court reporter took her hands off her machine, he said to Traxel, "Let's not make a mountain out of a molehill when we both pledged to function professionally as opposing counsel. You had plenty of time to prepare your client for this deposition, and just because he's not testifying the way you want is no reason for you to take him out in the hall and encourage him to testify in a way that you prefer. If you insist on taking a break now, then I'll recess the deposition, go back to Florida, file your Complaint and our

Answer, and we'll get a judge to supervise the continued deposition of this witness."

Muñoz couldn't understand the colloquy, but he accurately picked up the vibes of hostility between the lawyers. Traxel started to reply when Elizabeth tugged on his sleeve and whispered in his ear.

Traxel said, "Excuse me, I'm going out in the hall to consult with our translator. Mr. Muñoz will remain here." Turning to the court reporter, he said, "Back on the record, please." Then to Ted, he added, "Make sure that Mr. Stemler doesn't try to interrogate the witness while I'm out in the hall." Stemler rolled his eyes.

Out in the hall, Traxel asked, "What is going on?"

"I'm sure that either Cliff or Ted told you. Somebody threatened Leonicio that they'll kill his wife and child. There is nothing you're going to be able to say that can reassure him. Just let him answer the questions, and we'll resurrect him at trial if we can figure out how to rescue his family before then."

They re-entered the conference room, and Stemler completed his questioning of Muñoz.

To all of his questions, Muñoz either equivocated or denied any wrongdoing on the part of *La Galissionière's* officers and supervisors.

Chapter 36: Depositions Of Defendants

TRAXEL INVITED TED BRUNER TO accompany him to the depositions in Miami. Finding two qualified Greek and English translators had been something of a chore, but the firm's co-counsel in Miami, Anthony Brindle, found the translators and also attended the depositions, mainly to show the flag in hopes of intimidating the defendants and their lawyers. He had, after all, won the case, big time, that Lauren had observed... or at least the hearing on the appeal from that verdict, that she observed. The Circuit Court of Appeals had affirmed the verdict.

As expected, Felix Benteen only admitted that he was the CEO of Greenport Shipping but kept insisting that Greenport was merely an American subsidiary of a Greek corporation, *Hestia Etoupeia*, and that Greenport had neither authority, nor responsibility, and certainly not liability, for anything that happened on ships in the Eastern Hemisphere. In fact, he contended, Greenport's charter specifically limited the company's maritime activities to North America. He adamantly claimed that Greenport was punctilious in complying with all United States statutes concerning maritime activities, including the treatment of seafarers and that it also voluntarily complied with IMO recommended standards for the merchant ships it owned in Canada, Mexico, and Central America.

When pressed by Traxel, Benteen explicitly denied that he ever sent orders to *Hestia*, nor to any of the officers of the ships that service Europe or North Africa under *Hestia*'s umbrella, and that, because of the language difficulty, correspondence between *Hestia* and Greenport consisted almost entirely of inquiries from *Hestia* about budget targets, and financial statements that Greenport's CFO mailed to *Hestia*.

When asked if he had any knowledge of the wages paid, working conditions, safety compliance, and food provisions on *La Galissionière*,

Benteen answered, "I would have no reason to know of those things, precisely because I work for a subsidiary here in America."

"My question, sir, is *not* whether you would ordinarily have a reason to know, but, rather, IF you do know about wages, working conditions, safety compliance, and food provisions, on *La Galissionière*."

Benteen hesitated only for two seconds and then answered, "No."

"Did anyone connected with *La Galissionière*, with *Hestia Etoupeia*, or any other source communicate anything to you about events that have taken place on *La Galissionière* in the last six months."

"No."

"Has anyone communicated anything to you about Rocky Stonebrook, Julián Arroyo, or Pedro Fishkin?"

Benteen looked briefly at his attorney and then answered. "I read the Complaint and saw Fishkin's name as a Plaintiff and learned from that document that he used the name Julián Arroyo when he signed on to *La Galissionière*. The only other communication about him was in a conversation with my lawyer, and I know that you don't want to inquire about that."

Traxel decided not to comment on Benteen's smart-ass answer and framed the next question calmly. "So that the record is complete, is it your testimony that other than the Complaint and discussions with your lawyer, you have not had, and have never seen or had, any letters, reports, phone calls, emails, text messages, telegrams from, or conversations with, *anyone* concerning events that have transpired on *La Galissionière* or about Pedro Fishkin or Julián Arroyo?"

"Yes, that is my testimony," Benteen answered very smoothly.

The rest of the deposition concerned technical details about IMO's suggested practices, demands of the International Seafarers Union, U.S. statutes concerning minimum wages, limits on working hours, safety rules, and that sort of thing. Benteen was fluent in his answers.

Captain Aristedes Eliopoulos was clearly unhappy and palpably out of his element answering questions in a deposition. Through the translator, he testified about his background and how he climbed the ranks on merchant vessels to become a Captain; about who hired and promoted him ("a committee from the *Hestia Etoupeia* company"), and who gave him his orders about what merchandise to pick up and unload in which ports ("the *Hestia Etoupeia* company"), who decided the wages of the other officers and the crewmen ("the *Hestia Etoupeia* company"); and the working hours on board ("the *Hestia Etoupeia* company").

"Captain, you have answered four consecutive questions with the answer, 'the *Hestia Etoupeia* company. Who, specifically, at the company gave you orders?"

"It varied. Sometimes Alexis Mitsitakis, the Chief Financial Officer, communicated a budget for food and wages and supplies; sometimes Constantine Tsipras, the Operations Vice resident sent orders about the itinerary and the merchandise we were to carry; occasionally, Panagiotis Zolotas, the External Relations Vice-President sent instructions about dealing with various local authorities and law enforcement; and once in a while, I received orders, or inquiries anyway, from the Personnel Director, Andreas Simitas, about certain individuals who had requested to be placed as officers or supervisors under my command and if I knew anything about them."

"What were your standing orders about paying wages to crewmen who died while serving on board *Hestia* ships?"

"The standing order was to inform the finance department, so they could send money owed to the widows, but no one ever died on board ship while I have been captain."

"What about a man named Jesús López?"

"I would certainly remember a crew member whose first name was Jesús, but no one by that name ever served on *La Galissionière*."

"And what about a man named Francisco Quintana?"

"Never heard of him."

"Did you know the names of all the crew members, including deckhands on your ship?"

"Oh, yes, container vessels operate with crews of 20-25. So, I always learn, and insist that my officers learn, every man's name. We never had a Quintana or a Jesús López."

"Did you maintain a roster of crew members on board?"

"Of course."

"Would you send a copy of the roster of crew members on your last trip from the Canary Islands to Algiers, Algeria, to Mr. Stemler, so that he can forward it to me?"

"As soon as we finish a voyage, I send the roster back to the *Hestia* Personnel Department in Athens. So, I don't have it anymore."

"Well, could you, on the record, promise to obtain a copy and send it to Mr. Stemler?"

"No, I can't promise to obtain it. I can ask, but I don't have any power over the Personnel Department."

Traxel turned to Stemler. "I certainly can include such a request in a formal Request for Documents, but since we're here at Captain Eliopoulos's deposition, I am making the request here, on the record, for you to obtain that roster and provide it to me."

"I'm sorry, counsel, as the attorney for Greenport, I could insist that my client provide any pertinent documents to you, but Greenport doesn't have any employee rosters on ships that *Hestia* sends into the Mediterranean, I don't have any connection to *Hestia Etoupeia*, so the best we can do is to ensure that Captain Eliopoulos carries through with his assurance that he will make the request to the *Hestia* Personnel Department."

Traxel looked over at Charlene Nelson because he respected her integrity and wanted to let her know non-verbally how unhappy he was with her co-counsel. She pretended to be flipping through some exhibit documents and declined to make eye contact with Traxel, who stated, "Is that your notion of maintaining a professional, adversarial relationship in this case, Stemler?"

"Yes, counsel. I can no more guarantee that the *Hestia* Corporation provide a document than I can guarantee that the Greek Parliament will pay its dues to the European Union."

Traxel was steaming. "Let's take a 10-minute break."

During the break Traxel said to Bruner, "My hunch is that this Captain will never show up at trial, so he feels free to lie through his teeth. When we get back, your top priority will be to figure out how we get documents out of *Hestia*."

When they returned to the conference room, Traxel continued his questioning of the Captain. "Do you admit that you have not paid Mr. Arroyo/Fishkin for the work that he performed on the ship?"

"Mr. Arroyo is technically AWOL – he left the ship in Algiers and never returned. Other crewmen had to take over his duties, and we had to pay them overtime. So, it's the company's position, one with which I agree, that we owe Arroyo nothing."

"Isn't it a fact, Captain, that you had the *Casa Blanca* police take Mr. Arroyo into custody and deliver him to your ship?"

"Absolutely not! I have no control whatsoever over local law enforcement in any port."

"Have you had a chance to read Mr. Fishkin/Arroyo's deposition that Mr. Stemler took a couple of weeks ago?"

"Yes, I read it."

"Are there matters in there with which you disagree?"

"Almost everything he said about *La Galissionière* is a pack of lies."

"Do you have an opinion about why he would fabricate all those events?"

"Obviously, he wants money, and he figures the *Hestia* corporation has deep pockets."

"Is it a lie that you and your officers locked him up in the infirmary while the ship was powering between *Casa Blanca* and Algiers?"

"Yes. Why would I want to lock up a crew member when every single person, especially deckhands, is needed to. perform the work?"

"Is it a lie that the boatswain punched him in the face?"

"I never saw the boatswain punch him in the face, and I never noticed a black eye on Mr. Arroyo. So, based on those two facts, I'd have to say 'yes.'"

"Is it a lie that you kicked the four Moroccans off the ship because they complained that most of the meat served was pork and that they had been promised food that adhered to Muslim dietary laws?"

"Yes, it's a damned lie. We never take on Moroccan crew members, in part because the few who speak Spanish speak it poorly, and in part because our budget requires that we mainly serve pork, and we can't afford to comply with Islamic dietary rules."

"Is it a lie that you sexually abused the 17-year old Moroccan, named Mahmoud Nimri?"

The Captain's eyes grew large, and his neck turned bright pink as the interpreter translated the question into Greek. Then he recovered quickly. "Since we didn't have any Moroccan crew members, I couldn't possibly have abused one, could I?"

"Are you denying that you sexually abused Mahmoud Nimri?"

"As soon as we finish a voyage, I send the roster back to the *Hestia* Personnel Department in Athens. So, I don't have it anymore."

"Well, could you, on the record, promise to obtain a copy and send it to Mr. Stemler?"

"No, I can't promise to obtain it. I can ask, but I don't have any power over the Personnel Department."

Traxel turned to Stemler. "I certainly can include such a request in a formal Request for Documents, but since we're here at Captain Eliopoulos's deposition, I am making the request here, on the record, for you to obtain that roster and provide it to me."

"I'm sorry, counsel, as the attorney for Greenport, I could insist that my client provide any pertinent documents to you, but Greenport doesn't have any employee rosters on ships that *Hestia* sends into the Mediterranean, I don't have any connection to *Hestia Etoupeia*, so the best we can do is to ensure that Captain Eliopoulos carries through with his assurance that he will make the request to the *Hestia* Personnel Department."

Traxel looked over at Charlene Nelson because he respected her integrity and wanted to let her know non-verbally how unhappy he was with her co-counsel. She pretended to be flipping through some exhibit documents and declined to make eye contact with Traxel, who stated, "Is that your notion of maintaining a professional, adversarial relationship in this case, Stemler?"

"Yes, counsel. I can no more guarantee that the *Hestia* Corporation provide a document than I can guarantee that the Greek Parliament will pay its dues to the European Union."

Traxel was steaming. "Let's take a 10-minute break."

During the break Traxel said to Bruner, "My hunch is that this Captain will never show up at trial, so he feels free to lie through his teeth. When we get back, your top priority will be to figure out how we get documents out of *Hestia*."

When they returned to the conference room, Traxel continued his questioning of the Captain. "Do you admit that you have not paid Mr. Arroyo/Fishkin for the work that he performed on the ship?"

"Mr. Arroyo is technically AWOL – he left the ship in Algiers and never returned. Other crewmen had to take over his duties, and we had to pay them overtime. So, it's the company's position, one with which I agree, that we owe Arroyo nothing."

"Isn't it a fact, Captain, that you had the *Casa Blanca* police take Mr. Arroyo into custody and deliver him to your ship?"

"Absolutely not! I have no control whatsoever over local law enforcement in any port."

"Have you had a chance to read Mr. Fishkin/Arroyo's deposition that Mr. Stemler took a couple of weeks ago?"

"Yes, I read it."

"Are there matters in there with which you disagree?"

"Almost everything he said about *La Galissionière* is a pack of lies."

"Do you have an opinion about why he would fabricate all those events?"

"Obviously, he wants money, and he figures the *Hestia* corporation has deep pockets."

"Is it a lie that you and your officers locked him up in the infirmary while the ship was powering between *Casa Blanca* and Algiers?"

"Yes. Why would I want to lock up a crew member when every single person, especially deckhands, is needed to. perform the work?"

"Is it a lie that the boatswain punched him in the face?"

"I never saw the boatswain punch him in the face, and I never noticed a black eye on Mr. Arroyo. So, based on those two facts, I'd have to say 'yes.'"

"Is it a lie that you kicked the four Moroccans off the ship because they complained that most of the meat served was pork and that they had been promised food that adhered to Muslim dietary laws?"

"Yes, it's a damned lie. We never take on Moroccan crew members, in part because the few who speak Spanish speak it poorly, and in part because our budget requires that we mainly serve pork, and we can't afford to comply with Islamic dietary rules."

"Is it a lie that you sexually abused the 17-year old Moroccan, named Mahmoud Nimri?"

The Captain's eyes grew large, and his neck turned bright pink as the interpreter translated the question into Greek. Then he recovered quickly. "Since we didn't have any Moroccan crew members, I couldn't possibly have abused one, could I?"

"Are you denying that you sexually abused Mahmoud Nimri?"

"I deny it because there was no such person aboard my ship!"

"Is it a lie that you bribed the *Casa Blanca* police?"

"A complete fabrication."

"What about your or your First Mate's selling Mr. Arroyo/Fishkin at a *souk* south of Algiers?"

"That question embeds at least three lies. First, neither the First Mate nor I left the ship while it was docked in Algiers. Second, we didn't have Mr. Arroyo under our control. He left the ship without permission and disappeared. Third, perhaps North African *souks* sold human beings during the 18th or even the 19th centuries, but perhaps you have seen too many Errol Flynn movies. That doesn't happen in the 21st century."

"In his deposition, Mr. Arroyo states that when you docked *La Galissionière* in *Casa Blanca,* a deckhand was crushed between the ship and the pier, an eventuality that would have been avoided if the crew had tossed the safety blocks over the side. Is that true?"

"The reason we have safety blocks is exactly to protect against the possibility that a deckhand might fall off the pier and be crushed between the ship and the pier, Mr. Arroyo had the assignment to toss the safety blocks over the side when we docked in *Casa Blanca*. He apparently neglected to do that; but I have already testified that no crewman died. So, Arroyo is lucky: His negligence *could have* resulted in someone's death."

Eliopoulos did acknowledge that, as Captain, he was in charge of discipline, of appointing supervisors, of deciding which other officers could serve with him, and of deciding whether to discharge crewmen. He conceded that Fishkin had served briefly on *La Galissioniere* but that he had forged the name of another man, Julián Arroyo, on the contract. The Captain also denied that any crew member was required to work more than eight hours a day, except when docking. He testified that the water was pure, the food was nutritious, and that there were a sufficient number of toilets.

"Will you make yourself available at trial?"

"When's the trial, Mr. Traxel?"

"It hasn't been set yet."

"Well, I can't promise to be available without a date certain. I *do* have a job, after all, which requires me to be on board ships for months at a time. If I'm captaining a ship, then there's no way that I can leave the ship and fly to Minneapolis. As a courtesy to our subsidiary, Greenport Shipping, *Hestia* allowed me to come to Florida for this deposition. But I'm not sure where I'll be when you have your trial. I may be at sea."

Stemler bit his cheek in order to hide the smug expression. Traxel caught it and nodded, signaling that he recognized that the syrupy Stemler on the phone had given way to the cutthroat litigator, who planned to give no quarter.

"I have no further questions. The Court Reporter will send a copy of the transcript to Mr. Stemler, Captain. You will have 14 days to review it and make any corrections. Otherwise, her transcript will constitute your sworn testimony."

With that, they adjourned the deposition.

Chapter 37: Fig Newtons

"BRISTOL HERE," HE ANSWERED ON his special telephone.

"Elliot? This is Frederika Roxon. Are we on a secure line?"

"Of course. But if you need to mention the name of the organization, you should still use the term 'Fig Newtons' instead of NHS." NHS was the National Hitpersons Society, on whose Executive Council Elliot Bristol and Donna Putrell, using her professional name, Frederika Roxon, both sat.

"I need to ask a special favor," she began. "Instead of taking someone out, I want to order a rescue. I'll pay for it by waiving my compensation on my next assignment."

"That would be a first, Frederika. A rescue is not within the Fig Newtons' bailiwick."

"Look, I know you're going to have to clear this with President Pallo, but this is important to me."

There was a pregnant pause. "Assuming Pallo okays it, what's involved, who needs to be rescued, where does the job start, when and where does it end, and do you have someone in mind to take the assignment?"

She let out a breath. He hadn't rejected her request. "The rescue is of a woman and her five-year-old daughter. The woman's name is Sofía Muñoz, and the little girl's name is Valentina. They live in the municipality of *Arucas* on *Gran Canaria* in the Canary Islands. I shall send you their descriptions and their exact address as follow-up. Because they speak Spanish and live on an island that belongs to Spain, I would want Thurman Dixon to get the assignment because he speaks Spanish and Portuguese."

"You didn't say where you would want the delivery made?"

"I left it out because it will probably cause you to rise up out of your chair." She paused. "I want the two to be delivered to a Commodore Costaign of the U.S. Coast Guard, currently in Gibralter."

"Holy shit! You are absolutely right – I am out of my chair and incredulous. Not only do you want a gig that manifestly departs from our ... er, regular activities, but you want us to cooperate with the American military. This is so far-frigging out, I am speechless."

"The reason I called you, Elliot, is precisely because I know that you think outside the box. I concede that this is waaaay out of the box. But Thurman can pull it off, and both he and the Fig Newtons will get his/your regular cut. I'm paying it forward."

Before Bristol could sputter any more, Donna went on: "This is also kind of a rush job. I know that Thurman is a careful planner, and he will have to get out from under his docket, but he has to do that every time he gets an order for.. you know... some 'fig newtons.' I would appreciate it if you would use your charm to get Pallo's approval and then call Thurman and see if he can get away in the next two weeks."

"Why don't you do the rescue job yourself, Fred?"

"In the first place, I don't speak Spanish. In the second place, right now I'm in Lisbon and am scheduled for some major roles in ballets over the next two weeks; and in the third place, I don't want to have any face time with Commodore Costaign."

"You know, Fred, if you weren't so good at what you do, I would tell you to take a flying leap. But you are good. So, I'm going out on a limb. You owe me big-time."

Chapter 38: Summary Judgment Preparation

THE LAWYERS FOR BOTH PARTIES exchanged Requests for Admissions and demands for documents, and each side complained about the opposing counsels' responses. Each side had sought to back the other side into a corner by eliciting admissions to "facts" crafted intentionally to squeeze the adverse party; and the replies invariably admitted facts distantly related but avoided conceding the truth of the factual statements sought.

Each side complained that the other side failed to provide documents requested, as well: Plaintiffs answered that they couldn't provide most of the documents the defendants wanted about Delgadinho and Muñoz – birth certificates, seaman certificates, work histories, proof of wages earned on other vessels --- because they were in the United States and didn't have access to them and couldn't contact their families for them because *Hestia* officers had told their relatives that they were dead. For their part defendants claimed that they couldn't provide the documents that the plaintiffs wanted because those documents were in the hands of *Hestia Etoupeia*, over which Greenport Shipping had no control.

So, they moved inexorably toward a hearing on summary judgment. Dornan, Frager filed the Complaint, and the Stevens firm filed the defendant's Answer. Charlene Nelson tried to be professionally courteous even though negative tension was high between Stemler and Traxel. She called Traxel to seek a mutually convenient date for a hearing on Summary Judgment, and they jointly selected one six weeks in the future. Nelson scheduled the hearing with the judicial clerk to the judge newly assigned to the case, Roberta Mattson. Both sides devoted their energies on this case to the preparation of Briefs.

To the chagrin of the defense counsel, both in Miami and Minneapolis, the Dornan firm didn't just prepare a negative brief but also sought affirmative relief, partial summary judgment on the issue of liability, leaving the amount of damages for the jury. Traditionally, defendants in civil cases seek to get rid of lawsuits in hearings before the judge, arguing that the law as applied to the facts requires dismissal of the case; and plaintiffs focus on demonstrating that there are critical facts in dispute, thereby precluding a grant of summary judgment.

But in this instance, the Anagnos and Stevens firms, representing the defendant, didn't bother with trying to show that there were no genuine factual disputes (there were, after all, plenty) but, rather, just aimed at getting the Court to declare that Greenport Shipping legally had no responsibility or liability for whatever may have happened to the plaintiffs. Dornan, Frager, for its part, was asking the Court to declare, as a matter of law and fact, that Greenport Shipping was indeed the appropriate defendant and to enjoin Greenport from denying at trial any assertions to the contrary.

Judge Mattson's clerk set up a telephone conference among the judge, Traxel, and Nelson. After pleasantries, Judge Mattson said: "This appears to be a very complex case. Is there any chance of mediating this before you argue your respective summary judgment motions?"

Nelson spoke first. "I'm ordinarily a big fan of mediation, but mediation's goal would be to find a figure on which plaintiffs and defendant can agree. Here, our client contends that plaintiffs have chosen the wrong defendant. If Greenport Shipping is indeed the wrong defendant, then there's no reason that it should agree to pay a dime. If, and only if, the Court declines to grant our motion for summary judgment would it make any sense, and not be a total waste of time, to mediate."

Traxel spoke up. "I'm inclined to agree with Ms. Nelson."

After a pregnant pause, the judge said: "I would like to have an in-chambers conference with all the attorneys who will be involved in trying this case if there is a trial after the disposition of the summary judgment motions. That includes the Florida attorneys for both sides. My clerk, Eric Marcus, will provide you three or four hour-long times when I can make time in my schedule, and then you two find out from your Floridian colleagues the least inconvenient one when you can all make it." She disconnected but had her clerk tell the two lawyers the four options, and then he disconnected.

"Are you still there, Charlene?" "Yep."

"My reading is that Judge Mattson is not terribly pleased to have been assigned this case."

"I got the same impression."

"Well, of the four alternatives, which are the two you like the best? I'm afraid that if we give our Floridian colleagues four choices, we'll be spending untold hours trying to agree on one. If we just give them two, it is possible that we can cut the calendar games to a minimum."

"I agree," she said with a soft laugh. So they selected two and passed the information on to Stemler and Brindle. With just a few telephone calls, back and forth, they all agreed on one of the dates, and relayed the information to the judge's clerk.

Brindle called Traxel and said that he was preparing a supplemental motion and accompanying brief to request an evidentiary hearing on the summary judgment motion.

"Clearly, in order for us to prevail, we have to demonstrate the corporate veils hiding Greenport's true role in a way that would be more difficult just on paper. A live witness would be better. I'll write up the case law, you prepare your investigator, Lauren Marlo, to be the witness."

At the in-chambers conference, attended by Traxel, Rehmel, Brindle, and Bruner for the plaintiffs and by Nelson, Stemler, Wentworth (the one who had argued the appeal in Miami that Lauren had observed), and the Florida firm's associate, Emily Cadwalader (next to whom Lauren had sat in Miami), the judge acknowledged that she knew both Mr. Traxel and Ms. Nelson.

She said that she was happy to meet the other attorneys and then explained that "this gathering is informal, but it may eventuate in an order, so the court reporter is here to take down what everyone says.

"Mr. Traxel, are you the lead attorney for the plaintiffs in this case?" And when he affirmed that he was, she began her inquiry. "I have never heard of an evidentiary hearing on a summary judgment motion. Why do you want it, and what's your authority for it?"

"Judge, as I'm certain that you and your clerk have already discerned from the large amount of paper that has floated into your chambers from both sets of lawyers, this is a complicated and convoluted case. There are huge numbers of disputed facts, which is why the defendant did not attempt to argue in its brief that there were no disputed facts. The only questions that the Court really needs to decide at this juncture are whether Greenport Shipping is the appropriate defendant and the ancillary question whether, if you determine that it *is* the appropriate defendant, to enjoin it from asserting at trial that it is not.

"The paper trail of the ownership of *La Galissionière* is jungle-thick, and the number of corporate veils that have to be pierced in order to recognize how Greenport has carefully concealed its true ownership of *La Galissionière* is manifold. It will surely create a gigantic judicial headache to try to make sense of it based on attachments to briefs. It would be the equivalent of three aspirins for that headache if you allow us to have a witness testify about the connections."

Stemler interposed. "Judge, I have to rely on my colleague, Ms. Nelson, about the, um, special customs in Minnesota, but I've been a litigator for 25 years, in federal and state courts, and I have never, ever experienced an evidentiary hearing on a motion for summary judgment. I would like to formally object at this time." He had almost said "the *peculiar* customs in Minnesota" but had thought better about it and had substituted the word "special" for "peculiar." Judge Mattson intuited what the "um" meant but did not comment.

"Is there any precedent, Mr. Traxler?"

"If I may, Judge...." It was Brindle. "I can understand why there might not be any precedent in Minnesota, given that few admiralty cases are venued here. However, the attorneys signed a Stipulation of jurisdiction and venue in Hennepin County, Minnesota, so we are here, in your Court. In preparation for this in-chambers conference, I have brought some cases from state courts in Florida, Virginia, and Texas and some federal courts in the Fourth and Eleventh Circuits. One of them was a case that Mr. Wentworth and I litigated in federal district court for the Southern District of Florida. In all five of these cases – and I've made copies of the decisions which, with your permission I'd like to distribute to you and to the other attorneys here – - the courts recognized that the complexity of the matters contained in the briefs impelled an authorization for testimony to help the Court cut through the problems"

"Is that right, Mr. Wentworth?" Judge Mattson asked.

Wentworth, who had flushed crimson, responded, "Well, yes, but Mr. Brindle made precisely the same argument there, and Judge Holden told us that he wrestled with the issue because he didn't think that the cases cited by Mr. Brindle were pertinent."

"What did Judge Holden eventually decide, Mr. Wentworth?" the judge asked.

"He did allow the evidentiary hearing, but he told us in chambers that he did so reluctantly because he wasn't sure that it would be upheld on appeal."

"Then why did he grant it?"

"May I answer that, Judge?" It was Brindle who had spoken. "What Judge Holden told us was that he had read our briefs a couple of times and felt confused, and he thought that oral arguments were unlikely to clarify matters, so he was hoping that testimony might help him untie the 'knots,' as he called them, in the case."

"Is that accurate, Mr. Wentworth?"

"Uh, yes."

"And how did the Eleventh Circuit treat the issue?"

"They affirmed the denial of summary judgment and ignored the question of the appropriateness of an evidentiary hearing."

"Ms. Nelson, have you had an opportunity to research the question?"

"No, Judge, but I would like that opportunity."

"Back to you Mr. Traxel, who would provide testimony?"

"A private investigator we hired did the leg-work and has produced a chart that traces the corporate connections."

"Wait a minute!" It was Stemler. "I deposed your man Fishkin, and there was no mention of his having done any work on corporate tracing." His voice was at a higher timbre than is usual in in chambers.

Traxel quietly replied. "It is not Fishkin. The witness would be Lauren Marlo."

Stemler was steaming. "Your Honor, this is an unfair surprise."

"Mr. Traxel, where does this Ms. Marlo live or work?" asked the judge.

"In Cleveland, Judge."

"Mr. Stemler, when would you or Ms. Nelson like to depose her?"

"As soon as possible."

"Would you prefer to depose her in Cleveland or here in Minneapolis?"

"Umm. I suppose Minneapolis."

"Here's what we're going to do: First, Mr. Brindle, you may pass out the copies of the decisions you brought along. Make sure my clerk, Eric Marcus, gets a package. Second, agree on a date for the deposition in the next 10 days, and, Mr. Traxel, you make sure that Ms. Marlo is present for the deposition. Third, provide Ms. Nelson with a copy of the chart you mentioned, at least three days before the deposition. Fourth, I assume that the deposition will take place in the Stevens law office, so let my clerk know when the deposition will take place. Even if I'm in trial, I shall excuse myself to rule on any disputes counsel may have arising out of that deposition, but I will not be a happy camper if you impel me to recess a trial or a hearing to referee attorney squabbles. Fifth, after the deposition, I shall entertain a brief from defense counsel containing any counter-arguments to plaintiffs' request for an evidentiary hearing on the summary judgment motion.

"I promise that I shall give it priority attention. And I will issue an order whether or not to permit the testimony. If I grant plaintiffs' motion, will defense want someone from Greenport to testify?"

The question elicited prolonged silence. "Uhh, we hadn't thought about it, Judge," said Stemler, "but yes, if you do decide to allow testimony, then, yes, we would want the CEO of Greenport to be able to testify as well."

"Fine. Make sure that the CEO can clear his calendar on the date we have scheduled for the argument on the motion."

Nelson spoke up. "Judge, if you decide to allow an evidentiary hearing, and both Ms. Marlo and Mr. Benteen – the Greenport CEO – testify and will be subject to cross examination, I don't see how we can squeeze all of that, plus oral argument, into an hour."

"You're quite right, Ms. Nelson," said the judge. "Eric, would you please get the calendar, and see what else is scheduled that day?" He brought it to her, and she examined it.

"I would have to move a few things around. But I'm not going to do that now because I've not made a decision on whether to extend the hearing to include testimony, nor will I until I have reviewed Ms. Nelson's Reply Brief and any case law that she appends to it.

"Is there anything else we need to discuss?" The attorneys all understood that the question was a polite way of saying that the meeting had concluded.

Chapter 39: Offer

"PHIL TRAXEL SPEAKING."

"Hello, Phil, this is Charlene Nelson. How are you today?"

"Copacetic. How about you?"

"I'm good, thanks. I'm calling because our client is willing to make an offer before you pay for an airplane ticket for Ms. Marlo to fly to Minneapolis."

"I have a yellow pad in front of me.. What do you have?"

"Greenport offers $500,000. We would allocate it anyway you want it designated among compensatory damages, punitive damages, attorney fees, and out-of-pocket costs. In exchange we'd want a full release and a confidentiality clause."

"I'll of course have to ask the clients, and I'll get back to you within a day or two."

"Phil, will you recommend to your clients that they accept?"

"I don't think that I want to divulge to opposing counsel how I shall advise my clients, but I'm not offended by your question. Thank you for the offer."

A secretary arranged a conference call among the Dornan lawyers in Minneapolis, attorney Brindle in Miami, Stonebrook in his office in Cleveland, and the two original plaintiffs, who gathered in Pastor Elizabeth's office in Wayzata. Traxel explained the offer and asked Elizabeth to translate for Moises and Leonicio.

"What would the split be, Phil?" asked Stonebrook.

"We'd return the $10,000 to St. Edwards that was the retainer; your company would earn an additional $30,000 in investigation fees beyond the $10,000 you've already spent and another $10,000 that

Cliff mentioned as the 'bonus' for the 'combat duty'. The residue is $440,000, of which the law firm is entitled to 1/3, or $145,660, some of which would be shared with Farrell and Brindle in Florida. That leaves $295,000 to be divided three ways among the three plaintiffs, or about $98,000 apiece."

Elizabeth translated in Portuñol to save time, and said, "They both think $98,000 American is a lot of money, but they want your advice since this kind of negotiation is way out of their depth."

"This is Cliff Rehmel speaking. Let me talk about risks and gains. The reason that Greenport has made an offer is that there is a risk to Greenport that we will win on our summary judgment motion, and, if so, they would not be able to argue at trial that Greenport is not the owner. They would look like liars at trial because Felix Benteen denied it under oath in his deposition.

"They obviously fear that they might lose big and are willing to spend a half million dollars now and be done with it. If the Court were to grant their motion for summary judgment, then we'd have to find a way to sue *Hestia* in an American court, or in a Greek court, and that may not be so easy. On the other hand, based on what transpired in the chambers discussion, given the fact that the judge may be willing to hear Lauren's testimony at the hearing, we have a good chance of her granting our motion, or at least allowing the jury to decide the question.

"If we hurdle summary judgment, then it's all a matter of credibility – if the jurors believe Moises and Leonicio and Rocky and don't believe defendant's witnesses, we can ask for large sums for all three plaintiffs for pain and suffering, violation of IMO regulations, bad food, inadequate sanitation, safety compliance failures, unpaid wages, an amputated finger, putting Moises and Leonicio out on the ocean to die, and threatening to harm their families if they returned to their homes. We can also ask for what's called 'punitive damages' to punish Greenport. The good news is that if the jury awards punitive damages, you three get to keep them. Another thing you should think about is that if the jury makes the award after a trial, you are free to run the story in the newspapers and tell everyone you know. But if you accept the offer, then you are bound to keep it a secret. That's a condition of their offer."

After translating, Elizabeth spoke: "Leonicio is inclined to accept the offer, but Moises would like you guys to say more about the odds."

"My turn," said Anthony Brindle. "There are no guarantees, but there are likelihoods. I think that there is no more than a 15% chance that Judge Mattson is going to grant summary judgment to defendant. Lauren's testimony is so good that it almost *has* to create factual doubt. "Now, whether the judge will grant us summary judgment is maybe 25%. But there's a 60% chance that she will deny both motions, and therefore allow the case to go to trial. If that happens, then we have great witnesses – Leonicio, Moises, Rocky, Lauren, Ambasssador Grindon, and Commodore Costaign. The other side has an arrogant CEO, and a bullying Captain who will do everything he can to be 9,000 miles away during trial. They could bring the Mates, but my hunch is that they'd prefer not to. So, we have an... oh, 80% chance of winning *something*. The odds are that it would a lot more than $500,000, and the odds are also that the defendants think so too, or they would have started much lower."

Traxel asked, "Rocky, what do you think?"

"I think a bird in the hand is worth two in the bush; however, it's worth letting the one bird go if there are a whole flock of birds around the corner."

"So, may we presume that your preference is to turn down the offer?"

"Yes."

"Moises, how about you?"

[**TRANSLATION**]: "I am a gambler and am willing to risk it. I just feel a pang of guilt that if we turn it down, and we lose, then I remain dependent on St. Edwards."

Elizabeth assured him that that should not be a consideration.

[**TRANSLATION:**]"Is it possible," asked Leonicio, "to separate out – so that I could settle, but the others stay in?"

Rehmel: "We have a right to ask, and we will. But I don't see what the defendants would gain from it. The fact that they made an offer means they are afraid of losing big-time and want to get off as cheaply as possible. A jury would be just as appalled by what Leonicio and Rocky say. So their risk doesn't go down by paying $100,000 to one plaintiff and then have to face the possibility of millions at trial."

Elizabeth said in English, "You guys know why Leonicio is dragging his feet. He would be in an entirely different place if we could ensure the safety of his wife and child."

"We're working on that, but we don't have anything to show for our efforts yet," said Traxel. "Although I was unprepared for Leonicio's deposition testimony, it may actually work in our favor because the defendants are now convinced that they have scared him and that he will hurt our case and help theirs at trial."

"Phil," asked Stonebrook, "what's your hunch about what happens if we turn down their offer. Is it a one-time dealy?"

"Probably not. If they lose on summary judgment, they are likely to raise the stakes. If the jurors seem to be grooving on our case and they look angry at Greenport, then there will be another offer. That's what we have done when *we* represent defendants. We have even made offers while the jury is out."

"Then," said Stonebrook, "I want to propose that we counter with $1,000,000; and if they accept, then the law firm would get about $313,000, and each plaintiff would net about 210K."

Through Elizabeth, Moises readily agreed. Leonicio was undecided, but she told him that he had performed the way the man asked him to, so his family would not be in danger unless he testified differently at trial, which might be months away. He hesitated but finally assented.

Rehmel said, "There's one more thing: Phil and I need to know what kind of authority you three will give us to negotiate during the upcoming stages. If they turn down our counter-offer, then we have the hearing on summary judgment. If the Judge rules against Greenport on summary judgment, they are likely to make a slightly higher offer, and if we turn that down, a slightly higher offer still. How comfortable are you in relying on our judgment? We have a big stake too, so we don't want to throw our money away either. But our highest duty is to the three of you. The problem will arise when the three of you are not on the same page."

Stonebrook came back in. "What if, fellow plaintiffs, we let the lawyers negotiate based on their experience and their sense about the defendants during the litigation, up to $5,000,000. At that point they have to come back to us. Does that sound fair?"

Moises: "*Sim!*" [**Yes**]

Leonicio: "*Supongo que sí*". [**I suppose so**] (sigh).

Stonebrook: [**IN PORTUÑOL**]: "Elizabeth and Moises, please do a group hug with Leonicio."

Traxel returned Nelson's call: "Charlene, we have a counter-offer of $1,000,000." Charlene answered, "I don't have authority to accept that, and based on the conversation with Greenport, I won't get authority either. I guess we're going to have Marlo's depo and the hearing."

"Which of you will be deposing her, and when do you want her here?"

"Not sure on which attorney will depose. If you can have her here either Thursday or Friday, we'll accommodate. Just let me know ASAP, so I can alert Stemler, who will want to be here no matter who has the wand."

"Oh, one other thing, Charlene, does Greenport have any interest in settling separately with any of the plaintiffs?"

"That's not going to happen any time during the pendency of this case. If we settle, it will be just one lump sum."

"Just checking. See you at the depo"

Chapter 40: Summary Judgment Hearing

"ALL RISE," INTONED THE CLERK, "Judge Roberta Mattson presiding."

"Good afternoon, counsel. Please be seated. This is the matter of *Delgadinho et al v. Greenport Shipping*. The Court has changed its schedule to allow a total of three hours this afternoon and, in a previous order, has granted plaintiffs' motion to allow both the plaintiffs' witness, an investigator named Lauren Marlo, and defendant's witness, Felix Benteen, the CEO of Greenport Shipping, to testify. If we take two 15-minute breaks today, each side has a total of one hour and 15 minutes. That includes cross-examination time. My clerk will keep track of each party's time and will give you warnings when you have only 15 minutes left. Mr. Stemler, you may proceed."

Rising from his chair, Stemler began to stammer. "Umm. Excuse me, Your Honor, I, uh, had assumed that ... umm... plaintiffs would go first because of the deposition of Ms. Marlo."

"Things may very well be different in Florida, counsel, but here in Minnesota the party that files the motion first speaks first at the hearing."

"Yes, of course." (Pause) "May it please the Court. This case concerns...."

"Before you begin, let me telegraph to counsel for *both* parties my preparation for this hearing. I have read your briefs carefully, twice. And Mr. Marcus has adroitly prepared summaries of your arguments and of the cases each of you has cited. Accordingly, neither of you should feel any compunction to act like briefs-wired-for-sound. What would be most helpful is if each of you would direct your comments toward what you think are the two or three most salient points and toward your strongest rebuttals of opposing counsel's key arguments."

Stemler swallowed hard. He was unaccustomed to judges who asked attorneys to abbreviate their oral arguments. He covered his mouth and thought fast. "May it please the Court; there is only *one* salient point in this case: Greenport Shipping is entitled to summary judgment because it is merely a subsidiary of *Hestia Etoupeia* in Athens and has no responsibility or liability for what might have happened in the Mediterranean Sea on a ship over which Greenport has zero control.

"The leading cases in support of that proposition are the 1986 U.S. Supreme Court case, **Celotex Corp. v. Catrett**, and the 2015 Minnesota Supreme Court case, **Morris v. 3M**; citations, of course, are set forth in our brief. The Answer, our responses to Requests for Admissions, our Answers to Interrogatories, and the deposition of the CEO of Greenport all make clear that Greenport is merely a subsidiary of *Hestia*. The Court should take judicial notice of the fact that plaintiffs are having trouble bringing an action, assuming one is merited, against a foreign corporation, so they seek a shortcut, an improper shortcut, by suing a subsidiary that has nothing to do with the matters set forth in the Complaint. Rule 56 of both the federal and Minnesota Rules of Civil Procedure was designed precisely for this kind of situation where the plaintiff has joined the wrong party as a defendant. As the Court will observe when Ms. Marlo testifies, plaintiffs have a *theory* but no facts to contradict the sworn statements of defendant Benteen. Thank you, Your Honor."

"Is Mr. Benteen here ready to testify, counsel?"

"No, Your Honor, we decided that his testimony today would merely duplicate what he stated in his signed Answers to Interrogatories and in the excerpt from his deposition, attached to our brief, where he denies, under oath, that Greenport has any authority or control over *Hestia Etoupeia*."

"All right. Mr. Traxel, it's your turn."

Traxel rose. "Mr. Brindle will argue on behalf of plaintiffs."

The judge nodded. Brindle rose. "May it please the Court before I launch into an argument, I should like to use some of our allotted time to raise a question about adverse witnesses. I had hoped to cross-examine Mr. Benteen today, but he has obviously chosen not to appear. During the deposition of Captain Eliopoulos, I explicitly asked him if he intended to show up at trial, and he made it clear that he would probably be at sea, no matter when the Court scheduled the trial date. And we had subpoenas for the First Mate, Adolfo Vidaña, for the Second Mate, Manuel Fuentes, and for the Third Mate, Joâo Cano, delivered to Greenport Shipping. Mr. Stemler replied that since none of those gentlemen was employed or contracted by Greenport Shipping, the delivery was ineffectual, and he returned the subpoenas."

"May I presume, counsel, that none of these potential witnesses lives in the United States?"

"As far as we can tell, that is correct."

"Well, what is it that you expect this Court to do since it has no power to require foreigners not living in the United States to appear in our courtrooms?"

"I recognize that if you were to grant summary judgment to defendant, then the issue would be moot. However, if you were to grant *our* motion and declare that Greenport shipping is *in fact* the proper defendant, then the Court could order Greenport to produce the witnesses at trial."

Judge Mattson sat back and pursed her lips. "Mr. Stemler, do you have anything to say on this subject?"

Stemler hestitated and then said, "No, Your Honor. As Mr. Brindle conceded, a grant of our motion for summary judgment would eliminate the issue altogether."

"Mr. Brindle, are you ready to make your argument now?"

"With the Court's permission, I'd like to call Ms. Marlo to the stand first."

"Very well. Mr. Marcus, please swear in the witness."

After Lauren was sworn in, Brindle began his examination. "With the Court's and Mr. Stemler's consent, I shall save time by opening with leading questions that are non-controversial. May I?"

Stemler dropped his jaw and showed his palms, face up..

"You may begin, Mr. Brindle, but Mr. Stemler has the right to object if he so chooses."

"Ms. Marlo," Brindle asked, "you are a domiciliary of Ohio and a graduate of Case Western University in Cleveland, having majored in Law Enforcement and Political Science; you are a private investigator, employed by Stonebrook Investigations; your employer uses 'Rocky Stonebrook' as a professional moniker, but his real name is Pedro Fishkin; and he is a plaintiff in this case. Is all that all accurate?"

"Yes."

"Is it also the case that the law firm of Dornan, Frager & Paloma hired you and Mr. Stonebrook to conduct an investigation in connection with this case?"

"Yes."

"That's the end of the leading questions, counsel and Your Honor. Ms. Marlo, what were your specific assignments in this case?"

"The firm asked Mr. Stonebrook to verify the allegations of Mr. Delgadinho and Mr. Muñoz, and I was assigned to do three things: (1) Check out the International Maritime Organization in London and find an expert witness; (2) go to Miami, and find a co-counsel who was a plaintiffs' lawyer experienced in admiralty law litigation; and (3) go to Dover, Delaware, and do whatever other research necessary to establish the corporate relationship between Greenport Shipping and *Hestia Etoupeia.*"

"And did you carry out all three assignments?"

"Yes, I did."

"Who is the expert witness you found?"

"His name is Alfred Grindon, and he is an Ambassador to the IMO."

"How did you find him?"

"Through an employee of the IMO's Library staff."

"How did you find an experienced plaintiffs lawyer in admiralty law?"

"I observed you arguing before the 11th Circuit Court of Appeals in a case where Mr. Stemler's firm represented the defendant." Stemler opened his mouth but quickly closed it.

"How did you go about researching the corporate relationship between Greenport Shipping and *Hestia Etoupeia*?"

"I began by retrieving a copy of the corporate documents on file in Dover, Delaware, where Greenport is incorporated. I did some further research on its website, and I managed to find records of some lawsuits in which Greenport was a party. Through those records I discovered that Greenport has a subsidary Mexican company, called *Marina Mercante Mexicana, Inc.*

"With the help of a bilingual librarian, I was able to send for incorporation papers in Mexico City, and those papers acknowledge that Greenport is the parent company and that *Marina Mercante* has its own subsidiary, a French company called *Porte-Conteneurs Francais, Inc.* I do speak French, and I was able to make inquiries in Paris and learned that *Porte-Conteneurs Francais* is what the French call a *societé anonime.*"

"Why is that important?"

"The French have three different kinds of corporations. The important difference for this case is that a *societé anonime* can have a corporate owner, but it must also have an individual shareholder listed as co-owner."

"So, who are listed as the owners of *Porte-Conteneurs Francais?*"

"The corporate owner is *Marina Mercante Mexicana, Inc.* The individual owner is Felix Benteen."

Stemler. "Objection, Your Honor. The witness is testifying about alleged documents, but there are no documents being offered into evidence."

"Mr. Brindle?" asked the judge.

Brindle turned to Marlo. "Did you bring the documents with you."

"Yes." She opened her briefcase and pulled out a thick binder. "I have the documents from Dover, Delaware, which, as you instructed me, I pre-marked as Exhibit 1; the documents from Mexico City, pre-marked as Exhibit 2, and the documents from Paris, pre-marked as Exhibit 3."

"Do you have a copy for Mr. Stemler?"

"Of course." She handed a batch to Brindle, who gave half to the court reporter and half to Stemler. "I offer Plaintiffs' Exhibits 1, 2, and 3, Your Honor."

Flipping quickly through the batch, Stemler said, "Wait a minute; the documents are in Spanish and French."

"Am I allowed to speak?" Marlo addressed her question to the judge.

"Is it in response to Mr. Stemler's statement about the documents not being in English?"

"Yes, Your Honor."

"What is it that you wish to say?"

"I realize that Mr. Stemler hasn't had a chance to read the documents carefully, but appended to Exhibit 2 is an English translation from the Spanish, with a certification from the translator of its accuracy; and appended to Exhibit 3 is an English translation of the French with a certification of its accuracy from the translator of that document."

The judge turned to Stemler. "Mr. Stemler, would you like to take some time to examine the documents?"

"Yes, Your Honor. Thank you."

"In that case, we'll take a 15-minute break at this time."

During the break, Brindle whispered to Lauren: "You're doing great, Lauren. Remember, on cross-examination, unless Stemler specifically asks you, do not volunteer that you know the names of the directors of any of the companies except the Italian company and the Greek company."

"Got it," she answered.

After the break, Judge Mattson asked Stemler if he had any objection to the exhibits offered. "Well, she didn't provide these documents to us at her deposition."

"Mr. Brindle?" asked the judge with her eyebrows cocked.

"Your Honor, I have a copy of the deposition transcript. Nowhere in the deposition did Mr. Stemler ask Ms. Marlo if she had copies of the documents I am now offering."

"Is that accurate, Mr. Stemler?"

Stemler flipped through his copy of the deposition transcript. "Apparently, yes."

"Did you have time during the break to read the English translations?"

"Yes, Your Honor, but I have no way to independently verify that the translations are accurate."

"How about this, Mr. Stemler: Suppose that I receive these exhibits now conditionally; but if you want to subsequently challenge the accuracy of the translations, I'll make time on my schedule for you to do that?"

"Yes. That would be reasonable. Thank you, Your Honor."

"Then Plaintiffs' Exhibits 1, 2, and 3 are provisionally received."

Brindle continued his direct examination. "What else did you find, Ms. Marlo?"

"I found that the French company, *Porte-Conteneurs Francais*, itself, had a subsidiary, an Italian corporation called *Navigazione Commerciale Italiana, Incorporato*."

"And why is that pertinent?"

"The members of the Boards of Directors of the *Navigazione Commerciale Italiana Incorporato* and of *Hestia Etoupeia* are exactly the same. And the few copies of Minutes I was able to find show that the Boards invariably meet on the same day in the same city."

"Do you have copies of those documents?"

"Yes." She pulled out another batch of papers from her briefcase. "I have pre-marked these documents as Exhibits 4, 5, and 6; and the translations are appended."

Passing one copy to the court reporter and one to Stemler. Brindle said, "I offer Plaintiffs' Exhibits 4, 5, & 6."

"Mr. Stemler?"

"If the Court will allow us time to confirm the accuracy of the translation, as it has with the earlier exhibits, I shall provisionally refrain from objecting."

"Very well. Plaintiffs' Exhibits 4, 5, and 6 are provisionally received."

Brindle went on. "Ms. Marlo, did you make a chart mapping the connections?"

"Yes, I did, and I pre-marked it as Exhibit 7." And she pulled out a chart.

Brindle gave one to the court reporter and one to the judge. "Is this the same chart that we provided to Mr. Stemler prior to your deposition?"

"Yes."

"I offer Plaintiffs' Exhibit 7, and I have given one to the Court to follow along as Ms. Marlo testifies."

"No objection," said Stemler without the judge having to inquire.

"Ms. Marlo, will you please walk the Court through your chart?"

"Surely. In the upper left hand corner is *Hestia Etoupeia* with a line indicating that Greenport is its subsidiary. Underneath, there's a line across the page under it. Above the line is what defendant claims is the corporate relationship. Below the line, the rectangles show the connections that plaintiffs assert. Greenport owns the Mexican company; the Mexican company and Mr. Benteen together own the French company; the French company owns the Italian Company; and the Boards of Directors of the Italian company and of *Hestia* are exactly the same people and always meet at the same time in the same city."

"No further questions."

"Cross, Mr. Stemler?"

"Thank you, Your Honor. Ms. Marlo, You testified that you speak French. How much French have you had?"

"Two years in college."

"Have you ever been qualified by a court or any certifying agency to be a translator or an interpreter?"

"No."

"And you don't speak Spanish or Italian, do you?"

"No."

"So, you can't guarantee to the Court that these translations are correct, can you?"

"I sought out formally qualified translators in all three languages, and they certified that their translations are accurate."

"That isn't what I asked you ma'am. I asked if YOU could guarantee their accuracy."

"No, I cannot personally guarantee their accuracy."

"I notice from your chart that you have thick lines drawn from Greenport Shipping to the Mexican company, from the Mexican company to the French company, and from the Mexican company to the Italian company, right?"

"Yes."

"And those lines apparently represent an ownership relationship, am I right?"

"Yes, that's correct."

"Now, you did *not* draw a thick line from the Italian company to *Hestia*, did you?"

"No."

"And the reason you included only a dotted line is that you did not unearth any proof that the Italian company has any ownership interest in *Hestia*, did you?"

"What I discovered, as I've testified, is that the Boards of Directors...."

Stemler interrupted. "My question was framed to elicit either a 'yes' or 'no' answer."

Lauren paused. "I concluded that because the Boards of Directors are the same...."

"Excuse me, Ms. Marlo, but I asked about proof. Do you have any proof?"

"I am not a lawyer and don't know what the law says about proof, but, as a layperson, I inferred that the same Board of Directors and the same meeting dates and places constituted proof."

"You are correct that you don't know what the law says. Why did you not draw a thick line from the Italian Company to *Hestia*.?"

"I was demonstrating that the *level* of proof was not as strong."

"Indeed. I have no further questions."

"All right, Mr. Brindle. Are you ready to make your argument now?"

"Yes, Your Honor."

"Please take to heart what I said to Mr. Stemler before he began."

"Yes, Your Honor. Unlike most summary judgment motions, neither side has attempted to persuade the Court that there are no genuine issues of material fact. Either Greenport Shipping is merely a subsidiary of *Hestia Etoupeia*, or, through a series of carefully concealed veils, it is the actual *owner* of *Hestia*. Defendants contend that it is a long distance subsidiary with no power, responsibility, or liability for what takes place on ships nominally owned by *Hestia*.

"Now, the only predicate for that assertion is the signature of Felix Benteen on Answers to Interrogatories and his denial in his deposition. He is hardly a disinterested, objective observer. If the Court grants plaintiff's motion for summary judgment, as I urge it to do, then Mr. Benteen and the various companies he secretly controls are at great economic risk, and he comes off as a perjurer. Even though the Court expressly authorized Mr. Benteen to testify at today's hearing, he declined the invitation.

"Ms. Marlo's investigation, however, has pierced the corporate veils to reveal that Mr. Benteen has gone to a great deal of trouble to disguise Greenport's ownership of *Hestia* through three other companies in three other countries. It can be no coincidence that the Boards of Directors of the Italian company and of *Hestia* are precisely the same, have their meetings on the same day, and in the same city.

"Mr. Marcus's bench summary surely tracks the key cases that provide a legal basis for the proposition that this Court has the power to declare that, as a matter of law, Greenport Shipping is the *de facto* and the *de jure* owner of *Hestia Etoupeia*, and, through it, of *La Galissionière*, on which the horrendous events took place. At the very worst, the Court might determine that there is a genuine issue of material fact about Greenport's ownership of *Hestia Etoupeia* and permit us to proceed to trial, allowing the jury to decide. Thank you."

Judge Mattson nodded and turned to Stemler. "You have plenty of time left in your allotment, Mr. Stemler. Do you wish to make a rebuttal argument?"

"Yes, thank you, Your Honor. During my cross-examination of Ms. Marlo, she admitted that she intentionally did not draw a thick line from the Italian company, *Navigazione Commerciale Italiana* to *Hestia Etoupeia*, precisely because, as even she conceded, what she terms 'the LEVEL' of proof was insufficient. Just because it thunders does not mean that a hurricane is about to hit. Just because two companies have the same members of their Boards of Directors does not mean that one owns the other one. Plaintiffs have offered no evidence to contradict Mr. Benteen's sworn statements except Ms. Marlo's conclusory guesses. She is hardly a disinterested, objective person either, since she is an employee of one of the plaintiffs and an independent contractor of the law firm representing the plaintiffs. Without demonstrative proof of Greenport's ownership of *Hestia*, this Court should declare, as a matter of law, that the proper defendant in this case is *Hestia Etoupeia* and should grant our motion for summary judgment. Thank you."

"Anything further, Mr. Brindle?"

"No, Your Honor."

"Thank you all. We are adjourned."

Chapter 41: The Judge's Order

JUDGE MATTSON'S ORDER WAS OUT in a week. It was carefully crafted to withstand an appeal and contained all of the appropriate predicates and legal citations. The decisions set forth in the Order comprised: **(1)** she denied Greenport's motion for summary judgment; **(2)** she denied plaintiffs' motion for partial summary judgment as well, adopting Brindle's alternative argument that the corporate relationship was a factual question, left to the jury to decide; **(3)** since it was not clear if Greenport had any authority over the officers of *La Galissionière*, the Court would not order that they be present at trial; **(4)** however, if the jury were to determine that Greenport was, in fact, the actual owner of *Hestia,* and through it, *La Galissionière,* then plaintiffs would be entitled to a jury instruction that the jurors could make an adverse inference about defendants' refusal to honor the subpoenas for the three Mates and plaintiff's request that the Captain appear as well; and **(5)** the trial was scheduled for seven days, eight weeks hence.

Rehmel bought a bottle of champagne and invited Frank Bear, Ted Bruner, and the other associates working on the case to celebrate in his office. They immediately notified Brindle, congratulating him on his excellent argument. They also called Pastor Elizabeth, so that she could pass the good word on to Muñoz and Delgadinho; and they called Stonebrook, mainly to let him know how crucial Lauren's testimony had been but also to congratulate him on his role as co-plaintiff. "Let us raise our glasses to congratulate ourselves and our clients," sang out Rehmel.

After a few more sips and good cheers, Traxel said, "I'm pretty sure that Charlene Nelson will be calling tomorrow to raise the ante in her settlement offer. How shall I respond?"

Rehmel answered. "Stemler and company were relying on the Court's granting summary judgment. They have to know that their client has lied through his teeth. I can't imagine any jury that's not going to be sympathetic with our clients. I say that even if Nelson offers the one million you countered with last time, you answer that the offer of a million was valid before the hearing on the summary judgment motion, but now the cost has gone up."

"And what should the counter-offer be?"

They both looked at Bear, the chair of the Litigation Steering Committee. "Okay, you won on summary judgment. How strong is your case going to trial?"

Traxel answered. "On a scale of 1 to 10, I would say '9.'"

"I agree, Frank," said Rehmel.

Bear stuck his tongue between his teeth and upper gum, took a deep breath, and said,

"All right, let's go for five million. That was the threshold the plaintiffs agreed we could negotiate without re-consulting them, correct?"

"Exactly so."

When Charlene Nelson called the next day, she congratulated Traxel on the "procedural victory" and said that Greenport was now willing to accept the counter-offer of a million dollars.

"I appreciate that, Charlene. But we made the counter-offer before the hearing and without knowing for certain what the outcome would be. Now that we're going to trial, the needle has moved. The plaintiffs will settle for $5,000,000."

He could not see her blanch over the telephone. "You don't think that five million dollars is a very large amount when you haven't had to prove a single nickel of damages?"

"Actually, we'll be asking for a lot more if we go to trial. If I were in your shoes, I'd tell my client that five mill is a bargain."

"Phil, I have authority to go up 500K -- to $1.5 million. But that's it."

"I understand, and I recognize that you're just the messenger when it comes to settlement and not the decision-maker in this case. It might be different if you were lead counsel."

She decided not to respond to that comment. "I'll pass on your declination and your counter-offer, but I'm quite certain that Greenport will not agree to pay five million."

"All right, Charlene. If I don't see you in the meantime at some bar association meeting, I'll see you month after next in Judge Mattson's courtroom. Bye."

Chapter 42: Grand Canary

THURMAN DIXON WALKED OFF THE plane at the *Gran Canaria* airport, wearing sunglasses. It was a lot less noticeable how often he looked around when he wore shades. He went over to the first rental car company and asked to rent a car. When the clerk asked him for his driver's license and a credit card, he showed them a license and credit card in the name of his hitman persona, Dion Washington.

[IN SPANISH]:

Clerk: "You will be returning the car to this airport, right?"

Dixon: "Actually, I want to make a special request and will willingly pay extra for it. I want to be able to leave the car at the wharf. Just tell me where I should place the key?"

Clerk: "Under the floor mat by the driver's seat. I'll write it down on the contract. That will be an extra 25 euros."

Dixon: "That's fine. The other thing is that I don't know whether I shall be using the car for two days or for three. I'll pre-pay for three, but you might want someone to hunt for it two days from now."

He found an inexpensive hotel and then scouted the area. He drove by the address he had written down for Ms. Muñoz and parked down the street from her house. After about 25 minutes, he noticed a woman dressed in clothing one might wear to an office walking on the sidewalk. She turned onto the walk toward the house and opened the front door with a key. A few minutes later she emerged from the house in more casual clothes and walked two houses to the north and came back out with a little girl, obviously the daughter. He found a restaurant several blocks away, had a meal, and then returned to his stake-out. He saw a light go on in what apparently was a bedroom and then, after enough time for the mom to have read the daughter a story, the light went out.

After waiting for just enough time for the child to fall asleep, he knocked on the woman's door. "Señora Muñoz?"

[IN SPANISH]: "Yes?"

"I bring a message from your husband, Leonicio."

She cried out. "You can't. He's dead! Who are you?"

"That's why I have come. Leonicio is alive and has sent me here. I know that it's evening, and you have no reason to trust me, but I don't want to say anymore out here where someone might overhear us. So, I'm willing to come back in the morning, but I know that you go to work."

"You speak Spanish, but you don't sound like a *Canario*."

"No, I'm not. I'm from the United States, and that's where Leonicio is."

She cried out again. He was patient.

"How can I know that what you say is true?"

"First, I can tell you things that most strangers wouldn't know: Leonicio grew up in Tenerife and moved here when he was 21. Your first name is Sofía, and you met him here and got married. You have a five-year-old daughter named Valentina, and your neighbor two doors down watches her while you work."

Sofía put her hand to her face. Dixon went on: "Leonicio signed on to be a steward on the ship *La Galissionière*, plying the Atlantic Ocean. Second, he may have sent you letters saying that he got demoted to deckhand and that he had made one good friend on the ship, a man from the Azores named Moises Delgadinho. Lastly, some man from the *Hestia* corporation told you that Leonicio was dead and probably gave you a few hundred euros, saying that it was Leonicio's back wages."

"All that is true. You may come in." She still looked a little wary.

"Would you like something to drink?" she asked.

"No thank you. What I have to tell you is very important. At one point the officers of the ship got mad at both Leonicio and his friend, Moises, and put them on a row boat in the Irish Sea. The Captain told them that if they ever told anyone about what they saw on board or if they came back to their homes, they would be killed — after they watched their families be murdered."

She withdrew into her chair and put her hand to her mouth.

"With great luck they made it to Wales, part of Britain, and an Episcopal priest from the United States, who happened to be there, arranged for them to fly to America and stay with families that belonged to her church. He and Moises are there now.

"The church people hired a law firm to sue the ship company, but someone found out. A man came to the house where Leonicio is staying and threatened him. He said that if Leonicio said anything bad about *La Galissionière* or what happened on it, they would kill you and Valentina."

She began crying. He waited.

"Leonicio has sent me to take you and Valentina to him."

"How....where.... what....?"

"Yes, I know this is a lot of information all at once. But you are in danger. I want to give you some time to absorb all of this. You may ask anyone you want for advice, but neither you nor I know if the people who would hurt you live here, or not. To show you that I am a friend, I want to show you a photo of Leonicio that someone sent to me on my telephone." It was a photo of Leonicio and Moises with Pastor Elizabeth.

"Who is that woman?" she asked.

"She is the priest who rescued the two men. In the Episcopal Church, women can be priests."

When that seemed to calm her down, he said, "Here's what I propose. You think about this overnight. In the morning, call in sick to work. Send Valentina to the neighbor's while you pack. One suitcase for each of you, no more. Then tomorrow night, I will come by after dark and take you to the boat. If you are still not sure, I'll give you another day, and I'll come back the next night. If you say 'no,' I'll go away, and I'll let Leonicio know that you did not believe me and would not come to America."

Sofía got up and began pacing the floor. Dixon sat quietly.

"Where will this boat take us?"

"It is an American boat, a submarine, which will have a private room for you and your daughter. It will bring you to Lisbon, Portugal. Someone there will take you to the American Embassy, which will arrange for you and Valentina to fly to Minneapolis – that's the city where Leonicio is – and will take you to the courthouse where Leonicio will be."

"What if this is all a lie? Maybe you're the one who wants to kill me and Valentina!"

"It is okay to be angry and afraid. I understand. I would be too if I were in your shoes and someone came to my door and told me what I have told you. But if I had wanted to kill you, you would be dead now. I am here to rescue you and to take you and your daughter to your husband."

She sat down and began to cry seriously. Dixon touched her gently on her shoulder.

"I shall leave now. I will return after dark tomorrow. If you decide I am telling the truth, then, come to the door with your two suitcases. We'll get Valentina from her bed, and we'll all drive to the wharf and get you on the boat." And he left.

The next night, Dixon drove up a half hour before dark. No one else seemed to be on the street. He waited for the light in Valentina's bedroom to go off and waited 10 minutes. He went to the door and knocked. Sofía's eyes were red, but she had the two suitcases packed and standing by the door. "I will put the suitcases in the car; you get Valentina."

Once they were all belted, he drove in circles to make sure that no one was following, even though he had not seen anyone. Eventually, he arrived at the wharf, put the key under the driver's seat mat, and grabbed the suitcases. Sofía and Valentina followed. As they approached the gangplank to the sub, two men came running down the pier with guns, shooting. Some sailors on the sub fired back, and the two men collapsed on the pier.

Sofía began screaming, and when she heard her mother scream, Valentina began wailing as well. Dixon comforted them as much as he could, helped them board the sub, and led them to the cabin reserved for them. "If you need anything, say 'Washington' – that's my name. Very few of the sailors can speak Spanish. Practice it —'Wa-shing-ton.'"

She did practice the name, but she didn't need to call him that night. She and her daughter soon fell asleep..

Chapter 43: Voir Dire

IN MINNESOTA STATE COURTS, ATTORNEYS do most of the jury selection, called *voir dire*. The judge does only the very preliminary screening, asking those called to jury duty (the "veniremen") only if any of them knows any of the attorneys or is familiar with the plaintiffs or the defendant, or if any of them has any opinions about merchant ships or admiralty law.

The clerk called 13 veniremen to the jury box. No one among those first 13 veniremen knew anybody involved in the case, and none of them was even sure what admiralty law was about.

When the judge told them that the trial might last a whole week, or longer, and asked if anyone had a reason he or she could not be available for the entire seven days, one woman who was eight months pregnant explained that she was likely to need to run to the bathroom every half hour or so. The judge excused her. A hygienist who said that her boss, who owned the dental clinic, would have to reschedule over two dozen teeth-cleanings if she were gone for a week elicited a grudging excusal from the court.

A sole practitioner lawyer stated that he, of course, wanted to do his citizen duty and would willingly cancel hearings, mediations, and depositions scheduled for the ensuing week, but, neither party's attorneys believed him, nor did they want him on the jury. Traxel gave a subtle shoulder-and-eye signal to Stemler, who nodded just a scoche. Traxel rose. "Your Honor, may we approach the bench?"

Looking quickly at Stemler, who nodded affirmatively, the judge answered, "yes" and beckoned them with her right hand. Just Traxel and Stemler came to the bench and, out-of-the-hearing of the veniremen, both said that they thought the lawyer-venireman should be excused but that neither side wanted to use up a peremptory challenge.

Peering over her glasses, the judge asked, "What is the basis of the challenge for cause?"

Thinking fast, Traxel answered, "Dishonesty."

The judge straightened up. "What do you mean, counsel?"

"Despite his 'good citizen' response, this venireman obviously would rather have his wisdom teeth extracted without any anesthetic than serve on this jury. If he can't even be honest about that, during *voir dire*, then how can we trust him not to give mendacious legal advice to his fellow jurors, who already know that he is a lawyer?"

The judge suppressed a giggle, but before she could say anything, Stemler chimed in, "I'm in accord."

"Well," she answered, "I hope that this private chat foreshadows other agreements between and among counsel during the trial. I shall grant your joint request for a challenge for cause." Then, aloud, she announced, "Venireman Number 9 is excused."

The clerk called three more veniremen to replace the three who had been excused. None of the new three had any conflicts, nor did any of them have any excuses for not serving.

"All right, now the attorneys may ask you questions to check for biases. Mr. Traxel, you're up first."

Over the years, Traxel had learned that although the *voir dire* was a useful tool in eliminating potential jurors with strong opinions and whose prejudices would be helpful to the other side, veniremen did not like being asked questions that they perceived to feel like cross-examination. They sometimes took their revenge in the verdict against lawyers who had embarrassed them during *voir dire*. So, he was circumspect.

"Good morning to all of you. My name is Phillip Traxel. I am one of the attorneys representing the plaintiffs, Moises Delgadinho, Leonicio Muñoz, and Pedro Fishkin. Mr. Delgadinho speaks Portuguese, and Mr. Muñoz speaks Spanish. Neither understands or speaks English. So, when they testify, we shall have headphones for you for simultaneous translations. I just need to be sure that no one among you will have a problem being fair and impartial because of the language difference. I don't want to pry unnecessarily into anyone's background, but please raise your hand if – for any reason – you're not sure that you could be impartial as a result of their not being able to speak English."

It was a well-calculated question because it had been articulated anonymously rather than having been directd at any specifid venireman. And at the same time, it implied that any other attorney who might pry into an individual venireman's backgrounds was somehow out of bounds.

After a protracted silence, one venireman in the back raised his hand. "My parents were immigrants from Greece, and when I was a kid, I observed native speakers making fun of them. So, I am sensitive to people who don't speak English."

Traxel nodded. "Thank you for sharing that, Venireman Number 11. I assume from your statement that you would have no problem, then, serving impartially on this jury. Am I correct?"

Juror Number 11 answered, "Yes, that's right."

"Thank you, again, sir," he said, mentally concluding that Stemler would surely use up one of the defense's three peremptory challenges on Venireman Number 11. "Let me pose another general question: Has anyone here ever been on a cruise ship or a sailing ship of any kind?"

A woman in the front row raised her hand. "Three years ago, I went on a four-day cruise from Ft. Lauderdale to the Bahamas."

"Thank you, Venireman Number 3. Let me ask a follow-up question, if that's all right?"

The woman smiled. "Uh, sure."

"In weighing conflicting testimony between a seaman and a ship officer, would you give extra weight to the testimony of a ship officer just because he had the title or rank of supervisor or a Third Mate or Captain?"

Stemler wanted to interpose an objection but didn't have a good basis to object, and being fairly certain that the judge would overrule the objection, kept quiet.

The woman thought for a moment and then replied. "No. I don't think so."

"I don't want to push this too far, but may I ask how you think you would go about weighing conflicting testimony if you didn't use rank or title as a basis to decide who was being more truthful?"

The woman put her hand on her chin. "Umm. I would try to make a decision based on how consistent that person was in his testimony, on the person's body language, and all the other signs that everybody uses to determine if someone is being honest."

"Very good, Venireman Number 3."

This time Stemler *did* object. "Counsel is making editorial statements in between his questions."

The judge nodded. "Yes, Mr. Traxel, you will have an opportunity to editorialize during your closing statement."

"Yes, thank you, Your Honor." Traxel had known that his comment was likely to provoke an objection and that it would be sustained. But it was merely a venial sin, and he had communicated to Venireman Number 3, and to all of her colleagues, that the appropriate method of weighing testimony was precisely how Venireman Number 3 had answered. "Let me pose the question to the other twelve of you: Would any of the others of you, in weighing conflicting testimony between a seaman and a ship officer, give extra weight to testimony because of his rank or title of supervisor, or Third Mate or First Mate or Captain?"

No one raised a hand or said anything. Three or four of them shook their heads from side to side.

Traxel smiled broadly but refrained from commenting this time. "Somebody has to tell you the bad news," he began and then paused, "so let me forewarn you: In order for you to reach a fair verdict, you're going to have to hear a lot about container ships and cargo vessels, and contracts between shipping companies and seafarers, and discipline aboard ships, and unions, and a lot of it may seem, frankly, boring. Is there anyone among you who thinks you won't be able to pay full attention to all that stuff?"

There were some audible sighs, but no one said anything... until the white-haired man in the second row, Venireman Number 12, raised his hand. "I need to admit that boring stuff makes me sleepy. I usually nap in the afternoon, and if I'm watching something boring on TV, like the news, after lunch, the sandman usually wins the internal battle to stay awake."

All the veniremen laughed.

The judge intervened. "Venireman Number 12, does that mean you will or will not try to stay awake for the afternoon sessions?"

"I'll do my best, Your Honor," he answered, "because this sounds like it's going to be an interesting case, but I sure hope that this lady next to me will elbow me in the ribs if I start to snore."

This time everyone in the courtroom broke into laughter.

"Counsel, approach, please." When Traxel and Stemler came up to the bench, the judge asked, quietly, "Does either of you want to challenge Venireman Number 12 for cause?"

Both attorneys shook their heads and replied, "No, Your Honor."

"All right. Step back." Once they had returned to their respective tables, she asked:

"Mr. Traxel, do you have any more *voir dire* questions?"

"No, Your Honor, I'm satisfied. Thank you." He had been careful not to say 'I'm satisfied with this jury,' as it might have elicited another objection and another cautionary statement from the court.

"Your turn, Mr. Stemler," she said.

"Good morning to you all. My name is Brian Stemler. I'm the lead attorney for the defense, but you will later meet some of my colleagues who will be conducting part of the trial. We represent Greenport Shipping Co., and I hope you don't mind if I ask several of you some questions. As the judge explained, each side wants to make sure that the jury is fair and impartial. And the only way we have of doing that is to inquire about your backgrounds and belief systems."

He paused and made eye contact with each juror. "Nobody comes into a courtroom with a blank slate. We all have unique experiences, but certain experiences can possibly influence how we view facts...."

"Objection," said Traxel, standing. "If editorializing is improper for the goose, it's also improper for the gander."

"Indeed," answered the judge. "Mr. Stemler, why don't you get into the interrogative portion of your *voir dire*?"

"Quite so, Your Honor. Let me begin with Juror Number 1. According to the information you provided to the Clerk of Court, you are married and you work as a sales clerk in a store on Town Square, is that right?"

"Yes, that's correct," she answered.

"What does you husband do?"

Venireman Number 1 crossed her arms. "I don't have a husband. I have a *wife*."

"Ah," was the best that Stemler could do. "What does you *wife* do for a living?"

"She's a veterinarian."

"Is there a union among the employees at your store or at the veterinary clinic?"

"No." Venireman Number 1 was not able to keep the edge out of her reply.

"Have you ever had a dispute with your current boss or any previous boss?"

"What do you mean by a dispute?"

"A disagreement over wages or weekend hours or working conditions, things like that?"

"Not with my present boss."

"A previous supervisor?"

"Yes. In a job I had in Montana, a co-worker kept making derogatory remarks about gays and lesbians. I complained to the boss, but he waved it off as trivial."

"So, what did you do?"

"I quit and found another job."

"Will that experience make you be more favorable to seaman than to the supervisors on the ship?"

"No, not unless they're bigots."

"Thank you." He had already determined to knock her off the jury. "Let me move on to Venireman Number 6. "Mr. Eche<u>VER</u>ría. Is that right?"

"Yes, but it's pronounced 'E-chey-veh-RIA.'"

"Thank you for the clarification. Is that a Spanish surname?"

"No, it's Basque."

"Is Basque part of Spain?"

"The area of northwest Spain we call 'Visconia,' and Basque people call themselves Euskaldanak — E-U-S-K-A-L-D-A-N-A-K."

"But it's part of Spain now, right?"

"So far."

"Do you think that you can be impartial if one of the parties to this case is a fellow-Spaniard?"

"I am an American. My grandfather was Basque. And he didn't think of himself as a Spaniard but rather, as a Euskaldun - E-U-S-K-A-L-D-U-N."

"I see. Let me turn now to Venireman Number 8. You are Ms. Tenneston, correct?"

"Yes."

"And you are a free-lance writer and a volunteer for a civil rights organization, is that correct?"

"Yes."

"What exactly do you do as a volunteer?"

"I arrange meetings; I help in fund-raising; I draft and edit articles for magazines; I diddle with the group's web-site, things like that."

"The entity where you volunteer is essentially an advocacy organization. Is that a fair statement?"

"Yes, that would be fair."

"And what are the kinds of groups for whom you advocate?"

"Groups that are discriminated against or are under-served in our society – poor people, minority groups, women, tenants who have been evicted from their homes, people who have lost their jobs, members of the LBGTQ community."

"Is it fair to say that you see yourself in an adversarial relationship to landlords, employers, and large corporations."

"In specific cases, yes, but not to *all* landlords, *all* employers, or *all* large corporations."

"Well, here's the bottom-line question: Do you think that, given your volunteer work, you can be fair and impartial in deciding a case that involves seamen who claim that they have been mistreated by a shipping company?"

"I think that I am very analytical, that I can examine the facts, and make an accurate and impartial assessment of a situation by listening carefully to testimony and reading whatever documents are submitted in support of testimony."

"Thank you, I have no further questions of this panel."

"All right," announced the judge. "Let's take a break. The panel members are excused. When we return, the attorneys will have selected the final members of the jury. Please come back in 20 minutes. Counsel, I'll see you in chambers in 10 minutes. Please have your selections ready."

Attorneys don't really *select* a jury; they *remove* the veniremen who they think will be most unhelpful for their clients' case. They can remove for cause any number that they can convince the judge should be excused because of conflicts of interest. And in most trials, each gets two peremptory strikes, with no reason having to be offered. Judge Mattson, however, had told the lawyers that to make sure there was a fully impartial jury, she would allow each side three peremptory strikes in the *Delgadinho* case.

At the counsel tables, the attorneys huddled with their respective jury consultants. At the defense table, the consultant said: "You have six people you do *not* want on this jury: Number 1, the lesbian; Number 3, the cruise-ship lady; Number 6, the Basque Spaniard; Number 8, the civil rights-nik; Number 11, the child of the Greek immigrants; and Number 12, the after-lunch napper."

"But we are only permitted three peremptory strikes."

"Are there some you might persuade the judge to excuse for cause?"

"I shall try to challenge the Basque-Spaniard and the civil rights-nik. If that works, I would then knock off the lesbian, the cruiser, and the son of the Greek immigrants with ut peremptory strikes. That means we'll have to try to keep the napper awake in the afternoon."

One of the junior attorneys asked: "What if the judge declines to grant your challenges for cause? Then which three will you knock out?"

The consultant jumped in: "The lesbian, the civil rights volunteer, and the Basque-Spaniard."

"I'm not sure," said Stemler. "The Basques don't really like Spaniards. I'm more worried about the Greek immigrants' son."

The junior lawyer persisted. "If the napper snores through important testimony, then the plaintiffs could claim a mistrial."

"That's true," answered Stemler; "however, there will be an Alternate. And if the napper sleeps, we'll ask the judge to excuse the napper at the end of the trial and let the Alternate sit in."

At the plaintiffs' counsel table, Traxel said: "I think that the most important venireman is Number 3. She's smart and has a handle on how to look at evidence. My hunch is that she would likely become the most influential person on the jury if she makes the cut; but I'm afraid that Stemler will remove her."

Ted leaned over. "If I can put my two cents in, I think that Stemler really pissed off Number 1 as well as Number 6 and probably Number 8, too.. He's going to need to zap all three of them."

"Well, he'll try to challenge one or more of them for cause. Our strategy has to be to convince the judge to turn down the challenges, so that Stemler has to knock out the Greek immigrants' son, the lesbian, and the civil rights lady and leave Number 3 in the pool."

The consultant asked: "Which ones do you intend to remove?"

Ted jumped in. "Just so you'll know, the others consist of Number 2, a dispatcher at the St. Louis Park Police Department; Number 4, a lab technician at Methodist Hospital; Number 5, the private school administrator; Number 7, the owner of a snowmobile company; Number 9, a real estate broker; Number 10, the sculptor married to a chamber of commerce executive; Number 12, the napper; and Number 13, a bus driver."

"I think," replied Traxel, "that I'll want to remove the business owner, who is likely to identify with the shipping company, and the wife of the chamber of commerce executive, just because the chamber generally takes positions in favor of business owners. Even if she were convinced that the plaintiffs should win, my hunch is that her pro-business leanings would cause her to be parsimonious when it comes to damages. I'm open for suggestions about the third 'zap.'"

"I agree with those two suggestions, Phil." It was Cliff Rehmel, who had been silent up until now. "And I recommend that you eliminate the administrator at the private school but that you challenge the napper and the chamber of commerce spouse for cause, just so the judge can feel even-handed if she denies all the challenges for cause."

"All right. We have a plan."

Chapter 44: In Chambers

ALTHOUGH ALL THE ATTORNEYS CAME into the judge's chambers, she addressed her comments just to the lead attorneys, Traxel and Stemler. "Well, gentlemen, who are the winners of the raffle?"

Speaking first, Traxel said: "I have not conferred with opposing counsel on this, but I have some alternate lists here, depending on how you rule on my challenges for cause." Traxel purposefully spoke first so as to preempt Stemler.

"Actually," said Stemler, "we did the same thing because we have some challenges too."

The judge stuck her tongue behind her upper lip. "Okay, let's hear yours first, Mr. Traxel. And let's put this on the record." She signaled to the court reporter to be ready.

"Plaintiffs challenge-for-cause Veniremen Number 10 and Number 12. We challenge Number 10 because it is clear from the data on her Jury Information Form that she devotes an inordinate amount of time to attending chamber of commerce functions, playing hostess for the chamber, and sitting on a number of chamber committees, ostensibly as a member through her sculpting business but, in fact, as Second Lady of the chamber, married to the Deputy Executive Director. And we challenge-for-cause Number 12 because he has admitted to napping in the afternoon, and his doing so will likely impel defendant to claim a mistrial if the jury awards plaintiffs a substantial verdict."

"As I recall, Mr. Traxel, I gave you the chance to have Venireman Number 12 excused, and you declined."

"That's true, Your Honor, but after further deliberation, I have concluded he is unlikely to stay awake during this trial, and I just don't think we can confine all the boring testimony to the morning sessions."

"What say you to that, Mr. Stemler?" asked the judge.

"Those are preposterous challenges-for-cause. Obviously, plaintiffs want to strike five veniremen and are hoping to get you to strike two of their choices."

"Umm," she commented. "And what are Defendant's challenges?"

"We challenge-for-cause Veniremen Numbers 1, 6, and 8. We challenge Number 1 because she is clearly prejudiced against defendant owing to my having asked her what her *husband* did during *voir dire*. The acid in her voice was palpable. We challenge Number 6 because he's of Spaniard descent and is likely to be biased in favor of Plaintiff Muñoz. Finally, we challenge Number 8 because her conceded biases, as a civil rights advocate, are in favor of plaintiffs."

"How do you respond, Mr. Traxel?"

"Defendant's challenges against Numbers 1 and 6 are the 21st century version of 20th century Southern attorney challenges to African-Americans. Essentially, those challenges would keep Number 1 off the jury because of her sexual orientation and would strike Number 6 because of his ancestry. As for Number 8, Mr. Stemler asked about her bias, and Number 8 responded that she was analytical and that she could view the facts impartially. So, Mr. Semler has no basis except that he *surmises* that Venireman Number 8 *might* be sympathetic to people who have been beaten on-board ship."

The judge took a deep breath. "I believe that Mr. Stemler hit the nail on the nail on the head when he observed that plaintiffs' challenges were attempts to get rid of five veniremen by having this Court assist in removing two."

Traxel swallowed hard, and Stemler couldn't help smirking.

"However," she continued, "I think that his observation applies equally to defendant's challenges. I'm denying *all* the challenges-for-cause. Now, let me pass the official veniremen list between you two. Please use your peremptory challenges, each side striking one at a time, and then passing the list to opposing counsel. Plaintiff first"

When they completed the process, no one was surprised that plaintiffs' attorneys had removed the business owner, the private school administrator, and the wife of the chamber of commerce executive nor that defense counsel had removed the lesbian, the civil rights advocate, and the son of the Greek immigrants.

"All right. That leaves us with seven, one of whom is an Alternate. Unless the two attorneys can agree on the Alternate, it will be the last venireman to be called, who was Number ...9, the real estate broker, of whom neither attorney asked any questions during *voir dire*."

Stemler looked over at Traxel. "I'm willing to make the napper the Alternate, so if he *does* fall asleep, there is an ostensible excuse for eliminating him after the trial."

Traxel thought about it for five or six seconds and then said, "Agreed."

"Fine," said the judge. "No one is to reveal that one of the seven is an Alternate. At the end of the trial, if Mr. Traxel and Mr. Stemler stipulate on the record that the jury can consist of seven jurors, they can all participate; however, if either attorney objects, then I shall excuse Mr. Krause, the name of Venireman Number 12, to whom you both have referred as 'the napper.' I think we're done here. Let's return to the courtroom."

They all did, and the judge read off the names of the seven veniremen who would constitute the jury. She excused the other six and thanked them for exercising their civic duty by being willing to serve.

Chapter 45: Opening Statements

~ Plaintiffs' Opening:

"GOOD MORNING, LADIES AND GENTLEMEN," Traxel said. "This is called 'Opening Statement.' It's equivalent to a preview of coming attractions in the movies. It's my opportunity to tell you what this case is about, what evidence we will show you, and what we hope to prove to your satisfaction.

"My name, again, is Phillip Traxel. There are a couple of other attorneys at counsel table, whom you'll get to meet later; but right now I want to introduce you to the three plaintiffs who have brought this lawsuit, Moises Delgadinho, in the green shirt, from the Azores, who speaks Portuguese; next to him is Leonicio Muñoz in the brown shirt, who is from the Canary Islands and whose native language is Spanish; and the tall man at the end of the table is Pedro Fishkin, an American who happens to be tri-lingual in English, Spanish, and Potruguese.

"About seven months ago Mr. Delgadinho and Mr. Muñoz, who didn't know each other at the time, individually signed up to work on a commercial container ship called *La Galissionière*. You will hear testimony that, although the ship has a French name, it flies under a Bolivian flag, it has a Greek captain, a Burmese supervisor, deckhands from Morocco and from islands belonging to Spain and Portugal, and from other third world countries. It delivers merchandise to cities situated along the Mediterranean Sea, in northern Africa and southern Europe as well as to ports along the north Atlantic coast.

"You will hear from experts from as far away as London, England, that there are a variety of agencies and organizations that try to make sure that the ship is safe, that it doesn't pollute the ocean, that it treats its workers, generally called seafarers, fairly. However, the plaintiffs Delgadinho, Muñoz, and Fishkin will all tell you that *La Galissionière* was a living nightmare.

"All three will tell you (1) that the food for the workers was sub-standard; (2) that depriving deckhands of food was used as a disciplinary measure; (3) that workers who did something that displeased officers and supervisors were subject to beatings with billy clubs and whips; (4) that the men were overworked and underpaid; (5) that the drinking water was brown with rust; and (5) that there were not enough toilets and showers for the crew.

"Mr. Delgadinho will testify that there was no doctor or nurse on board, and the men who got injured were bullied and made fun of. Mr. Muñoz will testify that he witnessed the officers throwing overboard one man who was too sick to work and another man whom the officers thought to be a trouble-maker.

"Mr. Delgadinho and Mr. Muñoz will both testify that because they had witnessed these murders on the ocean, they were put off on a rowboat with one day's rations and told that they would probably die. The officers threatened that if, somehow, they survived they could never return to their families because, if they did, their families would be tortured in front of them and then killed. They will tell you that they luckily made it to a port in Wales and were rescued by an American Episcopal priest named Elizabeth Sánchez Ríos, who brought them back here to Minnesota and who managed to pull some strings to get the Attorney General of the United States to grant them special, temporary immigration status. Paastor Sánchez-Ríose will also testify, verifying how she came to know these two men.

"With the help of the St. Edward's-by-the-Lake Episcopal Church in Wayzata, the two men hired our law firm to represent them. Because the allegations sounded so incredibly like what you see in films about the horrible mistreatment of sailors on 17th century ships, we hired a private investigator – plaintiff Pedro Fishkin – to verify the claims of our other two clients.

"Because he speaks Spanish without an American accent, Mr. Fishkin was able to go undercover by signing on as a deckhand. He will tell you what he saw – cabin mates being beaten by supervisors, seafarers who had reasonably expected to work eight hours a day forced to work at least 10 hours a day. He will testify that two cabins down were four Moroccans, one of whom, a 17-year-old, was being sexually molested by the captain, and all four of whom were very unhappy because, even though they had been promised food that adhered to Muslim dietary laws, most of the meat served in the mess was pork, forbidden by their religion.

"Mr. Fishkin will tell you that the Moroccans were dumped from the ship in *Casa Blanca* with no money, no provisions, and no pay for their labor. Mr. Delgadinho will explain that he has not been able to see or even contact his brothers and parents in the Azores because he fears if he contacts them, that will be their death warrant. Mr. Muñoz will testify that he has not seen his wife or five-year-old daughter, who were told by a company representative company that he was dead.

"Mr. Fishkin will further testify that not only did he verify what Delgadinho and Muñoz had told Pastor Sánchez Ríos but that at some point, the ship's officers figured out that he was an undercover man and did everything to make his life miserable. Mr. Fishkin will tell you he was determined to get off the ship in *Casa Blanca* because of the horrible conditions but that the officers got the *Casa Blanca* police to arrest him – not for breaking any laws – but just because the ship captain had called and made it worth their while for the cops to deliver him to the ship. Once there he was locked for two days in what they called the infirmary, into which they slid a tray of gruel once a day and where he was told to urinate in the sink, to defecate in the wastebasket.

"Mr. Fishkin will tell you that they drugged him and took him to a modern-day slave market in Algiers, Algeria, and had planned to sell him to some Tuareg camel drivers, but they were outbid by a mysterious Arab, who knew his name, knew where he was from, and who created an elaborate con to try to convince Mr. Fishkin to reveal the whereabouts of Moises Delgadinho and Leonicio Muñoz. When he refused to tell him, they amputated a finger on his left hand with an unsterilized hatchet.

"By this time, you will surely wonder who did all this, and how did they get around laws and rules and regulations and standards? It turns out, as our expert witness, Mr. Grindon, will tell you, that some companies take a variety of steps to avoid anyone's looking over their shoulder. To avoid paying the kinds of wages that American laws require ships to pay seafarers, they get a flag from a country that doesn't have those kinds of laws, which doesn't send out inspectors to check on safety equipment or the condition of the men or the quality of the food.

"You will hear testimony that *La Galissionière* flies the flag of Bolivia, a country that is totally landlocked and never inspects ocean-going vessels for safety, pollution, food quality, water quality, adequacy of sanitary facilities, work hours, or discipline...and is hundreds of miles from any ocean. You will hear that ownership is a major issue in this case. Defendant Greenport Shipping doesn't exactly deny that these things happened, but it claims to have no authority over, responsibility for, or liability to anyone as a result of these actions.

"One of the questions you will be asked to decide at the end of the trial is whether the named defendant, Greenport Shipping, should be held liable. During all of the pre-trial hearings and activities, Greenport not just says, but its officers swear under oath, that it is a mere subsidiary of a Greek corporation named *Hestia Etoupeia.* One of our witnesses, an investigator and a colleague of Mr. Fishkin's, will testify that she spent a huge amount of time poring over documents that show that, through a carefully drafted scheme, Greenport Shipping has created three shell companies. Through these paper companies, Greenport actually owns *Hestia,* hires the officers, sets the policies, authorizes tossing overboard employees who don't jump fast enough when given orders, and blithely ignores all the standards of the International Maritime Organization.

"Now since we represent the plaintiffs, we have to prove (1) that all these terrible things happened; and (2) that the defendant Greenport Shipping is behind these awful practices, responsible for what happened to these plaintiffs and to the ones who are now dead, and in the language of the law is 'liable' for the wrongdoing.

"As both sides present evidence, you, members of the jury, will surely come to the conclusion that the truth really can't be half-way between our position and the defendant's position. Someone is seriously lying. If you decide that it is the officials of Greenport Shipping who are lying and who are responsible for what happens on *La Galissionière,* you will need to have a calculus for determining how to make these three plaintiffs whole. So, we have another expert witness who will walk you through some steps for making appropriate calculations.

"Thank you for your attention."

~ Defendant's Opening:

"Good morning, everyone. My name is Charlene Nelson, I'm one of the attorneys for the defense and a colleague of Mr. Stemler, whom you met during *voir dire.* Just before you retire at the end of the trial to examine the documents and to discuss the testimony you heard, the Judge will read the law to you. The judge decides the law; the jury decides the facts.

"The plaintiffs put their case on first, and they no doubt will testify, as Mr. Traxel has forewarned, that they were mistreated on board *La Galissionière*, that they were overworked, underpaid, and unhappy with the jobs for which they signed contracts. Soldiers, sailors, and merchant marine seafarers have complained about those things since Julius Caesar was a sophomore. But they didn't bring lawsuits. How many hours are too many when a ship pulls into dock, and the merchandise all has to be unloaded? What discipline is warranted on a ship in the middle of the ocean when a worker refuses to do his job?

"Most important, what should be the standard of proof for the most outrageous of the claims? And whose burden is it to prove it? The judge will tell you at the end of trial that there is no doubt that the burden is on the plaintiffs.

"If the plaintiffs say that they observed other sailors getting beaten, is that enough to be called 'the truth' if the sailors who were supposedly beaten don't show up to corroborate it?

If a worker says he had to work 10 hours, but the records show that he actually worked only eight hours, how do you decide who's right? And we will have a witness from *Hestia* with the records who will testify that, except when docking, the seafarers were never worked more than eight hours per day.

"Here's what defendant's witnesses will tell you: First that plaintiff Pedro Fishkin lied about his name, forged someone else's signature on a contract, smuggled a teenager off the ship for who knows what kind of shenanigans, assaulted a supervisor, punched the boatswain in the face without any provocation, and breached his contract by getting off in Algiers with the intention of quitting his job without notice, leaving the crew with one fewer deckhand. The local law enforcement authorities did bring him back to the ship because he had no business wandering around Algiers since he was off the ship without permission.

"Mr. Fishkin will no doubt testify that his finger was cut off while he was in Algeria, almost 75 miles away from where *La Galissionière* was docked, but he's asking you to decide that the ship owner should pay him for his injury. Others will testify that plaintiff Muñoz is still sore that he got demoted from dining steward after he spilled chili all over the Second Mate's lap. Subsequently, he had to do much harder work on deck and, for the rest of the voyage, he was belligerent, angry, and uncooperative.

"The boatswain from *La Galissionière* will testify not only about Mr. Fishkin's having sucker-punched him but, also, that plaintiff Moises Delgadinho was what soldiers and sailors for generations have called 'a goldbrick.' He did his job in slow motion, often hid during the least pleasant tasks, like chipping and painting, falsely claimed that he was sick in order to get out of work when it was raining, and constantly complained. Our witnesses will tell you that plaintiff Delgadinho and plaintiff Muñoz asked -- no, *demanded* -- to be let off the ship in the middle of their contracts. And even though their absence would put more work on everybody else, the captain allowed them to take a lifeboat rather than have them be a continual source of discontent. By the way, you may have gotten the impression from what others have said that *La Galissionière* is a cruise ship with hundreds of crew members. In fact, as our witnesses will testify, *La Galissionière* had a total crew of 25, and that included four officers, the chief engineer, and the boatswain. So, one person not doing his job or leaving the ship in the middle of a voyage put a huge burden on those who were honoring their contract.

"But, so far, I've been forecasting testimony and evidence which will raise questions about the credibility of the plaintiffs and their work styles on the ship. Here's *the most* important fact of all for you to decide. Assume for the moment that everything the three plaintiffs and their expert witnesses will tell you is absolutely true and that the plaintiffs were harmed, set adrift, beaten, overworked, and that they heard some of their Muslim colleagues complain that the ship served too much pork. Does that mean that because these three plaintiffs were harmed in some way that our client should have to pay for it? How about the United Nations – should the UN have to pay for it? What about the Seafarers Union or Ford Motor Company? Surely, you would think that requiring any of those entities to pay for it would be absurd... precisely because they had nothing to do with the things that allegedly harmed the plaintiffs. I would agree with you. But in this trial, the plaintiffs want you to impose liability – that means make somebody pay – on Greenport Shipping, which had about as much to do with what went on aboard *La Galissionière* as Ford Motor Company.

"You will hear testimony that the owner of *La Galissionière* is a Greek company called *Hestia Etoupeia*. *Hestia* is a large company with several subsidiaries. One subsidiary, located in New York City, is Greenport Shipping, whose ships ply the Caribbean and the waters off the east coast of the United States. Its ships *never* go to Europe or Africa or the Mediterranean. Greenport is incorporated in the United States and is, therefore, easier to sue than *Hestia*. Perhaps that's why plaintiffs chose to sue them. It will be your decision.

"Thank you."

During the recess that Judge Mattson declared after the opening statements, Ted Bruner leaned over and asked Traxel, "A lot of what Charlene Nelson said sounded like closing argument rather than opening statement. Couldn't you have objected?"

"You are correct, Ted. First, it was a smart move to have Charlene give the opening statement because she comes off as much nicer than Stemler. And if I had objected, what would that have accomplished? The jury would just assume that we didn't want her to say whatever she was saying. It was better to let her speak. The proof is in the pudding of evidence."

Chapter 46: Morning Witnesses

THE ORDER IN WHICH WITNESSES testify represents strategic placements by the attorneys.

No boring witnesses right after lunch, spread out the most important witnesses, sandwich expert witnesses between civilian witnesses, have a strong opener and a dynamite closer.

Traxel had Alfred Grindon, the expert witness whom Lauren had found in London, testify first. He was crisp, articulate, and having been warned against being too wonky, fairly brief in his answers. He gave the jurors a clear picture of what the IMO does, the efforts it makes on behalf of safety and of seamen's rights; but he was candid about the problems of enforcing their high standards precisely because the agency had no enforcement powers and because wealthy shipping companies had learned to use "flags-of-convenience" – pretending to be under the auspices of tiny countries that really had no merchant marines, e.g. Bolivia, but were happy to charge shippers money for registering there while promising no inspections, no enforcement, no minimum wage, no maximum hours, no limits on corporal punishment. Even the napper stayed fully awake for Grindon's testimony.

On cross examination, Wentworth (the defendants were spreading out the courtroom action among their attorneys) asked, "Mr. Grindon, you have never seen *La Galissionière*, much less boarded her, have you?"

"That's right," answered Grindon.

"You don't have any specific knowledge about the work hours, the quality of food, the nature of discipline, the number of crew members, the merchandise which the ship transported, its ports of call, its safety compliance, or even its itineraries, do you?"

"I did check out that *La Galissionière* flies a Bolivian flag and that there had been a number of complaints filed against *La Galissionière*, but I personally can't vouch for the validity of those complaints."

"When you did this 'checking,' Mr. Grindon, did you notice who the owner of *La Galissonière* is?"

"The registration records indicate that the owner is *Hestia Etoupeia.*"

"And did the records you inspected mention the name 'Greenport Shipping'?"

"No."

"No further questions, Your Honor."

Judge Mattson looked over at the plaintiffs' counsel table. "Any re-direct?"

"Yes, thank you, Your Honor," Traxel answered. "Mr. Grindon, in your time with IMO, has it ever been your experience that the registered owners of ships are actually controlled by other companies?"

"Frequently."

"Do you know why that is?"

"Usually because the true owners want to minimize liability or to escape worker protection laws. Sometimes, for some political reason, they wish to conceal their connections with the nation under whose flag the ship operates."

"When you say 'usually,' how many cases have you personally investigated or supervised or overseen where that was true?"

"Somewhere between 70 and 80."

"Thank you; no further questions."

Wentworth rose. "One re-cross question, Your Honor, if I may."

The judge having nodded affirmatively,Wentworth posed this question: "Is *La Galissonière* one of the 70 or 80 you personally investigated or oversaw or supervised?"

"No, it was not."

"Thank you. That's all."

Delgadinho testified next. The jurors were given headsets, so that they could listen to the English translation of his testimony in Portuguese. The translator was a woman, so it took some adjustment for the jurors to see a burly witness but hear his testimony from a very feminine voice. Additionally, the translator chose not to say "umm" or "uh" when Delgadinho hesitated in his answers. So his testimony sounded smoother that it really was. Charlene Nelson put her hand on Stemler's arm to restrain him from objecting. He looked at her with snake eyes, but she shook her head, just barely, to signal that it would be imprudent to make an objection complaining about the translator's omission of hesitations.

Since Traxel was asking questions, Rehmel watched the jurors' reactions to Moises's testimony. He saw that they all listened intently, kept their eyes on Delgadinho the whole time, and he was certain from their facial expressions and body language that they found what he said to be both believable and shocking.

Traxel had prepared Delgadinho for cross examination, so he was not intimidated by Stemler's questions, and sounded forthright, i.e. he maintained a comfortable, physical presence, and the translator sounded confident. Stemler got nothing out of cross.

Stemler was expecting that Muñoz would be up next, but, to his chagrin, Pastor Elizabeth was called next. She wore her clerical collar, of course. As Traxel walked her through her experiences, everyone in the courtroom could tell that she made a very favorable impression on the jury. She sounded sincere and honest and admirable. After all, she had effected the rescue of two of the plaintiffs and had reached beyond what might have been expected in order to convince the Attorney General of the United States to grant them temporary admission to this country.

Stemler's objections first emerged during her testimony about Leonicio's visit to her office. "Pastor Sanchez-Ríos," Traxel began, "where do Mr. Muñoz and Mr. Delgadinho live while they are here?"

"Each of them lives with a family whose members are parishioners at St. Edward's-by-the-Lake."

"And who took the lead in those placements?"

"Well, I saw it as part of my job, but the credit goes to the two families that took them in, especially since neither family knew Spanish or Portuguese."

Stemler rose. "Your Honor, may we have a proffer about where this line of questioning is going and how it's relevant to the issues in this case?"

"Well, Mr. Traxel?" the judge asked.

"My next two questions will illuminate that, Your Honor."

"I'll be listening," she said.

He went on. "Did you ever move either Mr. Muñoz or Mr. Delgadinho to a different family?"

"Mr. Delgadinho is still living with his original family, but I *did* move Mr. Muñoz."

"*Why* did you move Mr. Muñoz?"

"He had come to my office seeking my help."

"What was the nature of the help he sought?"

"Leonicio – Mr. Muñoz – told me that a stranger came to the house when the family was not there and threatened him."

"What kind of threat?"

"He said that the stranger told him that his wife and daughter would be killed if he testified negatively about what happened on *La Galissionière*."

Stemler was on his feet, and his face was lobster-red. "Objection, hearsay. Move to strike, and I ask for a special jury instruction to disregard that last answer as in response to an improper question."

Judge Mattson remained calm. "Mr. Traxel?"

Traxel was just as calm. "Actually, it's not hearsay if the purpose of the testimony is to explain why she took steps to move him to a different family. Secondly, it is a prequel confirmation of the conversation between this witness and Mr. Muñoz, who will be testifying later today."

"We're going to take a break now," the judge announced. "I'll see counsel in chambers." Everyone rose as the jurors left the courtroom, and the lawyers trooped into the judge's chambers. Even before all the attorneys were seated, Stemler, who was still highly agitated, started talking. "This is an outrage...."

The judge cut him off. "Please wait until the court reporter is ready to take down what you're about to say, counsel."

With that delay, Stemler was able to lower the volume and to slow down the pace. "This may be cause for a mistrial, Your Honor, and the Dornan law firm should be financially responsible for the time it will take to select a new jury."

"What would be the basis of a mistrial motion, Mr. Stemler?" Judge Mattson asked.

"Counsel deliberately elicited an inflammatory answer from the witness which he knew was hearsay."

The judge turned to Traxel. "What is the support for the notion of a 'prequel confirmation,' Mr. Traxel?"

Traxel looked at Bruner, who withdrew from his briefcase several copies of two cases, which he distributed to the judge and to the three defense attorneys. "The first, *Kessler v. Schramm Industries, Ltd.*, is a Seventh Circuit case, in an opinion authored by Judge Richard Posner, in which he coined that expression. Defense counsel in that case had objected on precisely the ground that Mr. Stemler has made his objection today, but the Court overruled her.

Defendants appealed to the Seventh Circuit, listing that ruling as one of the predicates for the appeal. The Seventh Circuit affirmed the district court, holding that since another, later witness, corroborated the first witness's testimony, it constituted a 'prequel confirmation' and was, accordingly, not hearsay and admissible.

"The second case, *Schneider v. Miserocchi Enterprises*, just last year in the Second Circuit, dealt with a very similar situation and affirmed the district court's admission of the testimony, citing Posner's opinion and the term 'prequel confirmation' in the *Kessler* case."

After a poignant silence, Judge Mattson turned to Stemler. "Let me ask you this, Mr. Stemler: Suppose Mr. Muñoz had testified first and had stated that a stranger had threatened him if he testified negatively about *La Galissioniere*; and suppose, further, that on cross examination, you attempted to challenge his testimony. If Mr. Traxel had then called Pastor Sánchez-Ríos to confirm, would that be hearsay in your mind?"

Stemler pursed his lips. "Perhaps not."

"Then does your objection arise merely from the timing of the witnesses?"

"Only partly, Your Honor. We have reason to believe that Mr. Muñoz will not corroborate what Pastor Sánchez has said."

"And what reason would that be, Mr. Stemler?" It was Rehmel, and no one in the room had any doubt from Rehmel's tone of voice the implication that Stemler had inside knowledge about the threat. Stemler cast a glance at the judge to see how she was reacting, but the judge took pains to maintain a neutral expression. Then Stemler answered. "You will surely recall from Muñoz's deposition that he had very little to say about what happened on *La Galissionière*, and he even contradicted what was attributed to him in the Complaint."

Very softly, Traxel responded. "According to the time-line about which Pastor Sánchez-Ríos testified, you took his deposition *after* he came to her office to disclose the threat."

"What are you implying, counsel?" Stemler was in high dudgeon.

"I'm implying nothing except that Muñoz's behavior at the deposition becomes more explicable if he actually received a threat before that time."

Judge Mattson took control of the gathering. "I'm going to overrule the objection when we return to the courtroom. If Mr. Muñoz does *not* confirm Pastor Sánchez's testimony about the threat, however, defense counsel will be free to point out the lack of corroboration in the closing argument. Mr. Traxel, so that the jury can hear both the prequel confirmation and the potential corroboration on the same day, you do intend to call Mr. Muñoz to the stand today, correct?"

"Yes, Judge, we shall."

With that Judge Mattson got up from her chair, and so did everyone else.

Back in the courtroom, Judge Mattson had the court reporter read back Traxel's last question and Stemler's objection. "Objection overruled," she said.

Traxel continued questioning Pastor Elizabeth. "Did you attend Mr. Muñoz's deposition?"

"Yes, I did."

"What prompted you to attend?"

"The nominal reason was that I was there to make sure that the interpreter hired by defendants was accurate in his translation."

"Was he accurate?"

"There were one or two places where he made his own interpretation, but they were not serious. By and large he did a good job."

"Did you verbalize your observation that the translation was imperfect?"

"As politely as I could, yes, but only those two times."

"You said the 'nominal' reason. Was there another?"

"Well, the nominal reason was genuine. But I also wanted to attend in order to provide moral support."

"Why did you think he needed moral support?"

"His affect was anxious, nervous, distressed."

"Could that have been because of the deposition?"

"No doubt the stress of being deposed was additive. But I drove him to the deposition, and he was highly agitated."

"Was that your observation of his body language, or did he say something?"

"Both. He said that he was afraid for Sofía and Valentina. Those are the names of his wife and daughter." One of the jurors put a handkerchief up to her nose.

"No further questions."

Stemler was careful on cross-examination,. He could tell that the jurors liked this witness and would not be pleased if he tried to tear her apart. "Is it true, Pastor Sánchez, that Mr. Muñoz and Mr. Delgadinho are being financially supported by your congregation?"

"Yes, that's true."

"How long are your parishioners willing to continue supporting these two men?"

"No one has suggested imposing a deadline."

"If the jury awards money to these two gentlemen, then the congregation would no longer have to be the source of their financial support, is that correct?"

"Yes."

"But if the jury *doesn't* award them money, then the congregation remains on the hook, isn't that right?"

"I doubt that anyone who is part of the St. Edward's congregation would characterize it as 'being on the hook,' Mr. Stemler. We all see it as helping people in need."

"*Touché*, Pastor. You would like to see them prevail in this case, though, wouldn't you?"

"Yes."

On re-direct, Traxel asked, "Do you know why both Mr. Muñoz and Mr. Delgadinho have stayed all this time in Wayzata and have not returned to their respective homes in the Azores and the Canary Islands?"

"I know what they told me?"

Stemler was on his feet. "May we approach, Your Honor?"

Judge Mattson waved them to the bench. The three of them huddled so that the jurors could not hear. "What is it, Mr. Stemler?"

"I'd like a proffer. Is this another 'prequel confirmation'?"

When the judge turned to look at Traxel, he said, "Yes, it is. Same argument, same case law."

"I'm going to object on the record," said Stemler.

The judge asked Traxel, "Am I correct that this time there is no hearsay exception because she wouldn't be explaining why she took a particular action like moving somebody?"

"Uh, yes."

"And on this subject, Mr. Delgadinho has already testified that he is staying in Wayzata because someone warned him that his brothers had been told that he was dead and that if he returned, he would be killed. Correct?"

"Yes."

"So, you can ask Mr. Muñoz why *he* has stayed when you put him on the stand, can't you?"

"Yes."

"Then why do you need Pastor Sánchez's testimony?"

"It confirms their states of mind."

"If you wish to withdraw your question, you may. Otherwise I intend to sustain the objection."

The attorneys returned to their seats. Traxel said, "I withdraw the last question. I have no more questions for Pastor Sánchez-Ríos."

"You may step down, Pastor Sanchez-Ríos," said the judge. "It is now 11:45. I think the jury may have had enough for this morning. We shall recess for lunch. Please return by 1:00 p.m."

Chapter 47: Afternoon Witnesses

Muñoz DIDN'T SEEM ANY READIER after lunch than he had before. So, Traxel called Stonebrook to the stand first. At Traxel's insistence, Stonebrook wore a tie, borrowed from a Dornan associate.

On direct examination, he explained his private detective business, that verifying allegations was a natural part of his line of work, that going undercover was the only way to dig out the facts in this particular case. He also testified about all the things he had observed and had experienced, including the deaths, the beating, the extra-long hours — while at sea as well as while in port.

He explained the take-it-or-leave-it contract denying him the right to complain to a Union; he told the jury about Mahmoud Nimri, who had sought his help dealing with the captain's sexual abuse, about his arrest in Algiers, and about what he called his 'false imprisonment' by Babar, including the amputation of his finger, and the rescue in the nick of time.

Still watching jurors, Rehmel was quite pleased. They were practically open-jawed in their rapt attention.

On cross-examination, Stemler started right out to attack Stonebrook's credibility.

"Is it fair to say, Mr. Fishkin, that in your line of work, you often have to dissemble in order to achieve your goals?"

Pretending not to understand, Stonebrook answered, "What does 'dissemble' mean?"

"It means to prevaricate, to discard the truth, to tell lies."

Stonebrook didn't look fazed. "I would characterize it as disguising my true intentions, just as company owners do, on television, in that program, *Undercover Boss*."

"So, in your mind, you have a right to dissemble if it advances your goals?"

"Not as a general proposition, Mr. Stemler, but...."

"In this instance, you felt justified in ... disguising the truth, correct?"

"If I had said at the recruiting office that my name was Pedro Fishkin and that I was a private investigator, attempting to verify allegations of mistreatment, I never would have been allowed to board *La Galissionière*."

"So, you felt justified in lying about your name?"

"I felt justified in using a different name."

"You don't want to call it a lie, do you?"

"I don't think of it as lying, any more than a woman's wearing make-up is lying about her appearance or a man wearing elevator shoes is lying about his height." Stemler bit his teeth: Fishkin had guessed correctly that Stemler himself was wearing elevator shoes. Two of the jurors stared at Stemler's shoes.

"Let's count the ways you... 'disguised the truth' in your journey. You disguised the truth about your name, right? You disguised the truth about your work background... because you had, in fact, never worked on ferries; you disguised the truth about your nationality. Am I accurate so far?"

"Yes."

"You forged someone else's name on the contract, didn't you?"

"No. Since Julián Arroyo is a fictitious name, it was no more a forgery than Samuel Clemens was guilty of forgery when he signed his name 'Mark Twain' on his book, *Tom Sawyer*."

"You lied to a superior officer when you said you were carrying laundry off the ship when you were really smuggling a human being, isn't that right?"

"Smuggling is an inappropriate word. I was rescuing a boy who had been abused by the highest ranking officer on the ship."

"Is it accurate to say that you assaulted your supervisor, Mr. Thura."

"No."

"You did purposely bump into him, though, didn't you."

"Yes."

"And, then, you... 'disguised the truth'... when the Third Mate accused you of assaulting Mr. Thura, didn't you? You said that it was an accident."

"Yes."

"Isn't it true, Mr. Fishkin, that you punched the boatswain in the face without any provocation?"

"I disagree with your premise. I did punch him, but there was provocation. The boatswain was keeping the boy locked up so that the captain could use him as a sex toy."

"You don't have any firsthand knowledge of any sexual relationship between the captain and the boy, do you?"

"I never observed the captain fondling young Nimri, but the boy did tell me that the captain was abusing him sexually."

"So, your answer is 'no,' you don't have any firsthand knowledge."

"On the contrary, my answer is what I just testified – the boy told me that the captain was abusing him and asked for my help."

"Not to put too fine a point on to it, Mr. Fishkin, isn't it....?"

"He's badgering the witness, Your Honor," claimed Traxel.

The judge peered over her glasses and said, "You've made your point Mr. Stemler; move on to something else, please."

Stemler looked at his notes and then turned to Stonebrook. "This story you told the jury about being drugged, sold at a market, imprisoned in a fake village, escaping into the wilderness, then hitching a ride to a town, being captured, and having your finger amputated – is it fair to say that you have a vivid imagination?"

"I didn't imagine it. It all happened."

"No embellishments, no ... what you like to call 'disguising of the truth'?"

"No."

"Is there anyone else in the entire world who can corroborate your story?"

"I suppose the man named Zaki, who cut off my finger, but I doubt that you intend to make him available to testify."

"Ah, yes, you want the jury to believe that Greenport Shipping company in New York is responsible for what supposedly happened to you in Algeria, don't you?"

"Yes."

"Do you have any facts that show a connection either from Greenport Shipping or even from the officers of *La Galissionière* to this fellow Zaki?"

"I know that the Captain or the First Mate sold me to the man who called himself Babar, and that Zaki was an employee, colleague, or henchman of Babar."

"According to your story, Babar is an Azerbaijani name, right?"

"Yes."

"But you later decided that he was an Algerian, and not an Azerbaijani or even an Armenian, isn't that so?"

"Yes."

"So how have you selectively accepted some things – about the supposed sale at the *souk,* for example – when your entire escape was based on your having determined that Babar had lied to you about almost everything else?"

"I do think that Babar lied about my being in Nagorno-Karabakh, about his name, about his nationality, and about his interest in buying a container ship. However, he wanted to know the location of Leonicio Muñoz and Moises Delgadinho. There's no way he could have known their names without having been informed by someone connected to *La Galissionière* because that is the only connection that Muñoz and Delgadinho have to each other."

"This finger that was supposed amputated. Do you have any documents from the hospital in Tangier that they treated you?"

"No"

"You didn't even use the right name at the hospital, did you?"

"No."

"Do you have any medical records from the Cleveland Clinic?"

"I didn't bring any with me, no."

"Yet, you want the jury to believe the story, even though you have admitted that you disguise the truth if it advances your goals, isn't that right, Mr. Fishkin, Mr. Arroyo, Mr. Stonebrook?"

Stonebrook did not rise to the bait. He calmly answered, "I lost a finger, I think that I'm entitled to compensation, and I believe that Greenport Shipping is responsible for it."

"You don't even have any proof that the finger might not have been amputated two or three years ago and that you are merely disguising the truth in order to extract money from Greenport Shipping Co., do you?"

"Yes, I do."

"What proof, Mr. Fishkin?"

Stonebrook reached into his pocket and pulled out a plastic bag in which was a decomposing finger. "This was my finger. If it had been amputated more than several weeks ago, it would be totally black." There were gasps from several of the jurors.

Stemler thought about objecting, but he figured that if the judge overruled him, it would look worse. "So, you carry around this amputated finger to remind you of your voyage?" He was hoping to neutralize the shock value of the detached finger.

"No. I just brought it with me today because I anticipated that you would try to make me out to be a liar."

This time Stemler was less reserved. "Move to strike as non-responsive."

Traxel interposed. "Mr. Stemler opened the door with his question."

Judge Mattson announced, "The witness's reply *was* responsive to the question posed. Objection overruled"

"No more questions," said Stemler, unable to disguise his anger.

"You may step down, Mr. Fishkin," the judge said.

Traxel was on his feet. "Before he does, Your Honor, I'd like to ask the Court Reporter to mark the plastic bag containing Mr. Stonebrook's finger, and then I would like to offer it as an exhibit."

"You may." He did, there was no objection, and the finger was received.

Traxel then called Alice Lee, an economist and an accountant, to the stand. Rehmel conducted her direct examination, first qualifying her as an expert witness, walking her through her education, publications, and previous forensic testimonies in other cases. She had done the calculations of back pay for all three plaintiffs, the value of a lost finger (based on a compilation of court cases in a variety of jurisdictions), the value of being kept away from one's families on a *per diem* basis, a range of compensatory damages for two of them being cast out on a raft, compensatory damages for Stonebrook's having been kidnapped and falsely imprisoned, and then ranges of punitive damages from which the jury might select. She had put all of these numbers on charts, which Rehmel showed on an overhead projector, and also in charts which were received as exhibits.

On cross, the most that Stemler could elicit was that the ranges of punitive damages were at the suggestion of the Dornan lawyers and that the ranges were selected from cases where the punitive damages were among the highest ever awarded and that Dr. Norton had no idea of the amount of assets of Greenport Shipping.

The judge called for a recess, during which Traxel decided that he could only postpone Muñoz's testimony a little bit longer. After the recess, he called a man from the International Seafarers' Union, whom he told to be brief. And he was. The witness explained in quick sentences what the Union was, that it attempted to protect sailors on ships in international waters, advocating for decent wages, reasonable work hours, a nurse or ex-military corpsman to provide medical services, decent food, and no corporal punishment. That worked in the democracies and with those companies flying U.S., European, Australian, and New Zealand flags. However, many companies were now flying the flags of Palau and Bolivia and Paraguay and Lesotho, which had no navies and no ships.

When asked about complaints, the witness testified that the most came from ships owned by *Hestia Etoupeia*, including *La Galissionière*, but because *Hestia* forced its crew to sign contracts promising not to complain, the Union had not yet won a court case. The seafarers who were brave enough to be plaintiffs invariably got blackballed from working on any other ships flying flags of convenience.

On cross-examination, he admitted that he knew nothing about the specific voyages of *La Galissionière* (on which Delgadinho, Muñoz, and Fishkin had worked). He also had admitted, again, that not a single court, to his knowledge, had ever ruled against *Hestia*.

It was now 3:40 p.m., and Traxel reluctantly called Muñoz to testify. On direct, Muñoz said that he had signed the Complaint but wasn't sure what he signed because it was in English.

He said that he had a cloudy memory of what had occurred on *La Galissionière* because he drank beer and whiskey every day with his meals.

"Do you remember coming to Pastor Sánchez-Ríos's office to ask for help?"

[THROUGH THE TRANSLATOR]:

"I came to her office several times. She is a very good person, and she helps me a lot.

"Were you sitting here when she testified this morning that you came and told her that you had been threatened?"

"Yes." He said it very softly and hesitantly.

"Was her testimony truthful."

He sat silently, and Traxel repeated the question.

"It was a confession to a priest, and it was not right for her to talk about it." That brought murmurs among the jurors.

"Did the officers of *La Galissionière* put you and Muñoz into a skiff in the Irish Sea?"

"We asked to be let off because we wanted to go to our homes, and they let us use one of their lifeboats."

"Why are you still living in the United States?"

"I'm trying to save enough money to go back to *Gran Canaria*." He was bent over and obviously in psychic pain. Traxel knew there was nothing to be gained from further questioning.

"No more questions."

Stemler could hardly suppress a grin. "In fact, Mr. Muñoz, you never saw anyone tossed overboard, did you?"

"No."

"You never saw anyone beaten, did you?"

"No."

"You didn't work more than eight hours a day, did you?"

"No."

"You thought the food on the ship was better than you got in *Gran Canaria*, isn't that so?"

"Yes."

Stemler paused for effect. "Would you like to withdraw as a plaintiff in this case?"

Muñoz hadn't expected that question. He sat back and tried to delay by pretending he didn't understand. "What does it mean to 'withdraw?'"

At that moment the door to the courtroom flew open, and Donna Putrell came through, followed closely by Sofía and Valentina Muñoz. Valentina, ran up the aisle and through the gate separating the gallery from the area of the counsel tables, yelling, "PAPA! PAPA! PAPA!"

Her father jumped out of the witness chair to embrace her, and then Sofía joined them in a group hug. All three of them were sobbing.

The judge gently rapped her gavel. "Would the Spanish translator please ask Mr. Muñoz to return to the witness stand and explain to Mrs. Muñoz that she and her daughter must sit in the gallery."

Muñoz returned to the chair, tears streaming down his cheeks. Mrs. Muñoz sat down in the gallery, and Donna gently led Valentina out of the courtroom.

Judge Mattson asked the clerk to read back Mr. Stemler's last question, and the translator said it in Spanish. Muñoz sat up straight and practically shouted, "No, no, absolutely no! I do not want to withdraw. Now that I know that my wife and daughter are safe, I can tell the truth. I was afraid ....."

As pleasantly as he could manage, Stemler said, "Your Honor, there is no question before the witness, and I ask that you explain decorum to him."

Stemler's intervention had the effect of quieting Muñoz, and the judge asked, "Do you have any more questions of the witness, Mr. Stemler?"

"No, Your Honor."

"Mr. Traxel, any redirect?" she asked it as if it were a genuine query.

"Yes, Your Honor, thank you. Señor Muñoz, you were in the middle of a sentence when Mr. Stemler interrupted you. What were you about to say?"

"A man came to the house where I was living in Wayzata and told me that if I said any bad things in the... de-po-si-tion or in the trial that my Sofía and my Valentina would be killed. I was very scared. I went to see Pastor Elizabeta and told her. She asked me if I wanted it to be a confession, and I told her 'no.' I did not tell the truth to the lawyer a few minutes ago when he asked because although I know that telling the truth is important, I decided that it is not as important as saving the lives of my wife and daughter."

He paused, and Traxel knew that he should be asking questions rather than letting Muñoz ramble on, but he was certain that Stemler would not be so stupid as to make an objection, so he just sat there. Traxel nodded at Muñoz, signaling that he could go on.

"Pastor Elizabeta said that she would try to reach Mr. Stonebrook – the man who everybody calls Mr. Fishkin here in court – but she wasn't sure he could do anything. So, when Mr. Stemler took my de-po-si-tion, I said that nothing bad happened on *La Galissionière,* and here today I lied again – to protect my beautiful wife and daughter. But now I can tell the truth."

He was crying, all the female jurors were crying, and the male jurors were pinching their noses or coughing into their handkerchiefs in order not to be seen crying. Traxel decided he ought to enter the conversation. "Señor Muñoz, you have just said that you lied in the deposition, and you lied today when Mr. Stemler asked you questions. Did you understand that you were under oath?"

"Yes."

"Do you know the importance of telling the truth under oath?"

"Yes. It is very important – but just not as important as saving lives. I could not live with myself if I found out that by telling the truth I would cause the deaths of Sofía and of Valentina. They are here, somehow they are here; and I am grateful to Mr. Stonebrook and to whoever he got to bring them here."

"As you were hugging, your wife said something to you. Can you tell us what she said?"

"She said, 'I am so happy to see you. A man from the ship company came and told me that you were dead'."

Stemler rose. "May we approach, Your Honor?" She beckoned both lead counsel and had the clerk turn off the speaker system.

"Uh, this is obviously hearsay," Stemler said, "but I don't want to make a scene."

"Mr. Traxel?"

"If you were to sustain an objection on hearsay grounds, Your Honor, then I would put *Mrs.* Muñoz on the stand and ask her what she said to her husband during the hug."

Judge Mattson: "Mr. Stemler, do you still wish to make a hearsay objection?"

He rubbed his forehead and then said, "I suppose not."

"Step back, please, gentlemen."

"You may continue with your redirect, Mr. Traxel," she said.

Traxel took Muñoz through the litany of abuses and the circumstances surrounding their being put on the raft and why he really was still in the United States. It was at 4:28 when he said, "No further questions, Your Honor." Stemler declined the invitation to conduct re-cross.

Chapter 48: That Evening And The Next Morning

STEMLER, WENTWORTH, NELSON, AND CADWALADER met in a conference room at the Stevens law firm. It was a somber gathering. Nelson brought out a bottle of scotch and poured them each a glass.

"That's the worst day in court I have ever had," said Stemler. "Everything that could go wrong did."

Wentworth took a long sip and then said. "All right. It is clear that we are dead in the water on damages. If the jury gets to damages, they're going to nail us to the yardarm. Our only hope, a narrow path, is to head 'em off at the pass of liability. We don't need or want anybody to testify about what did or did not happen on the ship. The jury wouldn't believe them even if Mother Teresa and Nelson Mandela were our witnesses

"Our only chance is to prevail on liability; then it doesn't make any difference what the damages might be. We have to be able to convince the jury – or an appellate court – that Greenport is the wrong defendant."

"How're we going to do that?" asked Nelson. "The captain is 20,000 leagues away across the sea, and Felix Benteen has already told us he wouldn't show up... and, frankly, I'm not sure it would help us if he did."

"How about," Wentworth asked, "if you, Charlene, call up Traxel, and tell him we'll pay the five million they asked for last time?"

She shot him a look. "After today, would you take five million if you were Traxel?"

"No, I wouldn't. But these plaintiffs might. And you can always rattle the cage about our chances on liability."

"What do you suggest I use as a rattle?"

Stemler jumped in. "Tell him that neither the Captain nor Benteen is available; however, we're planning to bring in *Hestia's* Personnel Director, Andreas Simitas, and the Operations Vice-President, Constantine

Tsipras, both of whom will testify that the only relationship between *Hestia* and Greenport is that Greenport is the subsidiary of *Hestia.*"

"Well, it's worth a try," answered Charlene. "I'll do it from my office."

"Why not do it from here... on speaker-phone?" Wentworth asked.

Charlene hesitated just a few seconds too long but recovered quickly. "Sure, why not."

Since it was after business hours, the telephone operator at the Dornan firm had gone home, and Traxel picked up the phone himself. He and his colleague shad been reviewing the events of the day in his office. "Good evening, this is Phil Traxel."

"Good evening, Phil. This is Charlene Nelson." Traxel put the call on his speaker phone, so that everyone in both offices was listening. "Hello, Charlene."

"Well," she said, "I have to hand it to you. You had a terrific day today, and the timing of the arrival of Mrs. Muñoz was magical."

Traxel was tempted to explain that the timing was fortuitous, but he decided just to say, "Thank you." He had a pretty strong feeling that she was calling to make another settlement offer, but he was determined to let her make her offer on her own without his urging.

"Here's where we stand, Phil. If the jury gets past liability, I think you'll do well on damages. The big question is 'IF.' Even if everything that every one of your witnesses said about what occurred on *La Galissionière* happened, you still haven't proved that Greenport has any responsibility for the activities of the parent company, nor is there any proof that what happened to Fishkin is the result of either *Hestia* or Greenport."

She paused, hoping that he would make some sort of response, but he didn't and figured that he could out-wait her. She punctured the silence with an offer. "We think it's a toss-up right now, so my clients are willing to accept your last offer of five million dollars." She held her breath.

"Is Benteen going to testify, Charlene?"

"Probably not. He seems to be out of the country at the moment."

"And let me guess – Captain Eliopoulos is somewhere on the Indian Ocean."

She grimaced. "We haven't heard from him, but the *Hestia* schedules indicate that *La Galissioniere* is due to dock in New Zealand six days from now."

"So, are you guys planning to have anyone from *Hestia* testify?"

"Well, if you turn down our offer, then we'll fly the Operations Vice-President and the Personnel Director here from Athens, and they're going to testify that the only relationship between Greenport and *Hestia* is that Greenport is the subsidiary; but that won't be necessary, of course, if we settle."

"Right. Well, I shall relay your offer to our clients and get back to you tomorrow at the courthouse just before trial resumes."

"Good. And, oh," she added, as if it were an afterthought, "if you turn it down, how much longer will you be putting witnesses on – so we can know when Tsipras and Simitas should get here."

"Another day or two. But we'd be willing to agree to a break for a day while they're en route. The jury would probably appreciate a day off."

Yeah, she thought to herself, but didn't say aloud, *so they can spend the time processing and mentally replaying all the testimony so far.* "We'll draw up a Settlement Agreement and Release, with multiple copies, just in case."

"That's fine."

"Good night, Phil."

When she got off, Stemler asked, "What's your gut feeling, Charlene. You have worked with this guy before."

"I'd guess there was a 20% chance of their saying 'yes,' only because those two sailors never dreamed of that kind of money. But, if I were wagering, I think the odds are four-to-one they'll say 'no' because they figure that they have the jury on their side and will ask for even bigger bucks."

"But," Wentworth commented, "Traxel didn't seem to be concerned about the liability question – even though all they really have to go on is that Marlo chick's chart. And, even if they turn down our offer, they don't know if Greenport has enough money in order to even suggest a punitive damages amount."

"They will if the Operations guy and the Personnel dude testify." It was Cadwalader, who, precisely because she was the junior-most person in the room, had been quiet.

The other three made involuntary head motions but had no answer to her comment.

That night, after the discussion among the plaintiffs that resulted in the rejection of the latest offer, Stonebrook said to Donna in their hotel room: "You are amazing. I don't know how you pulled it off, but it was expialidocious that you managed to get Mrs. Muñoz and her daughter into the country, *and* to the Twin Cities, *and* into the courtroom. *Plus,* the timing was absolutely exquisite."

"I had help from your, uh, friend Pastor Elizabeth. She knows a senator who knows someone in the Attorney General's office who arranged for special visas for Sofía and Valentina. That little girl is precious. Even though we don't share a language, I would happily take her home."

"Well, if you can pull off one more supercalifragilistic trip – on Dorkan and Forken's nickel – I want to ask you to bring someone else here, this time from Morocco. You'll need an interpreter to go with you, preferably bilingual in Arabic and English, but bilingual in Portuguese and English would be adequate."

"How am I supposed to do that?"

"I have no idea. I would do it, but as a plaintiff I have to be in court. I don't know whom else to ask."

"Wow! Who's the person, where is he or she, and why do you need him or her?"

"His name is Mahmoud Nimri. He's 17-years old, and he lives in a village called Temara. It's apparently close to Rabat, the capital. I have a hunch that the *Hestia* witnesses are going to say that there never were any Moroccans on *La Galissionière*, and Nimri would be able to contradict them."

"When do I need to bring him here?"

"Yesterday would be best. But no later than three days from now."

"Holy shit, Pedro. How do you expect me to do that?"

"If I were free, here's what I'd do. First, I'd ask Pastor Elizabeth to pull her political strings again. Second, I'd find an interpreter willing to leave on a moment's notice and then take him – better a him than a her – since you're going to be in a Muslim country; third, fly into Rabat, rent a car and go to Temara; fourth, bring a letter, written in Arabic and English, for Nimri's father to sign, authorizing his minor son to travel with you; fifth, convince the kid that you're legitimate and not somebody in the pay of *Hestia*; and then get here on the double."

"I can't speak either Arabic or Portuguese. How am I going to convince the kid that I'm legit?"

"Here, show him this." He took the medallion from around his neck and handed it to Donna. This will convince him. He gave it to me as a 'thank-you' gift."

She looked at him and pulled him to her. "Let's go to bed. I may not see you for three days."

The next morning, the lawyers got to the courtroom early. Nelson approached Traxel. "Do we have a deal?"

"I'm afraid not. Your client continues to be a day late and a dollar short. The five million counter-offer was good before the first two days of trial. Given the developments, it's off the table."

"Do you have another counter now?"

"Yes. And, assuming that we can still allocate the amounts, our clients will settle for 10 million."

Nelson looked at him with incredulity. "For future reference, when I represent plaintiffs, how do you convince two broke sailors to turn down five million dollars?"

Traxel smiled "The best way is if someone threatens their wives and daughters with death, and you can bring the family to safety during the trial."

She turned red and bit her teeth. "I'll pass on your counter-offer, I'm guessing that it will never fly. Is there any flexibility?"

"Charlene," he answered, "you're asking the plaintiffs to bid against themselves, something that I've heard you say, in other instances, is unreasonable."

She nodded, and he changed the subject. "Before you arrived, I asked the judicial clerk if we could have a chambers conference this morning."

"What's the subject?"

"Defendant's witnesses." He said nothing more.

The clerk conducted the lawyers into Judge Mattson's chambers. "Good morning, everyone. What is the occasion for your visit to chambers?"

Traxel spoke up. "Defendants have told us that neither the owner of Greenport Shipping nor the captain of *La Galissionière* is available to testify."

"And why do plaintiffs care, counsel?"

"We want to be able to cross-examine them. Also, as we pointed out during the summary judgment hearing, we did serve subpoenas on Greenport for all three Mates on *La Galissionière*, but Greenport sent them back, saying that they had no control over them."

"Yes. I recall. And in my order, I wrote that if the jury found that Greenport *were* the parent corporation, you would be entitled to a jury instruction that they could make an adverse inference about the defendants' failure to produce the witnesses."

She turned to Stemler and his colleagues. "I don't want to tell you how to try your case, defendants, but is there a reason neither the captain of the ship nor the owner of the defendant company plans to be here?"

"They are both out of the country, Your Honor, and the Captain had told Mr. Traxel during his deposition that he'd very likely be at sea during the trial."

"Ummm," she said. And, then, after a pause, she asked Traxel, "What is it that you want from the Court?"

"Two things, Your Honor. First, defense counsel apparently intend to fly two officers of the *Hestia* corporation to Minneapolis to testify, but neither is the CFO. We want to be able to ask questions about the financial status of *Hestia*."

"Again, why do you care? Throughout this case your argument is that Greenport is the real parent company."

"Correct, Your Honor. We want to have a basis for the amount of punitive damages we shall be asking the jury to award. But since no one from Greenport is apparently going to testify about anything, including its financial situation, we at least want to have some testimony about the financial value of its subsidiary, *Hestia Etoupeia*."

"That won't be a problem, Your Honor," said Stemler. "One of the two officers who will testify will be the Vice-President of Operations, and he will have all the financial information."

The judge turned to Traxel. "Will that be satisfactory, Mr. Traxel?"

"Yes, Your Honor. Now, the second request is that we be allowed to have Ms. Marlo do a reprise of the testimony that she gave at the

pre-trial hearing but *after* we hear what the two officers of *Hestia* have
to say."

"Is that acceptable to defendants, Mr. Stemler?"

He hesitated. "Well, that does seem sort of odd. Why don't the
plaintiffs do what is normal, i.e. put on their affirmative witnesses and
rest, and then we can put on our witnesses, and if they have any rebuttal
witnesses, they can put them on then?"

Traxel was ready for that. "If the defendants had the owner of
Greenport here, that would be perfectly reasonable. He is on their
witness list. But we just learned from them last evening that Mr. Benteen
can't, or won't, make himself available. Since we had no advance notice
of Mr. Benteen's failure to participate in the trial and since we did not
have a chance to depose any of the officers of *Hestia,* we think it's not
an unreasonable request."

"Well, Mr. Stemler. Other than 'we've always done it that way,' is
there a valid reason why Ms. Marlo shouldn't be allowed to testify after
your two *Hestia* officers?"

"I suppose not, Your Honor."

"Very well, then. I'll see all of you in the courtroom. Bring in the
jury, Eric."

Chapter 49: Testimony Of Commodore Costaign

"CALL YOUR NEXT WITNESS, MR. Traxel," said the judge.

Traxel rose from his seat. "I call Richard Costaign to the stand, and my colleague, Mr. Brindle, will conduct the direct examination." A tall, ramrod-straight man in starched dress whites with a star on each epaulet got up from his seat in the gallery and strode to the witness stand. He was about 6' 2", sported a well-chiseled and handsome face, deep blue eyes, and a well-trimmed moustache.

After the clerk swore him in, Brindle began. "Please state your name for the record."

"Richard Costaign."

"You are wearing a uniform. Can you tell the jury your branch of service, your duty station, and your rank."

Costaign turned to the jury. "I am a career officer in the United States Coast Guard; my duty station is Gibralter, which is British territory at the southern tip of Spain. I hold the rank of Commodore."

"Should the attorneys and the Court address you as 'Commodore'?"

Costaign smiled. "Well, that would be respectful."

"What would be the equivalent rank in the army for Commodore?"

"Brigadier General."

"In what section or division within the Coast Guard are you assigned?"

"Counter-Intelligence."

"Can you tell us what your specific duties are?"

"No, sir. I'm sorry, but that's classified. I am not permitted to disclose that information."

Brindle nodded, signaling non-verbally to the jury that it was perfectly reasonable for this witness not to reveal classified information. "Do you know a man by the name of Rocky Stonebrook, also known as Pedro Fishkin?"

"I know *of* him, but I have never met him."

"Please tell the jury the circumstances of your involvement concerning Mr. Stonebrook."

Again, Costaign turned to the jury before answering. "A few months ago, I received information, from sources that I cannot reveal, that Mr. Stonebrook, of whom I had never heard at the time, was being held captive somewhere in Algeria. I was told that he had a tracking device embedded in his teeth but that it had not been activated yet. I was asked to arrange a rescue for him if and when we picked up the tracker signal."

Brindle looked at Ted Bruner and gave him a thumbs-up gesture. Bruner turned on the overhead projector and put on an acetate showing a map of the Mediterranean Sea. "This is Plaintiff's Exhibit No. 18, already received into evidence. Can you identify it, Commodore?"

"Yes, that is a map of the area around the Mediterranean Sea, southern Europe, and northern Africa."

"Please come down from the witness stand and use this pointer to show your duty station and pertinent places in Africa." Costaign did so and said, pointing, "Here is Gibralter, marked in blue. On the southern side of the Strait is Tangier, Morocco, marked in orange; and to the east is Algeria, the capital of which is Algiers, marked in green."

"Thank you, Commodore. You may return to the witness chair. How did you know that Mr. Stonebrook was in Algeria?"

"I didn't. Nor do I think that my source knew. The source *surmised* that Stonebrook's location was in Algeria."

"Did you know how far you could pick up the tracker signal?"

"The source wasn't certain but thought that it might extend between 100-150 miles."

"And how far is Algiers from Gibralter?"

"About 468 miles and, obviously a good deal farther if he were being held captive in central or southern Algeria."

"Then how did you expect to receive the signal in Gibralter?"

"We couldn't. That's why I dispatched a ship to the harbor outside Algiers."

"At some point, did the ship you dispatched receive the signal?"

"Yes, it did; and the captain radioed me in Gibralter, indicating its reception and its presumed location at a location southwest of Algiers."

"Did it indicate a precise location?"

"Well, it's a little complicated: Because of the Atlas Mountains, there are reverberations that make it difficult to ascertain the precise location."

"So, what did you do then?"

"I intercepted a text message in Arabic indicating that Mr. Stonebrook would be coming to a town called Blida."

"And then what?"

"I ordered the rescue crew to helicopter from the ship to Blida and retrieve Mr. Stonebrook."

"And did they?"

"Yes. Once we knew he would be coming to Blida, we were able to ignore the reverberations and knew exactly where he was being kept."

"Where did the rescue team take him?"

"As I had ordered, they dropped him at the Emergency Ward of a hospital in Tangier, Morocco, indicated on the map in red."

"Did the rescue team encounter any resistance?"

"Yes. But they were under strict orders not to kill or permanently injure any locals, so they merely tasered a local who had fired a pistol at the rescuers."

"What was Mr. Stonebrook's condition when the rescue crew picked him up."

"He was in good condition, but the pinky of his left...."

"Objection!" Stemler had stood up. "Hearsay!"

The judge turned to the witness. "Commodore, you testified that you had never met Mr. Stonebrook. Does that mean that you did *not* accompany the rescue team?"

"That's correct, Your Honor."

"Then the objection is sustained."

Traxel moved on. "Do you know how Mr. Stonebrook made it back to the United States?"

"He stayed overnight in the hospital in Tangier, and the next afternoon he took a ferry to Gibralter, where the American Consul arranged his passage."

"And how do you know this?"

"I had made sure that the rescue crew was supplied with a ferry ticket to hand to Mr. Stonebrook, and I had personally contacted the American Consul in Gibralter to arrange for Mr. Stonebrook to fly back to the States. I received a report from the captain of the ship that carried the rescue crew that the ticket had been delivered and from the American Consul that Mr. Stonebrook had boarded the plane."

Stemler rose again. "Move to strike. The witness's last sentence was entirely hearsay, forbidden by Rule 803 of the Rules of Evidence."

Brindle responded: "It's actually an *exception* to the hearsay rule, Your Honor, under Rule 803(8). The testimony was not offered for the purpose of the truth of the matter asserted but, rather, for the witness's state of mind. Alternatively, it falls within the exception of Rule 804(a), namely that the declarants are unavailable."

Stemler said, "We don't agree that the declarants are unavailable – plaintiffs *could* have produced the leader of the rescue team or the American Consul to provide first-hand testimony, but neither is on the plaintiffs' witness list."

Brindle started to respond, but the judge put up her hand. "Both counsel, please take your seats." She turned to the jury. "Let me try to translate for the jury what just transpired and surely sounded to you like an arcane and probably an incomprehensible set of arguments.

"The hearsay rule is a frequent source of confusion for jurors. The supreme courts of both the United States and the State of Minnesota have promulgated, that is, *issued*, formal Rules of Evidence which are binding on lawyers and judges. One of them is the rule against hearsay and is designed to make sure that we don't admit into evidence testimony about which the witness has only second-hand knowledge. There are, however, a number of exceptions to the hearsay rule set forth in the Rules.

"Mr. Stemler argued that Commodore Costaign's testimony about the delivery of the ferry ticket and the American Consul's having accompanied Mr. Stonebrook to the airport constitute hearsay. Mr. Brindle counters that they fall within either of two legitimate exceptions. Mr. Stemler is technically correct that those two pieces of testimony are indeed hearsay. So, I must instruct you that you may accept as factual the statement that Commodore Costaign personally took steps for the rescue crew to deliver a ferry ticket to Mr. Stonebrook and for the American Consul in Gibralter to arrange for air transportation to the United States for Mr. Stonebrook; however, you are to disregard the assertions that the rescue crew actually delivered the ferry ticket and that the American Consul actually procured air transportation for Mr. Stonebrook."

Costaign suppressed a grin. The judge had sustained Stemler's objection but in doing so had exquisitely made clear to the jury how silly some lawyerly arguments in court are about unimportant facts. Because of Stemler's objection, the jury was left only with the assumption that Stonebrook might still be in the hospital in Tangier, even though he was obviously in the United States because he was sitting 10 feet away, at counsel table. She had also demonstrated to the attorneys that she was perfectly capable of exposing their pettiness in what otherwise sounded like a neutral, reasonable explanation to the jury.

After a certain amount of silence for what the judge had said to sink in, Brindle replied, "Thank you, Your Honor. Let me move on to another matter for this witness. Commodore Costaign, do you know two individuals named Sofía and Valentina Muñoz?"

"Yes."

"Who are they, and how do you know them?"

"Sofía Muñoz is the wife of the plaintiff Leonicio Muñoz, and Valentina is their five-year-old daughter."

Stemler was tempted to object, arguing that the assertion that they were the wife and daughter of the plaintiff was hearsay, but he decided to keep silent since he sensed, correctly, that the jury already had a reason to think that he was overly persnickety.

"And how did you come to meet them, Commodore?"

"I had received a request to have a submarine available in the port of *Las Palmas* on *Gran Canaria* island in the Canary Islands on a day certain in order to take on two passengers, namely Ms. Muñoz and Miss Muñoz. The Canary Islands are marked in purple on the map."

"And did you fulfill that request?"

"I did."

"Where did the submarine take them?"

"To Lisbon, the capital of Portugal, which is marked in brown on the map."

"Were you personally aboard the submarine?"

"Yes, I was."

"Was that usual for you to accompany a submarine crew?"

"No, it was not."

"Then why were you aboard?"

"It was also very unusual for us to be requested to transport foreign civilians from Point A to Point B. So, I decided to be present personally."

"From whom did the request for the submarine come?"

"From the IMO, the International Maritime Organization."

"And what precisely is the IMO?"

"It is an agency of the United Nations, headquartered in London, and concerned with maritime safety, pollution, and fairness to seafarers."

"And what is your connection to the IMO, Commodore?"

"I represent the United States Government on the Council of Forty that governs the IMO."

"Into whose hands did you deliver the mother and child?"

"Clara Lobo Antunes, the Portuguese Ambassador to the IMO."

"Did you have any difficulty with the passengers?"

"Not with the passengers, but we did have some trouble as we were boarding them and their escort."

"What kind of trouble?"

"Two men, wearing masks, came running down the pier with machine guns and began to fire at Ms. and Miss Muñoz."

"What did you do?"

"I ordered my men to return fire, and both masked men were killed."

"To what country do the Canary Islands belong?"

"Spain."

"Did you have permission to kill Spanish citizens?"

"Of course not. But we were protecting our passengers. Besides, when we examined the bodies after the gunfire ended, we found evidence that they were Moroccans, not Spaniards."

"How did you know that?"

"One of them had written instructions and the address of the Muñoz home."

"In what language were the instructions?"

"Arabic."

"What did you do with the bodies?"

"We bagged them and delivered them to Moroccan military officials in Tangier on our way to Lisbon."

"Were there any repercussions?"

"No, the Moroccan military officials identified both corpses as members of a terrorist group on their 'Wanted' list, and they thanked us."

"No further questions, Your Honor."

Chapter 50: Cross Examination Of Costaign

THE JUDGE LOOKED OVER AT Stemler. "Do you wish to cross examine the witness, counsel"

"Yes, Your Honor," Stemler said as he opened a file. Then addressing Costaign, he asked: "Tell me if I have correctly summarized your testimony, as follows: You want the jury to believe that you are an officer in the Coast Guard, with the rank of Commodore, stationed in Gibralter, performing duties the specifics of which you refuse to reveal, but with which you have the power to send ships to Algeria and submarines to the Canary islands, to send armed rescue teams to rural Algeria, to order men to kill people from countries with whom we are not at war, and to transport foreign civilians in American ships at the request of a UN agency. Is that a fair summary?"

"That's close, counsel. It is not the case that I *won't* reveal my specific duties; I am forbidden by federal law from disclosing the information. Second, Blida, Algeria, is more exurban than it is rural; and third, the authority for lethal gunfire only applies when someone has attacked our forces or people for whom we are responsible. Other than those three corrections, and your omission of some important details, your summary is fair."

"And the validity of this testimony depends on the jury finding you to be a credible witness, wouldn't you agree?"

Without hesitating, Costaign answered. "I should think that your observation would apply to *every* witness in a trial."

"Quite so, Mr. Costaign. Let me ask you a few preliminary questions before we reach the credibility issues." He looked at the jurors, many of whom were squeezing their eyebrows, indicating curiosity about where this line of questioning was going. "Do you speak Arabic, Commodore?"

"No, sir. I do not."

"Did any of the submarine crew members speak Arabic."

"No, sir."

"Do you know where the Coast Guard Academy is located?"

"New London, Connecticut"

"Have you ever been there?"

"Yes."

"Umm. Did you ever actually *live* on the campus of the Coast Guard Academy?"

"Yes."

"Now, I have here a document – - before Mr. Brindle objects, Your Honor, it is not an exhibit yet, but it is a document which I would like to ask the Commodore to identify."

"Show it to Mr. Brindle," said the judge.

Stemler did. Brindle looked at it briefly and then said, "I have no objection to counsel's showing this document to the witness."

Stemler asked, "May I approach the witness, Your Honor?"

"Yes, you may."

Coming up to the witness chair, Stemler handed the document to Costaign and asked him to identify it.

Costaign read it briefly and answered. "It is a copy of the Executive Order abolishing the rank of Commodore in both the Navy and the Coast Guard, and the date is 1950."

"Have you seen that document before, Commodore?"

"I know *of* it although I don't recall having read the Order before today."

"Do you know of any Executive Order, statute, or Regulation that *restored* the rank of Commodore since that time?"

"I do not."

"I offer Defense Exhibit Number 1."

"No objection," sang out Brindle.

"Defense Exhibit Number 1 is received," said the judge.

"Did you ever have another name besides Richard Costaign?"

"No, that's always been my name."

"You testified that you actually lived on the campus of the Coast Guard Academy, isn't that right?"

"Yes, that's correct."

"I'm showing you what I'm marking as Defense Exhibit Number 2. It's a letter from the Registrar of the Coast Guard Academy, and it says that Richard Costaign never graduated from the Coast Guard Academy, and, in fact, Richard Costaign never even matriculated as a student to the Coast Guard Academy. Do you have any basis to refute the Registrar's letter?"

"No, I don't." There was a palpable murmur among the jurors.

"Your Honor, I offer Defense Exhibit No. 2."

"No objection," Brindle said, almost cheerfully.

"Defense Exhibit Number 2 is received."

"Commodore, Your testimony included two mentions of documents written in Arabic – one a text message that you supposedly intercepted and a set of directions to the Muñoz household which guided your actions, isn't that right?"

"Yes."

"But you testified moments ago that you don't speak Arabic. Are you changing your testimony now?"

"No, I still can't speak Arabic."

"Lastly, I want to show you what your counsel listed on Plaintiffs' Exhibit list but has not introduced into evidence, namely your resumé. Did you prepare this document?"

"Yes, I did."

"The resumé states that you are a Commodore in the Coast Guard, that you are stationed in Gibralter, that you are assigned to the counterintelligence unit, and indicates that you have previously captained naval vessels. Is that right?"

"Correct."

"Apparently, Mr. Brindle doesn't intend to introduce this resumé as an Exhibit. I can understand why. So, I'll offer it as Defendant's Exhibit Number 3."

The judge looked at Traxel. "Counsel?"

"No objection, Your Honor."

"Defense Exhibit Number 3 is received."

Stemler continued. "But that's all there is in this resumé, right?"

"That's correct."

"The resumé does not assert that you speak Arabic or any other foreign language, does it?"

"No, sir."

"Nor does this resumé even mention where you went to college, does it?"

"No, sir."

"And why is that?"

"I didn't think it was relevant to my testimony here today."

Stemler practically guffawed. "Oh, so you didn't. think it was *relevant*. Well, Commodore, you may very well know how to steer a ship, but you don't get to decide what's relevant. That's a legal question."

"Objection, Your Honor." It was Brindle. "Counsel is arguing with the witness. There's nothing interrogative about his statement."

The judge looked over her glasses. "Both attorneys are correct. Mr. Stemler is right that it is this court's prerogative to determine what evidence is relevant, and Mr. Brindle is right that Mr. Stemler *was* arguing with the witness. Pose a question, Mr. Stemler."

Looking like a Cheshire cat, Stemler moved in. "Even though the judge gets to make the decision about what's relevant, since you used that word in your answer, let me inquire: How do you define 'relevance'?"

Judge Mattson looked at Brindle, anticipating an objection, which she would have sustained. But Brindle kept silent, and she decided that she wasn't going to run his case for him.

"Relevance," Costaign began, "is the tendency of a given item of evidence to prove or disprove one of the legal elements of the case, or to have probative value to make one of the elements of the case likelier or not."

Stemler was momentarily taken aback. "And what is the source of your knowledge, sir?"

"*Black's Law Dictionary.*"

"And did someone advise you to look at that tome prior to testifying here today?"

"Objection," said Brindle.

"Sustained. You know better than that counsel. Do you have any more questions for this witness?"

Stemler opened his file. "Let's see," he answered, looking at his notes. "I just want to pose a summary question: You have admitted that there are no Commodores in the Coast Guard; that you never attended the Coast Guard Academy; that you don't speak Arabic, and that your resumé is a mere half page, with no mention of your educational background or the ability to speak Arabic. That's all correct, isn't it?"

"Yes."

"I have no more questions of this witness." He sat down, looking very satisfied with himself. He looked over at the jurors, who were all staring at Costaign with a kind of suspicion.

REDIRECT

"Any redirect, Mr. Brindle?" Judge Mattson inquired.

"Indeed, Your Honor. Commodore Costaign, is everything about which you testified both on direct and cross examination the truth?"

"Yes sir. I have sworn to tell the truth, and I did."

"Can you explain why you refer to yourself as 'Commodore' if the Navy and the Coast Guard both abolished that rank in 1950?"

Costaign nodded. "During World War II, 'Commodore' was an official rank in both services. But five years after the war, with the reduction of military forces, and the fact that all the Commodores had either retired or been promoted to Rear Admiral, both services formally abolished the designation. However, in order for the Navy and the Coast Guard to maintain equivalence with the Army, i.e. with the rank of Brigadier General, the Navy and the Coast Guard divided the rank of Rear Admiral into Rear Admiral Upper and Rear Admiral Lower. No one really wanted to be a 'Rear Admiral Lower.'" There were titters among the jurors.

"Eventually, both services decided that senior captains, that is those who have supervisory command of more than two vessels, could use the honorary rank of Commodore. Since I am a senior captain, supervising the command of more than two vessels, I am entitled to wear the star on my epaulets and to be called 'Commodore,' which is how everyone in the Coast Guard, including the Commandant, addresses me."

Stemler's face started a slow burn.

Ignoring Stemler, Brindle went on. "Could you explain to the jury how it is you could testify that you actually lived on the campus of the Coast Guard Academy without ever having attended school there?"

"Surely. I attended, and graduated from, the *Naval* Academy, in Annapolis, Maryland. I spent a number of years in the Navy, serving on ships in a variety of capacities, including those of Executive Officer and Captain; and then I was placed on the faculty of the Naval Academy. There is a Concordat between the Navy and the Coast Guard that certain professionals who are officers in either service can, with the approval of both organizations, transfer to the other. I formally transferred to the Coast Guard and eventually taught at the Coast Guard Academy, which is why I lived on campus in New London, Connecticut."

Stemler involuntarily put his hand up to his neck... until he noticed that three or four of the jurors were watching him.

Brindle went on. "Mr. Stemler kept pressing you on the point that you admitted that you can't speak Arabic, but you testified that you intercepted a text message in Arabic and that you found the Muñoz's address, written in Arabic, in the pocket of one of the terrorists. How do you explain that discrepancy?"

"It's not really a discrepancy: After graduating from the Naval Academy, I was awarded a Fulbright fellowship to study Islamic Law at Punjab University in Lahore, Pakistan. The Navy authorized my leave of absence on condition that I extend my term in the Navy, which I readily did. In order to study the *Quran,* we graduate students had to learn to *read* Arabic, but speaking it was never emphasized. So, today, I can read the language, but I can't speak it."

"Did you earn a degree at Punjab University?"

"Yes, a Masters Degree in Islamic Studies."

"You haven't explained why you transferred to the Coast Guard."

"The Coast Guard was expanding its Counter- Intelligence section in North Africa and wanted someone who had some background in Islam. They made me an offer and persuaded the Navy to let me transfer."

"Mr. Stemler was interested in how you knew the formal definition of 'relevance.'

How is it that you were able to trip that definition off the tip of your tongue?"

"One of the courses that I was teaching at the Naval Academy was International Law, and the chair of my department suggested that to attain credibility as an instructor on international law, I should really have a law degree. So, I went to law school at Georgetown University."

"Did you take another leave of absence from the Navy to attend law school?"

"No, sir. I taught at the Naval Academy in Annapolis in the daytime, and I attended law school at Georgetown, in Washington, D.C., in the evening."

"How long did it take you to graduate law school if you were working full-time?"

"Three and a half years, including summers."

"So, did you use the law degree just to enhance your status as an international law instructor?"

"No, I transferred to the Judge Advocate General division, where I prosecuted criminal matters, represented the Navy in civil matters, and eventually served as a judge."

"And you gave that up to join the Coast Guard?"

"Not exactly. At the time, the Coast Guard didn't have an overt Counter-Intelligence unit, so my cover work was in the Coast Guard's Judge Advocate General corps. I continued to try cases and to preside over trials as a judge half-time while I spent the other half carrying out counter-intelligence activities."

"How did you come to be appointed Ambassador to the International Maritime Organization of the United Nations?"

"Before I got the job, the President, with the advice of the Secretary of State and of the Secretary of Defense, decided that the Coast Guard would be the appropriate governmental unit to represent the United States at the IMO. When my predecessor retired, the Commandant of the Coast Guard invited me to take his place."

"You said that senior captains who supervise command of more than two ships can be called Commodores. Over how many ships do you have command?"

"That's classified... but I *can* tell you that it's more than two."

"And from your earlier testimony, at least one of those vessels is a submarine, correct?"

"Yes."

"Commodore, do you have a longer resumé of your educational and military accomplishments?"

"Yes. But, as I told Mr. Stemler, I didn't think it was relevant for purposes of my testifying about the rescues of Mr. Stonebrook and Mrs. Muñoz."

"Showing you what is marked as Plaintiffs' Rebuttal Exhibit Number 1, is this your long-form resumé?"

"Yes it is."

"How long is it?"

"Well, it's eight pages because it includes books and articles that I've published as well as conferences where I've given speeches or made presentations."

Judge Mattson interposed, "Are you going to offer the exhibit, counsel?"

"Yes, Your Honor, as soon as Mr. Stemler has had a chance to look at it." He nodded his head, and Ted handed a copy to Stemler, who flipped through it and grudgingly said, barely above a whisper, "No objection."

"Plaintiffs' Rebuttal Exhibit Number 1 is received." Judge Mattson said it quietly.

The courtroom was dead silent, and Brindle milked the silence for as long as he thought reasonable and then said, "No further questions, Your Honor."

RE-CROSS

"Do you wish to conduct re-cross, Mr. Stemler?" asked the judge.

Stemler rubbed his forehead for a long moment. "Uh, ... yes, I think I will." He remained seated. "You did that on purpose, didn't you Commodore?"

"Did what, sir?"

"You deliberately declined to explain after answering 'yes' or 'no' to my questions about your rank and your knowledge of Arabic, about your not having attended the Coast Guard Academy, and about how you happened to learn the definition of 'relevance' from Black's Law Dictionary. You chose to string me out because you thought that by embarrassing *me* you could give the plaintiffs a leg up in this case, even if the facts were not in their favor. Is that how they do things in the Judge Advocate General Corps?"

Judge Mattson was on the verge of cutting Stemler off, but Brindle was sitting there with an almost-smirk on his face. She figured, correctly, that Brindle had no need to protect this witness, who obviously was very comfortable around a courtroom. She sat back.

Costaign looked directly at Stemler. "No, that isn't the normal procedure in the Judge Advocate General corps, either in the Navy or in the Coast Guard."

"Then why did you lead me on?"

"You don't want to know."

"Yes, I *do*. That's why I asked the question."

"All right, if you insist," replied Costaign. "In my years as a judge in the Judge Advocate General corps, I took umbrage at lawyers who were mean-spirited, especially those who bullied witnesses and cut them off in the middle of sentences when they didn't like the answers to their questions. I thought that that kind of behavior skated on the edge of unethical conduct. As I was sitting in the gallery yesterday, in civilian clothes, I saw how you treated plaintiffs' witnesses, and I was appalled. So, I decided to answer your questions but to wait for Re-direct to explain them."

Stemler was on his feet. "Objection. Move to strike as unresponsive."

"Mr. Stemler asked the question, Your Honor," Brindle said. "Commodore Costaign even gave Mr. Stemler an opportunity to withdraw it, but counsel persisted. Commodore Costaign's reply was appropriately and precisely responsive."

'Objection overruled," Judge Mattson said. "Commodore, you may step down. Court is in recess."

Chapter 51: Defendant's Witnesses

TRAXEL HAD AGREED TO A two-day break that Stemler requested so that his witnesses, Constantine Tsipras and Andreas Simitas could fly to Minneapolis and be ready to testify without jet-lag. Judge Mattson cautioned the jury not to discuss the case with anyone, including their fellow jurors.

After the two days off, and before the defense called the two *Hestia* witnesses, Traxel had asked, out of the presence of the jury, for permission to have actors testify as if they were Felix Benteen and Captain Eliopoulos. He explained that he would only ask questions that he had posed during the deposition and that the actors would merely answer as the deponents had.

"What would be the purpose?" the judge asked Traxel.

"Since neither Mr. Benteen nor the captain intends to appear at trial, we want to have a record of their testimony under oath."

"Any problem with that, Mr. Stemler."

Stemler was suspicious of Traxel's motives but, having read the deposition transcripts, he could not think of anything harmful. "None, Your Honor."

The Captain

Traxel had hired two actors from the Guthrie Theatre. The one playing a ship captain was rotund, unshaven, and appeared in a pea jacket and what looked like seafaring clothing.

Judge Mattson explained to the jury: "This man is *not* Captain Eliopoulos. He is an actor. The real captain is presently at sea. With the consent of Mr. Stemler, Mr. Traxel will ask him questions that he had asked at the captain's deposition, when Mr. Stemler was present, and the actor – playing the captain – will answer by saying or reading what the captain answered, under oath. There will be no questions from the defense because in depositions the attorney representing a deponent rarely asks questions, and Mr. Stemler asked none. Both Mr. Stemler and I will be following along with the transcript that the court reporter created to make sure that the actor's testimony follows word-for-word what the Captain actually said in his deposition."

Traxel began: "Captain, you have answered three consecutive questions with the answer, 'the *Hestia Etoupeia* company.' Who, specifically, at the company gave you orders?"

"It varied. Sometimes Alexis Mitsitakis, the Chief Financial Officer, communicated a budget for food and wages and supplies; sometimes Constantine Tsipras, the Operations Vice-President sent orders about the itinerary and the merchandise we were to carry; occasionally, Panagiotis Zolotas, the External Relations Vice-President, sent instructions about dealing with various local authorities and law enforcement; and once in a while, I received orders, or inquiries, anyway, from the Personnel Director, Andreas Simitas, about certain individuals who had requested to be placed as officers or supervisors under my command and if I knew anything about them."

"What were your standing orders about paying wages for crewmen who died while serving on board *Hestia* ships?"

"The standing order was to inform the finance department, so they could send money owed to the widows, but no one ever died on board ship while I have been captain."

"What about a man named Jesús López?"

"I would certainly remember a crew member whose first name was Jesús, but no one by that name ever served on *La Galissionière*."

"And what about a man named Francisco Quintana?"

"Never heard of him."

"Did you know the names of all the crew members, including deckhands on your ship?"

"Oh, yes, container vessels operate with crews of 20-25. So, I always learn, and insist that my officers learn, every man's name. We never had a Quintana or a Jesús López."

"Did you maintain a roster of crew members on board?"

"Of course."

"Would you send a copy of the roster of crew members on your last trip from the Canary Islands to Algiers, Algeria, to Mr. Stemler, so that he can forward it to me?"

"As soon as we finish a voyage, I send the roster back to the *Hestia* Personnel Department in Athens. So, I don't have it anymore."

"Well, could you, on the record, promise to obtain a copy and send it to Mr. Stemler?"

"No, I can't promise to obtain it. I can ask, but I don't have any power over the Personnel Department."

"Do you admit that you have not paid Mr. Arroyo/Fishkin for the work that he performed on the ship?"

"Mr. Arroyo is technically AWOL – he left the ship in Algiers and never returned. Other crewmen had to take over his duties, and we had to pay them overtime. So, it's the company's position, one with which I agree, that we owe Arroyo nothing."

"Have you had a chance to read Mr. Fishkin/Arroyo's deposition that Mr. Stemler took a couple of weeks ago?"

"Yes, I read it."

"Are there any matters in there with which you disagree?"

"Almost everything he said about *La Galissionière* is a pack of lies."

"Is it a lie that you kicked the four Moroccans off the ship because they complained that most of the meat served was pork and they had been promised food that adhered to Muslim dietary laws?"

"Yes, it's a damned lie. We never take on Moroccan crew members, in part because the few who speak Spanish speak it poorly, and in part because our budget requires that we mainly serve pork, and we can't afford to comply with Islamic dietary rules."

"Are you denying that you sexually abused Mahmoud Nimri?"

"Yes, I deny it.... because I never met anyone named Mahmoud Nimri, and we didn't have any Moroccans aboard *La Galissionière*."

Felix Benteen

That was it for the captain's testimony. The actor stepped down. "I call the actor playing Felix Benteen." A different actor came forward. He was 6'1," had an Errol Flynn moustache and a cleft in his chin.

The judge repeated her cautionary explanation about the actor and the testimony.

"What is the connection between Greenport Shipping and *Hestia Etoupeia*?"

"Greenport is merely an American subsidiary of a Greek corporation, *Hestia* Etoupeia, Greenport has neither authority, nor responsibility, and certainly not liability, for anything that happened on ships in the Eastern Hemisphere. In fact, Greenport's charter specifically limits the company's maritime activities to North America."

"Did you ever send orders to *Hestia*, or to any of the officers of the ships that service Europe or North Africa under *Hestia*'s umbrella?"

"No, never."

"How often do you correspond with *Hestia* officials?"

"Because of the language difficulty, correspondence between *Hestia* and Greenport consists almost entirely of inquiries from *Hestia* about budget targets, and financial statements which Greenport's CFO mailed to *Hestia*."

"Do you have any knowledge of the wages paid, working conditions, safety compliance, and food provisions on *La Galissionière*?"

"I would have no reason to know of those things, precisely because I work for a subsidiary here in America."

"My question, sir, is *not* whether you would ordinarily have a *reason* to know, but, rather, IF you *do* know about wages, working conditions, safety compliance, and food provisions, on *La Galissionière*?"

"No."

"Did anyone connected with *La Galissionière*, with *Hestia Etoupeia*, or any other source communicate anything to you about events that have taken place on *La Galissionière* in the last six months?"

"No."

"Has anyone communicated anything to you about Rocky Stonebrook, Julián Arroyo, or Pedro Fishkin?"

"I read the Complaint and saw Fishkin's name as a plaintiff and learned from that document that he used the name Julián Arroyo when he signed on to *La Galissionière*. The only other communication about him was in a conversation with my lawyer, and I know that you don't want to inquire about that."

"So that the record is complete, is it your testimony that other than the Complaint and discussions with your lawyer, you have not had, and have never seen or had, any letters, reports, phone calls, emails, text messages, telegrams from, or conversations with, *anyone* concerning events that have transpired on *La Galissionière*, or about Pedro Fishkin or Julián Arroyo?"

"Yes, that is my testimony."

Constantine Tsipras

Wentworth conducted the direct examination of Constantine Tsipras, the Operations Vice-President of *Hestia Etoupeia*. Through a Greek interpreter, Tsipras testifed that *Hestia* had a number of subsidiary companies in different parts of the world, including Greenport Shipping in the United States. He further testified that *Hestia*'s net worth was about $2.5 billion, but Greenport's net worth was only about $400,000 owing to a high amount of debt. He corroborated that Captain Eliopoulos was, indeed, currently commanding a ship in the Indian Ocean and added that Mr. Benteen, the owner of Greenport, was attending a mandatory meeting in Istanbul of the various owners of the *Hestia* subsidiaries.

On cross-examination, Traxel asked this question: "If Greenport were the parent company of *Hestia*, then its net worth would be at least $2.5 billion, is that correct?"

Tsipras laughed, almost avuncularly. "But it isn't."

"My question, sir, was *if* Greenport *were* Hestia's parent company, its net worth would then be more than $2.5 billion."

"That's a theoretical question."

"Yes. But since you are testifying about financial matters, I assume that your command of mathematics is such that you can answer the question."

Tsipras frowned. "Yes, theoretically, that is correct."

Addressing the judge, Traxel said, "Your Honor, I have no further questions for the witness at this time, but I ask that he be required to stay available in case we need to recall him."

"Mr. Stemler," the judge asked, "will you ensure that Mr. Tsipras remains available for the rest of the trial?"

"Uh, yes, Your Honor."

"Please call your next witness, Mr. Traxel."

When Tsipras stepped down, Traxel asked for a bench conference. He and Stemler approached. "If it's all right with Mr. Stemler, I'd like to call Ms. Marlo to the stand now."

Stemler was puzzled. "You said that you wanted to wait until after our *Hestia* witnesses."

"Yes, I did. But, if you don't mind, I think it would be easier for the jury if Ms. Marlo testified now, in between the two *Hestia* witnesses, because I'm going to be asking questions related to organizational matters on cross-examination."

"Well, Mr. Stemler?"

Stemler raised his arms in the surrender sign. "Okay."

They returned to their seats, and the judge explained to the jury that Mr. Traxel had requested that he be allowed to call one last witness before the second *Hestia* officer testified and that Mr. Stemler had consented.

"You may call your next witness, Mr. Traxel."

Brindle stood. "I call Lauren Marlo to the stand." Brindle's questions and her testimony were virtually word-for-word the exact same questions and testimony as at the Summary Judgment motion hearing. When Brindle offered the exhibits and their translations, Judge Mattson said: "I provisionally received these exhibits during the pre-trial hearing, subject to defense counsel's right to challenge the translations. Mr. Stemler, you have had time between that hearing and the trial to have the translations verified. Do you have a challenge to any of them?"

Stemler sighed, a little too loudly. "No, Your Honor."

"Then they are received into evidence today. The court reporter will re-mark them for this trial."

The questioning about the chart intentionally took longer, so that the jury could absorb the testimony and the relationship among the corporate entities. Rehmel noticed that practically all the jurors were leaning forward to scrutinize the chart.

"Your Honor," asked Brindle, "we have made copies of the chart – may I distribute copies to the jury, so they don't have to squint to read it?"

"Mr. Stemler?"

Stemler desperately tried to think of a good reason for opposing the request. Finding none, and figuring the dotted line on the chart to be helpful to the defense, he said, "No objection." Bruner handed a copy of the chart to each of the jurors.

Brindle chose to steal Stemler's thunder. "Ms. Marlo, I notice that on the chart you have drawn thick lines from Greenport Shipping to the Mexican company, from the Mexican company to the French company, and from the French company to the Italian company. However, you have only a dotted line from the Italian company to *Hestia Etoupeia*. Why is that?"

"I was trying to be as objective as possible. I found hard evidence of ownership between Greenport and the *Marina Mercante Mexicana*, between *Marina Mercante Mexicana* and *Porte Conteneurs Francais*, and between *Porte Conteneurs Francais* and *Navigazione Comercial Italiano*. However, because the only connection between *Navigazione Comercial Italiano* and *Hestia Etoupeia* was that they had identical Boards of Directors, I thought that my chart should reflect the difference in the level of evidence." She not only had taken away the defendant's major point on cross-examination, but she had come across to the jury as fair-minded.

Stemler decided to let Emily Cadwalader do the cross-examination, ostensibly because it would give her a chance to get some trial experience under her belt but, actually, because he didn't have much to ask.

"Ms. Marlo," Cadwalader began, clearly nervous at her first foray into courtroom action, "are you a law student?"

"No."

"Isn't it true that you told me in Miami that you were starting law school?"

Brindle: "Objection. Either Ms. Cadwalader is going to be an attorney or a witness, but she can't be both. The only possible reason for asking that question is if Ms. Cadwalader intends to testify and attempt to contradict Ms. Marlo."

"Ms. Cadwalader," asked Judge Mattson, "do you intend to testify as well as to cross-examine the witness?"

"Umm, no, Your Honor."

"Then can you provide the Court with a proffer as to where this line of questioning is going?"

"Er, it was an attempt to test the witness's credibility."

"And how did you plan to challenge it, using this question?"

"I was going to ...umm... I was just planning to, er, press the witness on the point."

"Objection is sustained. Move on."

Clearly rattled, Cadwalader checked the notes on the yellow pad that she was holding and then asked, "Where did you obtain these documents?"

"Some from the IMO, some on-line, some from commercial registration offices in Mexico City, Paris, and Rome."

"And you did say, did you not, that the dotted line between the Italian company and *Hestia* represented a lower level of evidence?"

"That's correct."

"You said that you wanted to be objective, but you are employed by the Stonebrook detective agency, aren't you?"

"Yes."

"And Mr. Stonebrook's *real* name is Pedro Fishkin, isn't that right?"

"Pedro Fishkin is the name his parents gave him. Rocky Stonebrook is his professional name. Both are 'real.'"

"And Mr. Fishkin, or Stonebrook, is a plaintiff in this case, true?"

"Yes,"

"So, you would indirectly benefit if the jury awarded him money, isn't that correct?"

"I don't think that I have any right to money that he is awarded because allies of the defendants amputated his finger; but I sure hope that I get a bonus for the careful work I did in ferreting out information about the corporate veils."

"When you say 'corporate veils,' what do you mean?"

"It's pretty obvious that Greenport owns *Hestia*, and that the other three companies are fig-leafs to conceal that relationship."

"When you say 'obvious,' you mean that that's what *you* have concluded, true?"

"Correct. But my conclusions are the result of the analysis of data."

"Your analysis, right?" She said it so fast that it sounded like "urinalysis," and a couple of the jurors giggled.

"Analysis that I was trained in college to use when examining data."

"And where did you attend college?"

"Case Western University in Cleveland."

Cadwalader flipped through pages of her yellow pad but could find nothing else to ask.

"No more questions."

"Any re-direct, Mr. Brindle?"

"No, Your Honor. "

Chapter 52: Andreas Simitas

STEMLER ROSE. "I CALL ANDREAS Simitas to the stand."

Personnel Director Andreas Simitas was quite competent in English and did not need a translator. After inquiring about his background and his duties, Stemler proceeded: "Mr. Simitas, do you maintain the records of all the crew members who work on *Hestia* ships?"

"Yes, sir. Every ship is required to send the names of every crewman, how he was recruited, and what his background is."

"Why is that necessary?"

"We want to make sure that officers are not hiring their brothers-in-law or their friends who are not qualified."

"Are there posted criteria for employment?"

"They are not posted, but the Third Mate on every ship is assigned the duty of checking on each attempted hire, and all of them know that the expectation is for prior experience on ships or boats or, in the case of stewards, experience in serving food."

"Are there any *dis*qualifications besides lack of experience?"

"If they have poor records on other ships with discipline or work ethic. Also, if they can't speak the language of the ship. On *La Galissionière*, the language is Spanish, so we don't let anyone on who can't speak and understand Spanish."

"There was some testimony by Mr. Fishkin about some Moroccans being on board *La Galissioniere*. Is that true?"

"No, it is not. At your request, I double-checked the crew list for *La Galissionière* when Mr. Fishkin was aboard, posing as Julián Arroyo. There were no Moroccans. In fact, because of our experience with North Africans on other ships, all of whom spoke Arabic, and some of whom could maybe get along in French, but almost none of them could speak Spanish, we have a policy against taking on North Africans. Where they had signed on, on previous voyages, it was constantly a problem. They couldn't understand simple commands, and when there was an emergency, like a storm, or lifeboat drills, or someone in danger, they couldn't react fast. So, we had a rule that no North Africans could be hired unless they passed a Spanish language test."

"What happens if a crew member dies while on board a *Hestia* ship?"

"It rarely happens because they have to pass a physical to be employed, but on the only occasions that I can recall in the past ten years, we have sent the widows the amount of money which the deceased would have earned if they had not died in the middle of their contract."

"Were there any deaths on *La Galissionière?*"

"None."

"How do you know?"

"The Third Mate submits a report at the end of each voyage, indicating any deaths or injuries and if any of the crew departed from the ship while in port and didn't come back."

"What did the Third Mate's report say about Mr. Fishkin, alias Mr. Arroyo?"

"It said that he had been recommended by a screening outfit in the Canary Islands, that he lied about his previous experience, that he had assaulted his supervisor, had punched out the boatswain, and that he left in Algiers and never came back."

"At my request, did you review the roster on the shp when Mr. Delgadinho and Mr. Muñoz were employees on *La Galissionière?*"

"Yes, I did."

"Did that refresh your recollection from some months ago?"

"It did. One of them signed on in the Azores, and the other in the Canary Islands.

One was employed as a mess steward, but because of poor performance was demoted to deckhand. They were both poor workers, complainers, and obviously unhappy."

"This is all from the Third Mate's report?"

"Yes, I was not on the ship myself."

"And what did the Third Mate say in his report about why these two men left the ship early?"

"They asked to be let off when the ship was near the west coast of Wales."

"Is that normal for *Hestia* ships – to allows crew members to leave upon request in the middle of the ocean?"

"No, it's not normal, but the First Mate had radioed our office. These two characters were troublemakers, were not carrying their load, and it was easier to honor their request than to deal with the morale problem that their laziness and whining had been causing."

"Didn't that leave a gap in the deckhand crew?"

"It did. We had to hire on two replacements in Scotland."

"Did *Hestia* pay those men for the time they had worked?"

"We sent the money to their homes, minus the cost of the lifeboat they took."

"Do you know if the families actually received the money?"

"I just know that somebody cashed the checks."

"No further questions, Your Honor."

CROSS EXAMINATION

Without prompting from the court, Brindle began his cross examination after turning the overhead projector back on with Lauren's chart of the various corporate entities. "Mr. Simitas, is the Personnel Director's position a political appointment or a merit selection?"

Simitas puffed up his chest. "It is *not* political. I was hired based on qualifications."

"What were the qualities that you think won you the job?"

"I had experience in what you Americans call 'Human Resources.' I had been a crew member on boats, so I knew my way around ships, and I had good recommendations from previous employers for competence and efficiency."

"Does the Personnel Director have to have a good memory?"

"Indeed. It is an essential skill."

"Who exactly hired you?"

"The President of *Hestia*."

"What's his name?"

"Fotis Bouros."

"And do you and Mr. Tsipras and the Chief Financial Officer, Mr. Alexis Mitsitakis, and the External Affairs VP, Panagiotis Zolotas, as well as Mr. Bouros all office together in Athens?"

"Well, Mr. Tsipras and Mr. Mitsitakis and Mr. Zolotas and I all have offices in the same suite. President Bouros has other companies in which he's involved, and so he travels a lot and is not in the office frequently."

"Do you have tenure, Mr. Simitas, or are you an employee-at-will?"

"There is no tenure. We can all be fired if we don't perform well. But all the officers work very hard and are efficient. That's why *Hestia* has a net worth of $2.5 billion dollars."

"Well, who could fire you?"

"Either the President or the Board of Directors."

"Is anyone in charge when Mr. Bouros is not around?"

"We all work together very well, and we have our respective assignments, We don't need anybody to be acting in charge."

"Is it a fair statement that the Board of Directors sets policy for the staff?"

"Of course."

"Who are the members of the Board of Directors of *Hestia*?"

Twisting in his chair, Simitas answered, "I'm trying to remember all their names."

"You told us that a good memory was an essential skill for a Personnel Director. Surely, you can remember the names of your bosses on the Board of Directors."

Simitas brought out a handkerchief and wiped the sweat off his forehead. "I am blanking out here. Maybe the names will come to me soon."

"Isn't it the case, Mr. Simitas, that you, yourself, are a member of the Board of Directors?"

As if a lightbulb suddenly went on, he answered, "Ah, yes, now I recall – there are so many entities and subsidiaries, even with my prodigious memory, I sometimes have to consult documents to keep them all straight."

"Would a document help you remember?"

"Yes, but I didn't bring any with me."

"That's okay. I have one." Brindle turned to Marlo, who, as pre-arranged, handed him three copies. He gave one to Stemler, one to the court reporter to mark as an Exhibit, and one to put on the overhead projector. "Showing you what has been marked as Plaintiffs' Exhibit 28, do you recognize the document as a list of members of the *Hestia* Board of Directors?"

"Where did you get this?" Simitas blurted out.

"No, Mr. Simitas, in court the lawyers ask the questions, and the witnesses answer them, truthfully. Is Exhibit 28 a list of the Board of Directors?"

"Yes." His answer was grudging, something no juror missed.

"I offer Plaintiffs' Exhibit 28, Your Honor."

Stemler said, "May we know where Plaintiffs obtained this document?"

"It shouldn't matter, Your Honor," replied Brindle, "the witness has identified the document as genuine."

"The exhibit is received. You may proceed, counsel."

"It shows that you are a member, does it not?"

"Yes."

"And let's look at the rest of the list. What is the next name?"

"Alexis Mitsitakis."

"And he is the Chief Financial Officer, isn't that right?"

"Yes."

"The next name?"

"Panagiotis Zolotas."

"And he is the External Affairs Vice-President, isn't he?"

"Yes."

"And the next name is Constantine Tsipras, isn't that right?"

"Yes."

"And he is the Operations Vice-President and the witness here with you today, right?"

"Yes."

"And the final name is Fotis Bouros, the President, isn't that correct?"

"Yes."

"So, the five key staff members are also the members of the Board of Directors?"

"Yes."

"You are your own bosses, aren't you?"

"Well, this is common in Greece for the Board and the officers to be the same."

"How often does the Board meet?"

"Whenever the President calls a meeting."

"Is that likely to be monthly, quarterly, semi-annually, annually, what?"

"It varies. Generally, quarterly, but it could be more frequent or less frequent."

"Does the Board always meet in Athens?"

"No, we like to inspect the ships that we own and that our subsidiaries own, so we have Board meetings all over the world."

"And when was the last meeting the Board had?"

"About two months ago, in Athens."

"And the one before that?"

"Maybe three months prior to that one, in Rome, if I remember correctly."

"Are you on any other boards of directors, Mr. Simitas?"

"I am on several committees and boards and international exchanges. It's part of my job."

"Can you give us a list of those committees and boards, and exchanges?"

"Not without a document to review."

"All right." Turning to Marlo, who handed him another packet of three, Brindle gave one to Stemler, one to the court reporter to mark, and put one on the overhead projector. "Perhaps this will help you recall. Showing you what's been marked as Plaintiffs' Exhibit 29, can you identify the document?"

"It is a list of the Board of Directors of *Navigazione Comerciale Italiano*."

"That's the name of the Italian company identified by Ms. Marlo on her chart, isn't that correct?"

"Yes."

"Aren't the members of the Board of Directors exactly the same five fellows, including you, as the members of the *Hestia* company?"

"Yes."

"I offer Plaintiffs' Exhibit 29."

"I am going to interpose an objection here, Your Honor," said Stemler. "None of these exhibits was among those that plaintiffs told defendants and the court that they intended to offer."

"They are rebuttal exhibits, Your Honor," said Brindle. "In each case, the witness has said that he couldn't remember who was on either Board of Directors without a document to remind him, but he didn't have the document with him. Then, when we supplied the document, it refreshed his recollection."

"Objection overruled. Plaintiffs' Exhibit 29 is received."

"And the last Board meeting of the Italian company was five months ago, in Rome, on the very same day that the Board of Directors of *Hestia* met, isn't that so."

"I'm trying to remember. I'm not sure."

"Isn't it a fact that you met in the same building, in the same room?"

"Probably."

"Not probably, Mr. Simitas. Please apply that prodigious memory of yours. You met on the same day in the same room in the same building in the same city, didn't you?"

"Yes."

"Now, you were sitting in the gallery when Ms. Marlo introduced documents that showed that the Italian company was in fact owned by the French company, *Porte Conteneurs Francais*, weren't you?"

"Yes."

"Do you acknowledge that the French company owns the Italian company?"

"Yes."

"And are you a member of the Board of Directors of the French company?"

"I believe that's one of the boards on which I sit."

"I want you to be sure, Mr. Simitas." Turning again to Marlo, he retrieved the packet and distributed copies as he had with the other two. "Showing you what's been marked as Plaintiffs' Exhibit 30. Is this a list of the Board of Directors of the French company?"

"Yes."

"The same five gentlemen who make up the Board of *Hestia* and of the Board of the Italian company. Isn't that correct?"

"Yes."

"Except that the French company requires an individual owner as well, isn't that right?"

"Knowing the laws of all the countries where we have ships is not in the job description of the Personnel Director."

"But you are aware that Felix Benteen is listed as the co-owner, are you not?"

"I think that's right."

"I offer Plaintiffs' Exhibit 30."

The judge looked at Stemler, who just shook his head. "Hearing no objection, plaintiffs' Exhibit Number 30 is received."

Brindle went through the same routine with the Mexican company and with Greenport Shipping. Simitas admitted that all five companies had the exact same members on their respective Boards of Directors, that they coincidentally met on the same day in the same city.

"Who presides at these Board meetings?"

"The President."

"Can you describe President Bouros for the jury?"

"Describe him?"

"Yes."

"He's handsome, very smart, speaks English and Greek, and some Spanish; he...."

"How about a physical description?"

"I'd say about 6'1," a long nose, brown eyes, sideburns, a little cleft in his chin, a narrow moustache."

"Very good, Mr. Simitas. Let me show you a photograph." This time he turned to Ted Bruner, who handed him three copies of a photo. After marking the photograph as an exhibit, he showed it to Simitas. "Is this a photo of President Bouros?"

"Yes."

"I offer Plaintiffs Exhibit 31."

Looking at Stemler, who said nothing, the judge announced, "It is received."

"Now, Mr. Simitas, please describe Felix Benteen, the CEO of Greenport Shipping."

Simitas looked like he was about to have a heart attack. "I'm not sure that I can. I don't see him very often."

"If he is the co-owner of the French company, doesn't he attend the meetings of the French company's board of directors?"

"Occasionally."

"And none of these companies seems to have a General Counsel. Why is that?"

"I never gave it much thought since I don't have to deal with legal issues."

"Isn't it true that Mr. Benteen is a lawyer and functions as the General Counsel?"

"That's possible. You'd have to ask the External Affairs Vice-President about that."

"Are you able to dredge up a description of Mr. Benteen, now that you've thought about it?"

"I'm trying to remember him."

"If I said, 6'1," long nose, brown eyes, cleft chin, narrow moustache, does that refresh your recollection?"

Simitas turned the color of vermillion. "NO!" he shouted. "He's different."

"Okay, describe him."

"Well, he's maybe 5'10," blue eyes, glasses, has a beard."

"Mr. Simitas, after you step down, I'm going to call as a rebuttal witness the person who took the photograph that you identified as the photo of Fotis Bouros. That witness will testify that he took the photo in New York at Mr. Benteen's deposition, and it was of Mr. Benteen. Now, I want to give you a chance to remove any taint of perjury. Isn't it true that Felix Benteen and Fotis Bouros are the same person?"

Simitas put both hands on his face and wheezed. Finally, he answered, "Yes."

"No further questions, but I offer Plaintiffs' Exhibit 31."

"Hearing no objection from defense counsel, Exhibit 31 is received."

Stemler prudently decided not to conduct any re-direct. He knew that Simitas was beyond rehabilitation.

"Mr. Stemler, do you have any other witnesses?"

"No, Your Honor."

"Mr. Traxel, have plaintiffs rested?"

"We have a rebuttal witness who will be ready to testify tomorrow morning."

"I'll see counsel in chambers. Court is adjourned until tomorrow morning."

Chapter 53: In Chambers

"Who is this rebuttal witness, Mr. Traxel?"

"Mahmoud Nimri."

"Has he arrived?"

"Not yet."

"Can we have a proffer about his testimony?" asked Stemler.

"Yes," replied Traxel. "He will testify that he was a deckhand on *La Galissionière,* that the captain sexually abused him, and that he was being held captive on the ship until Stonebrook/Fishkin got him off."

The judge spoke. "My concern is about time. We already took two days off for the witnesses from Greece. I'm not inclined to take another break-day. So, what do we do if your witness doesn't make it by tomorrow morning?"

"I propose that the Court read its instructions to the jury before closing arguments and explain that before the jurors retire they get to hear one attorney for each side make a closing argument in which they hope to persuade the jury. If Mr. Nimri arrives before my closing argument, then we'll put him on before my closing. If he doesn't make it here, then he won't get to testify."

"I'm opposed to that plan," Stemler interposed. "The normal procedure is for the Court to read its instructions to the jury *after* both closing arguments, and I shouldn't be expected to make my closing before we hear from this putative, rebuttal witness."

Traxel replied before the Judge could rule. "You already know what he's going to say, and you will have the opportunity to cross-examine him. I am willing to let you supplement your closing to say anything you want about Nimri's testimony and cross-examination."

"I still formally object."

"Well, Mr. Stemler," inquired Judge Mattson, you requested two days of break so that your witnesses could get here and even overcome jet lag. What alternative would you offer except to take another day off, or to apply the Traxel Plan?"

"Tomorrow's Friday. We could postpone everything until Monday. If the witness isn't here by then, he doesn't testify."

Traxel said, "Why don't we be really creative: Let the jury spend Friday morning examining the exhibits that have been admitted. That way when we make our closing arguments, they will have a context."

"Oh, no. That absolutely breaks the rubber band of elasticity. I would oppose that."

"Well," the judge said, "I actually think that in *every* civil trial, that would be a good idea. However, I'm not going to institute it here over the objection of either attorney, in this case, defense counsel. But I do think that plaintiffs deserve the same consideration that defendant got about a continuance for overseas witnesses. So, I'm going to let Mr. Stemler and his colleagues confer and then make a choice: Either accept the Traxler Plan, or allow the jurors to review the exhibits on Friday and have the closing arguments and possible testimony on Monday.

So, that there's no possibility of *ex parte* communication, I'm going to ask the defense counsel to go into the courtroom, and the plaintiffs' attorneys to stand out in the hall. When defendants are ready, we'll come back here."

The plaintiffs' attorneys all got up and left. In the courtroom, Stemler asked his colleagues for advice. "You know," Nelson began, "I think the judge is right. It does make a lot of sense to let the jurors review the documentary evidence on Friday, so they won't have to plow through it while they're trying to reach a verdict."

Cadwalader said, "Uh, we probably would not be happy if the Moroccan kid gets to testify. If we take the Traxel Plan, then if he's not here by tomorrow at noon, the jury will never hear him."

Wentworth demurred. "I think that you ought to go back in there and decline to make this Hobson's choice. It will give us another hook when we appeal."

"So," answered Stemler, "you think we're going to lose, and you're already planning the appeal?"

"I'm just being realistic, Brian."

Stemler rubbed the back of his neck and frowned. "I think we still have a chance on liability. For the record, I'll say that I don't like either option, but if we're forced to choose the lesser of two evils, we'll do what

Emily suggests and take the Traxler Plan in hopes that the Moroccan kid doesn't get here by tomorrow."

They went back in, and that's what Stemler said. "All right," said Judge Mattson. "When do you want to work on the Verdict form?"

"How about this evening?" asked Traxel.

"We're frankly exhausted, Judge," said Stemler. "Why doesn't each set of lawyers come up with a proposed Verdict Form tonight, and tomorrow we can all get here at, say, 8:30, and you can help us merge the proposed forms?"

Wanting to give Stemler at least one procedural victory, Judge Mattson said, "That's a very good idea. Go home, all of you, work on your proposed Verdict Forms, get some rest, and come back tomorrow at 8:30."

Chapter 54: Temara, Morocco

THE DAY BEFORE, RIGHT AFTER Stonebrook had left for court, Donna called Thurman Dixon. "Thurman, this is Frederika Roxon. Is our conversation on this line private?"

"Well, it's private, but I cannot guarantee that it's secure. So, let's be discreet. What can I do for you?"

"First of all, I haven't had a chance to tell you how absolutely thrilled I am about how you handled the...uh... Canaries. You deserve whatever special award the ...uh, Fig Newton Society reserves for outstanding performances. As the newest members of the...er, Society, you and I have been ripping up old traditions. Your proposal about sending an umpire to Wyoming two years ago saved my fiancé's life. And now your... Canary work helped two stranded sailors who deserve compensation. Thirdly, maybe we've inadvertently invented a new line of work for the Fig Newton Society – rescues. Our members are all resourceful, smart, and think outside the box."

"Maybe so. I have to admit it was a fun gig."

"Good. Because in addition to thanking you, I'm calling to extend the favor on an emergency basis. Of course, I don't know what your court schedule is there in New Jersey, but I need to get a 17-year-old boy out of Morocco and back to the Twin Cities by Friday morning.

My plan is that we two go together."

"Your plan, eh? Why don't you do it yourself this time. You're not dancing, are you?"

"No, but given Morocco's sub-culture, a woman can't just waltz in alone. Besides I don't know Portuguese."

"Fred, they don't speak Portuguese in Morocco; they speak Arabic."

"I know, Thurman. But the kid spent his childhood in Portugal while his father worked there, so he knows Portuguese. My only alternative is to find some bilingual Arabic-English person to go with me, and I have no leads, no idea, and the clock is ticking." Dixon was silent for a while, and Donna wisely chose not to say anything else.

"Is this a paying gig?"

"Yes, just not as much as for...figs."

"Understood. When would we leave?"

"I'll get a travel agency here to whomp up a couple of tickets, yours from Philadelphia, mine from Cleveland, and we'll rendezvous in Madrid and fly from there to Rabat. I don't think that Morocco is as bad about women driving as Saudi Arabia, but why don't you call a rental car agency in Rabat, and get us a car in one of your names. Meanwhile, I'll get someone to draft a letter in Arabic for the father to give permission for the boy to travel with us; and I have a contact here in Minneapolis, where I am now, to grease the wheels for the kid to zip through customs. Also, I need you to find somebody who can forge a passport for the kid."

"And we're going to do all this in three days?"

"I hope it's *fewer*. You and I will meet in Madrid tomorrow, get to Rabat the day after, drive to the kid's village, convince the father, grab the son, zoom back to Rabat, fly to Madrid and to Minneapolis, dropping you off in Philly."

"Wow! Try *not* to get a return flight into any of the New York airports. I don't care how much clout your contact's friend has, we would not be able to get the boy through customs very fast in either Newark, Kennedy, or LaGuardia."

"Okay," she replied. "When you want a favor, even if it involves my swimming across the Atlantic Ocean, I'm going to say 'yes.'"

Donna actually managed to find someone who drafted the letter of permission in Arabic and English, got Pastor Elizabeth to dip into her political well one more time, and obtained the plane tickets for Dixon and her and for Nimri. She even bought a *hijab* to wear in Morocco.

All the connections worked, even though the plane over the Atlantic was an all-nighter, and the plane from Madrid to Rabat was at 7:00 a.m. They rented the car and drove to Temara.

Finding the Nimri home was not difficult because the village was fairly small, and the second person they asked knew of the Nimri family.

When they came to the Nimris' home, however, there was a language barrier. Mrs. Nimri answered, and she only spoke Arabic. Dixon tried Portuguese, but, although the lady had spent the same amount of time in Portugal as had her son, the boy learned Portuguese in school whereas the woman mainly spoke to other Moroccan women and had learned only a few Portuguese expressions. Donna said, "Let me try, Thurman." She turned to the woman: "Mahmoud, Mahmoud."

The woman was uncertain. Here was a dark-skinned man speaking Portuguese and an Asian-looking woman, who seemed to be speaking English, asking for her son. She had temporarily lost him once before when the ship recruiter came by, so she was wary. She closed the door and went inside. After a few minutes, she came back with Mahmoud.

[TRANSLATION FROM THE PORTUGUESE]: "May we come in?" Dixon asked.

"Who are you?"

"We are friends of Julián Arroyo. He needs your help."

"Who is the woman?"

"She is his fiancée. I am a work colleague of the woman."

Mahmoud looked from one to the other. "How do I know that you tell the truth. Another man came by some months ago, saying that he was a recruiter for a ship. I went, and it was the worst mistake of my life."

Donna lifted the medallion from her neck and showed it Mahmoud. He grabbed his chest. "How did you get this?"

"Julián lent it to me precisely so that I could prove to you that we are friends. He wants it back though because he said that it was a gift from you in *Casa Blanca* after your terrible experience on *La Galissionière*." Dixon translated it into Portuguese, and Mahmoud kissed the medallion.

"Yes, it is from him. You may take it back to Julián because it *was* a gift. How can I help?"

"We have an airplane ticket for you to fly to the United States with us and testify in a court trial."

"I have never traveled on a plane, and I have never been in a court, and I don't have any papers to leave the country."

"How did you get on the ship?"

"They don't seem to need papers to work on a ship."

"Well, we have a passport for you. I shall take a photo of you now and put it on this IPad, which has a handy little printer, and if you have some glue, we'll paste it in. Go explain to your mother, and then pack. We leave right away. Also, please send a brother or sister to get your father."

"I don't have a suitcase like I saw other deckhands have on the ship. I only have a small bag. The other one I had is still on *La Galissionière*."

"We brought one with us for you," and he handed the boy a suitcase.

They heard the boy speaking Arabic. The mother screamed, but a younger sister came running out the front door to find her father.

When the father arrived, Mahmoud had packed. The parents sat in their living room, listening, but the mother understood nothing because Dixon and the father conversed in Portuguese. Even though Dixon knew the clock was ticking, he found the inner patience to speak slowly and to act as if they had all the time in the world.

Finally, the father said: "I will sign, and I will let Mahmoud go. He says that he is going to help the man who saved his life. So, we repay the debt."

Donna said, "Please translate Thurman: 'We have an airplane ticket for Mahmoud, and we shall feed him while he is in the United States. He will return next week at the latest and will arrive at the Rabat airport. Is there a taxi from Rabat to Temara?'"

After Dixon translated, the father answered, "Yes, but it is very expensive, about 250 *dirhams*."

"How much is that in dollars, Thurman?"

"The exchange rate is about 10 *dirhams* to a dollar, so that would be $25."

"We will arrange for enough money to be left at the Iberia airlines counter for Mahmoud when he returns from Madrid. He can take a cab home."

Mahmoud gave his parents and his sister big hugs and then got into the car. They had no trouble getting to Madrid; however, even though Donna booked a flight that would land in Detroit, instead of New York, there was still some hassle at Customs in Madrid. It was the middle of the night and too late to call Elizabeth. Dixon, speakingSpanish, showed an I.D. card that he was a judge and asked to speak to a Spanish judge. The officer found a supervisor, who examined the ID card.

[TRANSLATION:] "This ID is different from your passport. Why?"

"I am on a special judicial mission that requires secrecy. This boy needs to testify in court in the United States tomorrow. I intend to let the President of the Supreme Court of Spain, Juez Carlos Lesmes, know that you were very helpful if you are... and to tell him who was *not* helpful if you are not." He conspicuously wrote down the officer's name.

The customs officers, whose eyes had doubled in size when Thurman mentioned the name of the Chief Justice, conferred briefly and then let them through.

Once airborne, Donna said, with Dixon translating, "Mahmoud, it is important that you sleep on the plane because you have to be alert tomorrow."

"But what will I say?"

"Arroyo's lawyer will ask you questions about what happened on *La Galissionière*. Just tell the truth. Then a different lawyer, one who works for the shipping company, may ask you questions too. He may try to trick you. Again, just tell the truth."

"I don't know if I can sleep."

"Try." She turned off the light.

In Detroit, the Assistant A.G. had apparently made a call. They had no trouble getting through customs there. They bade farewell to Dixon, who flew back east to Philadelphia.

Chapter 55: Back In Minneapolis

ALTHOUGH DONNA AND MAHMOUD DID not have a language in common, they found ways to communicate and to build a bond. They made it to Minneapolis by 11:00 a.m. on Friday and Donna called Rocky. He left the courtroom and went out into the hallway when his cell phone buzzed. Donna told him that they were at the airport and were taking the metro to downtown and would get off at the courthouse.

Stonebrook immediately told Traxel. At 8:30 that morning, the attorneys and the judge had had a conference about the Verdict Form, but it took a little over an hour and a half to reach an agreement and put it on the record. It included the adverse inference that the jurors could construe from the absence of Greenport's CEO, the ship captain, and the three Mates. The attorneys also formally stipulated to seven jurors since the napper had stayed awake the whole time.

The Court reconvened at 11:00 o'clock, and the judge explained that she would read the instructions and then make a written copy available in the jury room which the jurors could consult if they had any questions about the applicable law. She read the instructions slowly, ...so that they would absorb, thought Traxel, ...and intentionally to delay, thought Stemler.

After a break, Stemler gave his closing argument: It was a lot shorter than his usual closing arguments: "Ladies and Gentlemen of the jury. Thank you for your rapt attention to this long trial. We have heard the testimony of several witnesses, and almost all of you took notes, so that you have something to remind you of important things you heard. I have no doubt that Mr. Muñoz and Mr. Delgadinho underwent a lot of difficulty while working on *La Galissionière.* "They seemed credible. I feel as bad as you do that Mr. Fishkin lost one of his fingers while checking out the stories of the other two plaintiffs.

"However, as you just heard the judge explain, the first question on the Verdict Form is the following: 'Is Greenport Shipping liable for any damages suffered by the plaintiffs?'

"If you answer 'no' to that question, there is nothing more to do. Now, I know that you may be tempted to say 'yes' just so that you can award damages to the plaintiffs, for whom I would guess that you feel a lot of sympathy. But your job is to apply the law to the facts. Put aside, for a moment, how you may feel about the plaintiffs having gotten a raw deal. The key question, though, is who should pay?

"The defendant is Greenport Shipping, headquartered in New York, whose ships only ply the sea in and around the United States and Central America. Mr. Tsipras testified that the company's net worth is about $400,000. When Mr. Traxel speaks to you, he will want you to decide that Greenport owns *Hestia*, which has deep pockets, and that, therefore, you should make Greenport disgorge geysers of cash.

"But what *evidence* is there of that ownership? The best that plaintiffs could do was to demonstrate that the Boards of Directors are interlocking. That is true of corporate America and corporate Greece and corporate Europe. People who own companies generally want people on their Boards of Directors who are knowledgeable about the industry. If you ran a company that owned cattle ranches, would you put vegetarians on the Board, or civil servants who are comfortable with bureaucracy but who have no experience in business? Of course not. You'd want people who were familiar with what goes on in the cattle business.

"Container ship companies are complicated and expensive operations. So, of course you want board members who understand how the business operates. Naturally, a number of companies want the same people sitting on their boards. The fact that five companies in five different countries share board members is not proof that any one owns another. The only testimony that you have concerning the relationship between *Hestia* and Greenport is three-fold: (1) the deposition of Felix Benteen, (2) the live testimony of Mr. Tsipras, and (3) the live testimony of Mr. Simitas. All three testified that Greenport is merely a subsidiary of *Hestia*.

"Remember, the foremost function of this jury is to decide if the *named* defendant should pay for whatever plaintiffs have suffered. You don't really have the power to impose liability on some *other* corporation that the plaintiffs *might* have sued but chose not to. Regardless of any emotional tug to reward plaintiffs, this is not therapy; rather, you jurors are participants in a court of law. The law is that only a defendant whose employees or agents or contractors did something wrong should be required to pay. Greenport's employees, agents, and contractors did nothing to hurt, harm, or injure any of the plaintiffs.

"Accordingly, if you apply the law objectively, you will answer the first question on the Verdict Form in the negative and, thereby, fulfill your constitutional duty. Thank you."

"It is now 11:40," said the judge. "We'll recess for lunch. Please be back by 1:00 p.m."

After the jurors had trooped out, Wentworth and Nelson shook hands with Stemler, congratulating him on his "outstanding" closing argument. The judge had been conferring with her clerk at the bench and was about to go to her chambers when Donna and Mahmoud came rushing in to the courtroom.

"Here he is!" Donna said, to no one in particular.

Judge Mattson beckoned Stemler and Traxel to the bench. "Is that Mr. Nimri?"

"I believe so, Your Honor," answered Traxel.

"If he's from Morocco, his native language is Arabic. We don't have an Arabic interpreter available here in the Hennepin County courthouse."

Traxel answered, "That's all right, Your Honor, he speaks Portuguese. Please ask the Portuguese interpreter to translate."

"Very well. He's on at 1:00 p.m."

Over the recess, Rehmel called someone at the law firm to ferry in some sandwiches, and Stonebrook translated while Traxel prepped Nimri with questions in the law firm's conference room in preparation for his upcoming testimony. At 1:00, the jurors filed back to their seats, and the judge called the court to order. "Call your rebuttal witness, Mr. Traxel."

"I call Mahmoud Nimri to the stand." Nimri went up to the witness chair, and before he sat down, he turned and looked, wide-eyed at the jurors.

"Where do you live, Mr. Nimri?"

[**IN TRANSLATION**]: "In Temara, Morocco."

"How old are you, sir?"

"I am 17 ½."

"Have you ever worked on a ship?"

"Yes. *La Galissionière*."

"How were you recruited?"

"A man came to our village and bought five of us some clothing and food and got a few of the older fellows to agree to go with him for jobs on ships. He invited me to ride in his car to Rabat, the capital, when he took my friends. When we arrived in Rabat, he said that I had to work off the price of the clothes and the food by being a deckhand on *La Galissionière*."

"Had you ever been a deckhand before?"

"No, I never was on a ship before."

"You are testifying in Portuguese. How do you know Portuguese?"

"When I was of elementary school age, my father took a job on the wharf in the Algarve section of southern Portugal. My sister and I went to school there and learned Portuguese that way."

"Were you the only Moroccan on *La Galissionière*?"

"No, there were three others, and we were all put in the same cabin."

"What was the language of the ship?"

"Spanish."

"Did any of the four of you speak Spanish?"

"One man, Hamdi, understood some Spanish, but he didn't speak it very well. He translated the orders for the other three of us."

"How'd that work out?"

"Most of the time we figured out what we were supposed to do, but the supervisors yelled at us if we didn't move right away. Mostly, we didn't move right away because we didn't understand right away."

"What had the recruiter told you about the work?"

"He said that because I was young, I would get to be a steward and serve food in the dining room. He also said that the ship was used to having Muslims on the crew and would make sure the food adhered to Muslim dietary law."

"Did that turn out to be true?"

"No. Neither one. I had to do deckhand jobs. And most of the meat they served was pork."

"Did you complain to the supervisors or the Mates or the captain?"

"I could not, but Hamdi, the one who knew a little Spanish, *did* complain that the ship was not honoring its promise to make sure we did not have to eat pig meat."

"What did the officers do?"

"The Third Mate told Hamdi that...."

"Objection, hearsay," Stemler called out, mainly to let Traxel know that he wasn't going to let him get away with anything.

"Sustained."

"Did anyone else on the ship speak Portuguese besides you?"

"The Third Mate... and Mr. Arroyo."

"Did you talk to the Third Mate?"

"NO! He was very mean to all of us Moroccans. I was afraid to talk to him."

"How did you learn that Mr. Arroyo spoke Portuguese?"

"I went from cabin to cabin, asking if anyone spoke Arabic or Portuguese. No one spoke Arabic, and only Mr. Arroyo could speak Portuguese."

"When you say 'Mr. Arroyo,' to whom are you referring?"

"That man sitting next to you," he said pointing to Stonebrook.

"Why were you wandering around looking for someone who spoke Arabic or Portuguese?"

"I needed help, and the three Moroccan men could not help me."

"What kind of help?"

"Every night the Third Mate brought me to the captain's cabin so that the captain could...touch me ... sexually."

"Did you tell the captain to stop?"

"Every night – both in Arabic and in Portuguese. I also tried to resist with my fists."

"How did the captain react to that?"

"He laughed and slapped me. Then he put his hands on me some more."

"What did you want Mr. Arroyo to do?"

"I didn't know. But I was desperate for someone to get the captain to stop."

"What did Mr. Arroyo do to help you?"

"When we came to the pier in *Casa Blanca*, he put me in a laundry bag and told the officers that he was carrying his laundry off the shp to do laundry in the port because the water on the ship was full of rust."

"Where were you when he came to put you in the laundry bag?"

"The boatswain was keeping me prisoner in the room... I don't know how to say it in Portuguese... the room where there should be medicines."

"Why do you say 'prisoner'?"

"Because he wouldn't let me out. I tried to go, and he pushed me down,. We did not have a language together, but he let me know with his fists that I could not leave."

"So, how did Mr. Arroyo get you out?"

"He pushed the door open, punched the boatswain, and tied him up, and put a handkerchief in his mouth. Then he took me in the laundry bag and was the first man off the ship, and me in the bag, I was next."

"Do you know how Mr. Arroyo got to be the first man off the ship?"

"Yes. On the first day of the voyage, the First Mate had what he called 'Quiz Hour.' He asked hard questions about the ship, and the winner got to leave the ship first in *Casa Blanca*. Mr. Arroyo was the winner."

"Did you understand the questions?"

"No, but Hamdi translated later what he understood."

"All right, once you were in *Casa Blanca*, what happened?"

"When we were out of sight of the ship, Mr. Arroyo put me down and let me out. We walked and walked until we saw a mosque. I went in, and talked to the *imam khatib* there. He said that he would get me to my village."

"Did you ever see Mr. Arroyo again?"

"Not until an hour ago, and I was really happy. He saved my life."

"Your witness, counsel."

Stemler got up and stood in the well of the court.

"How did you get here, Mahmoud?"

"Objection." It was Traxel. "Even though the lad is 17 ½, he deserves the respect to be addressed as *Mr.* Nimri."

"Why don't you do that, Mr. Stemler?" asked the judge instead of sustaining the objection.

"All right, how did you get here, *Mr.* Nimri?"

"On three airplanes, one from *Rabat* to Madrid, one from Madrid to a place called 'Dee-troy,' one from Dee-troy to this city, whose name I cannot pronounce. And then we took a train to the courthouse."

"Let me try again... Mr. Nimri. *Who* brought you here?"

"Her name is Donna. I don't know her family name."

"Where did you meet her?"

"She and a man who spoke Portuguese came to our village and asked my father for permission for me to go to America."

"And just because she asked, your father said 'yes'?"

"No. At first, my father was suspicious, and I did not believe. I thought it was another bad recruiter."

"So, what convinced you?"

"When Mr. Arroyo and I said good-bye at the mosque, I gave him my most precious possession, the medallion I wore around my neck, which my parents gave me when I became 12 years old."

"And?"

"Donna was wearing it around her neck, so I knew that she was a true friend of Mr. Arroyo. So, then I believed her."

"Did they offer you any money to testify?"

"They said they would put enough money at the Iberia Airlines counter in the Rabat airport, so when I flew back to Morocco, I could take a taxi to my village."

"Is that it?"

"Is *what* it?"

"Did they give you anything else in exchange for your testimony today?"

"An airplane ticket. And a sandwich for lunch. Oh, and the airline gave me breakfast."

"No further questions."

"You may step down, Mr. Nimri," said the judge. "Mr. Stemler, do you wish to add anything to your closing argument now that Mr. Nimri has testified?"

"No thank you, Your Honor."

"Then, Mr. Traxel, you may proceed with your closing argument."

Chapter 56: Traxel's Closing

"GOOD AFTERNOON. YOU SEVEN HAVE all been both patient and attentive. As you have surely figured out, a lot is riding on your verdict. The paramount question is: Can an American corporation escape liability for heinous actions of its agents and employees by dancing the dance of seven veils, or four veils in this case, and pretending not to own the ship on which the bulk of the terrible things about which you heard testimony in this trial happened?

"In some cases, a jury can play Solomon and cut the baby in half – half way between what the plaintiff asks for and what the defendant asserts is fair. In some other cases, a jury can decide that the plaintiff wins on the law but is entitled only to nominal damages, say $1. Neither of those outcomes is likely in this case. Either Greenport Shipping is liable because it owns *Hestia*, or it is not liable because it is merely a subsidiary of *Hestia*. As Mr. Stemler told you in his closing argument, if you indicate that Greenport is *not* liable, that's the end of your work. If, however, you find that it *is* liable, then you must fix the amount of damages.

"So, let me address liability first: The basis for the defendant's claim that it is not liable is the assertion that it is merely a subsidiary and has no responsibility, authority, or liability for what happens on *La Galissionière* in the Mediterannean Sea.

"Who makes that assertion? Felix Benteen does in his deposition, but he declined to show up for the trial, and the judge has explained that you may make a negative inference from that. Second, the captain does in his deposition, but he refused to show up also, and the instructions allow you to make a negative inference from that, as well. The Operations Vice-President also asserted that Greenport is merely a subsidiary of *Hestia*, and, to give him credit, he at least showed up. But his own fellow officer, Personnel Director Mr. Simitas, admitted, finally, that the boards of what I call 'the veil companies,' the Mexican company, the French company, and the Italian company, are all the same; and these same board members are also the board members of both Greenport Shipping and *Hestia*. And who are these board members? As Mr. Simitas testified, and as the documents admitted into evidence show, they are the five officers of *Hestia*.

"And who is the President of every board? The President of *Hestia*. And what's his name? Well, he has two names, Fotis Buoros and.... Felix Benteen, the CEO of Greenport. Greenport owns the Mexican company, the Mexican company owns the French company, the French company owns the Italian company, and the Italian company, with the same board members and the same president, meets on the same day in the same room as *Hestia*. And who is the top guy in all five companies? Felix Benteen, in the empty witness chair over there.

"Now, what are the consequences of completing the logical circle that Greenport owns *Hestia*? It means that the defense witnesses all lied under oath. Benteen lied in his deposition and then chickened out at trial. The captain lied in *his* deposition and also chickened out. We subpoenaed the First Mate, the Second Mate, and the Third Mate, but Mr. Benteen sent back the subpoenas, saying, *falsely*, that he had no authority or control over those officers. And Judge Mattson has told you in her instruction that you may make negative inferences from their refusal to appear.

"Even Vice-President Tsipras lied here in this courtroom under oath. And Personnel Director Simitas at first lied; then when he was confronted with the list of board members for the five corporations, his response was to ask where we got the documents. Not that they were false, not that the boards of directors had other names, but to ask where did we get the documents. He clearly did not expect to see the documents that exposed the truth.

"And, finally, under cross-examination, he admitted, after first pretending that he didn't know the names of the board members, that he himself was a member of that board of directors and of all four other boards of directors and that his fellow officers of *Hestia*, along with the President, Mr. Bouros, constituted the boards of directors of *Hestia* and of Greenport, too.

When we showed him a photograph, he acknowledged that it was of President Bouros. And then when I told him that the photographer was in the courtroom and would testify that he took the photograph of Felix Benteen during his deposition, Mr. Simitas broke down and told the truth.

"Fotis Bouros and Felix Benteen are one and the same person, the president of all five boards, the CEO of *Hestia*, and the CEO of Greenport. What should be abundantly clear is that the Mexican company, the French company, and the Italian company are not real shipping entities; they are merely the false covers for the fact that Greenport owns *Hestia*, and the only reason for Mr. Benteen to use the name of Fotis Bouros is to conceal that he is the CEO of both companies.

"Now, with all that evidence, if you answer the first question on the Verdict Form that Greenport **IS** liable, then you need to fix the damages. Some things are easy – the amount of pay withheld from all three plaintiffs. You know that from the expert economist witness.

"But for most of the damages, there are no handy measuring sticks.

"How much does it take to compensate Mr. Delgadinho and Mr. Muñoz for being put out on a skiff in the Irish Sea with the distinct possibility that they would die – of starvation, of exposure, of shark bites?

"How much does it take to compensate Mr. Delgadinho and Mr. Muñoz for being told that they could never return to their homes, to their families, or to their homelands because if they did, they would die after watching their family members be tortured to death?

"How much does it take to compensate Mr. Muñoz for being threatened by a company official here in Hennepin County that if he dared to say anything negative in his deposition or at trial about what happened on *La Galissionière*, his wife and daughter would be murdered?

"How much does it take to compensate Mr. Delgadinho for being beaten and for the permanent scars on his back from the whippings?

"How much does it take to compensate Mr. Muñoz for having two teeth knocked out with a blackjack by an officer of *La Galissionière*?

"How much does it take to compensate all three of the plaintiffs for having to work under substandard conditions, failing to meet even the minimal IMO standards, having to work long hours, without overtime pay, having to put up with spoiled food, having too few bathrooms, having to drink water brown from rust?

"How much does it take to compensate Mr. Fishkin for having his finger involuntarily amputated because he wouldn't reveal the location of Mr. Delgadinho and Mr. Muñoz?

"I will offer some numbers for your consideration, but you are free to increase the amounts if you think more is required: "For Mr. Delgadinho – $55,000 back pay; $75,000 for the vicious beatings and permanent scars, $250,000 for being set adrift in the Irish Sea, $300,000 for not being able to see his family because of the threats of death; $75,000 for the horrendous working conditions on *La Galissionière*.. That's a total of $755,000.

"For Mr. Muñoz - the same amounts as I suggested for Mr. Delgadinho for back pay, horrerndous working conditions, being set adrift, and the threat of death if he returned to his homeland, i.e. $755,000, ...*plus* another $25,000 for having two teeth knocked out, plus an additional $500,000 for being threatened with death for telling the truth, in this trial, a total of $1,280,000.

"For Mr. Fishkin - $20,000 in back pay, $25,000 for being held prisoner between *Casa Blanca* and Algiers, $100,000 for being sold to the terrorist colleague of Greenport/*Hestia*,

$75,000 for being kept captive by the terrorist, and $400,000 for having his finger chopped off.

Total of $620,000.

"Now, those are what the judge described as 'compensatory damages,' the amount it takes to make the plaintiffs financially whole. But the damages don't end there. Her instructions also authorize you to award punitive damages.

"A jury awards *punitive* damages when it finds that the conduct of the defendant was egregious, flagrant, shocking, notorious, scandalous, deplorable. How about treating its crews as if they were wretches on a Roman galley ship, complete with whips and bad food and corporal punishment? How about having its witnesses lying under oath in depositions and here in court? How about throwing people overboard and then denying they ever existed? How about threatening to kill the plaintiffs' immediate families if they tried to return home? How about selling the investigator to a terrorist? How about letting the captain sexually abuse an underage seaman, who was Shanghaid onto the ship? How about totally disguising the ownership arrangements and then having company officers shamelessly lie and disguise the truth here in court?

"Under our law, punitive damages are not to compensate the plaintiffs but, rather, to punish an evil defendant. The amount should be enough to make a dent in the defendant's wallet. The Operations Vice-president, Mr. Tsipras, acknowledged that *Hestia* was worth $2.5 billion dollars, even more if, theoretically, Greenport owned *Hestia*, which it does. What's going to hurt Greenport? $25,000,000? – that's a measly 1% of its net worth. Of course, 'net' means after debts, after paying big salaries to the five officers, and after paying for them to fly around the world to have meetings when they all office in the same suite.

"I'm going to ask you to award for 2% of the net worth – fifty million dollars.

Thank you."

Chapter 57: Aftermath

TRAXEL AND HIS COLLEAGUES WERE in a conference room at the law firm with Frank Bear and Stonebrook, Lauren Marlo, Donna Putrell, Pastor Elizabeth, and Anthony Brindle. They were replaying some of their favorite parts of the trial. They all congratulated Traxel on his closing argument; complimented Anthony Brindle on his contributions to the team and said how glad they were that he had joined them.

"I'm partly ashamed to admit it," Brindle responded, "but I really enjoyed sticking it to that law firm of Anagnos, Iken, and Goldthorpe. I don't respect them at all. I think you can see why."

Rehmel tried humor: "May we assume that the one word in your last paragraph that doesn't ring true is the word 'partly'?" It took a moment for everyone to mentally replay what he said, and then they all laughed.

Traxel said, "Once again I cannot over-emphasize how important the 'Cleveland Three' were in our case. I have already complimented Rocky and Lauren, and they deserve accolades with oak leaf clusters, but we didn't even know about Donna, who somehow, against all probabilities, produced Sofía Muñoz, Valentina Muñoz, and Mahmoud Nimri for dynamite appearances. I am very curious, but I won't even ask, how you did it. We certainly expect to pay you a generous fee out of the verdict."

"Speaking of the verdict," said Bear, "I retract my reluctance to approve taking on this case because you guys did a spectacular job. Having acknowledged that, I need to ask a question. Even if the jury awards everything that Phil asked for, we know that Greenport's not going to pay that amount. What's our plan?"

Rehmel answered. "Let's assume that the jury awards the entire $2,655,000 in compensatory damages that Phil mentioned and only *half* of the punies he asked for. That would be a total of $27,655,000."

"Exactly so, Cliff," responded Bear. "Greenport's going to bring a motion for remittitur, then they're going to appeal to the Minnesota Court of Appeals, and if they lose there, they'll seek review by the Minnesota Supreme Court. If they lose theire, they'll try federal court. They'll drag this out for years before we, much less our clients, see a dime."

Just then the phone rang. It was the law firm operator. "Phil, there's a Judge Mattson on the phone."

"Please put her through here." He put his index finger to his lips, so that everyone would be quiet.

"Mr. Traxel, This is Judge Mattson on a conference call. I have Mr. Stemler on, as well. The jury has sent a note to me, asking a question. I am aware that you both the know the answer to it, but I am obliged to inform both lead counsel if a jury contacts me before it completes its deliberations. The note asked how they, the jurors, are supposed to compute attorney fees and costs when Mr. Traxel did not mention any amounts."

All the lawyers in the room covered their mouths to smother their shouts of joy.

"I shall have the clerk bring a note back to the jurors, saying that if the jury makes an award for the plaintiffs, the Court will decide attorney fees and costs. That's it. My clerk will call you when the jury signals it is ready to render its verdict."

Traxel hung up, and all the lawyers jumped up and shouted like cheerleaders. Rehmel explained for the non-lawyers what that was all about. "That's almost as good as the question that the jury asked in the Paul Newman movie, *The Verdict*, if they could award more than the plaintiff's lawyer had asked."

Bear took the floor again. "All right. Good news. But once more, what's the plan when Greenport will surely do everything possible to delay and not to pay?"

"My guess," answered Traxel, "is that Charlene Nelson will call again, offering the 10 million that we demanded on the last round. What's the consensus of what I should say?"

"Well," Rehmel said, "you could do what you said last time – 10 mil was on the table before the verdict."

"Yes, but then what's our counter? And do I negotiate or just give a number like I have every other time in this case?"

Bear spoke. "I think that I have the most objective vantage point here. All of you are high on your litigational derring-do, and that's all well and good, but I'd like to be able to count the money. Besides, I'm confident that the plaintiffs would rather see something for sure this year than *maybe* something more next year or two years from now."

"So," said Rehmel, "what's your notion, Frank?"

"I say, counter with $16 mill, and then compromise at 13 mill. It's a number I think Greenport will accept. And we can certainly live with 13 million dollars, right?"

The others snickered.

"Well, Stonebrook, you're a plaintiff, what do you say?" Traxel asked.

"I accept Frank's proposal."

"Elizabeth, can you speak for Moises and Leonicio?"

"I'll talk to them as we go back to court. From the judge's phone call, that should be soon, correct?"

The call from the judge's clerk followed five minutes later. "The jury's ready."

They walked through the skyway to the courthouse without their briefcases. The defense counsel were ashen, as if they were at a wake. The jury filed in, and the judge asked who was the foreperson. When Juror Number 3, the woman who Traxel had most wanted to influence the other jurors, stood up to say that she was the foreperson, Traxel smiled broadly and pumped his fist under counsel table.

They awarded as compensatory damages every dollar that Traxel had sought; and, just to show that they weren't captives of the plaintiffs, they awarded "only" $30,000,000 in punitive damages.

The judge thanked the jurors for their service and dismissed them. Traxel and Rehmel both mouthed "thank you" to the jurors as they walked out.

Charlene Nelson approached Traxel. "Phil, can we speak in private?"

"Of course."

When they were out in the hall, Nelson said, "Congratulations, Phil. You did a great job. Before we draft our motion to oppose most of your attorney fees and costs, and then file a motion for remittitur, and then an appeal, I wanted to take one last opportunity to settle. We'll pay you the 10 mill you requested prior to the verdict."

She expected him to respond with the "day late and a dollar short" cliché, but he didn't. Instead, he stared at her, making her wait, and then said. "We won't do it for 10, but we *will* do it for 16 if – and only if – Greenport pays within a week of the signatures."

"Eleven," she said, "plus a confidentiality clause."

"Fifteen," he countered.

"Twelve."

"Fourteen."

"Thirteen ... and don't forget the confidentiality clause."

"Deal," Traxel replied. They shook hands.

As she walked off, he said, "You can tell them you negotiated me way down."

She smiled and said, "I'll have the Settlement Agreement and Release signed by Benteen and Stemler delivered to you day after tomorrow."

"Indicate that the precise allocation is in 'the attachment;' I'll email you what should be listed."

"Fine," she answered.

"And, remember, payment in one week from the signings."

"Oh," she said, trying to be jocular, "thanks for reminding me; I had already forgotten."

She walked into the courtroom to deliver the news, and the plaintiffs and their legal team came out into the hall, where Traxel gave the 'thumbs up' sign.

Chapter 58: Algiers, Albuquerque, And Cleveland

Algiers

DONOHUE, HAVING DISEMBARKED *LA GALISSIONIÈRE* while in port for a little R&R, made his way south of the city to the *souk,* about which he had heard a good deal from the Mates.

As he browsed in the open air booths, two people followed him. In Arabic, Zaki asked Yasmine, "Is that the man?" She nodded.

They approached him, and Yasmine handed him a card, which read, in English,

"Are you Mr. Donohue from the ship, *La Galissionière?*"

He smiled, and nodded affirmatively. Zaki plunged a syringe into Donohue's neck.

He said, in Arabic, which Donohue could not understand, "This is in revenge for Walid Al-Sinan. You passed information about the IMO to Stonebrook. This is payback."

When he awoke, Donohue was in a cage, on the back of a camel, in what looked to be the Sahara Desert.

Albuquerque

At the semi-annual meeting of the Executive Council of the National Hitpersons' Society, in Albuquerque, New Mexico, President Pallo called the meeting to order. "Judge Dixon has asked for the floor to make a proposal."

Dixon rose. "I would like to propose that we extend our specialties to rescue operations." There was a general hubbub when he said it. "Hold your horses. You should know that Frederika and I, with President Pallo's knowledge, undertook two rescues this last month. No weapons. We got paid about the same amount as for a hit, except that there was a little less stress. I'd like to hear some reasoned arguments against the proposal, other than '*we've always done it this other way.*'"

S. Margaret Thompson, eager, as usual, to enter council discussions, said, "Let me ask a question first, Thurman. What do you think qualifies us to do rescues?"

"The same skills for liquidation: A keen eye, a willingness to travel to exotic locations, resourcefulness, flexibility, competence, efficiency, quick-wittedness, ingenuity, capacity for artifice, and adaptability." He went on to regale them with the two gigs in the Canary Islands and in Morocco, but he left out the part where he surrendered those whom he had rescued to the U.S. Coast Guard.

At the end, with Frederika's support, the Executive Council, by a narrow majority, adopted the Dixon motion.

Cleveland

Back in the office, with the money in the bank, Stonebrook called Lauren and Carol to his conference table. "I'd like to suggest some change of titles in this outfit," he said. "Carol, I'd like to offer you the job of Office Manager and Administrative Mancipal, with an appropriate raise. Lauren, I'd like to take you on as partner and change the name of the firm to 'Stonebrook and Marlo,' with a commensurate boost in compensation as well as a bonus for your supercalifragilistic work on the Delgadinho case." There were no objections.

Chapter 59: Tying Up Loose Ends

TRAXEL HAD SIGNED THE SETTLEMENT Agreement and had elicited the signatures of the three plaintiffs. He sent the executed Agreement over to Charlene Nelson with instructions that she hold on to the document until Greenport had wire-transferred the $13,000,000. The two lawyers had also determined that it was necessary to seek Judge Mattson's formal approval.

Because there had been no specific amount allocated for out-of-pocket expenses, Traxel sought submissions from all of those who had fronted money for litigation-related expenses: investigators' fees, airplane tickets, taxis, photocopying, deposition transcripts, hotel bills, food costs, translations, filing fees, a suitcase, courier fees, Stonebrook's shipboard clothing, rental car, hospital bill, clinic fees, Portuguese "translator" in Morocco, even for investment counselors on Grand Canary and in Lisbon for the non-Stonebrook plaintiffs (they couldn't find one in the Azores).

To be absolutely fair, Traxel asked Pastor Elizabeth to find an attorney in her congregation who was not connected with Dornan-Frager, to represent the interests of Delgadinho and Muñoz in signing off on the amount of the reimbursable fees, the attorney fees, and the allotment of damages to the three plaintiffs.

All of that took several weeks, by which time Delgadinho and Muñoz had returned to the Azores and the Canary Islands, respectively. The two firms decided to underwrite a catered affair in a nearby hotel in downtwn Minneapolis and included the plaintiffs, one of Delgadinho's brothers, Muñoz's wife, Pastor Elizabeth, Lauren Marlo, Attorney Brindle from Florida, members of the Litigation Steering Committee, Ted Bruner and the other two associates who had worked on the case, and the Dornan firm's Managing Partner, Diana Silverman-Enríquez. Traxel had also invited Commodore Costaign, but he demurred and, on behalf of the federal government, waived all cost reimbursements, explaining that the paper work involved in trying to get the feds to estimate and acknowledge the costs of two unofficial rescues would not be worth it. They had also invited Donna, but she was at some conference in New Mexico.

The firm sent first-class tickets for the plaintiffs and those who accompanied them and put them up at a hotel. They asked the plaintiffs to come to the law firm where they would be escorted to the party.

Leonicio Muñoz asked to use the restroom when he arrived, and as he was washing his hands, he noticed a man enter the men's room and go into a stall. It was the man who had threatened him!

He ran back to the conference room and told Stonebrook that "*el amenazador*" was in the men's room. Stonebrook hustled to the men's room just as the man in the stall was flushing the toilet. When the man exited, Stonebrook said, "*Buenas tardes.*"

The man started to answer but then said, "Why did you think that I spoke Spanish?"

"You're Tomaine, aren't you?"

"Tremaine. Norton Tremaine."

"Yes, I remember you from one of the strategy meetings during the trial when we were all conferring about matters related to the Delgadinho case. Since you're on the Litigation Steering Committee, you're on the invitation list. Aren't you coming to the party?"

"No, I have another engagement."

"Well, I'd like you to come to the conference room right now."

"That's very thoughtful of you, but I'm in a hurry to get home."

"I bet you are," said Stonebrook. He then took the man's index finger and bent it into his palm, as he done with Donohue on *La Galissionière.*

Unwillingly, Tremaine accompanied Stonebrook to the conference room, where Traxel, Rehmel, Brindle, Pastor Elizabeth, Lauren Marlo, Frank Bear, the Muñozes, Delgadinho and his brother, Muñoz and his wife, and the Managing Partner were all waiting.

[IN SPANISH] "Tell them what you told me, Leonicio."

"*That's* the man who came to the Andersens' house and threatened to have my wife and daughter killed if I said anything negative about what happened on *La Galissionière.*" Pastor Elizabeth translated.

"There must be some mistake," pleaded Tremaine.

[IN TRANSLATION]: "No, there is no mistake. I shall remember your face for the rest of my life. You threatened to have my Sofía and my Valentina murdered." Elizabeth translated again.

Tremaine's face turned a deep purple. There was dead silence in the room, until Silverman-Enríquez spoke. "Why, Norton?"

Tremaine put his hands to his face and began sobbing. "Benteen was blackmailing me and ordered me to vote against the case in the Litigation Steering Committee, then to let him know about the investigation, and later to threaten Muñoz."

"Why was he blackmailing you, Norton?" asked Rehmel.

"It doesn't matter, now. I'm finished." He sat down and covered his face.

Silverman-Enríquez said, "The rest of you go on to the party. I'll join you later. Phil, if your secretary is still here, I'll want to dictate a letter to her for Norton to sign which will say that he is resigning from the firm as of today and in doing so waives any rights he might have to a partner's share in the profits from the Delgadinho Settlement. Frank, tomorrow morning please ask Norton's secretary to prepare a list of all of Norton's pending cases and the names of the associates and paralegals working on them; then you'll have to assign those cases to other partners. Cliff, I'd appreciate it if you would find a law clerk to clean out Norton's desk, separating Norton's personal belongings from the firm's property and then have him or her deliver the personal belongings to Norton's house in Edina tomorrow afternoon.

"Norton, I'll want you to sign the letter and then leave and never return to this building."

"What if I don't sign?" asked Tremaine, almost petulantly.

"Then I'll place a a call to the County Attorney tomorrow and suggest prosecution."

After a brief hesitation, Tremaine nodded and said that he would sign, which he did.

Silverman-Enríquez joined the party after she got Tremaine to sign the letter of resignation. Everyone tried to be in a celebratory mood, even those who had heard Tremaine's confession.

The next afternoon when the law clerk arrived at Tremaine's home, there was yellow tape around Tremaine's front lawn. A detective told him that the occupant had shot himself.

THE END

CPSIA information can be obtained
at www.ICGtesting.com
Printed in the USA
FSOW01n2303170217
30947FS

9 781524 579753